FLAGS OF VENGEANCE

SECRETS OF STATE

Kenneth Wash

FLAGS OF VENGEANCE

SECRETS OF STATE

BY
KENNETH WASH

Kenneth Wash

WASHBOARD PRODUCTIONS

ISBN-13: 978-0-9851076-3-5

*To the 8,372 victims of the genocide
known as the Srebrenica Massacre
and their families*

ACKNOWLEDGEMENT

To my wife who has been at the helm of our family ship for 30 years, navigating in solitude during many of my duties and two long deployments. She is the anchor in the storm for our family, for whom she has dedicated her life, and yet, she has always recognized my individual goals and helped me to accomplish them. She is a wonderful wife and mother, a great friend, and a fantastic editor who has spent countless hours making what I write the story that I wanted to tell.

PART 1
The March to Potocari
Srebrenica, Bosnia, July 1995

Chapter One

THE T80 tank's track squeaked and groaned as the Serbian tank commander, Siri Ahmovic, held his binoculars to his eyes and scanned the surrounding hillside.

"Stop! Prepare to fire," he barked into his headset microphone, and for a moment his gunner appeared. The tank commander stretched an arm to his right and pointed. "There is movement over there, near that house."

The deeply wooded hills rolled away from the road and down into the Drina Valley below. Small fires burned in the distance marking the path of the Serbian general, Radislav Krstic and his tank company with plumes of smoke that drifted above the treetops. Siri recounted the most recent weeks of the war. A war that had now waged for more than two years since the struggling Yugoslavia had broken apart, its government collapsing as support from the defunct Soviet Union waned, leaving the Serbians with an unpromising future.

The Serbs were strong supporters of communism, and as the country buckled, the Serbians realized that they would no longer benefit from the wealth of the withdrawing, more westernized republics. The political structure was changing and with it came the loss of influence of the communist political machine. Simply put, the Serbs no longer dominated the crumbling Yugoslavia, and their political leaders knew, as the republics withdrew, Serbian political and economic existence would cease to exist. They saw their own Serbian failure as a direct result of the successes of their geopolitical neighbors.

On the morning of July 8, 1992, on the day that Bosnia would be the first separatist state to secede from the failed Soviet Union, the first volley of howitzer shells whistled through the crisp morning air, exploding in the streets of Sarajevo, ushering in the first major conflict on the European continent in nearly forty five years.

And now, almost three years later, the Serbians, under the control of Slobodan Milosevic, had nearly driven out all the Muslims from all regions of the former Yugoslavia. The valley below Captain Siri Ahmovic's position held the last vestiges of the filth that had been a plague on Yugoslavia. He, his tank platoon, and an attachment of mechanized infantry had them surrounded.

The tank shuddered as the first round of projectiles flew above the forested refuge of the fleeing Muslims and impacted on the far hillside. The exploding tank rounds filled the air with the stench of hot steel and burning gunpowder. The Bosnians had been on the move, seeking shelter in the towns and ethnic rich communities that dotted the Balkan countryside. They had been moving for months away from the war-ravaged city of Sarajevo, having had a short-lived peace in the U.N. protected town of Srebrenica. But that village, too, came under attack from the same forces that fired on them from the roads above the valley. It would appear that the United Nations' order to leave Srebrenica untouched meant nothing to General Ratko Mladic or his army.

CHAPTER TWO

NIKOLAI Sidorova moved forward and scanned the area to his left and right. He knew the forest well, having grown up in one of the towns close by. He felt heavily the responsibility of getting tens of thousands of Muslim men, women, and children from the towns surrounding Sarajevo, to Srebrenica, and then to the Dutch outpost, Potocari. He moved steadily forward through the ever thickening woods trying to keep his own children close to him. He looked back at them and yelled his encouragement. "Zlatko, Nikki, stay together. Try to keep up!"

His daughter jogged forward to catch up, her brother in tow. "Come on, Zlatco. You have to stay close. Follow our path." She stepped up next to her father. "Papa, Zlatco is having a hard time keeping up. How much farther is it to the place we are going?" she asked, somewhat out of breath. "Can't we move to the road yet? This path is very hard."

Nikolai stopped for a moment to give them a rest. He looked at the groups of refugees making their way through the woods behind him as he handed his canteen to Nikki. "Here, take a drink and then give it to your brother. Rest here while I go check on the others." He walked away, patting his son's head as he moved past him. "You are doing fine, boy. Stay with your sister for a moment. I will be right back."

Zlatco was afraid. His father could see the fear in the twelve year old's eyes. Zlatco tried to act brave, like a soldier, a warrior like his father, but his entire world had been turned upside down. He had never spent more than a day near the woods, let alone in the middle of a deep forest. But still, it was better than the streets of Sarajevo, seeing the dead bodies and listening to the screams of the wounded. And it was better than the incessant exploding shells that forced them from the last town, Srebrenica. He missed his mother mostly and could not stop wishing she were there now to hold him and make him feel safe.

The sudden thump of a tank firing across the valley startled him. He turned to look at Nikki and scrambled to her side as the round screeched overhead and impacted about a thousand meters away. The exploding shell was extremely loud. Within seconds another round, then a third and fourth, were impacting all around them. Zlatco felt an arm grab him and pull him off of his feet. His father had scooped him up at nearly full speed. He looked back for his sister just as a huge orange fireball exploded in the distance, silhouetting her body as she hurdled over a small creek bed. His father yelled frantically for her to follow him. "Move, Nikki! Lets go!"

Nikolai was sprinting, dodging the saplings and forest debris as he made his way farther from the impacting shells. Nikki was on his heels, vaulting over fallen trees and craggy outcroppings of rocks. She had never thought her years of Olympic gymnastics training would ever be used to outrun tank shells.

Her father turned to see the position of the rest of the refugees. They were on their own now. He was concerned solely for his family at this moment. He must get them to the Dutch base, Potocari, where there were four hundred Dutch United Nations soldiers. He had done his best to protect them, but Srebrenica had been over-run. General Ratko Mladic's forces had killed hundreds of people in the U.N. Protected community and many more died as they fled to the nearby base. The Dutch tried to intervene but were pushed back. The commander, a Dutch Colonel named Thom Karramans, had to secure Potocari, once a thriving local factory that employed many of the inhabitants of Srebrenica.

The U.N. force had taken control of the main office complex and some of the smaller warehouses. Those buildings were being used as sleeping quarters and the kitchen for the base. The factory building sat empty except for the materials and equipment left behind when the workers began to flee.

Karramans' forces built barriers and guard towers along the boundary of the factory's ten-foot fence and deployed coils of barbed wire. Most of the observation points overlooked the ravaged, and in some areas, still burning town of Srebrenica. It was from those towers that Colonel Karramans watched as General Krstic's tank company bombarded the surrounding hills. He could do nothing to stop the onslaught. The Dutch force could not protect the population from the psychological effect of the assault that was designed to drive the townspeople from their homes.

Srebrenica, a small town nestled in the Drina Valley of the Balkans, had been home to over nine thousand people before the war. Over three quarters of its population were Muslim. The rest, Christian Serbs who had migrated across the Serbian border and, until the outbreak of war, had lived peacefully with the town's Muslim inhabitants.

As war enveloped the country and moved out from the larger cities, thousands of people fled toward the small, U.N. protected community. Eventually over twenty thousand refuges had converged on the town. Homes in the town took in as many as they could fit inside their walls. In some cases there were twenty people living in houses that were built to comfortably support four. The village's single hotel was packed with refugees, eight to eleven in each room. Srebrenica's infrastructure could not support the overwhelming and growing population. Still they came, led by a promise of safety that Colonel Karramans' outpost simply could not provide.

Karramans had some help from the people of Srebrenica. A small faction of about a thousand men, led by the Muslim warlord Masa Orlich, provided some security and performed raids on the fighting positions of Krstic's tank company using guerrilla tactics and hit and run techniques.

Orlich was a huge figure. He was ruggedly handsome with a full beard and a vibrant personality who led his army of farmers and former businessmen from the back of a silver and white Anglo-Kabarda horse. He showed no mercy for those who threatened the lives of the Muslim people and, in an effort to make room in the village for those who had given him the title Defender of Srebrenica, he met with the Serbian councils and ordered non-Muslims to leave Srebrenica. To help convince the council of his intentions he proclaimed that those who refused to leave would be considered soldiers or spies and would be killed.

Masa Orlich publicly executed any captured Serbian soldiers. His mission was to protect his people, and that he did with vengeful enthusiasm. Before long he had a following of men who waged a war of stealth and speed against the technologically advanced and numerically superior army of General Ratko Mladic.

In response to Orlich's attacks, General Mladic placed Krstic's tank company and mechanized infantry regiment on the main highways, cutting off the supply routes to both Srebrenica and Potocari. With no food for his people, and running low on ammunition it became impossible to continue to resist General Mladic's forces and, in the best interest of his people, Masa Orlich had begun a mass exodus of the inhabitants of the Srebrenica safe zone to the Dutch base, Potocari.

Nikolai heard the sound of horses' hooves on the rocky surface of the hillside and turned to see Masa and some of his men heading toward his position. He raised his hand so Masa could recognize him among the masses of fleeing refugees, though he was a hard figure to miss. He was over six feet tall with blonde, short-cropped hair and green eyes and could be spotted easily among the others making their way through the shadows of the forest.

Masa Orlich pulled back on his reins and motioned for his men to stop. He dismounted while his horse was still moving, landing with a thud in front of Nikolai who was putting his son down after carrying him over a quarter mile. Nikolai was panting heavily as Orlich began to update him on their progress toward the U.N. Post.

"Nikko, they have surrounded the valley. Mladic's men have placed positions on the roads leading to the fort. We cannot go further until we find a way through safely."

Nikolai wiped his brow and took a drink from his canteen. "What do you suggest, that we attack the tanks with sticks and rocks? We have nothing left to fight with. How do you propose to make a hole in their line?"

Masa knelt down and cleared away the leaves to expose the fertile dark earth below. He used a stick to draw out his plan. "I have sent some of my men to secure rifles and grenades from the Dutch compound. We have a back entrance to the factory and have made contact with the soldiers. They have promised to supply us and help us with air support, but we must reconnoiter the positions and return to the base with grid coordinates."

Masa looked at Nikolai's children, then back into his eyes. "I need you, Nikko. I need your help to do this. It is our last hope to get these people to safety." He motioned to the hundreds of refugees as they trudged onward through the thick forest.

Another explosion lit up under the canopy of trees close enough for them to see bodies being lifted and hurled through the forest as automatic gunfire erupted in the distance. Nikolai looked at his seventeen-year-old daughter. "Nikki, you have to go on without me. Take Zlatco. Keep him safe in the Dutch fort until I come back. There is a building set aside for families and children. I will meet with you there." He could see that she was scared.

Tears welled in Nikki's eyes as she nodded her understanding. She hoped she was strong enough to get her brother and herself to the safe zone. She yelled over the gunfire to her father, "Papa, be careful!"

Nikolai knelt down and hugged his son who was crying hard, convulsing as he gulped air between sobs. "You will be OK. Stay with Nikki and do everything that she tells you. I will see you soon." He squeezed him tightly then released him to his sister.

Masa Orlich motioned to one of his men. "Yusek, give Nikko your horse and rifle. Stay with these people." Masa swept a hand toward the hundreds of people converging on his position, all wanting to get a glimpse of the great Masa Orlich, Muslim warlord and defender of Srebrenica. The man climbed from his horse and handed the reins and then his AK-47 to Nikolai.

Masa slapped the back of his new foot soldier. "Lead them to Potocari, Yusek."

He watched as Nikolai mounted Yusek's Arabian, then jumped onto his own horse. Masa tugged the reins around and walked the horse in a circle to face Yusek. "We will meet you at the base to make plans after our mission. Be safe, my brother. Allah Akbar!"

With that Nikko and Masa yanked their reins, and pulling the horses around, galloped back in the direction from which Masa had come. They disappeared over the rolling, forested hills. Yusek turned to the sea of people, raised his hand and yelled for them to keep moving.

He prodded Nikki and Zlatco to move. "Come on, my new family," he said with a grin. "We still have quite a way to go."

CHAPTER THREE

COLONEL Karramans sipped his coffee and looked at the information laid out before him. All the inhabitants of Srebrenica were moving to his location. Several thousand had already made it to the base and had been busy readying the warehouse and the assembly plants to accommodate the massive amount of refugees. No matter what preparations they made there would be no way to support the twenty five to thirty thousand people that would be descending on the base.

Karramans stepped out onto the deck outside the office and looked out over the forest. To his right the main entrance of the compound jutted outward to the gated entrance. A steady stream of refugees moved through the gates, *trudging like Moses' Jews,* he thought, as they moved under the overhanging deck and gathered in the empty fields and warehouses. He had no supplies for these people and no fuel for his vehicles to go get them any. The truth was he was just as much of a refugee as the thousands filling the compound.

He lit a cigarette and inhaled deeply. The sound of mortar and tank shells impacting on the hills, roads, and deep in the valley was getting closer to the post, moving with the flow of the exiled.

The sun was beginning to set, bathing the treetops with the reflected scarlet of the gloaming. Soon the darkness would come and with it the eerie silence, broken by the sound of tanks and mortar tubes, followed by sporadic small arms fire as the infantry moved through the woods and engaged with Masa Orlich's forces.

He had seen so much death already that he had become numb to the sight. His men were nervous and apprehensive. They could do nothing to prevent what was happening. There was so much chaos and fear that the Muslim forces had mistakenly attacked his men, tossing a grenade into one of the personnel carriers and killing one of his best gunners.

The colonel crushed out his cigarette and called for the phone. One of the privates pulled the receiver from its hook and handed it to Karramans as he set the body of the phone on the rail of the deck and carefully laid the cord out of the walking path. Pressing the buttons on the keypad, Colonel Karramans drank from his coffee. He downed the dark liquid relishing it for the moment, as it was the last of their stores. He guessed he'd be drinking tea tomorrow as the phone clicked and began ringing. Within two rings an unfamiliar voice answered. "United Nations Protection Force, Eight Nineteenth, may I help you sir or ma'am?" The voice was nearly robotic.

"I need to speak with General Jernvier, please. This is Colonel Karramans at Potocari Base." Karramans leaned against the railing.

"Yes, Sir, I will go get him. He has been waiting on your call." The phone rattled as the receiver was placed on the desk and the sound of the soldier running from the room could be heard. Within a minute, quickened footsteps and then General Jernvier's voice filled the earpiece. "Good evening, Thomas. How are you?" The general was French, but his U.N. mandated English was very understandable through a heavy accent.

Karramans was frustrated. He had requested food supplies and fuel several times in the past two days and had not gotten any confirmation of a planned delivery time. "General, Sir, I am not well. I am calling to let you know that the entire population of Srebrenica is overrunning my base as we speak and I still do not have the supplies that were requested more than forty hours ago. I have heard nothing from anyone."

"That is ridiculous, Colonel. We shipped the drops hours ago. You should have skids full of pallets containing food and bottled water. Are you sure it is not on your site?" The general spoke arrogantly, "Perhaps you should look again."

The Dutch colonel was trying to be patient, but he was already on edge. "Sir, the requested drop site is directly in front of me. I am looking at it and I am telling you that there are no supplies in that field, not one crate!" Karramans leaned on the railing and peered through the enveloping darkness out to the makeshift landing zone just beyond the fence line. "Unless your people have delivered pallets full of refugees, I didn't get them."

Jernvier turned and looked at his wall of maps. What the colonel was telling him didn't make sense. He traced a finger from the site of the hastily constructed landing zone near the factory at Karramans' current location, to the runway of a small airport. An uneasy feeling twisted in his stomach. "Colonel, are you at the factory, at Potocari Base itself or are you at landing zone Foxtrot?"

Karramans was losing his patience. "Sir, General Jernvier, as I told your radio operator and your desk sergeant, the captain, the major, and your colonel, I am locked down on Potocari. I cannot leave here. I have no fuel, I have very little ammunition and I am running extremely short on patience with your command. Tell me that your people did not send three thousand cases of MRE's and two thousand cases of bottled water, not to mention the fuel and ammunition, to LZ Foxtrot!"

13

General Jernvier was quiet for a long time. "Do you have any vehicles you can use to retrieve the supplies?" he asked quietly.

Karramans' heart sunk. "You have got to be kidding me! You guys dropped my shit over ten miles away?"

Jernvier apologized. "Colonel Karramans, I am sorry for the misunderstanding, but you will have to go get your supplies from that LZ."

Karramans could not believe what he was hearing. He was seething with anger now. Carefully he formed the words of his next sentence before speaking it. "Sir, are your men ready to support my requested air strikes? I will have exact coordinates soon and will resubmit the request forms as soon as the information arrives."

"Of course, Colonel, we are here to help you, you know that. We have aircraft on standby and your original request is under review by the Under Secretary General. We should get pre-authorization for any strikes you need based on that." General Jernvier spoke as if he were getting authorization for a weekend pass, not the strategic attacks on enemy positions.

Karramans hated the bureaucracy of the United Nations. Every move he made had to be reviewed and authorized by layer after layer of members from different countries. His original request had been denied because the wrong form was used for the request. He had to plead with the council to review it anyway so that they would have the gist of the mission to act immediately upon receipt of the exacting coordinates. They moved far too slowly for the fluid nature of the developing war. The fact that Yasushi Akashi, the Under Secretary General for Humanitarian Affairs of the United Nations, had anything to do with the authorization of force at Karramans' level was unbelievable. He was sure that by the time his request was submitted, the Secretary-General of the U.N. himself, Mr. Kofi Anon, would be making the final decision on the approval, or worse yet, the disapproval of his requested air attacks. Once again his hands were tied.

"Sir, I must get back to the situation here. I will have the coordinates relayed to your office as soon as they are received." With that he hung up the phone. He had to get the fuel from the drop site. Once he had the fuel he could get the food and water distributed to the refugees.

CHAPTER FOUR

MASA Orlich and Nikolai Sidorova, along with twenty other soldiers from the Bosnian Muslim Army or A.B.i.H., had split up into four groups of riders to reconnoiter the enemy positions and perform any disruption tactics they could to stop the bombardment on the refugees crossing through the valley below. The sun had set behind the mountains and for the forest night had arrived.

Nikolai crept forward, sneaking up on the 120 millimeter, M-74 mortar position. The four men were no longer loading and firing, but simply talking amongst themselves between blasts from a T80 tank's main gun that was less than thirty meters from them. Nikolai's men moved forward silently, each concentrating on a single target. He looked toward the tank and saw the silhouette of Masa Orlich who had climbed to the turret of the T80 tank, moving up slowly and quietly, directly behind the machine gunner who was laying down a steady stream of tracer rounds into the forest below.

Siri Ahmovic, the tank commander, had ducked down inside the tank to review his firing chart. Shell casings from the machine gun fell into his hatch as the gunner fired down into the valley. Siri hit the soldier in the leg to get his attention. "Stop! Stop! Quit firing! Take a break before you melt the barrel and break my eardrums." The machine gun stopped firing and for the moment, other than the ringing in Ahmovic's ears, there was silence. He unfolded the map and its plastic overlay, flattening it out on his legs as best he could.

The young commander leaned back in his lowered seat and started to ask the main-gun fire technician about his last salvo, to mark it on his map, when he heard a strange ticking sound and felt his map move slightly. He leaned up and searched for the source of the now rhythmic tick. At first his mind could not comprehend what he saw. The right corner of his plastic map overlay was covered with a dark fluid. He thought, *it must be hydraulic fluid,* and pulled the corner of the map closer to his eyes trying to discern its composition under the blackout lighting that flooded the compartment with a reddish hue. He pulled a small flashlight from his lapel and focused its beam as he swirled his thumb through the fluid on the plastic map overlay and was startled to realize that it was blood. Siri shone his penlight at his machine gunner and noted the blood running out of his sleeve, across the back of his hand that was hanging limp at his side, and then dripping from his fingertips to the floor of the tank.

Suddenly, a loud clank caught Siri's attention. He moved his leg to the left to discover a live grenade spinning to a stop between the outer hull wall and his lowered seat frame. Frantically, Ahmovic jumped to his feet and yelled, "Grenade!" as he threw himself upward, out of the open hatch in an attempt to escape from the turret.

The force of the explosion rocked the tank, peppering Ahmovic with shrapnel as he half jumped and was half blown from the hatch. An immediate secondary explosion ripped through the tank as the round the main-gun fire technician was preparing to set in the loading chute detonated, blowing the remaining ammo stores and sending the entire gun and turret twenty feet skyward.

Siri Ahmovic was blown ten meters away from the tank and lay on the ground, his life spared from the huge explosion by the thickness of the tank's hull, and the fact that he escaped milliseconds before the detonation of the tank rounds. He found that he was still clutching the map and overlay as he pushed himself away from the ground. Something was wrong. He couldn't move his legs. He tried again, forcing the thought, again and again, but he couldn't do it.

He struggled to turn himself over, and when he did he was shocked to see the extent of his wounds. He grimaced when he saw that most of his skin and muscle was shredded or blown away just above his boots. What was left hung uselessly. He yelled in agony as the full picture of his condition sank in. He was bleeding profusely from his wounds, his blood boiling and steaming from the superheated shrapnel embedded in his flesh. He dragged himself over to sit upright against a small tree, not hearing the footsteps of the two men who approached him, and was startled to suddenly see them standing near him.

Nikolai reached down and pulled the map from the tank commander's hand, shaking off the pieces of flesh and wiping the blood away. He took a quick look and saw that every current tank position, as well as their grid coordinates, was written on the map with a grease pencil, a stupid tactical error on the part of this young officer, he thought.

The flickering light from the flames illuminated the tortured look on Siri's face as he looked over his right shoulder to the slain bodies of his comrades, then up at Masa Orlich who was now standing over him. He raised a shaking hand and pleaded for help from the tall bearded figure. "Please, help me," he said, his words sounding muffled. He reached his hand to his ear and pulled it away. It was covered with blood. The concussion must have destroyed his hearing as well.

Orlich's huge figure squatted down and said something to Siri as he grabbed his jaw and rotated his head to either side to look at his wounds. Masa slapped him lightly on the cheek and stood fully, still talking to the Serbian officer. Siri could not hear what Masa Orlich was saying to him. He looked briefly toward Nikolai, then back to Masa and the Muslim warlord's raised pistol.

Masa glanced at the map. He saw the markings on the overlay and laughed at their luck. Siri looked at the map in the hands of his enemy, suddenly feeling deep pangs of guilt, knowing they now had the information that would probably lead to the deaths of his brothers in arms, and he would be responsible for their deaths. Tears welled in his eyes and streaked through the dirt on his face at the thought that he had been so stupid. As if Masa read his thoughts, he looked down, and in words that Siri couldn't hear, but could read on the lips of the smiling bearded man, thanked him for helping with his efforts to destroy Siri's own army.

Nikolai jumped at the sound of the shot fired from Masa's pistol through the forehead of the tank commander. "Masa, we must hurry and get back with this information before the positions change." He motioned to the map. "With this, the Dutch can call in the air strikes and destroy the Serb tanks."

Masa saw that the mortar tube and most of its ammunition had been collected by the others and was strapped to the horses or resting on the men's shoulders. There was no need to continue the reconnaissance. All the information they needed was on that map. He smiled at Nikolai and slapped him on the shoulder as they moved toward the horses. "Good work, my friend. We have been lucky tonight. Let's hope that this information only leads to more of the same."

CHAPTER FIVE

SIX kilometers away a convoy of Karramans' vehicles, driving on fumes, had just reached LZ Foxtrot. The plan was to fuel the vehicles on site with enough fuel to return to base with the supplies and remaining fuel stores. There they would top off the larger cargo vehicles and return in the darkness, throughout the night, as many times as possible, to retrieve the remaining supplies.

Sergeant Wallach stepped from his Mercedes truck and surveyed the area. The airfield was littered with thousands of boxes of food and gallon bottles of water. Some of the skids were intact, though most of the intact skids were at the far end of the short runway where they had slid to a stop against the chain link perimeter fencing. Others were completely empty, their contents spread across the width of the runway.

Wallach yelled to his squad leaders, "Get your men out here and get those fuel containers. Priority of work is refueling, then foodstuffs. Let's go! Move your asses!"

The last of the vehicles on site moved toward the end of the runway where the majority of the fuel canisters and the hand pumps had skidded to a stop. As some of the men worked to roll a fifty-five gallon container up into the bed of a pick up truck and set up a mobile fuel point, others began removing the straps securing the remaining cargo to the skids.

Lieutenant Dirk Linden, a twenty two year old graduate of the Koninlijke Military Academy, trotted across the runway trying to catch up with his men who had driven to the fence and were working to free the fuel containers. He scanned the empty pallets and the asphalt along the way and noted the straps that had secured the cargo to the pallets were not torn away or broken and the plastic wrapping lying near some of the empty pallets appeared to have been cut.

He stopped moving and looked toward the end of the runway at his soldiers who were struggling with the cargo straps and plastic on the intact skids. He then walked over to an empty skid and inspected the strap's ratcheting mechanism. They had been released, the metal handles pushed past their locking detents and the straps unwound from the hub.

He released the strap, letting it fall, and noticed a dozen or so discarded cigarette butts around the skid. On further inspection, around other skids, he found more indicators that someone had been there. Then he spotted it: a still smoking cigarette.

He unslung his weapon and pulled the charging handle to load a round into the chamber, pulled his weapon to the ready position, then called his lead sergeant over. "Sergeant Wallach, come here!" he yelled as he scanned the area on all sides of the runway.

Wallach could see the apprehension in his lieutenant's actions. He yelled to his men as he ran over to Linden's position, "Cover! Take positions away from the fuel drums! Ready weapons!"

The successive sounds of thirty weapons ratcheting into a ready posture, followed by platoon and squad commands, filled the air as the platoon took up defensive positions and began scanning sectors of fire from the strewn cargo to the tree line and back toward the access points of the road.

Sergeant Wallach stopped at Linden's position hoping that the young lieutenant was just overreacting to something. Linden pointed down at the smoking cigarette and then pointed out the released cargo straps and cut plastic. "That is not the work of our men, Sergeant. We have company. There is someone else in the area."

He continued to scan the tree line as Sergeant Wallach assessed the information around him. Given that Lieutenant Linden was a K.M.A. graduate, the Dutch equivalent of West Point in the United States, Wallach was sure he was not overreacting.

"Steady, Men, scan your sectors," Wallach barked as he walked the line through the boxes of cargo and the thick uneasy silence. It was almost nightfall and the dusk had overtaken the forest making it impossible to see the edge of the wood line. Wallach cursed that his unit did not have the new night vision equipment or any of the infrared scanners that were mounted on the tracked vehicles. Without the aid of visual light enhancement all they could do was wait for something to happen.

CHAPTER SIX

ON the north side of the Dutch base, columns of men moved along a muddy forest trail. The darkness of the forest suddenly opened to the artificial bright white lights of generator powered security lamps as Masa and his men emerged from the road on the edge of the wood line.

As they approached the rear gate to the factory turned military post, the true picture of the exodus emerged. The grounds of Potocari were filled with refugees as far as one could see. They stood silently or squatted, some knelt in prayer and others slept where they could. The entire open area, every square meter surrounding the factory, was filled with people.

It looked like a sea of people from Nikolai Sidorova's perspective atop the saddle of his Arabian. Still, he knew that the people gathered here represented only two thirds of those who had originally set out to flee the deadly bombardment by the Serbian

Army. Thousands of people were dead and others still wandered the hills hoping to find their way to the safety of the Muslim territory in Kosovo.

Nikolai searched for any sign of Nikki or Zlatco as the horses and men wedged through the throngs of people. Women in headscarves looked up at the soldiers on horseback and those following, searching for their husbands or sons separated from them during the journey. The area surrounding the gates was a meeting ground for those looking for someone they loved, a place where broken hearts and broken dreams were manufactured by the thousands each hour.

Masa looked at Nikolai whose eyes were darting back and forth from face to face, looking for anyone he might recognize from the journey through the forest with his children. "Nikko, don't worry, we will find them. Yusek is a good man, he would not leave them unprotected."

Nikolai did not look convinced. "I hope you are right, Masa, but I do not share your hopeful outlook." He motioned to the wailing, bleating people that surrounded them. "Look at these people. Their hearts are broken. Most wait here for someone who is already dead or dying in the forest."

Masa changed the subject. "Nikko, we must gather the men who can fight and prepare to move them. Once the air strikes have succeeded we will have to move through the area and clear out the remaining resistance. It is the only way to guarantee the survival of our people. We must destroy the Serbs or they will not stop until we are all dead."

Nikolai could see the hatred in Masa's eyes and wondered how different they really were from the Serbians. They rounded the corner of the main building and dismounted. Masa led his leaders into the headquarters building and up the steps to where Colonel Karramans was waiting. Masa stepped up to him with the captured map and tossed it down on the Dutch commander's desk. "Here is the information you need to destroy their tank positions. You must call in the air strikes immediately, before they can relocate."

Karramans looked exhausted. "The air strikes have been postponed. The weather in Italy is not cooperating. General Jernvier has promised to send F-15s from Aviano Air Base there, but they are talking in the morning at 0600. I will get the positions to them and push for an immediate strike, but I do not expect that it will happen until the morning." He sighed and continued, "It would surprise me if the information gets to the airbase before noon, actually."

Masa struck the table with his fist. "My people are dying while your U.N. have meetings and talk to the media about all the good you are doing. Where is the food and the water they promised us? Where are the ammunition and weapons to support us? It is all talk and no action." He leaned over the desk, "You and your Q.R.F. are nothing more than a failure."

Colonel Karramans stood up. He had tried to protect the Muslim population, and fail or not, he had invested the safety of his own men to do it. His unit was the pride of the Dutch Armed Forces and the United Nations had hoped that the deployment of the Quick Reaction Force, a modular force that could be structured to meet the requirements of the rise of asymmetric clashes around the world, would be the answer to the recent events of terrorism. But this mess they had been placed into was not a terrorist attack. It was conventional warfare against an indigenous population that was simply too overwhelming for his unit.

"Now hold on right there, Masa! My men are out there right now putting themselves at risk to help *your* people. They are picking up the supplies that were dropped over ten miles away, in the middle of *your* war!"

Karramans stepped around his desk as he spoke until he was standing face to face with the Muslim warlord. He was angry and it showed. "We don't have to be here! I could have pulled those men and moved them back to the safe zone, but I didn't. Do you know how tempting it has been to leave you to deal with all of this yourselves?" Karramans dramatically swept a hand outward, gesturing to the throngs of people and the abandoned town of Srebrenica on the other side of his walls.

He paused for a moment as the helplessness of their situation came to the forefront of his thoughts. "I have already lost one soldier, and that was to your own scouts. A mistake, you said. Well, I'm beginning to think that this entire mission is a mistake. We will probably all die here on the grounds of this godforsaken factory. But if indeed we do, we will die fighting beside *your* men, for *your* cause." With that he turned away, looking through the window at the thousands of people within his view. "Only history will tell whether what we do here will have been a failure or not."

Masa turned to leave, unmoved by Karramans' words. "When you have secured the supplies, notify me. I will send some men to help distribute them." He spoke more rationally now. "I will be needing ammunition and some weapons for my warriors. I am sending some of them into the woods for safety in case General Mladic's men appear on your doorstep tomorrow morning."

Karramans spun to face the two men. "When my men return you will have what you need. What is stored here is all we have at the moment and I will tell you that it is not enough to split between us."

Masa looked at Nikolai. "Nikko, I will go gather the men and what supplies we have." Masa knew that the only real hope for the refugees was to keep moving, to get them to the Muslim territory that was almost forty miles away. "You go find your family. Make sure they are safe. Meet us on the floor of the factory in the morning and I will let you know the plan."

Nikolai looked relieved. He nodded to Masa and slapped his shoulder, then turned to leave. As he left the building the realization of the amount of people there hit him again. It could take him hours to make it from one end to the other and even then, the people were a moving target. He hoped for the best and headed in the direction of the main warehouse. That building was supposed to be for families with children. He would go there first, hopefully Nikki had found her way there.

Nikolai pushed and shoved through the growing crowd of people. Women were beating their chests and wailing having heard the fate of their husbands. Some of the men were huddled together near the front of one of the buildings sitting on their belongings. Nikolai recognized a bright green backpack from the journey as one belonging to one of the men in his group. He stepped up to the group. "Who does this backpack belong to?" The men just stared at him. "One of you was with my group in the forest. I am looking for my children and I'm hoping that you can help me find them. Now, please, whose backpack is this?"

For a minute no one answered and then there was movement in the back of the group and a man stood. "That is mine, though I do not know the whereabouts of your children. We all got separated when the shelling picked up and many people were killed. Our guide, the one who replaced you, is dead. He was hit directly with a mortar shell."

"You mean Yusek, a red haired, bearded man, right? Were there any children with him?" Nikolai asked anxiously.

The man searched his memory. "If there were, they ran away, deeper into the woods like the rest of us. We scattered in all different directions. I came in by myself." His eyes welled with tears and his lip began to quiver. "My Myrna is out there. I left her behind." He began sobbing and turned away. Some of the other men stood to comfort him. They looked at Nikolai with a look of total despair.

Nikolai turned and pushed through the crowd to the warehouse. He entered the building and looked around, but could not see through the thick wall of people. He could hear children and babies crying, but none sounded like Nikki or Zlatco. He looked around to find something to stand on to look over the crowd of people and spotted a ladder that rose some twenty feet and ended at an opening to the roof access. Nikolai made his way to the ladder, climbed about halfway and then stopped to survey the area below.

Zlatco was sitting near the outside wall leaning against the building. Something caught his attention and he got to his feet, listening intently, thinking that he had just heard his father call to him. The sound of a thousand people talking, crying and yelling blended together into a single droning noise with no discernible conversations. He looked to where his sister stood talking with an older woman and then he heard it again. He saw Nikki turn around suddenly. She had heard it, too. Zlatco couldn't see anything through the wall of people. He only saw the expression on his sister's face go from bewildered and sad to one of surprise and happiness. He tried to see what she was looking at. Nikki waved her arms and jumped in place. It had to be their father. He must have returned. How Zlatco wished he could see. He spun around trying to look through the crowd, trying to find something, anything, to stand on. He looked at Nikki who was moving toward him. She was crying and, yes, he could hear her now, she was almost squealing the words, "Papa, Papa, Zlatco, it's Papa!"

The shoving and surging of the people around him increased, moving him as if he were floating in an ocean wave. He was being pushed back and forth as he tried to get to his sister, fearful that he would be trampled, when suddenly he was yanked from the crowd and pulled into a crushing hug by his father. Finally, at least for the moment, Zlatco felt safe.

CHAPTER SEVEN

COLONEL Karramans woke to the sound of explosions and the frantic yelling of his aid trying to get his attention. He had fallen asleep sitting in his chair and was trying to shake away the night and come back to full awareness.

Another explosion rocked the compound. He grabbed his aid, Sergeant Schmidt, by the arm as he made his way to the door to see what was happening. "What is going on?"

Sergeant Schmidt was obviously shaken. "We are being attacked. The guard posts have been destroyed and the gate has taken a direct hit." He flinched as another explosion lit up the early morning darkness.

Karramans looked at the clock on the wall over his desk. It was just after five o'clock in the morning. He had actually slept for several hours. "Where are the react teams? Why aren't they taking up their positions?" He scanned the hardened positions expecting to find his sergeant major directing the defense of the compound.

A sick feeling overwhelmed him, "Where are Sergeant Wallach and Lieutenant Linden? Tell me they made it back with the supplies."

Sergeant Schmidt yelled from the protection of the doorway. "They never made it back. I sent a recon team to find out what happened to them. They found the supplies, but no vehicles or personnel. Several of the fuel canisters were empty. I'm afraid they have abandoned us, Sir."

The Colonel refused to believe that his sergeant major would ever allow his soldiers to turn tail and run, let alone be part of such an act.

The explosions stopped suddenly and for several minutes there was only the sound of the scared and wounded refugees outside the building. The phone on Sergeant Schmidt's desk rattled to life, causing them both to jump. Schmidt ran from the doorway to his desk, grabbed the phone and ran back to the center of the two rooms answering the phone while moving, "Schmidt. Go ahead." The sergeant listened for a few minutes. "Yes, I will tell him." Schmidt looked pale as he hung up the phone.

"What is it? What's wrong?" Karramans asked as he lit one of his few remaining cigarettes.

The sergeant sat the phone's receiver down in its cradle and looked at Colonel Karramans. "General Ratko Mladic is at the gate, Sir. He sent word that he is ready to accept our surrender and wants to meet with you."

Masa Orlich ran through the warehouse looking for Nikolai. He surveyed the hundreds of cowering families seeking the shelter of each other, and whatever they could find inside to hide under. Nikolai was standing resolute in one corner holding his son. The explosions had stopped, but not long enough for even the dust to settle.

Masa stopped in front of him. "Mladic and his men are at the gate. He has several of his key leaders with him, including General Krstic. That can only mean one thing."

Nikolai completed the thought, "He is here for the surrender of Potocari and Srebrenica. There would be no other reason for them to stop at the gate."

Masa knew that if Karramans surrendered, Mladic would seize and kill all of his men. "We have to leave Potocari. We must lead the men out, disperse in the woods. They must move quickly to Kosovo."

Nikolai stepped back and set down his son. "That is over forty miles away. Most of these men could not walk half that. They need food and rest."

"Then they will die here," Masa said abruptly. "We do not have a choice. At a minimum we must evacuate the fighters and anyone who is of age to fight. The oldest and youngest can stay with the women and the children."

Nikolai looked down at his son and his daughter, then looked back at Masa. "When will we leave?"

Masa mulled the question over in his mind. "We will wait and see what comes of this meeting between Karramans and Mladic. He does not have enough soldiers with him to try anything drastic. He will probably give an ultimatum. We will wait until nightfall to move the brunt of our army, but until then we must feed them what we can and start releasing them to find their way."

CHAPTER EIGHT

KARRAMANS stepped out into the new morning's light. He scanned the sky for any sign of the F-15 jets promised by Jernvier, but there was no sign, nor any sound of aircraft. He walked briskly to the gate, or what remained of it. He saw his men standing with their weapons pointed at General Mladic and his entourage and motioned for them to lower their weapons.

Mladic was a large man. Not tall necessarily, but bulky. His shoulders were broad, supporting a thick neck and square jaw. He stood on the outside of the gated entrance with his arms folded on his barrel shaped chest. Karramans approached cautiously and rendered a salute to the Serbian General.

Mladic returned the salute. "Good Morning, Colonel, I am General Ratko Mladic and this is General Radislav Krstic. We are here to discuss the terms of an agreement to end our hostilities." He reached into his pocket and removed a pack of cigarettes, shook one loose, then held the pack out for Karramans.

The Dutch Colonel hesitated briefly and then reached out for the smoke. He pointed with the cigarette to the camera crew standing to the rear of Mladic. "What is all this?" He asked.

Mladic turned, gestured to the cameraman, "This is history in the making, Colonel. We are recording our triumph over the Muslim people. It is not everyday that a population rids itself of wretched parasites such as these." He motioned to the Muslims staring at his group. "Look at them. They also want this to end." He reached back to his aid who handed him a bottle of wine. Mladic handed Karramans and Krstic glasses and then filled them. He held the bottle out and proposed a toast.

"Tomorrow all of the Muslims will leave Bosnia and then only the English and Serbian language will be spoken here," he said, making reference to the N.A.T.O. soldiers and his own Serbian forces. He raised the bottle and met Karramans' and Krstic's glasses with a clink. "To a long life, gentlemen."

As if on cue two fast moving F-15s pierced the cloud cover and launched a salvo of munitions on the tank positions closest to Potocari base and then arced outward, disappearing back into the clouds. The missiles struck their targets illuminating the overhead cloud canopy brightly as the explosions destroyed two T-80 tanks and their crews. A thunderous roar erupted from the thousands of refugees as they cheered the sudden, successful strike. General Krstic threw his glass to the ground and bellowed as he took a step toward Karramans. "What the hell is this?"

Mladic stepped between the two, but faced Karramans. "Stop the air strikes! Call them off!" he screamed.

Karramans looked over at the black smoke billowing from the burning tank wreckage. "I do not have the authorization to start or stop an air attack. The request was input days ago."

Mladic was not convinced. "Call them. Tell your General Jernvier that I am holding thirty of your men and several of your vehicles, as well as the food and water for those you are protecting.

Tell him that I will kill your men if another of my positions is destroyed. Go. Call him and report back to me."

Colonel Karramans stared at Mladic, then down at the wine that was still in his hand. He growled angrily as he threw the glass, liquid and all, over the head of Mladic and his men. He did not want to kowtow to the murderer before him, but the alternative was far worse. This was not his country. He looked around at the frightened people. These were not his people, and although he had a responsibility to protect them, he knew he could not. For these people it was over, there was nothing more he could do for them. He could, however, save the lives of his own.

"I will make the call, but on the condition that my soldiers are returned and we have access to the supplies and the vehicles. These people need food and water."

Mladic stepped closer, causing Karramans to take a step back. "I will agree to your terms, but realistically, you are in no position to make demands." With that, Colonel Karramans moved back to the building and to his office to call General Jernvier.

Masa peered through his binoculars from his position atop a steel cargo container, looking on as the U.N. guards lifted the gate and let the Serbian leadership pass through. They were heading to the office of Colonel Karramans. He turned to the entrance of the building where Karramans was now standing and motioning for them to come into the building. He lowered his binoculars and handed them to Nikolai who was crouched at his side. "This does not look good. Karramans appears to be making some sort of deal."

Nikolai looked at what was concerning Masa. He spotted several men with weapons walking with Mladic, as well as General Krstic. Nikolai scanned the road and the wood line. He could see more soldiers and infantry vehicles parked under the cover of the trees. In the near distance the two tank positions that had been hit by the missiles were burning. Other tanks and armored vehicles had moved onto the road. "They are preparing to move. Why aren't they attacking their positions? It has been an hour since the first missiles struck."

A cloud of dust flared in the distance and a flash of light grabbed Nikolai's attention as the morning sunlight glinted off the windshield of one of over fifty large passenger busses, ordered by Mladic himself, sent to pick up the refugees and move them to the Muslim safe areas in Kosovo. He readjusted the binoculars and focused on them as they lined up along the road as far as he could see, disappearing over the hill crest. Looking back in the direction of the gate he saw there were several hundred soldiers converging on the red and white striped barrier. It was raised and several soldiers had already entered the compound. He handed the binoculars back to Masa Orlich. "We must get our soldiers out of here now. Karramans has surrendered the base."

Masa and Nikolai climbed down from their position overlooking the base. Masa ran toward one of the warehouses, jumped up on some crates and began yelling to his soldiers and anyone who could hold and shoot a rifle, to collect as much ammunition, water and weapons as possible and move to the rear of the compound.

Nikolai, like thousands of others, was concerned for his children. He could only hope that they would make it to the Muslim Territory and that he would be able to meet them there. All they had to do was survive. He sat down for a moment with his children. Zlatco, fearing what was coming, was sobbing as he latched his arms tightly around his father. Nikki felt sorry for her brother, but she was scared as well, afraid more for her father than for herself and Zlatco. She stood staring, then suddenly, she reached around the back of her neck and unfastened the necklace she was wearing.

"Here, put this on. It will keep you safe." The shining silver crucifix dangled in front of Nikolai's eyes. He glanced at the people closest to them, wondering what they would think to see the symbol, knowing it was the Christians who were murdering their families.

Nikolai Sidorova had no faith. Born to a Muslim family, traditional in every sense, but Nikolai could not believe the history of his people that was told as the story of Allah. He wandered through his life with no religion to guide him, but with the goal to treat people as he would want to be treated, respected and loved.

Then he had met Nikki's mother, Tijana. She was Serbian, a Catholic and very beautiful. They would discuss life and other matters over coffee and walk for hours in the evening after work. On occasion Tijana tried to convince Nikolai that he should choose a faith. Muslim, Catholic, or Orthodox Christian didn't matter, but he should have something that he could embrace to help guide him, "...to bring peace into your heart," she would tell him as she placed her hand on his heart and joked, "You do have one in there, don't you?"

Sarajevo was a beautiful country that both he and Tijana loved. They got married and vowed that they would never leave. Sarajevo would be home for them and the children they would raise together. Even after Nikki was born and then Zlatco, Nikolai never committed to the type of faith that Tijana had, and the faith that she so desperately wanted for her children, though he supported her in her decisions when it came to her Christian beliefs. But in the summer of 1992 the Serbian Orthodox Christians were not so tolerant, nor forgiving.

Yugoslavia was a dissolving entity. The nation encompassed three distinct ethnic groups: the Bosnian Muslims, The Christian Orthodox Serbs and the Catholic Croats. One early morning in July it all came to a head. That morning several groups gathered to stage a peaceful protest, attended by hundreds of people representing all three groups, rallying against the nationalistic policies of their politicians which they felt were driving their nation farther apart.

Tijana had been downtown that morning, shopping for a present for Nikki whose birthday was approaching. Serbian Nationals began firing on the crowd of protestors. Tijana, wearing the clothing popular with the Muslim women in the area where they lived, was mistaken for one of the Bosnian women. She had been killed for beliefs that she did not share.

For the briefest of moments Nikolai could see Tijana again on that day as he had brushed away her hair and wiped the blood from her face. He was holding her lifeless body in his arms, sobbing, while hundreds of people ran past.

And now his daughter stood before him, extending the very necklace that Tijana bought for her on the day that she had been killed. Nikolai leaned forward allowing his namesake to fasten the clasp behind his neck. Nikki took Zlatco's hand and pulled him to stand next to her as her father got to his feet. Nikolai stood looking down at his children. "Be strong. I will meet you in Kosovo. Try to sleep on the bus."

Masa Orlich called to him, "Nikko, we must go now." He motioned for him to move. Nikolai turned and ran to his position where Masa handed him an AK-47 and some ammunition. Masa noted the crucifix glinting in the sunshine and gave Masa a strange look, remembering that he was not a Muslim, yet he fought side by side for their freedom. One day he would know this man's story, he supposed, but for now he just wanted to continue with the mission of getting those who were in the most danger out of Potocari Base and into the woods. Masa poked hard at the crucifix with an outstretched finger, "You might want to put that away."

Nikolai looked down at the amulet and then back in the direction of his daughter who was now out of sight, swallowed by the masses as they milled about inside and around the warehouse. He slung his weapon and moved in the direction of the fleeing men as he grabbed the necklace and dropped it inside his shirt and closer to his heart.

CHAPTER NINE

GENERAL Mladic's men assembled at the gate, herded the refugees into groups, and awaited further orders. Word spread quickly through the twenty-three thousand that the refugees were to be being taken by bus to the Muslim territory. Nikki looked around one last time for her father, hoping for a final glimpse as she held her brother's hand so she would not get separated from him. A woman leaned down and yelled so that Nikki could hear, "It's over. They are taking us out of here! There are busses coming for us!" she exclaimed ecstatically.

People began moving outside. Nikki and Zlatco had no choice but to move with the crowd. As they gathered in the open area outside the building, Nikki guided her brother toward the edge of the massive group of people for fear of him being trampled. When she made it through she could see soldiers with weapons surrounding the people, holding them in line.

One of the soldiers reached into the crowd and pulled a man from his wife and children. The family wailed as they tried to hold onto him. Another soldier grabbed the man's son by the arm as the mother screamed for him to let him go. The soldier yelled, "How old is this boy?" The woman yanked on her son's arm. "He is a baby. He is only ten. Please, let go of him!" she pleaded. The soldier released his grasp on the boy and let him clamber into the crowd to safety.

A tall officer walked back and forth barking orders at the crowd. "Women and children will board the busses at the front of the convoy. All men and boys, twelve years old and above, will board those busses and trucks." He motioned toward the end of the first row of busses. "You will be taken back to Srebrenica where you will gather your belongings and put them in bags in front of your homes. We will send trucks to collect the bags." The other soldiers repeated the directives so that everyone got the word.

An older man, shuffling through the crowd, tried to move past the guards. He ducked down behind several women as they were herded to the next group awaiting a bus. Nikki looked at him, noting how afraid he was. He placed a shaking finger to his lips and shushed her, giving Nikki and her brother a wink and a slight smile. She recognized him. He was a doctor of some sort who had come from the college in Sarajevo and had been in meetings with her father and Masa Orlich at their home, both in Sarajevo and Srebrenica.

Suddenly, there was a scuffle and a Serb soldier burst into the crowd and yanked the doctor out. "What the hell do you think you are doing? Get your ass over here with the other men, you coward!"

The doctor yelled, "Wait. Wait. I am a doctor. I need to be with them to help them!" He tried to move back into the crowd, but the soldier grabbed him again, this time shoving a pistol in his face.

The doctor held up his hands. "I am a doctor. I care for many of these people." He mumbled over and over. "I must go with them."

One of the Serbian officers stepped in. Nikki thought for sure the man was going to be shot, as did he. He was cringing at the barrel being held against his temple. The officer yanked the woman and her son from the earlier altercation and forced her to stand in front of him. The doctor recognized her from the march through the woods, he had wrapped her ankle that she had twisted on the rough terrain. He looked down at her ankle and the wrapping that was still on her leg. It had fallen down loosely around her foot, exposing her now purple ankle.

"Tell me, woman. Do you know this man?" the tall officer asked, while pointing at the doctor.

She looked at him, afraid to speak, but did so loudly to be heard over all the noise. "He is Dr. Jovan Kovicevic."

Dr. Kovicevic hissed a loud sigh of relief. "Yes, you see, I am Dr. Kovicevic. I told you, I need to stay with these people." The doctor began to move toward the crowd, but was yanked back yet again.

The officer glared at Kovicevic, turned to the woman and pulled the boy from behind her, placing him in front of the doctor. "This boy here, he does not look ten years old to me. He is taller and stronger than most ten year olds, don't you think, Dr. Kovicevic?"

The woman reached over her son's shoulders and placed her hands onto his chest, trying to pull him closer to her, away from the Serbian. She stared at the doctor and silently pleaded for him to say the right thing. Kovicevic felt the pressure of the pistol increase against his skull. "Well, Doctor, how old would you say this boy is?"

Nikki looked at her brother. He was small for his age but he was stocky, sure to grow to the size of her father. He could pass for ten or twelve depending on who did the looking. She pushed him deeper into the crowd and out of sight of the two soldiers.

The officer was getting impatient. "Dr. Kovicevic, tell me, how old is this boy? He is not ten years old is he?"

The doctor looked into the mother's pleading eyes. He knew he should lie and tell them that the boy was only ten, but he feared for his own life. If he could prove himself useful to them, then perhaps he would survive long enough to make it to the Muslim territory in Kosovo. He unlocked his gaze from the mother and looked into the crowd of people. His eyes happened to fall on Nikki's as he answered. "He is thirteen. I know this because his mother told me that he had just celebrated his thirteenth birthday the day the bombs fell on Sarajevo."

Immediately the mother began to scream, "He is lying!" He has mistaken us for someone else." She pulled her son away and pushed him in front of her as they tried to disappear into the crowd. The soldier dove in after them, shoving the mother hard, knocking her to the ground and grabbing the young man by the arm. The teen struggled, broke free, and ran from the Serb, headed along the fence toward the rear of the mass of refugees gathered there. The soldier moved to the outside, pulled his weapon up, and without warning, took aim and fired several rounds, hitting the boy in the back. The young man stumbled and fell face first to the ground. He tried to get to his feet only to fall back to the ground. This time, he no longer moved. The woman wailed and ran toward him as her husband struggled to free himself, only to be grabbed by more soldiers and held at the end of their rifles. The father looked beyond his captors, helpless to do anything for his son or his wife. He spat on the ground at the feet of the Serbs as the soldiers guided him toward the bus.

Dr. Kovicevic was placed by the entrance to the busses where he stood with a soldier and pointed out those who were either too old or too young to be a problem for the Serbians. All of the women were allowed to board regardless of age.

Nikki moved to the front of the line. She held the hand of her brother and worried that someone would call to him. "Come on, Zlatco. Move." She prodded him as she stepped onto the first step of the bus.

"Hold it. Stop!" She turned to see one of the young Serbian soldiers standing near them. "How old is he?" the soldier asked, preventing them from boarding.

Zlatco, not fully understanding what was going on, began to answer. Before he could speak Nikki stepped back down between the Serb and her brother. "He is ten," she stated flatly. The Serb looked at Nikki who was now standing very close to him. He couldn't help but notice her green eyes and note the suppleness of her full lips.

Nikki spoke quietly, "Please, my brother is ten years old. May we board the bus now?" She looked around the soldier to where another Serb and Dr. Kovicevic stood. Kovicevic was speaking to the Serb, but was looking in the direction of Nikki and her brother. Nikki moved a bit closer to the soldier, allowing her breast to contact the soldier's chest. She looked up at him with pleading eyes. "Please, let us get on the bus now," she nearly whispered.

The other officer now stepped up to them. "Let her board, but put the boy on the other bus." The young soldier looked apathetically at Nikki, but pushed past her, moving toward Zlatco as he barked, "Come on boy."

"No!" Nikki screamed. "No! He is all that I have left. Please, let him go!" She stepped back to keep them from Zlatco, but the soldier pushed her aside and grabbed him, pulling him off the step of the bus. Zlatco pawed at the bus railing not wanting to let go, yelling and kicking at the soldiers. Suddenly the Serbian officer pulled out his pistol. "Enough!" he yelled.

Zlatco and Nikki both stared at the pistol pointing in their direction. Nikki relaxed her hold on her brother as he was removed from the bus, whimpering. Nikki told Zlatco, "I'm sorry. I will meet you in Kosovo," but somehow she knew this would be the last time she would ever see him. Quietly she stepped up into the bus and watched out the window as her brother was placed on the only black bus at the far end of the convoy. She had promised her father she would protect him, but she had let them take him. Her remorse suddenly turned to determination. She could not leave him, not after getting this far. No, she thought, she would not let them take him without a fight.

As the driver of the bus began to close the doors, Nikki bounded from the bus and scrambled around the front to the opposite side. She moved stealthily along the busses, sprinting from one to the other until finally she made it to the black bus.

Inside the bus Zlatco sat crying. He had never been so scared or felt so alone. Some of the people on the bus were standing, trying to get a look at something outside. Zlatco looked out his window and saw Nikki moving down the side of the bus trying to see through the darkly tinted windows. He tried to get up, but the bus was so full there was no room to move. He beat on the glass with his fist.

Nikki moved down the length of the vehicle to find Zlatco sitting almost all the way to the rear. Zlatco stopped hitting the glass and screamed her name excitedly.

Suddenly, Nikki heard the sound of the busses as they began to accelerate one by one out of the compound. She was not sure what to do, but she had to get on Zlatco's bus. Clouds of dust burst from under the busses as the expelled air from the air brake check valves chirped and groaned, blasting pressurized air against the dirt and gravel of the road.

The Serb soldiers moved away, backing up to escape the thickening clouds of dust and exhaust that permeated the air. Nikki used the distraction of the pollutants, jumping out from between the busses and then flinging herself through the door opening, just as the driver was closing the doors. The bus lurched forward as Nikki shoved and pushed her way through the densely packed people to her brother, who was still looking for her outside the window. She stooped next to his seat and called his name quietly, "Zlatco." Her brother turned toward her voice. He smiled a huge smile and crawled over the man sitting to his left to get to his sister. "What are you doing here? You should be on the other bus."

Nikki sat on the edge of Zlatco's bench seat. She had come to save him, to remove him from the bus and disappear back into the safety of the woods. Now though, she was heading back to Srebrenica, or so they said. She was just as much a prisoner as her brother.

"I didn't want to lose you. This isn't what I had planned, but...well, I didn't really have a plan, so this will do. Now, let me think about what we will do once we get to where we are going."

She offered her hand to Zlatco who latched onto it, squeezing it hard. He didn't care what her plan was as long as she was with him. That was good enough.

CHAPTER TEN

MASA Orlich walked at the head of a line of about fifteen hundred men and boys who had managed to make it out of the compound before being forced to board the busses. The man with the green backpack came running to the front of the line, out of breath. He moved up the line to find Nikolai Sidorova and pulled at him, yanking him from the row. Nikolai recognized him again by the backpack. The man bent at the waist, leaned on his knees and tried to catch his breath.

"Your children...," he began, "They...were put on the bus. They split everyone up. Your boy was put on the Srebrenica bus."

Nikolai's heart faltered. He stared at the men he was leading to safety.

The man straightened up and put his hands on Nikolai's shoulders, "That's not all...your daughter...she switched busses. She is on the same bus as your son, heading back to the village."

"Damn it!" Nikolai cursed. "You are sure of this?" Nikolai looked around, assessing his situation. He was already a mile north of Potocari base, leading fifteen hundred men on a journey to safety, yet his own family was heading back to Srebrenica. He had to go get them.

"Why are you still standing here? They are going to kill them. You know that. Go! Save your family! I will do what I can to take over here." Nikolai looked toward Potocari Base and beyond it, to the red clay roofs dotting the hilly countryside and then back at the people trudging past.

He turned back to the man with the backpack. "Tell Masa that I left to go get my children. Tell him I will catch up or meet him at the end of all this." He motioned with a sweeping gesture to the thousands of marching people, then patted the man on the shoulder, unslung his weapon and handed it to him.

"Thank you, my friend," Nikolai said. With that he set out running for Srebrenica.

CHAPTER ELEVEN

TWENTY or so busses lined the road just outside the town as the men and boys disembarked for their homes to gather their belongings. Nikki and Zlatco hid at the rear of the black bus under the last seats and waited for the crowds of soldiers and people to disperse. A soldier stuck his head into the bus and began to board, but the driver insisted that the bus was empty. When the Serb soldier stepped away the driver looked back to where Nikki and her brother were crouched. "You have to go now. If they find you here I will be arrested...or worse. It is clear now if you go around to the other side of the busses."

Nikki grabbed Zlatco by the hand and moved up the aisle, crouching low in case anyone was watching. The two moved out and around the bus. In order to get to the woods they would have to move north, along the edge of the town. That would also take them by the house where they had been staying. Nikki thought they could stop in and get some supplies to take with them. They needed food and water. She could maybe grab some clothes and hygiene items. By then it would be close to nightfall and they could slip into the woods undetected. She pulled her brother along from bus to bus until they had no choice but to dash across the road and hide along a low stone wall. Just as they made it across the road the busses began to drive away.

They arrived at the small house without incident. Nikki went inside and immediately began to collect food for the trip north. As she gathered apples, oranges and cheese she told her brother to get some clothes and anything else he needed. Zlatco ran up the steps to the room he had shared with two other boys. Out the window he could see neighbors putting their belongings in large plastic garbage bags and setting them in front yards.

Nikki moved through the house deciding what she should take with her. She needed shoes badly, the ones she had been wearing were not hers and hurt her feet. She slipped them off and kicked them away. She stopped briefly at the bottom of the stairs and lifted a crucifix from the wall. It was a heavy cast made of porcelain, hand painted by her and her mother and glazed at a kiln in Sarajevo. She looked at it, contemplating its meaning in her current situation. Given the events leading up to this moment, she had to admit to herself that the miracles of her mother's and her own Christian faith hadn't been very plentiful as of late. She placed the cross back on the nail. If she had room she would take it with her.

Suddenly, she heard the sound of the back door as it slammed against the wall and then the unmistakable sound of her father's voice. "Nikki, Zlatco, where are you?" He stepped from the kitchen to be met with a forceful hug from his teary eyed daughter. He held her tightly for a few moments, then asked her, "Why did you come back here? You should have gotten on the bus headed to Kosovo with the others."

Nikki pushed back from him to look into his eyes. "They separated us, at the last minute. I found Zlatco, but we couldn't get off the bus before it started to drive away."

The sound of gunshots could be heard in the distance. "Where is Zlatco? We must get moving. There are fifteen hundred people being led to the Muslim territories by Masa and his men. Some of them are armed. If we hurry we can catch up with them. We will be safer in the woods."

Nikki did not have time to respond before she heard a loud crash that seemed very close. They could hear people arguing as a shadow passed by the window, then another, and another.

Suddenly the door handle shook, and before Nikolai could get to the door, the thick timbers of the doorframe split and shattered as the solid wood door flung open forcefully, slamming against the wall and shattering the glass.

Nikolai yelled for his daughter to run. "Hide, Nikki! Get away!" His thoughts flashed to his son who was upstairs. "Get your brother! Hurry! Run!"

Nikolai threw himself at the first man entering the house. He slammed him hard against the floor and stepped onto his face, then, reaching back, grabbed a butter knife from the table behind him and plunged the knife into the man's chest.

Nikki screamed as a second soldier grabbed her father, only to be met with a forceful blow from Nikolai's huge fist, which knocked him off his feet. Her father pulled at the rifle in the soldier's hands as a third man entered the house.

Nikolai grabbed the rifleman, thrust a knee into his groin and pulled him toward him, slamming the soldier's face into his knee, subduing him for the moment.

The third soldier, an officer, recognized Nikolai as one of the most sought after Muslim leaders, second only to Masa Orlich, and lunged at him, gaining the advantage on Nikolai with an arm around his neck. "Help me, this is Sidorova! Nikolai Sidorova! Do not kill him. Capture him!"

Nikolai struggled to break the hold. He looked to his daughter who was standing in shock in the doorway. "Nikki, go! Run!"

The soldier looked up as the teen ran past and up the stairs. The distraction was enough for her father to turn the advantage in his favor. His strong hands were like a vice, crushing the man's face into a distorted mound of twisted flesh. The officer screamed as Nikolai dug his thumb in, blinding one eye. He kicked him away forcefully, but was grabbed by the second soldier who was now back on his feet.

Nikki ran up the stairs only to meet her brother standing frozen. "What is going on?" he asked frantically. Nikki grabbed his hand and yanked him into motion, yelling over her shoulder to him. "Soldiers downstairs. Come on, we have to go!" She ran from the room toward the rear of the house. As she neared the end of the hallway one of the soldiers met her at the top of the steps. It was the officer whose face her father had mangled. He was bleeding terribly from what used to be his left eye.

Without hesitating, Nikki ran toward him and kicked him full in the face. Disoriented from the loss of half his vision, he fell down the steps backward and landed hard on the floor below. Nikki caught a glimpse of her father, still breathing, but beaten badly, being led from the house, his wrists bound behind his back.

One of the two soldiers helping to secure Nikolai turned to help the officer as he struggled to get up. He yanked away from the soldier and yelled, "There is a boy upstairs. Get him!...and kill that little bitch!"

Nikolai heard the orders and struggled to free himself. He spun to the side giving his remaining captor a head butt, only to be met with a kick to the stomach. He fell to his knees exhausted and watched through swollen eyes as his daughter turned at the top of the stairs.

Nikki grabbed her brother and dragged him behind her. She ran down the hall with her brother in tow and stopped to open the window to put him out onto the roof when she heard him scream.

One of the soldiers pushed Nikki hard against the window causing the large casement window to shatter, dropping large, jagged shards of glass to the floor. Nikki howled as a dagger-like piece of broken glass sliced through the top of her bare foot.

The soldier grabbed Zlatco by the arm and flung him toward the stairs where he was collected by another soldier and whisked out of sight. She heard the man yell to the others to go as he dragged her screaming brother down the steps and out the door.

Nikki had no choice other than to escape through the window. She struggled to release the lock, cutting her hands as she hurriedly brushed away the glass . She threw herself up on the sill.

"No you don't, girl!" the soldier growled as he grabbed her by the shirt and brutally pulled her down. She fell to the floor with a thud, landing on her back on the broken glass. The soldier loomed over her, then knelt down and grabbed her by the throat, choking her and pinning her to the floor as he struggled to remove her pants with his free hand.

Nikki clawed at his face only to be met with a punch that nearly caused her to lose consciousness. The man screamed at her to be still. She tried to shake the dizziness away and struggled to free herself as the soldier forced himself on her. She felt the Serbian pawing at her and could feel the glass grinding into her back and shoulder blades as she tried to return to her senses.

She forced herself up onto her elbows and tried to shuffle away from the weight of the man on top of her. The soldier pushed her down again, slapping her across the face. Nikki was just about to give in to him when she felt the broken glass at her bloodied fingertips.

The man felt her relax suddenly and assumed that she was submitting to his desire. He pushed her shirt up to reveal her breast. He looked at her green eyes and began to caress her. Nikki smiled just a little as she maneuvered the knife-like glass shard into position.

The soldier was breathing hard from the struggle. "You are like a wild cat. You should relax and enjoy it." His breath smelled of garbage and whisky as it hissed through his crooked and missing teeth, making Nikki nauseous. She held back the urge to vomit and turned her head away as the man lowered himself down to kiss her.

Nikki picked up the glass and drove it hard into his neck, burying it deep in his flesh and severing his jugular. Blood spurted from the wound as Nikki hit the glass with her fist several times, forcing the jagged spear in as far as possible and slicing into the soldier's larynx.

The man rolled onto his back, his eyes wide with surprise and fright. He clawed at the makeshift weapon only to have it break in his hands, blood oozing through his shaking, bloody fingertips as he gargled a plea for help.

Nikki grimaced as she knelt in the pieces of broken glass, struggling to get to her feet. She stepped backward and then leaned against the wall. Panting and shaking, she stood there, staring at the soldier struggling on the floor in front of her.

The flailing legs of the soldier kicked the weapon he'd left lying on the floor, sending the AK-47 spinning to a stop at Nikki's feet. Without thinking Nikki picked up the weapon and, while the young Serbian soldier struggled to stop the pain and the bleeding, she aimed and fired. The kick from the burst of automatic fire caused the rounds to travel up the man's chest and through his neck and face, exploding through his back and skull.

The Serb soldier fell limp and the blood no longer gushed from his neck. Nikki pulled her pants up fully and smoothed her shirt back into place. She stepped over the man, glass cracking under her bare feet, and moved carefully to the stairs holding the rifle nervously as she peered down, afraid of what she might find. The house was empty. The soldiers were gone and her father and brother were nowhere to be seen.

"Papa?" Nikki called down to the emptiness of the floor below. "Papa? Zlatco?" She stepped carefully down the stairs leaving a bloody footprint on every other step. Nikki held the weapon tightly and scanned the rooms for any movement. She walked into the kitchen, set the weapon down on the kitchen table and scanned the area outside the window, staying low. She saw plumes of dark smoke outside and stepped up on her toes to see.

Nikki carefully stepped through the mess and out the front door. The neighborhood was wrecked. The items that had been collected and placed in the front of the houses in bags had been set ablaze, thick black smoke billowed from burning vehicles, and several dead bodies, some of them soldiers and all of them men, were lying where they had been shot. Otherwise, the village appeared to be empty.

She ran a few feet to the middle of the road and yelled for her father and brother. She spun around and looked in all directions, then toward the U.N. checkpoint that was down a long sweeping hill about a mile and a half away. The last of the convoy of trucks and busses were driving away from the town. The blue helmets of the U.N. soldiers could be seen as the Dutch soldiers stood along the road, weapons hanging from their sides, helpless to do anything to stop the vehicles.

She ran toward the checkpoint, screaming her father and brother's names, but it was no use. The vehicles were diminishing in the distance. The guards that were supposed to be protecting Srebrenica from the murderous Serbian nationalists were walking away. There was nothing left to protect. For them the war was over.

Nikki collapsed to her knees and sobbed. *How could this happen?* she wondered. They were supposed to be protected from this type of attack. The American leaders at the United Nations promised an end to the violence, but instead had allowed a deal with the Serbian general, giving him the town, the base, and worst of all, the people, to deal with as he desired. She thought about her mother's death in Sarajevo three years before. What was she going to do now?

She looked back at her home and thought about what had just happened. She thought about her would-be rapist, the man that she had killed. She knew he would have raped her and then killed her. She'd had to kill him and she was glad. There was no one who could have helped her.

She wiped at a tear that trickled down her bloodied cheek. There was no one else, she thought again, no one who could protect her, protect her home, her family.

She went to church, she prayed, asking for the war to end, asking for her family's safety. Her prayers had largely been ignored. Her father would tell her to be strong, to keep the Christian faith that her mother had taught her. She could feel her father's large hand touching the crucifix hanging against her chest and telling her, "It will keep her alive...in your heart." Yet her father followed no religion.

Nikki got to her feet. She placed her hand on her chest and felt only the pounding of her heartbeat. The necklace, given to her father, was no longer there. Her tears splashed onto her hand, evaporating quickly in the hot mid-summer sun. She took a deep, shuddering breath and walked back to her house. Her feet were a mess, cut on both the bottom and the top, but she was numb to the pain. She stepped into the kitchen to retrieve the AK-47 that now belonged to her.

Nikki picked up the assault rifle and held it, contemplating her relationship with God. Her mother had told her that Christianity was the way to heal the world, to stop the bloodshed, yet it was the Christian Nationalists that destroyed her life and the lives of countless others. In fact it was a Christian Serb soldier that had killed her mother, supposedly mistaking her for a Muslim, based solely on where she lived and how she dressed. Where was her God today? Where had he been when her mother died? She raised the rifle and aimed down the sights of the AK-47 at the cross that hung on the wall, the same symbol that lured her mother to Sarajevo in the first place, to buy her daughter a gift at one of the few stores that supported her Christian faith.

Nikki had kept her mother in her heart for three years. Her memories and love for her mother were strong, but the pain caused by her death and anger over the irony of how she died left little room. Her heart was heavy with the losses she had suffered. There was no more room for forgiveness, for understanding and faith. She felt only hatred and the need for vengeance.

She closed her left eye and concentrated on the front sight pin, centering it on the poorly painted figure of Jesus. She had to make room for the new pain and sadness that was filling her heart. She had to let her mother go.

Nikki pulled the trigger releasing a single round. The seven-point-six-two millimeter round struck dead center of the porcelain cross, shattering the symbol in a powdery explosion as the bullet continued on, through the thinly framed wall to some unseen destination.

A sudden feeling of relief washed over her as she closed her eyes and accepted the closure she had been looking for.

PART 2

CHAPTER 1

RECALLED

DOMODEVO AIRPORT, MOSCOW, PRESENT DAY

NIKKI Sidorova awoke suddenly, snapped to consciousness when the wheels of the Tupelov contacted the asphalt of the runway, yanking her from her past and into the present. That landing, her return to reality from a dream state, was always a rough one. It took her a second or two to realize where she was, her groggy feeling passing as she thought about her dream. She reached her hand up to her chest, feeling for the crucifix. Feeling only the smoothness of her skin, she dismissed the thought and turned her attention to the phone still clutched in her hand, noting the time.

Though she had been asleep only for a few minutes, it seemed like so much time had passed. It always did, she thought, and supposed she would never be free from the reminders of her violent past. It was probably best that she dreamt about her shattered life as a child in Bosnia rather than some of the more current events in her life.

The Russian-built aircraft taxied into position, coming to a stop as the walkway extending from the main terminal inched its way to lightly contact the aluminum airframe. Nikki unfastened her seatbelt and gathered her belongings. She hated trans-Atlantic flights. Twelve hours of wasted time, she thought, as she stood to remove her carry on bag from the overhead compartment, garnering a stare from the flight attendant.

The attendant pulled a microphone from its mount. "Ladies and gentlemen, please remain seated. The captain has not yet turned off the seat belt light." She spoke to everyone, but she glared at Nikki, the only passenger standing, breaking the rules.

The electronic chime sounded and the seat belt warning light blinked off, as if on cue. Nikki smirked at the timing and glanced at the attendant who was still giving her a look of disapproval. The flight attendant turned her attention to the duty of collecting blankets and headphones as the captain's voice came over the speakers throughout the cabin. "On behalf of myself and the crew I'd like to welcome you to Moscow. The time is two-forty, and for those of you who are suffering from severe jet lag it is Thursday, not Wednesday, as you are probably thinking." The passengers erupted in light laughter, followed by conversation and a contagion of watch checking.

Moscow's Domodevo airport was huge and very busy, a gateway from the drab, still recovering and expatriated, communist country to everything better that the West had to offer. Still, as Nikki's adopted home, Moscow had its charms, one being the recognizable faces of her friends and colleagues. Nikki's eyes found one of those familiar faces, Anatoly Vacjevic, standing just on the other side of airport security. She smiled broadly and adjusted her steps through the crowd to meet him.

Anatoly was tall, but not lanky by any means. He had the body of an athlete. He was wearing an expensive, tailored suit that showcased his wide shoulders and slim waist. His dark brown hair, over his traditional eastern European features, was trimmed in an almost military fashion, yet long enough to be wavy with a small strand that always seemed to hang across his right eyebrow, as if intentionally placed there to draw attention to his brown eyes.

Anatoly sighed as Nikki came into view. He recognized the deep red-brown hair in the crowd as she negotiated her way toward him. She was nearly six feet tall and very sexy. She was wearing what the Americans liked to call a little black dress. The cotton fabric hung from her body in such a way that he could easily make out the contours of her breasts, abdomen, and hips. The dress ended mid thigh, exposing Nikki's smooth, toned legs. Anatoly returned Nikki's smile while holding out a hand, an offer to take her carry-on.

"Welcome back, Nikki. It has been a long time. It is very nice to see you again," he greeted. Then, leaning forward, he offered the pleasantry of a light welcome home hug, one that Nikki willingly accepted. After a minute they turned into the flow of people who were rushing to collect their luggage.

Nikki split from the crowd and called to him, "No, Anny, "I only have that one bag," she said, motioning to the bag Anatoly had slung across his shoulder, "I left everything else back at the apartment."

Anatoly was relieved at not having to wait through the baggage claim process. Once again at Nikki's side, he motioned ahead to a set of double doors and, ushering her through, walked into daylight and the muggy seventy degree air. Dodging the terminal traffic, they hurried across the road into the cooler shadows of the underground parking garage.

In the darkness of the garage, Agents Nathan Marks and Hector Villacruze sat in a black BMW 328i watching as Nikki and her male companion emerged from the terminal and walked within ten meters of their vehicle.

Marks aimed a cone shaped device in the direction of his subject and started recording. The M.E.V., or Mobile Eyes and Voice, was a directional audio receiver that had the capability of making both audio and video recordings at a discreet distance and would go unnoticed due to their vehicle's position, parked in the darkest corner. Now that the two agents had visual confirmation of their subjects, it wouldn't be long before the surveillance ball would start rolling, utilizing the latest high tech gadgetry to increase the success of their investigation.

Hector Villacruze, also known as Vee, and his partner Nathan Marks were both veterans of America's war on terror. Both served in the Special Counter Operations Terrorism Teams, or SCOT Teams, while in Iraq, during the height of the surge, under the command of then Captain Alan Ramsey, a SPECOPS officer and head of the specialized teams, and were experts in marksmanship and clandestine counter terror operations.

Ramsey, who developed the SCOTs program, was again their boss, this time as head of the T2SCI or Terrorism Tracking, Surveillance and Counter-Intelligence Division. Known simply as T2T, the C.I.A.-managed Terrorist Tracking Division, originally a small component of the C.I.A., had grown exponentially due to recent successes. To fill his ranks Alan Ramsey called on specialized military members, such as Villacruze and Marks.

Villacruze spoke quietly into his Bluetooth headset. "This is Vee. We got them on the east side of the parking garage."

The other two teams checked in, acknowledging that information.

"Roger. It's about time we heard from you. I was wondering if maybe somebody didn't put you two kids down for your afternoon nap."

Vee smiled, recognizing the voice as Paul Jackson's, the security guard turned operative who, on his first mission with the T2T, surprised the agency with his adaptive skills and unwavering fearlessness while helping in the pursuit of a ruthless terrorist.

Before Villacruze could respond to Paul Jackson's verbal attack on his youth, the driver of the third vehicle responded.

"Moving," Bob Matthews stated flatly.

Villacruze toggled the microphone and directed a question to their resident technical geek, Rick White, who was working from an apartment three miles from the airport. "Rick, you got the GPS lock yet?"

White was an electronic genius. He could manipulate software and electronics better than anyone Alan Ramsey or the team had ever met, creating computer and mobile device programs and hacks on the fly.

White had been invaluable during their last mission, creating a program known as CHERI, an acronym for Controlled Hosting Enhancement and Recognition Imaging. The program helped gather information from within the three letter organizations' data bases, assess and summarize information within minutes instead of hours.

What had started as a hack, born out of necessity and refined for the agency under White's direction, was quickly integrated and eventually mandated into every D.O.D., clandestine, and civilian law enforcement agency by the Department of Homeland Defense, changing the face of interagency cooperation and becoming a cornerstone in the revised doctrinal operational procedures under the PATRIOT act.

Rick White acknowledged Vee's question. "I've got your phone, Jackson's and Matthew's all imaged and on the grid. How close are you to the subject?"

Vee estimated his distance from his subject and reported back, "Approximately one hundred meters."

Rick White needed to build a baseline. His tracking methods required using the cell phone signals in the area of operation as a grid of sorts. By locating all the phones in the area, identifying the known devices, such as Vee's and the rest of the team, he could build a virtual site picture of moving points. Once established, White would use the informational grid to locate Nikki Sidorova's phone. However, to make it work he needed someone on location to describe the real-time environment. That task belonged to Villacruze who would act as a spotter, describing his surroundings to White. "Ok, Vee, I'm ready. Give me the lowdown," White asked.

Vee scanned the area looking for any other people within his range of vision. "I've got two people near the entrance of the airport and one walking away from us toward the end of the parking lot."

White manipulated the images on the screen, touching and pulling at the virtual map to increase its size and the clarity of subject's positions. The satellite view expanded showing the GPS markers for Vee and the other two agents. He performed a couple of key commands overlaying the area between the agent's markers with a series of grid lines. Within a fraction of a second the grid was populated by red and blue markers, each one representing a GPS lock for every phone within the triangulated area of the three agents. One of the dots was moving east, away from Vee's red marker. All he had to do now was understand the picture as Villacruze saw it.

The radio crackled after a short silence with White asking, "Vee, which direction are you facing?"

Villacruze was pretty sure he was looking east. He ran through his mind the route he had taken to the airport. The highway was parallel to his position. He reported back to Rick White. "We are facing east. My subject of interest is to my left, ten o'clock, about one hundred meters."

Rick White used his multi touch interface to spin his virtual map to correlate it with the information Vee had just given him. He could see two markers within feet of one another.

White zoomed in on the markers. "Roger, I have two blue dots at ten o'clock and one hundred meters. Is your subject closer or farther from your position?"

Villacruze verified the ten o'clock reference, mentally acknowledging that his view and the picture that White was developing several miles away were the same before answering.

"Farther. She's moving toward the passenger side of the car. She's farther away."

Rick White touched the dot on the screen and placed a shaded circle around the marker. A text box was generated automatically and the phone number for Nikki's phone populated the fill. White added her name to the text box. "Got it. I'll give her a call and get the program running."

Anatoly opened the rear hatch of his Lada Priora. Nikki looked at the sleek lines of the sporty silver car as she dropped her bag in the back.

"Nice. When did you get this?" she asked as he closed the hatch, then stepped over to the passenger door.

"I've had it for about a year," Anatoly said as he slid in behind the wheel. "It's a little small compared to the Mercedes, but the performance is impressive and its fun to drive." Anatoly smiled at Nikki as if he were advertising the car.

Nikki smiled back. She liked Anatoly Vecjevic. He was handsome, rugged, and, he was good in bed. They were good friends and at times, lovers, despite the fact that he was married.

"How is Elena?" Nikki asked with a look of disdain and a sarcastic flutter of her eyelashes.

Anatoly frowned, rolling his eyes skyward as he started the car. The engine growled as it came to life then purred as the man reached above the visor for his sunglasses.

"She is the same as always, mean and controlling. Why I am still married to her is a mystery."

He shifted into reverse, flashing a big smile at Nikki as he turned to look over his shoulder. "I would be better off had I married someone like... oh, I don't know, Lenin, or maybe even Brezhnev. I think either of them might have been friendlier sometimes."

Nikki laughed at Anatoly's situation. "Yes, and the amount of sex would probably be the same," Nikki said sarcastically, laughing some more. "That is what happens when you marry for money and politics."

"Don't forget the big breasts. Money, politics and large breasts," Anatoly replied. He turned his head, looking at Nikki over his sunglasses, smiling a wicked grin before continuing. "Not that I don't like yours." He reached out to fondle Nikki's breast through the black cotton dress and leaned over to kiss her. Nikki leaned in, sighing and closing her eyes. She kissed him, drawing in on his bottom lip playfully, but then pushed his hand away.

"Stop. I am tired and grungy from the flight. Take me to the apartment, so I can take a shower. If you are well behaved I will let you stay for a little while, but not long. I have to get some sleep."

Anatoly grinned as he stepped down on the accelerator causing the tires to screech loudly on the concrete surface.

As Anatoly sped away CHERI began its algorithmic sequence, searching the local cyberspace for cellular artifacts that shared the same trace elements and electronic "fingerprint" as Nikki's Russian built Vladd cell phone, gathering bits and pieces of hundreds of her calls that had bounced from local cell towers to satellites thousands of miles above the earth, gleaning the information to identify the most commonly called number and sending that information back to Rick White's laptop.

On White's command a call would be placed to Nikki Sidorova's phone. To Nikki the call would seem normal, displaying the name of the caller as someone who was known and trusted, ensuring an answer. Once Nikki picked up, a re-engineering "virus" would be introduced into her phone. The virus, a type of malware, energized select components, such as the microphone on Nikki's phone, then transmitted the data to Agent Marks' receiver in the BMW using the phone's GPS signal as a sort of modified radio signal.

There was one drawback to the system. The voice over GPS protocol wasn't strong enough to support the data required for voice communications to be sent over long distances. Villacruze's BMW would act as a mobile relay station, staying close to Anatoly's Lada Priora to capture, amplify, and then broadcast the information to Rick White's location.

Nikki was contemplating whether she had the energy for anything other than a shower and sleep when the sound of her phone's ring tone interrupted her thoughts. She fumbled for a moment, digging in her bag and then lifted the phone. She frowned when she saw the name of her boss, Dmitri Gregorov, then showed it to Anatoly.

"It's the General," she said sarcastically, staring at the number and contemplating not answering. The phone played through the ring tone a second time. Nikki made a face and sighed deeply. "Hello, Dmitri." There was no answer.

"Hello?" Nicki said again, but still there was only silence.

She pulled the phone away from her ear and looked at the display. It was connected and her signal strength was good. She placed the phone back to her ear.

"Hello,.. Dmitri,.. Hello."

All she heard was a click and some electronic garble. "Oh, well, lost the call. Too bad." She threw her phone back into her bag.

Anatoly looked questioningly at her. "Aren't you going to call him back? Dmitri doesn't usually call unless it is important."

Nikki adjusted her seat to lean back a little. "To hell with Dmitri. He can kiss my ass today. If it was important he will call back."

Agent Villacruze pulled in a few cars behind the Lada and called in. "This is Vee. We're in position." He adjusted the zoom on his binoculars.

Alan Ramsey was monitoring the situation from White's location in the hotel room across town. "Vee, stay back. You don't want to spook them. Sidorova picked up the call, so you should have feed in a minute."

"Roger that, Sir. We're tracking only," Vee replied. Alan thought back briefly to his days as a team leader and captain in the Army Special Forces. He was glad that Staff Sergeant Villacruze, now Agent Villacruze, was still part of his team.

Ramsey picked up his phone and dialed the Russian Special Services liaison assigned to the American investigation.

"Hello, this is Russo."

"Ruslan Makovich, this is Alan Ramsey. I was told to give you a call when our investigation began."

"Ah, Mr. Ramsey, yes, and please, my fellow officers call me Russo. Please, call me Russo." The voice was loud and his English was somewhat choppy. Still, Ramsey appreciated that he spoke English.

"And you can call me Alan. I have to get back to what is going on here, but wanted to let you know our subject just got off the plane and has left the airport. We are following right now."

Russo answered, "Yes, I got a report from my men in the airport that she had arrived and that you had...," he paused as he thought of the phrase, "...eyes on your target."

Alan Ramsey didn't like that Russo and his men were observing. He was concerned that they would overstep the parameters of the agreement with the C.I.A. ambassador. He cut the conversation short.

"Ok, Russo. Gotta go. Make sure your agents stay way back. Remember, we have the lead on this. We need some room to breathe."

Russo replied flatly, "Thank you for calling. Let me know if you need anything else." With that his phone disconnected.

Jackson's voice suddenly broke the silence bringing Ramsey back into the game. "I just caught up with Vee. I'm on his ass, three vehicles back."

Jackson then called to Villacruze. "Hey, Vee. Is that a little silver car you're tracking?"

Villacruze replied, "Yeah, you got it." Vee looked in his mirror and spotted the dark blue Volkswagen Touareg SUV trailing his BMW. He wondered about Matthews. "Hey, Jackson, where's your driving buddy?" he asked.

Bob Matthews' voice suddenly entered the conversation. "I'm heading west on Leskiev. I'll jump on a cross street to switch out when you're ready. Let me know when they turn, and which way."

Agent Marks suddenly pointed forward and yelled, "Highway! They're jumping on the highway!"

Bob Matthews nearly missed the highway entrance. "Got it. I'm heading up the ramp now." Villacruze could hear the tires squealing in his headphones, protesting Bob Matthews' sudden maneuver to the entrance ramp.

Inside Anatoly's car the radio was on, broadcasting the news. More unrest in the Middle-East. Syria and Iraq were on the defensive against a faction known as ISIS, a group all but ignored by the last American administration and one allowed to grow exponentially. Now Jordan and Iran were entering the fight, trying to push back a force that was gaining support from groups like Al-Shabaab in Africa and growing stronger by the day. The ISIS movement had set the Middle-East on fire, it seemed, threatening the rise of a new Caliphate and promising to control the lands controlled by the Muslim people over 900 years before.

Nikki's closed eyes and relaxed posture changed suddenly when the news anchor began his next report.

"And finally, today in Srebrenica, officials there are closing the book on recovery efforts to find the last remaining victims of the 1995 slaughter, with a solemn ceremony, as the last identified remains of those killed were laid to rest, marking the closure of one of the worst atrocities in the history of modern Eastern

Europe. For more on this we go to Etovny Belaruz reporting live from Srebrenica."

"Thank you, Jon. I'm standing here, on the grounds of what was once the home of the 400 strong, United Nations Protection Force, Dutch Base, Potocari, overlooking the rolling hills of the Drina Valley, the site of one of the most grisly acts of genocidal cleansing. This lush green hillside, the location of fierce battles and destructive shelling during the Bosnian War, today is filled with the cries and chants of the local Muslims who have gathered here for a solemn ceremony."

The reporter's voice faded as the sound of ghostly wailing from the family members of those killed during the five year long war permeated the interior of Anatoly's car.

"From this vantage point one can see the rows and rows of green fabric draped coffins, five hundred in all, the last of the identifiable remains of those who were driven from their homes, interrogated, and savagely murdered, more than fifteen years ago, by members of the Army of the Republica Srpska, the forces loyal to then President, Slobodan Milosevic. Milosevic did not go to trial, instead, dying a suspicious death in prison before being able to speak at The Hague. An untimely end for the one man who could have shed so much light on the fifteen year long investigation."

Nikki's attention was drawn to the sound of the announcer's voice. He was droning on about the end of the search for more bodies, and how this mass burial would bring closure for hundreds, if not thousands of people.

"Closure? How could these be the last when my brother and father are both still missing?" she asked angrily. Nikki listened, seething as the reporter continued.

"That Milosevic was not tried and found guilty for his crimes may be the worst part for these people. Speculation about the cause of Milosevic's heart attack point to an assassination plot. Some even wonder if perhaps he was killed so he would not reveal others who were equally responsible for the attacks.

Only those who lie here today have the answers. Answers that they take with them, literally, to the grave.

With these five hundred coffins there comes the end of a decade long government search and identification process. Still, it is estimated that there may be at least another four hundred out there, somewhere, waiting to be found.

Reporting live from Srebrenica, this is Etovny Belaruz."

Nikki was furious. "What?" she screamed at the radio. She looked at Anatoly. "How can they stop looking? There has to be more!"

Anatoly tried to calm her. "Nikki, calm down. Tomorrow we can call the consulate and ask for a list of names. No, today we will go online and see if there is a list. Maybe Nikolai and Zlatco's names will be listed. If they are we will get you back home for the funerals tomorrow."

Nikki was nearly hyperventilating. Anatoly tried to take her hand but she pulled away abruptly and slammed her fist down hard on the console.

"And if they are not among the dead, then what? This is bullshit!" she yelled to nobody in particular.

Anatoly knew enough to leave her alone when she got like this. She was fuming. Tears tracked down her cheeks.

"What does Gregorov want?" Nikki asked suddenly, changing the subject. "Why did he bring me back to this place?"

Anatoly was relieved by the sudden change of subject.

"I am not sure. He said that he wanted you here when he met with Dr. Metelov in two days."

Nikki suddenly turned to face Anatoly. "You mean Vladimir Metelov, the one who built the bomb for the terrorists?"

Anatoly was not fully aware of what had happened in America while Nikki was on assignment there. He knew that there was a nuclear weapon and that the General had not only sold the warhead, but had transported it to the U.S. as well. What happened between the warhead leaving the arsenal and Metelov's return to Moscow he did not know, and, as Gregorov had told him, was none of his business. Other than securing the flight for Dr. Metelov and setting up an overseas account to manage the doctor's money upon his return, Anatoly was in the dark.

"Yes, I believe so. He helped the terrorists is all I know. That and the fact that he returned with over a million American dollars."

Behind Anatoly, two cars back, Agent Matthews was still trailing the Lada when Marks and Vee sped past him. Vee's voice came over his com set. "We need to move up. We're losing signal. Marks barely got that last conversation. It's bad enough the radio is on. Can't hardly make anything out."

"But, did you get it? The part about the warhead and Metelov?" Matthews asked.

Vee and Marks took the same exit as the Lada and were now directly behind Anatoly and Nikki. "Oh yeah, we got it."

CHAPTER 2

GREGOROV

ACROSS town Alan Ramsey poured a cup of coffee. He was thinking about Dmitri Gregorov and the upcoming meeting with Metelov. He took a seat at one of the computer terminals and scrolled a finger across the smooth surface of the touch-pad, bringing the system out of its sleep mode. The desktop was littered with files and folders about Gregorov. There were photos and videos from years past as well as the information that had been gathered in the last few weeks.

Alan studied the latest pictures and information regarding his subject, noting his age. Supposedly in his eighties, Gregorov appeared to be in excellent health and looked no more than sixty.

He scrolled through the electronic dossier reviewing what information he had about the ex-Soviet general. His past was made up of both heroics and scandal, making some of the Russian politicians of today look like saints. Although Gregorov was neither a politician nor a spy, he had connections to both, and had controlled some of them with bribes and special favors, and, assuredly, blackmail.

Dmitri Gregorov was one of Russia's youngest war heroes who began his military career in 1941, on the day that over a million German soldiers and nearly three thousand tanks of Gerd von Rundstedt's Army Group South smashed through Gregorov's hometown of Kiev, the third largest city in the Soviet Union, and the capital of the Ukraine.

The *Hero of the Soviet Union and the Order of Lenin Award* was the highest honor a soldier could receive in the heyday of the Soviet military. Ramsey read the translated text, the story of Dmitri Gregorov, the fourteen year old who watched as his father was gunned down by soldiers of the fast moving Sixth Army, backed by the deadly First Panzer Group, on the first day of what would become known as Operation Barbarossa.

Hungry and exhausted, after running south for two days, the young Gregorov met up with what was left of the 3rd Mechanized Corps, 11th Army, a company of Russian T-34 tanks. He had just climbed up on one of the tanks, accepting half a piece of bread from a soldier when German Panzers from the Army Group South formation exploded from well hidden positions in the tree line and began firing on the parked tank company.

The Russian tankers scrambled for their vehicles, literally jumping into their hatches. The machine-gunner of the T-34, the soldier who had offered the bread to Dmitri, sprang up to get into his hatch only to be met with screaming twenty millimeter rounds from one of the Panzers, cutting him in half as they rocketed toward a slow moving T-34 on the other side of the road.

Huge explosions reverberated all around, creating concussions unlike anything the teenager had ever experienced. He fell sideways against the thickly armored cupola as the T-34 under his feet jerked into motion over the rubble strewn road.

As machine gun fire whistled by only inches above his head, Gregorov scrambled up the turret of the tank and into the open gunner's hatch. He pulled his knees to his chest, ducking down low, struggling to regain some sense of composure when the first tank round was fired from his vehicle.

The tank shuddered as the round left the barrel. Within seconds the turret was spinning left. Gregorov heard the sound of electric motors and hydraulic cylinders energizing, the main gunner repeating the words of the tank commander, screaming some firing formula, and then the explosive force of another tank round being fired wracked his body.

Gregorov found himself in the midst of a fierce tank battle. He looked up through the open gunner's hatch at the quiet machine gun as it bounced and spun, unmanned, on the mount above him. Without really thinking, he stood up and started firing the machine gun in place of the dead gunner. He took aim at the Nazi infantry as they moved in like flowing water, behind the flanking Panzers and the newly introduced Tiger tanks, and killed nearly 100 special Nazi infantry soldiers and grenadiers. The battle raged on for more than an hour as the T-34 tanks continued to hold their ground against the German Panzer division until reinforcements could arrive.

The fact that Dmitri not only survived such an ordeal, but that he was integral to the success of the battle, left the young man stunned and grateful. With an overwhelming sense of success and pride, Gregorov stayed with the 3rd Mechanized Corps, 11th Army, proving himself both on and off the battlefield, earning a field commission and command of the company.

Twenty years later, the barbed wire fencing and the first of the thick concrete slabs of the Berlin Wall went up, separating the families of Europe into two groups: Communists and the West. The young armor officer poured himself into the communist military experience, becoming the epitome of the Soviet soldier.

Less than a quarter century later, General Gregorov watched as the wall and everything he knew and had worked for came crashing down around him. After a lifetime of steadfast support for the Soviet military, he would lose his pension, housing priority, and medical benefits, as well as other special privileges that were part of his *Hero of the Soviet Union Award* prize package. Suddenly the Cold War was over and he had no enemy for which he could plan defeat. For millions of post-Soviet civilians the future held the promise of peace, but for Gregorov and others like him, the future was undefined.

As a high ranking general with a glorious hero's history, Dmitri Gregorov had enjoyed the high class political scene. Throughout his illustrious career he had made many friends and an equal amount of enemies.

Yet, when the walls came down his friends and associates abandoned him, helping themselves to newly created political positions. And his enemies forgot about him, writing him off, leaving Gregorov without a future. Except for a modest amount of money he had saved, Dmitri Gregorov had nothing to show for over forty years of dedicated service.

So, for the last twenty years Dmitri Gregorov had lived off the profits of the sale of the government weapons he had protected throughout his military career, laying claim to abandoned arsenals of weaponry all but forgotten by his government. In the very early months following the collapse, Dmitri could literally drive his unguarded fortune away from the abandoned motor pools.

His collection grew to include S.A.S. missile trucks, mechanized infantry BMPs, T62s and the formidable T82 tanks. He had an arsenal of weapons from Kalashnikov automatic assault rifles to grenade launchers and shoulder fired missiles.

Gregorov was suspected of selling Scud rockets and chemical weapons to Iraq, AK-47s and RPGs to Iran, Turkey, Syria and Bosnia. The litany of charges was long and mostly unproven. But now, given that his last sale of a weapon of mass destruction, or WMD, was to a small faction of terrorists that nearly succeeded in destroying an American city, and it appeared that he was directly involved in the transportation of the Soviet-era nuclear warhead to the United States, the President had vowed to work with the Russian government to capture or kill their most wanted criminal.

Ramsey knew that the time to prove Gregorov's involvement, arrest him and have him extradited was limited. President Carlton had made it perfectly clear to the C.I.A. director that if Ramsey and his team could not take him down, he would turn the investigation over to the Russians. Ramsey was given a thirty day window to make it happen and he was already into the third week of the operation. He was running out of time.

Kenneth Wash

CHAPTER 3

HOME SWEET HOME

ANATOLY pulled through the gates that made up the entrance to the parking area for Nikki's apartment, maneuvering through the brick archway connecting two apartment buildings. The buildings were typical turn of the twentieth century architecture. Row after row of four and six apartment complexes, rehabbed a decade after the disintegration of the Soviet Union.

The Lada Priora stopped just across from the entrance to Nikki's apartment. Anatoly removed his keys and quickly got out and walked around the car to open Nikki's door.

Anatoly was still in love with this woman. He had tried to leave her in his past many times, but the sound of her voice, her laugh, and even just the trace of her scent could bring back memories that affected him much like the stimulus that would trigger a flashback suffered by a veteran of combat.

He took a long breath through his nostrils as Nikki stepped from the car and stood fully. Her green eyes expressed a sadness that Anatoly knew he could never fully understand. Her life had been harsh. She was strong and beautiful, but her childhood haunted her. It must be devastating, Anatoly thought, to get the news, after years of waiting, that all hope of finding the bodies of her father and brother were gone.

Anatoly reached out and pulled her into him. She accepted his comfort for the moment. He rested his chin on her shoulder, but lifted his head quickly when a black BMW drove past the entrance gates. The car was moving too slowly, he thought, as he released his arms from around Nikki. She pushed away and looked beyond the gates, then back at Anatoly. "What is it? What's wrong?"

Surely it was nothing, he thought. Who could know that he was with Nikki? He assumed it was just his paranoia.

"It's probably nothing, but I think Elena may have had me followed. I don't know why she would. She knows I don't give a shit about her. Let's go inside. I'm probably just being foolish."

Nikki spoke as she turned to head in the direction of the apartment. "And if she has someone following you, then what will you tell her?" She looked at him quizzically.

Anatoly's face lit up as he walked sideways and backward so that he could look into Nikki's eyes. "I will tell her that today I met a woman who is so beautiful and sexy that I couldn't help but fall in love with her, and now, I want a divorce."

Nikki smiled. She looked up at Anatoly, who was leaning his head to the side, as if to look around the wisps of her reddish-brown hair that hung in front of her, concealing one of her eyes. Nikki found her keys and shook them a little to make them jingle, holding them up as a sign of success after not having them in her hand for almost two years.

She smiled, then asked rather rhetorically, "So then what? Are you willing to give up all that you have, all of the money, the parties and your sporty little cars...for me?"

Anatoly paused at the door. "Wait, don't move."

Nikki stopped, turning to face him with a hand on her hip. Anatoly peered at her and then held up his finger emphasizing that she should wait. He turned, stuck his head out of the door and looked at his Lada Priora, then back at Nikki, eyeing her from head to toe, and again at the sports car.

Nikki sighed, tiring of his antics. "Anny, what are you doing? Come on."

He stepped through the door feigning a look of bewilderment and said, "It's...just...well, I *really* like that car. Such a tough choice. It is not fair to make me choose." Anatoly flashed a big smile.

Nikki punched him hard in the solar plexus, catching him totally off guard, causing him to double over with a sudden exhale and a grunt.

Anatoly watched her walk away admiring her strength, her glistening hair and her shapely body, all the while holding his chest, alternating between smiling, grimacing and gasping for air.

CHAPTER 4

MICROMANAGEMENT

GABRIEL Anderson moved quickly down the hallway. This was the second time in as many days that he'd been summoned to the Secretary of State's office. He thought that if this kind of meeting schedule kept up, he would have to get a secondary office nearer to the State Department building. He hadn't yet gotten to Secretary Erickson's office when the C.I.A.'s State Department liaison, Gene Patterson, met him.

"Morning, Gabe, glad you could get here on such short notice. Hopefully you've had some coffee. Erickson is pretty geared up this morning."

Gabe Anderson smiled as he shook Patterson's extended hand. Gabe studied the uncomfortable, almost scared look that Patterson wore. It was a new and permanent feature of his predecessor's appearance, due to his recent move from the position as Deputy Director to his current position as the C.I.A. liaison to the State Department, a position that he struggled to perform marginally at best. As much as Gabe Anderson respected the man, he had always felt he was the wrong pick for the position.

As the C.I.A. liaison to the State Department, Patterson was so far removed from his professional comfort zone and the C.I.A. element that he became ineffectual, unable to extend even the slightest influence of the office of the C.I.A. to that of the office of the Secretary of State. Gene Patterson had been effectively neutered.

Patterson was being treated by the Secretary of State, Jim Erickson, as his own personal C.I.A. errand boy, causing a flood of attempts by Erickson to use his position as SECSTATE and close friendship to the President to influence operations deep within the C.I.A. And now, with the successful operation of the C.I.A.'s T2T Division, and Gabe Anderson in the Deputy Director's position, it was Anderson who was battling the rising waters, but today Patterson seemed even more disheveled than usual.

"You been here long, Gene? Hate to say it, but you look like shit." Gabe said, jokingly.

"Yeah, about two hours. Erickson called me in at five this morning. He said he wanted some specifics about the last three weeks of your project. I gave him everything I have, but he still wanted to talk to you directly. Said he wanted to hear it straight from the horse's mouth."

Anderson scoffed, "Great thing, that trust and confidence. Are you sure he said horse's mouth, though, and not horse's ass? You know, Erickson and I don't exactly see eye to eye on this mission's objective...Wait, let me rephrase that, on *his* mission objective for *my* mission."

Patterson gave a smirk, "Ah, I do believe that I sense a bit of interagency hostility."

Gabe Anderson wasn't smiling when he stopped walking and said in a low tone, "Look, you and I both know that the Secretary of State has no business trying to tell us how to do our job. The C.I.A. doesn't even fall under his supervision. I don't get it. Why does this clown Erickson have the President's ear when it comes to this mission?"

He paused briefly, poked a finger in Patterson's direction and said, "I told the director, if he had any balls at all, he'd back you up and keep this prick out of our affairs."

Patterson looked around before speaking, "Gabe, I appreciate that and I understand your frustration. Remember, I'm here running defense all day long for all the National Clandestine Service divisions, not just the T2T."

Gabe shot back, "Yeah, well how much does he try to jump into the operations of the other N.C.S. organizations? Seems to me he's fixated on the T2T and, more specifically, this mission. Ok, Ramsey's program is new. We just came off a very successful operation, glory and confetti, I get it, but this guy needs to back down and let me, no, let us, do our jobs. Holding a meeting every five minutes doesn't help at all."

Gene Patterson prodded Anderson to keep moving, "Well, and trust me, I'm not just blowing off your concerns when I say this, but you've got one more week of surveillance and then a wrap up. Gregorov will be in custody, under C.I.A. protection, and I'll do my best to make sure Erickson is out of our hair at that point. He simply won't have a jurisdictional leg to stand on, no matter whose ear he's got." He patted Gabe on the shoulder as he urged him hurriedly along.

They reached Erickson's outer office door to find it open and walked in. Patterson made a quick attempt to look a little less worn as he stepped in. He ran a hand through his hair and turned to Erickson's secretary, "Hi, Betty. Is Secretary Erickson back yet?"

Betty was a veteran staffer who had been assigned to at least six other offices in the last fifteen years. Most everybody knew her, including the last four presidents. "He is, Gene." She looked up at Gabe. "Well, good morning, Mr. Anderson. Welcome back." She smiled broadly as she called to Jim Erickson on the intercom, "Mister Secretary, Mr. Patterson and Mr. Anderson are here."

The sound of footsteps preceded the opening of Erickson's inner office door. Jim Erickson stepped out smiling, hand outstretched. "Gabe, glad you could make it."

Gabe Anderson feigned a pleasurable look as he shook the Secretary's hand. "We start having these meetings any earlier in the day and I do believe I may have to move in. Hell, I think Gene already has."

Erickson was unmoved by Gabe Anderson's attempt at humor. "Would you care for some coffee? I've got fresh Starbucks," he offered, as he poured himself a fresh cup. "I'll try not to keep you too long. The President should be here any second."

Anderson was caught off guard as he picked up a cup from the table. "President Carlton is sitting in?" He glanced at the liaison.

Gene Patterson turned his hands upward and shrugged his shoulders, gesturing his lack of knowledge about what was going on.

Erickson saw the exchange. He could see the two men were surprised and explained, "I spoke with him after our earlier meeting. He asked to come down and get in on this one. What was I supposed to do, tell him no? He is the President."

His last statement seemed directed at Gabe Anderson. Gabe noticed the look on Erickson's face as he said it. He looked...spiteful, Anderson mused, taking a sip of his coffee. Suddenly, the door swung open. Gabe set his cup down and stood as the other two got to their feet.

"Oh, for Christ's sake, gentlemen, relax," the President said as he headed straight for Gabe Anderson and grabbed his hand to shake it. "Alright, glad you came. I'm excited to hear what's going on with your team. What is it again, the T2T?"

Gabe answered quickly, "Yes, sir. That's kind of a nickname for the acronym T2SCI or Terrorism Tracking, Surveillance and Counter-Intelligence."

President Carlton turned to face them all, smiling, "Got it," he said, shaking his head, "Too many damned acronyms. Hard to keep track of them all." He turned, coffee cup in hand and paused before sitting. "Please, gentlemen, take a seat."

"Ok, Staff. Let's talk some business. Mr. Anderson, if you could fill me in on your progress so far."

Gabe stood and opened his notebook in front of him. He handed a few pages of information to the President and the Secretary of State. "Gene, you have a copy of this already, right? It's yesterday's update, as of nineteen-hundred hours."

Gene Patterson acknowledged that he did and retrieved his copy and placed it in front of him.

"Ok, then," Gabe began, "I know that you know who General Dmitry Gregorov is, but do you know any of his history prior to his sale of the nuclear warhead to Hamza al-Muhajeer?"

"Mr. Anderson, how about I tell you what I know and you pick it up from there?" The President set down his coffee cup and began to explain all he knew.

"I know that he is retired from the Soviet Army and that he was some sort of Russian hero. I know that he sells arms to other countries and recently he sold the warhead to the terrorist that had plans to destroy one of our cities, probably this one if Ramsey's assessment is correct. And, I am aware that currently we are at the three week point of a mission to find him and remove him from his position as a dealer of weaponry to rogue and failing states." He looked up at Anderson and asked, "How am I doing so far?"

Before Gabe Anderson could answer, the Secretary of State interjected, "And, I would like to add, he killed one of our airmen, stole a Blue Force Tracker, and illegally entered our airspace with a Russian attack helicopter armed with missiles and who knows what else." Jim Erickson looked angry as he laid the litany of charges out before the men in the room.

Gabe Anderson held up a hand as if he were stopping traffic, "Now hold on a minute, Mr. Secretary. "Now, you're right about the stolen Blue Force Tracker, the helicopter and all that stuff, but where you're wrong is that General Gregorov didn't fly that helicopter or shoot that airman. Gregorov hasn't ever been to the United States, in a Russian helicopter or a Boeing 747 for that matter, that I assure you."

Gabe pulled out a couple photos and passing them to the President, explained, "The woman in that picture is Nikki Sidorova. She's been involved with the Russian Syndicate for about seventeen to twenty years. The last ten or fifteen years have been with Gregorov. We are just starting to get info on her. She's the one who killed Airman Beirman, not Gregorov. Of that we are positive. She conned Beirman into stealing the Blue Force Tracker and transponder that was installed on the Mi-24 helicopter.

That equipment is the only thing that ties the helicopter to Gregorov, and only because of Sidorova's involvement. We don't have the helicopter or the stolen equipment to prove it, not that we aren't looking. That bird went down in the Gulf, well into Mexico's waters, and we are working it. As for Beirman, again it was Sidorova who left the airman love struck with two bullet holes in his head at an apartment in Pensacola. We are currently tracking her. Ramsey and his team picked up her trail when she landed in Moscow."

Anderson's eyes burned into those of the Secretary of State as the President shuffled the two photos in front of him, placing Metelov's photo on top of the woman's. President Carlton saw the exchange of glances and could see that Gabe Anderson was not happy with Erickson. "Ok, tell me about this guy."

Anderson sat down and leaned toward the President. "That is Dr. Vladimir Metelov. He is a medical doctor and physicist who deals primarily in nuclear power and weaponry. We know that he is married and has two children and lives in Moscow. According to Metelov, Gregorov sold his name to the terrorists. He was blackmailed into assisting them to reconfigure the warhead. His family was being held hostage and he was threatened he'd be killed if he didn't help."

The President looked over the photo of Dr. Metelov, then asked, "So, this is the one who is working for us now, this Metelov person?"

Gabe continued, "Yes, Sir. The Russian Special Police unit picked him up at the hotel where his family was being held. One of the hotel staffers started getting suspicious with the comings and goings of the Middle Eastern men and the fact that they didn't want any maid services performed during their nearly three week stay. He was confronted as he was leaving and he and his family were taken in for questioning."

Gabe Anderson took a sip of his coffee before continuing. "All the family knew was that they were being held against their wishes. Metelov's wife was told that the terrorists would kill her husband and her children if she caused any trouble, so she kept quiet and kept the kids under control."

"And the terrorists not only released him, but paid him after he did the work. Amazing," the President interjected. "So, now what? What's the plan from here?"

"Well, Sir, the Russians have set up a meeting between Metelov and Gregorov. Based on our interceptions we believe that Nikki Sidorova will be there also. There are three or four places that Gregorov frequents and we have all of them plumbed with electronics waiting to flip the switch when we find out where the meeting will be held."

Gabe collected the photos from President Carlton. He placed the folder on the table next to his coffee. "We are hoping that this meeting will net information about the amount of chemical, biological, radiological, and nuclear weapons that Gregorov has at his disposal or the location of his weapons stash. We are pretty positive that he has assembled quite a collection. We just don't know where he's keeping them."

The Secretary of State got to his feet, interrupting Anderson. "Why are we pussy-footing around with these guys? You have them all in visible range. Take them out and we won't have to worry about whether or not Gregorov has weapons or if the physicist will help build another bomb. Kill them, kill the woman, and the world will be a better place."

Anderson shot back, "And then what? His mafia agents have a big garage sale and sell off everything? We gotta find those weapons before somebody else does! We need Gregorov and Dr. Metelov alive to get that information."

Gene Patterson stepped in to help with Gabe's argument, "Mr. President, Secretary Erickson, we can't just set up shop in Moscow and take it upon ourselves to go around and assassinate their citizens, no matter how guilty they may seem. Not only do we not work that way, but at the moment, we aren't even allowed weapons other than for personal defense on this mission. The Russians wouldn't allow it. Our agents aren't there for target elimination. This mission is about information gathering and that's all." He looked directly at the Secretary of State as he said it, as if to drive his point home.

Erickson wouldn't let up. He turned to face Anderson and continued, "Your people have been on site for over three weeks. What information do they have to show for their efforts?" he asked. "I'll tell you what they have. Nothing. They have nothing to show after three weeks. I could have had a team in there, eliminated Gregorov and Metelov, saved Nikki Sidorova the cost of a plane ticket and had her taken out before she got on the plane here in the United States. But, what the hell? You guys didn't even stop her, basically letting her flee the country!"

Gabe Anderson jumped to his feet and got well into Erickson's face, "You have no idea what you're talking about! You can't armchair quarterback a mission like this. Hell, even if we wanted to take out Nikki Sidorova we couldn't have. All we had was a first name and only a vague description. She didn't hit our radar until she was at the airport and her name came up in the security line, and that was after the plane was in flight, and only because one of the attendants recognized her from the composite that my people, not your people, sent out. We had about nine hours to build a plan based on that information."

He was fuming as he continued, "Now, I don't like all of this finger pointing bullshit, but had your departments done their job and forwarded the composites to the T.S.A. when we sent them out, we might have had a track on her when she bought her ticket, not after she boarded the airplane and already had her first in flight meal and a movie!"

Erickson started to speak, but Anderson would not yield to him. "I've just about had enough of you getting into my business. I can see that this program is not going to work very well if this is the kind of shit that I have to look forward to on a daily basis. We are not there to kill those people. We are there to collect data, manipulate their movements and get them in a position that best benefits the United States government, through, I might add, our judicial system. It is not our position to be the judge, jury and executioner."

The Secretary of State got right back into the fight. He stared at Gabe Anderson, but spoke to Gene Patterson, "Gene, you need to tell the director to start looking for another deputy. This man is disrespectful and out of line and obviously not performing in a manner that best suits the government of the United States."

At that point President Carlton stood. He placed a hand between the two men as if making a wedge, and nudged his Secretary of State back a bit. "Sit down, Jim."

Secretary Erickson stopped talking and looked at the President questioningly.

Carlton repeated himself, a hint of anger in his voice, "I said, sit down, Jim!"

With that, Erickson found his seat. "Gabe, you sit, too." President Carlton motioned to where Anderson had been sitting.

Gabe Anderson relaxed and sat as the President walked around the room thinking about what he was going to say. "Ok, look. Nobody's getting replaced or fired." Carlton gave Erickson a disapproving glance before continuing, "Gabe, you're right. It's your business, not ours, how you best manage your folks. You run the show when it comes to what you do, and by God, your directives were exactly what you stated: find Gregorov, find the weapons and stop any further sale or acquisition through his network. Period."

"Furthermore, I believe that by the end of next week we will be into the next phase of securing Gregorov's weapons cache. By that time Gregorov, and this Nikki person will be in custody because of Dr. Metelov's assistance and the world will be a better place."

He motioned toward Secretary Erickson. "But, I also believe that Jim has a good point. We don't know what will happen to Gregorov once he enters the custody of the Russians. This man has been working the system for years and I'd bet he's got friends in high places. Likewise, Gregorov has probably made as many enemies as he has friends, so you could flip a coin as to which way it might go for him."

Gabe Anderson began to get fidgety. He could see where the President was going and didn't like it. He began to stand, wanting to express his opinion, even if it meant interrupting the President of the United States.

President Carlton could see his uneasiness and held out a hand, "Let me finish, Gabe, and then you can argue your point."

"Gabe, my thoughts are this. Once you get the information you need, and your men are on their way to secure the weapons cache, I want you to contact our friends in the Russian Special Services and give them the opportunity to eliminate the possibility that Gregorov will ever buy or sell another weapon system. They can use their discretion on what to do with Nikki Sidorova, but you can make the suggestion that your government would prefer that she not be able to reenter the United States...ever."

Gene Patterson spoke up, asking for clarification, "So that I fully understand, Sir, we are not pulling the trigger."

President Carlton continued, "Our teams will not have anything to do with any follow on mission regarding Gregorov or Sidorova." He turned to Gabe Anderson. "In fact, your people are to turn over all their information,…and I mean all of it, to the R.S.S. Am I understood?"

Gabe bit his tongue. He didn't have to like it, but at least his people were not the ones who were going to mop up. He thought Alan Ramsey was not going to be so easy to convince.

"Now, as for Metelov."

Gabe suddenly tensed up.

"Here we have a man who willingly helped the enemies of our country build a bomb that would have killed thousands of people, not to mention the effect it would have had on the spirit and morale of our citizens. This country cannot afford another sucker punch…"

This time Gabe did interrupt. "Sir, he did not have much of a choice. They were holding his family."

President Carlton shot back, "And that's where we disagree then, because I believe that Metelov *did* have a choice. He made a conscious decision to save the lives of his own family over the lives of thousands. What if he has to make that choice again, Gabe? I think I know which way his bias leans and, personally, I don't want to take that chance."

He tapped a finger hard on the folder next to Anderson. "That man has a moral obligation, not an obligation to America, or to Russia, or to you and me as individuals, but an obligation to the world to understand that his specialty, his tacit knowledge and understanding of nuclear physics, puts him in a position of great personal responsibility to protect that information and keep it out of the hands of those who would do the world harm."

The President had walked a complete circle around the room. "Gentlemen, in my opinion, it is no different than if he had a nuclear bomb and handed it over to the terrorists. He chose poorly, and, because the possibility of future poor decision making on his part still exists, I believe that we have to do what is best, not only to defend our own country, but any country. We have the opportunity to save hundreds, if not thousands of lives if we act now. A thousand lives for the cost of a single bullet. That's a good deal the way I see it."

The room was silent for a moment. Breathing hard, the President was obviously passionate about what he had just said. He turned, grabbed his coffee cup and headed for a refill. "We, too, have an obligation, Gentlemen. I think we had better act on it before the opportunity eludes us. If there aren't any more questions, then I believe this meeting is at its end."

Gabe Anderson stood. "Gene, if there is nothing further I have duties to attend to." He walked toward the door.

Gene Patterson couldn't get up fast enough. "Wait up, I'll walk with you." Before he got the words out, Gabe had slammed the door behind him. Patterson followed him out to the hallway, but Anderson was already out of sight. He turned back to look at Betty, who was looking rather startled. She said quietly, "I guess things didn't go so well in there."

Gene Patterson closed the door behind him, ran a hand through his hair, sighed, and then muttered just under his breath. "No, as a matter of fact, things didn't go well in there at all."

CHAPTER 5

THE HEADS UP

IT was only nine a.m. and already Gabe Anderson was ready to call it a day. With the increased responsibility of the T2T Division, his staff had grown, along with the budget and his headaches. What started as a small portion of his daily responsibilities, and almost as a favor to an old friend to indoctrinate Alan Ramsey, had manifested into one of the most talked about and well-respected divisions within the C.I.A.'s Terrorist Defeat Operations Center, or T-DOC.

Anderson scanned the list of agents on his operations board. His eyes settled on Paul Jackson's name. He thought about his first meeting with Jackson in St. Louis. The man had a great attitude and a strange sense of humor, but what Alan Ramsey saw in him to want to bring him on board ended up being the perfect mix for his department. Gabe couldn't help but think how bad things would have been had Jackson not joined the team.

Jackson, wounded during the last mission, had made a quick recovery. His prior military experience, as well as his police background pretty much made the man as ready as he could be, but as soon as he was on his feet Gabe Anderson made sure that Jackson got some quick lessons on C.I.A. structure and protocol.

Gabe picked up his phone and thumbed through his contacts. He scrolled to Ramsey's contact info and stared for a moment before touching the entry. He knew Alan was going to have problems with the President's decision. He didn't like it himself.

Alan's phone buzzed in his pocket taking him away from monitoring the audio. He walked a few steps away from the electronic equipment and slid open his phone. He saw it was Gabe Anderson calling. Alan made the calculations for the eight-hour time difference before greeting his boss. "Good morning, Gabe. What's going on?"

Gabe told Ramsey about the early meeting with Patterson, Erickson, and the President. He explained how Ramsey's teams would not be involved in more than the information gathering of the investigation. Once the meeting between Metelov and Gregorov was complete, the operatives, including Nikki and any other associates, would be taken into custody by the R.S.S.

As Gabe had anticipated, Ramsey didn't like the plan at all. The fact that they were going to turn over an informant to the Russian Special Services angered him. The R.S.S. was a legitimate agency of the Russian government, but it was rife with cold war era criminals and politicians that simply could not be trusted, and certainly would not want someone like Gregorov to start talking.

Ramsey was vocal about his disagreement. "Gabe, they have to know that those agents will kill Gregorov and, more than likely, Dr. Metelov and Nikki too. There may still be information that we can glean from Gregorov, but it takes time."

Ramsey was staring at the photos and information on the project board. A photo of a young Gregorov was juxtaposed with one taken at some park somewhere a few weeks earlier during one of his clandestine meetings. The participant in that exchange, a Middle Easterner, was still an unknown.

"Who knows what we could find out if we could push this operation further, The administration has got to untie our hands so that we can squeeze as much out of Gregorov that we can."

Gabe clarified his position and the position of the President for Ramsey. "You're preachin' to the preacher, Alan. I tried to push back when Secretary Erickson initially suggested the elimination of Gregorov and the doctor. But the President is on Erickson's side on this one and feels strongly that we need to step back and let them do whatever they are going to do. He made it absolutely clear that Dr. Metelov chose the wrong side and, therefore, put this country and others at risk. He basically said if they do the dirty work, well then, that's on them. He's not going to lose any sleep over it."

Ramsey thought it odd that the President was so adamant in proposing a "shoot first, ask questions later policy" for the mission. "Why do you suppose President Carlton so closely has the back of his Secretary of State on this one? Generally the President wears the pants in the family, do you think he's just trying to save face with his SECSTATE, given that you and Erickson don't see it the same way?"

Anderson mulled the question over for a moment before answering. He was sure that the President was voicing his own concerns and nothing more should be read into it. "No, I'm sure that the President was on the same page as Erickson. Scary to think it, I know, but for whatever reason they seem to share the idea that the world would be better off without your three subjects in it."

Ramsey wouldn't let it drop. "I don't get it. Why? We have hundreds of GITMO detainees still in custody and everyday something new comes out of that prison that resets our compass and points us in a better direction to deal with terrorism, both at home and abroad. If we were to eliminate all the people that the world could do without, *just because*, then, we would never have a chance to work offensively against these bastards and we'd be worse sitting ducks than before 9-11."

He pulled his phone down to look at the date and time. "You've got a few more days to make something happen with this before I get the final plan from Patterson, who, I'm sure, is getting all his ducks in a row as we speak. Orders is orders Alan, and we got ours, so we'll just have to deal with it."

Alan shook away his thoughts on the subject and took a few moments to brief his boss on the status of their investigation. Gabe never got bored with the specifics and was aware of some of the most minute details. "So, what's the story with this Anatoly character? Have we figured him out yet?" Gabe knew only that he was a bit more than an acquaintance of Nikki's, given the talk being passed about the T-DOC.

Alan lifted his iPad from the table and pulled up the electronic dossier for the mission, scanning through the list of names of the players like a table of contents for a novel. He stopped when he got to Anatoly. The selected page appeared, populating with photographs, documents and links to other parts of the file.

Ramsey scanned the info and relayed it to Anderson, "His name is Anatoly Vodjosic. He's married to Elena Vodjosic. She's the daughter of Josip Hajseman, the head of Russia's Contemporary Labor Party."

Ramsey clicked on a link and the page switched to information about the Hajseman family. "Josip Hajseman has ties to a lot of the good old boys of the Soviet Union as well as the post Berlin Wall crowd. He's related to Boris Yeltsin somehow, hunts wolves with Vladimir Putin and caribou with some retired Cosmonaut. The guy is a jet setter, making appearances at political fundraisers and parties all over Russia."

He hit the browser's back button then continued, "Our boy Anatoly appears to be along for the ride. He likes fast cars and good-looking women. His wife Elena has both covered. She's got her daddy's money to buy whatever car catches Anatoly's eye and has the looks of a supermodel. Not sure why this idiot is out shopping around."

Gabe acknowledged the info with a grunt. "So, is he a playboy then, or is Nikki his only extramarital lover? And do you think his wife Elena, knows about his activities?"

"I don't have the answer. This is all new information. We started our research on him when he picked her up at the airport. We traced the plates. Once we got a name, the internet and the R.S.S. did the rest."

At least, Alan thought, the Russian Special Service was useful when it came to getting information on private citizens. It's the one area where the Russians excelled, intruding into the personal business of everyday people. The fact that the Hajseman's were a powerful, wealthy family only meant that there was more intrusion. That equaled more information for Ramsey's team.

Ramsey continued, "As to whether his wife knows, I would have to say yes. The R.S.S. handed us this information within minutes of our request. I would have to assume that she has him tailed. Not sure about any other women though. I'll ask the Russian liaison, Russo, and see what he knows. I found that if we don't specifically ask for it, the R.S.S. won't offer it."

"Same old Russians." Gabe commented, thinking back to his operative days. "Ok, well keep me posted. Make sure all of this is in your update. You seem to be OK with Carlton's directives. This is your last chance to give me something I can throw back at them that I haven't already put on the table."

There was a long pause as Ramsey thought. He had two issues, based solely on the promises he'd made and how changing course now would make him feel that his own words meant nothing.

The truth was, if it hadn't been for a phone call from Gregorov during the search for a suspected terrorist's bomb only months before, there would be a smoldering radioactive crater somewhere in the U.S. The phone call Gregorov made to Ramsey during the height of a fast moving investigation was pivotal to the success of that mission. Ramsey told Gregorov then, in an exchange for information, that he would personally direct any investigation that resulted from Gregorov's involvement. Although he hadn't broken his promise yet, he would, once he turned over the information to the Russians.

The second regarded the promise made to Dr. Metelov, by both Ramsey and the R.S.S., that he would be released and his family relocated, once he helped bring down Gregorov and locate the weapon cache. They also promised immunity from Gregorov's associates. None of which would happen without US intervention.

It pissed Ramsey off that the President had directed them to back out of the deal. Still, there was nothing he could do about the decision except act on it as directed. "You know that I think we should stay on plan. I don't get it, but who am I to second-guess it. Especially since you already took up the fight. I'll just suck it up and drive on."

Gabe was a little surprised, but knew that Ramsey was sensible enough to know when to fight and when not to. "If it's any consolation, I've been in your shoes more than I can count on my fingers and toes. Let me know when you get the meeting set up and where it's going to be."

Ramsey saw his opportunity to close the conversation and get back to work. "Roger that, Sir. Metelov is going to call Gregorov within the hour. As soon as we know I'll drop you a line." He looked at his watch and thought, "Time to get this show on the road."

CHAPTER 6

SECRETS OF STATE

ANATOLY walked around the large open living room for the third time. Nikki's apartment was sparsely furnished with contemporary furniture that was only a few years old, but looked as though it was from the seventies. Hung on the walls were photos dating back to her childhood. Several photos of Nikki at Olympic training in her Olympic uniform with the wide low cut neckline trimmed with red stripes. Gone was the USSR logo, dating the photo to just after the Soviet collapse, in its place the flag of Bosnia. How different life would have been for Nikki had there been no war, he mused. Next, there was a photo of Nikki and her mother. Anatoly examined the photo closely. The resemblance to her mother was amazing. Except for the green eyes, it was as if Nikki were a clone.

Anatoly was suddenly pulled from his thoughts by the telltale rattle of the water pipes indicating that the water had stopped flowing and that Nikki was getting out of the shower. The bathroom door opened and Nikki stepped out wrapped in only a towel. Steamy vapor wisped from the warm dampness of the bathroom.

Nikki glanced at Anatoly, her short wet hair hanging straight down clinging to her cheeks, water droplets dotting her shoulders and neck. She wore the towel around her waist, leaving her breasts uncovered except for the drops of water that clung to her skin. She smiled wickedly and stepped toward her bedroom, tossing the towel to the side as her naked body disappeared around the doorway.

Anatoly hesitated only for a moment. Quietly making his way down the short hallway, he stopped at Nikki's open bedroom door. The image of Nikki, naked, sitting on the edge of her bed greeted him. The smell of Nikki's freshly washed hair and her fragrant body lotion enveloped him.

Nikki lifted her foot to the edge of the bed and rested her chin on her knee as she prepared to paint her toenails. She pulled the glistening brush from the small bottle of dark red nail paint while looking up at Anatoly. He was staring at her, his eyes sparkling with excitement as she dabbed the brush against her toenail and slowly drew it outward, leaving a fresh wet coat of thick dark red paint across the opaque surface of her toenail.

Anatoly shuffled forward taking a knee at the edge of her bed. He took the brush from her, dipped it into the bottle and laid down a second coat of the glistening paint to cover the nail completely. With his free left hand Anatoly began caressing and massaging her right foot, kneading it from her toes to her ankle, gently rubbing, applying just the right pressure to evoke a sigh and light moan from Nikki.

She lowered herself onto the cool sheets, arm outstretched, holding the bottle. Anatoly finished the remaining toenails, all the while rubbing both the top and bottom of her right foot and each individual toe. He pulled her foot up higher and kissed lightly around her ankles, shin and calf.

Nikki was enjoying the moment. She remembered the attention to detail which Anatoly paid to every movement, every caress. He was masterful, and the thought that what he demonstrated with a simple foot massage, he would, within moments apply to the rest of her body, made her more excited with every touch.

She switched the bottle of paint to her other hand and maneuvered herself to extend the bottle again as close to Anatoly as she could. She switched the positions of her feet, placing her right foot in position for painting. Anatoly immediately began the massage of her freshly pedicured left foot, being careful not to disturb the wet paint. He inhaled deeply, taking in the scent of her perfumed body and the sharp contrasting smell of the nail polish, the two somehow combining to create an oddly erotic stimulant, enhancing the excitement of the moment.

It took considerably more concentration to apply the paint steadily on her toenails with his left hand. Again Anatoly massaged and kneaded her other foot, pushing hard into the arch and applying pressure to the ball of her foot and the soft areas surrounding her ankles and calves. Nikki moaned and breathed more rapidly as the caressing became more intense and targeted.

Anatoly dipped the brush into the paint for the last time, spreading the thick red liquid over her last little toenail. He then turned all his efforts to the task of her massage.

Nikki breathed in quick choppy breaths as Anatoly's massage, combined with kisses and nips, moved up her legs. She placed her feet on his shoulders and pulled him by his brown hair toward her.

Anatoly pulled at his shirt, unbuttoning and pulling it away from under the pressure Nikki was placing against his shoulders as she rocked close and then pushed away from him, as if she were teasing herself. Anatoly struggled to unfasten his pants, trying hard not to change the tempo of what was taking place. It had been nearly two years since they were last together and Nikki was shaking with each kiss and subtle touch of his lips and tongue on her body. She was overly excited. He knew her sensitivities and how to exploit them, teasing her with his touch.

Nikki could not wait any longer. He had toyed with her in such a way that she was ready to explode with passion. She was anticipating him, wanting his body against hers. She arched upward and pulled him toward her, his chest sliding against her breasts.

He ground against her, teasing her some more, but Anatoly himself was nearly overcome with passion too soon. Nikki's breathing was becoming more rapid with outburst of sighs and light moans. Her body shuddered under his, until finally, she could take no more. She pulled her lips away from his and held his face long enough to speak softly, "Please Anny, stop teasing me." She moaned loudly and sighed deeply as Anatoly complied, thrusting himself against her. Their movements became intense for mere minutes as Nikki succumbed to her body's desire to let go.

All of the sensations of the sexual encounter culminated into an explosive feeling that Anatoly just did not experience with any other woman, ever. For whatever reason, Nikki Sidorova drove him absolutely crazy.

Nikki slowed her movements and held him tightly against her. The still warmth of his body was soothing. She felt his heart beating and listened as his breathing slowed. After several minutes she allowed him to pull away from her.

Anatoly lay next to her, tracing her body with his palm and staring into her eyes. His strong desire for her returned to him as he contemplated their relationship yet again. He had always loved her and wondered why their paths had never fully come together. His expression suddenly turned solemn.

"Tell me again why you didn't marry me when I asked you?" He asked quietly.

Nikki stroked his cheek and kissed him again, lightly tracing his upper lip with her tongue. If there was ever anyone she would have married it was Anatoly. Truth be told, she was afraid to have a relationship with someone she truly loved after having lost all of the others who had a place in her heart, sometimes feeling cursed to never be happy. She just wouldn't allow herself to get that close. And, as Anatoly had so painfully experienced, when she felt that she was becoming too involved, she would just walk away. She felt that she owed him an explanation, but still, only repeated what she had told him every time he brought it up.

"I was just too young, Anny," she answered, nearly whispering, "I wasn't ready for someone like you. I didn't even know who I was back then."

She gently kissed him on the forehead and got up. Nikki stood in front of the mirror and looked at herself. First at her body, then, leaning forward on the dresser, at the slight crow's feet that greeted her each day.

"But now, I have waited too long and I am getting old." She turned around to look at her own ass, giving it a slap to check its resilience, happy to see that it was still firm enough to settle after the first ripple.

Anatoly slid toward the end of the bed were he had left his clothing. He cursed as he held up his pants and underwear, showing Nikki the reason for his displeasure, several spots of fingernail polish. "We will have to either wait for the paint to dry next time, or paint your toes after making love." They looked at each other and laughed.

Nikki held out a bottle of polish remover, along with a small rag for Anatoly to take. The strong chemical smell of turpentine filled the air immediately upon opening the bottle. "Here, it will be better to smell bad than to explain to your wife how you came to have red nail polish on your underwear."

She turned away and began the process of putting herself back together while looking in the mirror at the reflection of Anatoly, dabbing at the red paint and speaking to his reflection. "Anny, I need your help."

Anatoly drew on his trousers and walked over to stand next to her. He faced her in the mirror as he put on his shirt. Nikki was looking serious again.

"I need some information. It has to do with my brother and father's disappearance. Someone has to know where they are, or where they are buried."

Anatoly looked at her as if she was alien and asked, "You think they are alive? Surely you do not believe..."

Nikki interrupted him, stopping him from going further, her demeanor changing. She turned to look into his eyes. "Dead or alive does not matter. I want them back!" She said sharply. "and I want the people who are ultimately responsible to pay for what they did. I want to know who had the authority to stop the massacres. Who knew about it and did nothing to prevent it? I want to know who made what deal, and why people like Mladic are not in custody. Why aren't they being held accountable?"

Nikki's eyes narrowed as they danced back and forth from one of Anatoly's eyes to the other as her passion flared.

"You can get me that information. Your wife has the ties to the government that will allow you access. Please, Anny, do this for me."

Anatoly thought back to the moment in the car and how angry and frustrated she was at the news reports regarding the end of the search efforts for the victims of Srebrenica. One moment she was intensely angry and the next, it was as if she had flipped a switch, he thought. The sudden change could only mean that she had come to some sort of conclusion. She was not the kind of person to let something go, especially when it involved something so personal to her, and now, he supposed, he would have to help her.

It worried him why she wanted the information. He knew what she was capable of and whom she worked for, and was always concerned that each time he saw her would be the last.

The only reason he decided to be part of Gregorov's association in the first place was to be sure that Nikki was ok.

Though, there were never any details of whom she was with or what had transpired, Anatoly wasn't naive enough to expect that nothing happened in the relationships that she developed to help with the advancement of Gregorov's power and influence.

The fact that she had returned after several such missions meant that Nikki could no doubt take care of herself, but still, it caused him worry. He answered her with a question.

"And when I risk ruin and possible incarceration for you to get you what you want..." He paused to think of the right words "...these, secrets of state, then what? What will you do with the information?"

"I will use it to find them." She said defiantly as she picked a thong from the dresser drawer and stepped into it. Anatoly couldn't help but notice the superman emblem on the front patch of the material.

Anatoly could see the anger in her eyes as she thought about whatever plan was mulling around in her head. He motioned to her apparel, pulling slightly on the waistband and letting it snap lightly back in place.

"Do you think you are some sort of superwoman?" He asked. "Seriously, Nikki, some of those people are already dead and others, I'm sure, are high up in the governments of many different countries like France, Japan, the USA and probably twenty more." he said, rattling off the countries that he knew were involved in some manner or another.

"What are you going to do, fly around the world, wave your flags of vengeance and wreak havoc on anyone who had something to do with the destruction of Bosnia either directly or indirectly?"

Nikki looked angry. She seethed an answer that Anatoly didn't expect, but didn't surprise him either, "If that's what it takes, yes!"

He stared at her for a moment somewhat incredulously. He knew she had the fortitude to mount such an expedition, but Anatoly couldn't help but think about where she would get the resources for such an endeavor.

"Have you any idea how much that is going to cost?" he asked, not necessarily expecting an answer. "The airfare alone would take all of the money you have. All of it, Nikki...Not to mention any weapons, technology, and information you will have to buy."

Anatoly was a numbers guy. He related most every project to the bottom line. He knew that the deals she had made with Gregorov were not exactly profitable. She simply didn't have the kind of cash it would take to support her lone wolf plan.

Nikki replied, speaking rather too nonchalantly for Anatoly. "That is why I need your help. You are going to help me get into Gregorov's account."

"Oh no, no I am not...,"Anatoly began.

Nikki spoke over his objections. "Anny, You are his bookkeeper."

"No, Nikki, No! It will not happen!" He folded his arms in defiance.

Still Nikki would not listen, raising her voice to speak again over his remarks. "You have access to the information I need."

Anatoly became animated. He threw his arms up and spun around to walk a few paces away then turned back to face her.

"How far do you think I would get if I hacked into his account and stole his money? He would have me killed, and you too if he even thought you were involved."

Anatoly wanted to help. Information gathering and access was one thing, but taking the boss's money...he knew that was a ticket to a bullet to the head. He thought about the information Gregorov had on his computer, tons of documents and emails. There were physical documents stored in his safe as well. Information, Anatoly thought in retrospect, saved by Gregorov as his get-out-of-jail-free collection, information to which Anatoly had complete access.

Perhaps, he thought, there might be something there to satisfy Nikki's desire, and to buy him some time. "Here's what I will do. I will get you access to some information that may help you, but I will need time to get it done. Getting his money is too dangerous."

Nikki felt satisfied that he was going to help at all. "But you *can* access his account, right? And don't think I am done negotiating. I want access to his money." She knew well how to manipulate any man. She walked the few steps between them to stand within a foot of him. Nikki pulled him close and kissed him, darting her tongue against his. "I'm hungry," she said suddenly.

Anatoly, somewhat surprised by the kiss, stared into her green eyes and then at her still bare torso. He was no match for this woman and knew he would lose in the end. He jumped at the opportunity to change the subject. "Me too. How about you and I go to dinner, when we come back we can get you started on your search? I will have to make some configuration changes to your laptop to make it work."

Nikki agreed and began looking for something to wear.

Agents Marks and Villacruze hadn't heard any discernible conversation for at least an hour. They heard the two talking as they entered the house, but almost immediately the voices sounded like they were moving away from the phone. Marks suggested that Nikki must have her phone in the small bag she was carrying. It would explain the fact that the last sound they heard was the jingling of keys and the opening and closing of the door, along with some bantering. Then silence.

"Ten bucks says they're screwing." Marks said, lowering his binoculars to hang on the lanyard against his chest and breaking a ten minute silence.

Hector Villacruze opened his eyes and looked over at Marks. "Why you always wanting to bet on something that's so obvious? That's not how bets work, dumb shit."

"Whatever," Marks responded. "Too bad She didn't take her phone with her into the other room," he added with a grin.

Vee looked at him strangely. "You are a sick man. You need to get a girlfriend, dude." He paused for a second, smiled, then continued, "Would have been nice if we would have hooked up some video though." He smiled again, broadly.

Marks shot back, "Wait, who needs a girlfriend? You got a lot of room to..."

Vee stopped him from talking and cocked his head to try to listen to the system audio. "Shh, listen."

The sound of Nikki talking got closer to the phone. She was talking about Gregorov. She asked her boyfriend, about Dr. Metelov. Anatoly confirmed that he had Metelov's bank account information and spoke about setting up his account, and the million dollars he had in it.

Vee thought about the information they had received about the doctor. He knew the Russian Special Services had seized Metelov's account even though Alan Ramsey had tried to talk them out of it, and for the very reason Vee had just heard over the com-set.

Marks struck Vee's arm and pointed to the door of Nikki's apartment from their position at the farthest end of the parking lot. "They're moving." he said as he looked through his binoculars from his position in the passenger seat.

Nikki stepped out wearing a dark green sleeveless shirt with a low V-neck and a pair of OD-green capri pants, brown sandals and freshly painted toenails. Her short-cropped reddish hair exposed her slender neck, accentuating her strong, wide, shoulders. Marks whistled quietly as he watched her move toward Anatoly's car.

Vee grabbed the binoculars, pulling at the lanyard that Marks insisted he place around his neck, in turn pulling Marks closer and choking him at the same time. He raised them to his eyes to look at the woman in the distance. "Dude, that chick is too old for you," he began, but after focusing on her and getting a closer look, he agreed with Marks. "Why is it that all the good looking women are so much trouble?"

"They're all trouble," Marks replied, trying to pull the binoculars away and move from the uncomfortable closeness with his partner.

Villacruze released the binoculars causing Marks to slam against the door glass with a thud. "Ouch!," he muttered to Vee as he rubbed the pain away.

Vee laughed at Marks' impact with the door, "Dumb-ass, told you about putting that shit around your neck." He picked up his handset and got serious again. "They're moving. We're on them." He tossed the radio down on the console, placed the Beemer in gear and pulled out after them.

Kenneth Wash

CHAPTER 7

CONTACT

SECRETARY of State Erickson had to take a walk after his confrontation with Gabe Anderson. Situations like that made him antsy, a trait he never could fully get under control, and because it left him nervous and on edge, he had to burn off his pent up energy.

He walked quickly through the halls, his footsteps echoing ahead of him. He was deep in thought, ignoring anyone who passed him during his walkabout. He knew that what he was about to do would put him at odds with President Carlton and needed to think it through before committing to the call to his contact in Russia, Gordon Maxwell.

Unlike President Carlton, Erickson trusted the prior cold war spy. They met him at a pivotal time in both Erickson's and Ron Carlton's political careers, in 1995, during the Bosnian Conflict, when America was heavily involved trying to broker a N.A.T.O. sponsored peace deal.

President Carlton, the Secretary of State at the time, needed some help convincing the Bosnian President, Slobodan Milosevic, to concede to the terms of the Dayton Peace Accord, a deal Erickson was sure would not have been possible had Carlton been left to his own devices. And although the deal went south, it was the catalyst for the eventual fall of the Bosnian President. In a way, had it not been for the clandestine operators, known then as dark agents, Milosevic's war would probably had churned slowly onward and Slobodan would more than likely had seen another term as President. Still, Erickson knew that his boss would only remember the residual effects of an operation that had gone bad. With Carlton, it seemed, the glass was always seen as well less than half full.

Erickson's mind raced back to the present. He thought of how the methods of warfare changed over the years. In that time Maxwell developed his own way of doing business. He still worked with weapons suppliers, but instead of dealing only in the movement of stolen Soviet weaponry, Gordon Maxwell began to offer additional services, starting with guns for hire and mercenaries, which developed into the modern contracted security teams and specialized military operators.

The President would not be happy that he was about to reestablish contact with Maxwell, but then, President Carlton didn't need to know everything. After all, Maxwell could make shit happen, and right now, Erickson needed to know what was going on in Alan Ramsey's camp, and that's why he needed Maxwell.

Erickson was frustrated with the C.I.A.'s newest Deputy Director, Gabe Anderson, who wouldn't allow him to be privy to the information being gathered by Ramsey's team. Anderson considered the investigation, and any data collected, outside the range and scope of duties performed by a Secretary of State, driving his point home, on more than one occasion, when Erickson had asked for an update, that the information he was requesting was on a need to know basis and then, quite frankly, telling him, he simply didn't need to know.

"To hell with Gabe Anderson," Erickson muttered as he stepped into a darkened team room to make his call.

CHAPTER 8

LONG DAY'S END

AFTER dinner, Nikki and Anatoly headed back to her apartment. The Lada Priora circled through the parking lot and stopped adjacent to the door of the apartment complex. Vee and Marks slowed to a stop, sitting low in their BMW across the street. They had eaten fast food outside the restaurant. "McRuskie burgers," Marks had quipped at one point while they waited for the date to end, listening in on Nikki's conversation with her man, but the intercepted conversations for that last hour or so was merely bantering and playful chatter about each other as the couple prepared to part ways for the evening.

Nikki stared across the console at Anatoly. "It has been a long day. I'm glad it was you that came to pick me up. Did you get assigned the task or did you *want* to be the first to see me?" She smiled at her recent memory of seeing him when she stepped out of the walkway from the plane, and how he was trying to act professional, but really couldn't hide his excitement to see her.

Anatoly picked up his phone from the console's cup holder and displayed the calendar app. The day was highlighted indicating Nikki's planned return. "I was marking the days," he said, smiling. "I think Gregorov knows of our relationship. He asked if I wanted to pick you up."

Nikki leaned a bit closer to Anatoly and spoke softly. "You are going to help me, aren't you?"

Her voice was so alluring. Anatoly did not know how to say no to this woman. He looked at her eyes and her lips, sighing deeply before actually answering her question. "Give me some time to convince Elena that she should allow me into the archives. I will need a good reason, or she will tell me no."

Nikki placed her hand over his that was resting on the shift knob and stroked it with her fingertips. "Perhaps you can massage her feet. Who can resist that?" She smiled rather wickedly and then leaned further across the console to kiss him goodnight.

Her lips to him, were like candy to a child. He just couldn't get enough, and she knew it. Nikki darted her tongue against his while repositioning her right hand to his crotch to rub his growing erection. Then stopped suddenly, pushing herself away.

Anatoly opened his eyes fully, looking surprised and wishing she had not stopped. He flashed her a sly smile. "Are you sure you don't need my help tonight? Internet searches can be very frustrating." He raised and lowered his eyebrows and hoped for the answer to be yes.

Nikki reached for the door handle, pulling it to pop the door open. The light from the single dome lamp shone on her hair, face, breasts and shoulders, illuminating her stark beauty. She disappointed him with a shake of her head and one more peck on his lips. "Maybe you should give me Dmitri's information first. I promise I won't take his money yet." She paused before continuing. "I just want to look around so that I can start making a plan."

It wasn't a question of trust. Anatoly was afraid that Gregorov would somehow find out that an unauthorized user had accessed his account. If he could get to his work computer and verify that there was no activity on the network planned for the evening, he could hack Nikki's computer from his remote log in and change her IP address to make it look like someone from within Gregorov's organization was accessing the system. "I will call you with some information after I set it up for you. I have to make a few changes to the system to keep it safe," Anatoly agreed.

Nikki opened the door and stepped out of the car stretching somewhat before leaning down to give Anatoly one more directive. "Get me the doctor's information, too. If I am going to indiscriminately steal from my boss then I might as well take Metelov's money as well," she said, then closed the door and walked away.

Anatoly was dumbfounded for a moment. With Nikki he always felt like he had just lost at some sort of negotiation, yet still felt completely satisfied. Nikki gave one more wave as she entered her home, then closed her door, ending the evening.

Anatoly placed the shifter into first gear, wondering what exactly he was getting himself into, as he released the clutch to pull away from the curb.

Agent Marks was on his phone to Ramsey as the Lada drove out of the driveway. Alan Ramsey answered. "Yeah, Marks."

Marks was still not sure about calling Ramsey by his first name, having spent nearly two years as a special forces soldier under his command. "Sir, did you guys copy that last conversation, the one about the account information?"

Ramsey did hear the intercept. He was wondering why Nikki wanted into Gregorov's account, and before she even said the words, had figured out that she and her boyfriend were about to get really rich, really quickly. But Dr. Metelov's account was a surprise. He wasn't expecting that bit of info and neither was the Russian Special Services.

"Yeah. Gregorov's account I'm not worried about. She can take all of his money, as far as I am concerned, but we just got the R.S.S. jumping through hoops to get Metelov's account back on line. They had it locked down tight according to the agents here." Ramsey held his phone closer and spoke quietly. "If I had to guess, the Russians probably already spent his money and are scrambling to get something back in place, in case Nikki actually gains access."

Marks smiled at the thought. "Roger, Sir. Her boyfriend just left. We'll call back if anything new pops up."

"Good copy, Marks. Thanks for the update." With that Ramsey hung up his phone.

Marks turned a thumb toward Nikki's apartment, then offered, "That Anatoly dude ain't got a chance against that shit."

Vee sat back in his seat and reclined, knowing that they were more than likely going to be there through the night. "Yeah, he's done. Hell, I think I'm in love with her just listening in." He looked over at Marks, a serious look on his face and continued, "I love this job."

Marks replied, "No shit. Me too. Beats the hell out of getting sniped at in Afghanistan." He turned up the volume on the audio. "Not much going on now." The faint sound of a keyboard accompanied the hiss of static. "Better call White and see if he is going to hack her system or what. Either way, no reason to stay up all night listening to the tick of keys on a keyboard." He was getting tired. It had been a full day for Ramsey's two newest agents.

"Good plan. You take first shift. Wake me in a few hours," Villacruze said with a sly smile, as he leaned back, pulling the bill of his cap over his eyes to block the light from the streetlamp.

CHAPTER 9

CYBERSPACE

INSIDE the apartment Nikki put on water for instant coffee and sat down in front of her laptop to begin her perusing. She began with a search on Slobodan Milosevic. She read page after page of information that described a weak political system, manipulated expertly by Milosevic, rising to power by fanning the flames of an impending civil war, with rhetoric that only grew stronger as Communism collapsed throughout Eastern Europe.

The Warsaw Pact, a Soviet promise of protection for all within its borders, crumbled like the concrete walls that separated the East from the West. Milosevic used that failure to stir the dormant hatred for the Christian Nationalist, taking advantage of the frustration building throughout Yugoslavia and using it to propel him to power.

Resurrected were ideals and an environment of growing blame and retribution that began with the first battles fought between two rival Christian forces, Milosevic's Orthodox Christian Serbs and the Roman Catholic Croatians, led by their nationalist leader, Franjo Tudjman.

As the brutal civil war spread from Croatia into Bosnia-Herzegovina, the two Christian armies joined forces in a feeble truce, turning their efforts against the Bosnian Muslims. The "Bosniaks" were blamed for the strife in the war-torn countries. The unprovoked war and Milosevic's unchallenged ethnic cleansing tactics eventually led to the brutal death and murders of over two hundred thousand Muslims in the eastern Bosnian region.

Nikki never forgave the global community, N.A.T.O., for joining the fight against Milosevic's rampage too late to save those who were killed by the hundreds. She thought about the years following the disappearance of her father and brother, when Milosevic was no longer in power and N.A.T.O. was heavily involved in the peace keeping efforts. Too little, too late, she thought.

In the wake of the Muslim atrocities Nikki had risen to the position as the interim leader of a radical Bosnian Muslim group that waged sporadic attacks against the remaining Serb forces. Her hit and run tactics, vengeful executions and high level assassinations became legend among the locals in the Muslim communities and managed to catch the attention of the local arms dealer, Dmitri Gregorov.

Nikki was in the market for hard to trace Soviet designed, frequency-switching radios for her group. An American version known as SINCGARS had found its way into the arsenal of the Serbian forces, making it hard to hack into their network. It was unknown who authorized the sale of the communication devices to the Serbs, but Nikki suspected the C.I.A. had played a role in the purchase, as well as the training required to operate the sets. Regardless of how the Christian forces got them, their use gave them an advantage and Nikki wanted to even the odds.

Gregorov claimed to choose no side in the war politically, but as a businessman, he always placed his interest on the side of the winning force, selling the weapons that would, as Gregorov like to advertise, "Secure the crushing blow needed to win."

Dmitri was taken by the woman fighter and the callous manner in which she did business. He knew she would be an asset to his organization if he could convince her to work for him. She would be much more effective by getting the needed weapons and equipment out to the many who needed them, rather than commanding a group of insurgents. In return she could make sure that her people had the equipment they needed to strike the blows that were indeed slowing, if not stopping, the radical Christian groups.

Nikki agreed, and nearly two and a half years, and several operations later, she was told to report to Moscow, where Gregorov briefed her for a special mission.

She was flown to a high security prison located in The Hague, Netherlands. the prison was the home of ousted Yugoslavian leader, Slobodan Milosevic.

By then, the Balkan war was over, ending nearly ten years before, and Milosevic had resigned his presidency amid protests following the disputed presidential election of 2000. He was arrested by federal authorities on charges of corruption and abuse of power, but as the trial faltered due to lack of evidence, Milosevic was extradited to the former Yugoslavia to face charges of war crimes.

During the five year long trial, Milosevic, weakened by heart disease and under the care of a family physician, received medication for heart problems, and additional medications for a litany of ailments, ranging from asthma to arthritis.

In the summer of 2002 Milosevic became severely ill. He began to fear that he was being poisoned. After a brief investigation it was found that agents, bent on killing Milosevic, had infiltrated the prison kitchen help. They added arsenic and antifreeze to his food in amounts too small to kill him quickly, but were detected by a blood test when he was being treated for his strange illness.

The agents, upon hearing of Milosevic's hospitalization, disappeared from the kitchen, later to be discovered, each shot once in the head, almost two hundred miles away.

Nikki remembered walking from the medical van through the slush to the entrance of the massive prison structure. It was New Year's Day, 2006, the date chosen knowing that the holiday would provide an absence of prison staff, and those who were unfortunate enough to work would more than likely be recovering from their New Year's eve hangovers.

The guards eyed Nikki from head to toe, her traditional nurses clothing conforming to her shapely body. The white fabric was bright in contrast to her shoes, stained with the black slush from the street. She stepped up to the guards' desk and showed her identification and papers to the man who was more interested in her green eyes and shapely legs than the papers she presented. Asking for directions to the apothecary, she explained that she was new to the prison campus.

Both of the men on duty took their time to explain how to get where she needed to go. Neither of them bothered to check the bag that she carried. Had they looked they would have found only specialty medicines for the care of heart disorders, asthma and rheumatoid arthritis.

Less than three months later, on March 11th 2006, Milosevic suffered a massive heart attack and died in his cell, his five year long trial ending without verdict. Nikki thought back to the moment when Dmitri gave her the news. She sat staring at him, not speaking, as the news of Milosevic's death sunk in. She had difficulty believing that somehow she had a part in the death of Slobodan Milosevic, the worst war criminal since Hitler, and remembered asking herself why Dmitri would want Milosevic dead. She recalled wondering if he had done it for himself or had been paid by someone. The memories of her family bombarded her and the sadness must have showed on her face.

Dmitri broke the silence. He swirled the ice in his glass, then, setting the tumbler on the table, gave it a slight spin, something, Nikki noted, he did almost every time he finished a drink. He began speaking before the glass came to rest. "There will be more missions, more people who will die due to your involvement, but their deaths will not necessarily be…as personal as this one."

Nikki needed to understand her part. "Why did you want him dead?" she asked bluntly.

Dmitri looked at her intently as he fished a cigarette from the pack on the table and then asked in reply, "Didn't you? Tell me that I did not misjudge your hatred for Slobodan Milosevic."

He lit the cigarette and leaned back in his chair as he exhaled a large plume of gray-white smoke. "It is why I chose you for this mission." He pushed himself away from the table as he spoke.

"Many people wanted to see him dead. He burned many bridges, in a very short time, but you, Miss Sidorova, you had the motivation, the vengefulness. I saw it in your eyes. I knew that I could count on you to ensure that the mission was a success."

He inhaled again, this time allowing the smoke to come out of his nostrils on exhale. "I don't believe I have to point out that I was right."

Gregorov stood and walked toward the window as he continued to mentor his newest agent. "There is no profit in a man with no power. Besides, the information he possessed made him a liability to many people. It was merely a business decision…" He turned back toward Nikki as he continued, "albeit a risky one. But then, what type of businessman would I be if I didn't take risks now and then?" This time Dmitri smiled a broad grin showing his crooked, tobacco stained teeth.

In the darkness of her apartment Nikki's thoughts returned to the present. Why *would* he want him dead? She thought again.

What did he gain by it? She picked up her phone to call Anatoly and noticed that the battery light was flashing. She thought it odd that her phone was dead already as she placed it on the charging dock. The phone shut off automatically as the phone began to charge.

"Damn! There goes the signal," Rick White said in exasperation as he threw his headset down onto the table in front of him.

He turned to Alan Ramsey. "Sorry, Sir. There's nothing I can do until she takes it off charge. These Russian Vlad phones are screwed up, the way they work. They shut down completely, force the battery to discharge and then begin the charge cycle. We're out of business at least two hours at this point."

Alan Ramsey stepped over to the audio technician and placed a hand on his shoulder. "There isn't much going on right now anyway. At least no conversations to listen to."

He looked at the log covering the last couple of hours. What he saw supported his last statement. "Work on the internet stuff. Let's see what we can do to get into her computer. We need to see what she and her boyfriend are up to."

Rick acknowledged his boss' request with a nod. "I'll give it a shot, but we really need to get into her apartment. We are working blind until then."

Nikki stepped over to the apartment's land line phone. She couldn't remember the last time she had used it and almost caught herself looking for a contact list to scroll through. She searched her memory for the phone number and punched the keypad to call Anatoly. He barely got out the word "hello" before Nikki started talking. "When will I have access to Dmitri's account?"

Anatoly was surprised to hear her voice. "Nikki? I thought you were going to sleep. I specifically remember you telling me that you were tired and that you were going to bed. That is why I went to sleep. That is what I was doing, you know, sleeping." He looked at his cell, not recognizing the number on his display. "Where are you calling from?"

"My apartment phone, my cell is dead. Now, when will I have access? Also, how far do Dmitri's records go back?" She asked.

"Hold on a second. Give me a moment to wake up." He glanced at the clock as he got out of bed. It was nearly two in the morning. Nikki sounded anxious about something. "This can't wait until daylight, I take it?"

Nikki was getting impatient. "Anatoly, seriously, I have been searching for hours waiting for you to call and give me the access password. I thought you were going to work this issue when you got home."

Anatoly closed the door to his bedroom behind him and made his way down the hall as he tried to explain. "Elena was waiting for me when I walked in. She gave me the third degree. She knows I was with you, that I picked you up at the airport, and that we had dinner. She was angry. We had a bit of a fight before we went to bed. Somehow that turns her on..."

Nikki cut him off. "Stop! I do not want to know about your and Elena's on again, off again relationship. What I want is for you to help me. Otherwise I will do this alone."

Anatoly knew that she would. But if she did, it would surely expose him as a traitor to his boss. His best option was to help her, and then, once the money was secure, go away with her. If Nikki could support his lifestyle there would be no reason for him to stay with Elena. The thought was all too promising for Anatoly.

"Dmitri has records for every transaction he has ever made since the wall came down, and even before that. It's not all on electronic media. He had notepads and letters in boxes and stacked on shelves. There was so much that I had to hire additional help to transcribe or scan it all."

Nikki replied with another question. "Was he doing business with Milosevic? Selling weapons or information to him?"

Anatoly tried to remember the documents that he had seen. Hundreds, if not thousands of pieces of paper passed through his hands. "I would have to say that more than likely he was. He sold to everybody. It's how he made his money. War profiteering was his business. Why do you care how he made his money? What should matter to you is how we are going to get some of it and not get killed. Who cares where it came from?"

Nikki shot back an answer, "I care if he sold the weapons to the people who destroyed my home and my family!" She was getting angry. Nikki could feel her adrenalin pumping and wanted to scream at Anatoly, but she needed him.

"Gregorov had Milosevic killed. I delivered the drugs to his attending physician. I didn't think about it at the time, but he used me to help hide his involvement in the war crimes of Bosnia. Had Milosevic's trial continued, Gregorov's "business" would have been identified and shut down and he would be sitting in a cell rather than his office in Moscow. If Gregorov had access to mortars, howitzers, rifles, and the tanks that were used to kill thousands of people, including my family, and he sold them to Milosevic, then he used me to kill the one person that could have led to his arrest.

He used me, Anatoly, to cover up his role in the death of my own family. I need that information. Now, are you going to get it for me or not?"

Anatoly stepped into his office and sat down in front of his keyboard. Once his system was unlocked he opened up his program that could access Nikki's laptop remotely. "Ok, I am going to access your system for a moment. Once I get this set up, anywhere you go will show up on Gregorov's network as an approved log on. All history and cache will be recorded into his system."

After a few more minutes of typing Anatoly was in the network, "Ok, I have just set the parameters for you to log in. I am setting you up as the system watchdog. Basically the network should think that you are part of Gregorov's network security system. It will think you are simply an automated task set by the program, searching for virus' and malware." Again Anatoly thought how easy it was to fool the very programs that were written to keep the network safe.

A prompt suddenly came up on Nikki's screen and the voice of Alex, the computer generated voice of Apple began to speak. "You are about to access the GV4 domain." Nikki sat up straight and poised her fingers on her keyboard.

Anatoly's computer was set to monitor Nikki's. He could open and close files for her, input passwords and reset the ownership of any file or partition and the GV4 domain would think it was an authorized operation through the server he set up on Nikki's computer. The fact that Nikki's MacBook had the ability to hide the history, cookies and cache made the whole operation completely safe for him. There was no way they could trace anything back to his laptop and he hoped that it was the same for Nikki's.

Nikki watched as Anatoly negotiated the system for her. He spoke to her over the phone while she waited for her turn to go through the files. A prompt came up asking whether or not to show hidden files. Based on the size of the storage there must have been thousands of documents. Anatoly put in the password required to gain access and suddenly the monitor filled with folders.

"Nikki, these are Gregorov's personal files and account information. From here you can pretty much find anything and everything about him. I would suggest that you read through his personal journal. It reads like a novel and who knows, maybe it will be one day. He is a war hero, you know," Anatoly said.

By the time Anatoly was finished moving files, Nikki had a selection that would take her weeks to go through completely. She thought for a moment, and then asked, "Can I copy these files?"

Anatoly answered quickly as he placed new folders in for her to review. "Copy them, print them, do whatever you want, but do not get caught with them." He typed a couple more commands and then stopped.

"There. That should keep you busy for a while. Spend no more than an hour on his system and then log out. I can get you back in if needed, but not tonight. Now, I am going back to bed."

Nikki was already opening the journal. "I will be here. Thank you Anny. I will let you know tomorrow if I need anything else."

Anatoly wondered what this woman was about to do and wondered again if he was willing to help her commit her crimes of vengeance. He dwelt on it for a few minutes after his head met his pillow, but quickly went to sleep.

CHAPTER 10

PREPARATION

DR. Metelov sat nervously in front of the phone as the young audio technician, Rick White, gave a thumbs-up to Alan Ramsey that everything was ready. The young man gathered his equipment, winding some wire onto a spool to be placed with the other paraphernalia into a black gym bag. Before tossing it in he held it up, pulling loose a small strand and holding it out for Dr. Metelov to see.

Metelov gazed at what White was holding. Although he knew that it wasn't, it looked like fishing line.

"Ok, Mr. Metelov, try not to pull on the seam of your shirt. If it comes untucked, just leave it. As you can see, this wire is really tiny, in fact it's not even wire really, it's microfiber optic cable. I fished it up through the edging of the button hole side of your shirt. Pretty undetectable, if you ask me." White's excitement about the electronic gadgetry showed.

Metelov thought about correcting the techie for calling him mister. He preferred to be called Doctor, but before he could say anything White reached around behind him and lifted his jacket some.

Rick White poked at a near invisible square that was attached to the inside lower back of Metelov's dress shirt.

"This back here is the transmitter and battery. It's basically a battery like one you would find in an iPad, only this one is white, nearly impossible to see."

"The transmitter is here, along this edge. You can't make it out unless you were to cut open the casing. Very cool, high tech shit you're wearing. So James Bond like."

White let the jacket fall back in place, grabbed the straps of the gym bag and stood. He pulled Dr. Metelov's phone from his pocket and handed it back to him. "Here's your phone. It's your phone, has all your contacts in it. Nothing has changed except for a program that I put in to allow us to use it as a microphone. I'm a firm believer in redundancy. If you can, try to place the phone somewhere outside of your pocket, a table or the arm of a chair. If you can't, that's ok, but it works better when it's out in the open. Any questions?"

Metelov remained silent, scowling at Rick White.

White shrugged his indifference to of inquisitiveness on the part of Metelov and started to walk away. Snapping his fingers, he suddenly stopped short, remembering one more thing, and turned again to face the seated man.

"Oh, yeah, by the way, that battery will tend to put off a little heat. Not too bad, I mean it won't burn, but it might get a little uncomfortable. Try not to squirm around. You don't want to make them suspicious."

He stood and rolled his blue eyes skyward, as if searching his brain for anything else he'd forgotten. Satisfied that he had covered everything, he smiled and said, "Nope, that's it. Have a great day," just before walking away.

Metelov looked around the room. He hated that he was working with the American C.I.A. He had always felt that America was meddlesome with their in-your-face world leader status. For him and his family America was a failure and could not be trusted, though, in the case of his present situation, they probably saved his life. His arrest by the Russian Special Services would surely have led to a lifetime behind bars had the Americans not intervened.

Alan Ramsey stepped up, pulling a chair along to sit in front of the scientist. "Good morning, Doctor." Ramsey said cordially before continuing. "We're all set. We've got the Merinsk Street Cafe set up. You'll be covered by both camera and audio. I'm guessing Mr. White explained everything sufficiently."

Metelov let out a deep sigh. "Yes, as if he thought I could actually understand what he was saying."

Ramsey smiled a little and said, "Welcome to my world."

He could see Metelov was nervous and tried to reassure him. "You shouldn't have to worry. Aside from the device your wearing and your phone we have other devices planted around the Inn."

Metelov didn't look convinced. "Yes, well I have heard those words before, promises made by other Americans. You, and your government's good intentions do not always lead to good actions."

Metelov scowled again, gave a snort and asked, "What about my family? Are you sure they are safe? Can you promise me that no harm will come to them?" He leaned back fully in the chair, his eyes narrowing as he spoke with total disdain for the man sitting in front of him, "You don't even know Dmitri Gregorov, yet you think you can protect my wife and my children from his people. I'm sorry, Mr. Ramsey, but I do not share your confidence."

Ramsey was ready to move on with the instructions. "Look, Dr. Metelov, I understand the risk you are taking to help with this operation. I also understand that you don't have much of a choice." Ramsey glanced at the lead Russian R.S.S. agent, Russo, then looked back at Metelov. "Trust me when I say that you are in a far better position by helping us than not."

Paul Jackson was watching and listening from a few meters away, leaning back, half sitting on the windowsill. He didn't like Metelov, and Jackson's patience with the doctor had been pushed to its limits. As far as Jackson was concerned, Metelov's rights ended the moment he turned the bomb he built over to the terrorists.

Paul stared at him, his face drawn into a deep scowl as he listened to his boss try to reassure the man. He reflected on the lives that would have been lost had the terrorist attack succeeded, thinking to himself that the only thing that should have been offered to the scientist, as an alternative to his help, was a bullet to the head.

Uncrossing his arms, Jackson pushed away from the wall and stepped over to where Metelov and his boss were sitting. Jackson leaned down placing his face even with Metelov's to get the doctor's full attention, causing Metelov to lean as far back in his chair as possible, trying to gain some distance between him and the huge black man that was suddenly invading his personal space.

"The way I see it, you are lucky to be here at all. If it was up to me, I would have given the order to shoot you on sight."

Metelov cringed as Paul Jackson snarled. "Somehow, I don't think you were worried about my family's well being, or the thousands of other families that would have lost their lives to your handiwork. Why the hell would you think that we give a rat's ass about yours?"

He shoved the man back even deeper into his chair before stepping back across the room, only to glare menacingly at him from his perch at the windowsill.

Metelov turned back to Ramsey, noting the C.I.A. operative's obvious disapproval of his subordinate's last action. The physicist motioned to Paul Jackson with an outstretched hand, but spoke to Ramsey, brushing dismissively at his jacket with the other. "You cannot even keep your associates under control. Therefore, I am not convinced that you will not lose control of this operation as well," he said, somewhat arrogantly. The statement garnered Jackson another look from Ramsey.

The look on Jackson's face turned from one of contempt to intense anger. In a flash Jackson launched from his position against the window. Ramsey jumped up, intercepting him, stopping him with a hand on his chest. "Paul, what the hell has gotten into you?" he said quietly, diverting Jackson's movement to the side, and then backward, away from the doctor.

"That bastard pisses me off," Jackson began. "That son of a bitch has got some nerve bitching about his protection and his family's safety after what he did for those terrorists. He obviously didn't give a shit about ours." Jackson turned to look directly into Ramsey's eyes before continuing.

"We need to quit coddling these screw-ups and start treating them like they treat us, like shit." Jackson was visibly upset. He looked past Ramsey, thrusting a pointing finger toward the doctor and growled, "That's right, I'm talking about you."

"That's enough!" Ramsey barked loudly, then in hushed words continued, "You need to get yourself under control. Regardless of what Metelov has done, we need him. He obviously knows it. Don't let him get to you."

Ramsey turned a glance toward Metelov then turned back to Paul Jackson. "You think we can get back to work now?" he asked, ending the confrontation.

Jackson relaxed, his tension visibly ebbing. He spoke so that he was sure Metelov could hear, "Ok, but he better hope I don't have to take a bullet for him, cause that ain't going to happen." With that Jackson walked away to where Rick White was hooking up the video equipment.

Ramsey turned his attention fully to Dr. Metelov. Without apologizing for his partner's outburst, he began to explain how everything worked in the room, who everybody was and what part they played in the operation.

Metelov was surprised by the openness of Ramsey's briefing. He still had a few questions, but seemed a bit more relaxed after Ramsey explained what was about to happen.

"This location seems to be a bit far from the Inn. I could not tell for sure, but I was picked up only a few blocks from the Merinsk Street Cafe, yet we drove for quite some time before getting here. How quickly will you be able to respond, in the event that something does go wrong?"

Ramsey wished he could tell the man that it was all worked out, but that was not the case. Ramsey glanced again at the lead R.S.S. agent, Agent Russo and then said quietly, "The security issue is not under our control. The R.S.S. has total jurisdiction and has a plan in place to contend with any scenario,…or so they tell me."

"And do you trust that they actually have taken everything into consideration?" Metelov asked, thinking he knew the answer, but was curious what Ramsey's response would be.

Ramsey looked again at the three Russian Special Service officers and their "Official Liaison" before answering. They had been far from forthcoming and barely helpful. What information he'd gotten from them he all but had to pry from their skulls, yet he and his people in the states openly offered the R.S.S. every bit of intelligence that he had, to show them his commitment to complete cooperation.

He thought carefully how to phrase his answer. "If you are asking me whether I have complete faith in the R.S.S., the answer is no, but I'm afraid I don't have much of a choice, and neither do you. So, let's go over everything one more time to mitigate the effects of Murphy's law.

Metelov suddenly had a quizzical look on his face.

"Murphy's Law? Is that part of the U.S. legal system?"

Alan Ramsey couldn't help but smirk. "Unfortunately, it is," he said in jest before explaining.

"Surely, being a physicist, you are familiar with the different laws of physics: the theory of relativity, laws of gravitational force, and so on. Well, Murphy's law is kind of like that, an unwritten rule that says, anything that can go wrong, will go wrong."

The scientist stood, brushing at his clothing, smiling for the first time since they had met.

"Ah, yes. That one. Well, let us hope for all of our sakes that we are able to counter the effects of Murphy's law," he said as he was led from the room by one of the R.S.S. agents to a black S.U.V. for delivery to his hotel room.

CHAPTER 11

DUTY SHIFT

ACROSS town, Anatoly Vecjevic was awake and drinking his first cup of coffee. Sitting in front of his computer monitor, he logged in to see if Nikki was still actively searching the network and was glad to see that she was no longer logged on through his system. Hopefully, she heeded his time warning. He took a quick look at the system's log. She was right. The only discrepancy, and a minor one at that, was the amount of time that the system was active. No change in the system cache or history was detected. As far as anyone who might have actually noticed the amount of time that the system was in use through the night could tell, they would probably assume it was going through one of the many back ups or updates that are scheduled during the off peak hours.

Anatoly logged back out of his computer and shut it down, only to restart it again in an attempt to clear his own system cache. He was startled by the sound of his cell phone ringing. He walked quickly to where it was hooked to the wall charger and looked at the screen, recognizing the number as one of Gregorov's security phones. Odd, he thought as he answered, "Hello," he said, almost questioningly.

A deep Russian voice greeted him. "Anatoly, good morning. I am calling for the General. He has been trying to reach Nikki, but has not been successful. I know you two have...a...ah...history, so I thought, maybe she is there with you?"

Anatoly could hear the sarcasm in the man's voice. "No, she is not here. As far as I know she is at her apartment where I left her yesterday after picking her up at the airport." He wondered why Dmitri would be looking for her and worried that it may have had something to do with her internet activity.

"Why does he need her? If I see her I can give her a message... if you like."

The voice on the other end was silent for a moment. The man contemplated just how much of a confidant Anatoly was to his boss. He knew he was trusted with Gregorov's money and his account information. He guessed that if Gregorov could trust him with his money then he could trust him to deliver a message to another associate. Besides, it would pass his burden of responsibility on to someone else, alleviating him of his duties, therefore allowing him more time to screw off.

"The General said he wants Nikki to meet him at the Merinsk Street Cafe, at the Dreslev Inn, at one o'clock today."

Some of Gregorov's men had served under him in the defunct Soviet Army. They easily gave away their history by referring to their boss as the General rather than Dmitri or Gregorov.

The deep voice continued, "He has put her in charge of putting the security team together. He looked at the note he held in his hand. "Tell her Bryzncec and Stransky are up. They got duty today. Any questions?"

Anatoly had none. He was relieved, remembering that Nikki had been recalled for a possible meeting with the physicist. "Got it, one o'clock, Merinsk Cafe, bring some friends," He said, yawning, summing it up for the agent.

"Funny," the deep voice said in response, then the phone went dead.

Anatoly thought about Metelov and found it interesting that Gregorov was meeting with the man. If what Nikki had told him in the car was true, that Metelov was the one who had built the bomb for the terrorists, and he were Gregorov, he would stay as far away from Metelov as he could. The Americans would find out who the bomb builder was. It would only be a matter of time before they came for Gregorov, if he got too close.

Anatoly contemplated what it would mean for him if Gregorov was picked up for questioning. He was only a book keeper and had covered his tracks well, plus he had the protection of Elena's family. Oh well, not his concern.

He shook away his thoughts and dialed Nikki's cell, but got no answer, the phone going straight to voicemail. He remembered that she had called him from a different number the last time. He scanned his phone's call history and selected the second number, Nikki's apartment phone, from the list and was surprised when she picked up so quickly, simply greeting him with, "Hello."

"Good morning. Did you have a productive evening last night?" Anatoly asked cheerily, but Nikki's reply was all business.

"Anatoly, I need Gregorov's account information," she said flatly. "I am ready to take it all."

Anatoly was taken aback, "Whoa, give me a minute to wake up. You're breaking the morning speed limit. I haven't even finished my first cup of coffee yet," he joked, sitting straight up in his chair.

Nikki wasn't in a joking mood. "Listen to me, Anny. I need your help. I want all of it, Anny, weapons, money, everything. Gregorov used me. He played me for a fool working both sides of the war and it pisses me off. He sold tons of weapons to Milosevic's commanders through his crooked political cronies."

Anatoly sighed, "I take it you were up all night. You sound a little crabby this morning. Speaking of Gregorov, he called just now looking for you. Well, actually, one of his men called. Today is the meeting. He wanted to tell you where to meet him later today and at what time. You are supposed to be in charge of his security team. One o'clock at the Merinsk Street Cafe. The one at the old Dreslev Inn..."

Nikki cut him off, asking, "Who has the duty shift?"

"He said someone named Bryzncec and Stransky. I don't know them so you will have to get hold of them."

"I know who they are," Nikki said disparagingly. "They both have their heads up Gregorov's ass. They can't breathe on their own unless he takes a breath for them. I have their contact info in my cell." With that Nikki set the phone down and walked away to retrieve her cell. She unplugged the charge cord and pressed the power button to turn it on.

Suddenly the audio feed was back. Rick White motioned to the others in the room.

"We're back in business, gents," he said as he turned the volume up. Nikki's voice came over the speakers on his console. She was talking to someone, but the conversation seemed one sided. White increased the volume some more, still not hearing the person she was speaking to.

"Can you turn it up?" Ramsey asked, but Rick White shook his head.

"That's as loud as it gets. I think she's talking to someone on a different phone. Maybe it's a land line. Probably not gonna get anything."

When Nikki came back to the phone Anatoly reminded her that the meeting was with Dr. Metelov. "I think you should be careful around this Metelov. Gregorov should be staying way clear of him, too. If this man did help the terrorist in the U.S. it seems odd to me that Gregorov would agree to meet with him so soon. If I was a betting man I would bet that Gregorov did not really expect the doctor to return to Moscow after his mission. Something seems strange about the whole thing. I guess the lure of an extra million dollars in Dmitri's bank account is too appealing to turn away."

Nikki reflected on the last mission and her memories of what she thought she knew about Metelov against some of the information that she gleaned from Gregorov's files during the night.

"No, if anything, Gregorov is loyal. They go back a long way. There are pictures of the two together, when Gregorov had hair…" Nikki suddenly stopped talking.

Anatoly waited several seconds before saying anything. "Hello, you still there?"

Nikki was thinking about the images of the doctor with Gregorov. Suddenly he seemed familiar to her. Where did she…? "Hold on," She said as she flipped her laptop open again.

Nikki opened the folders that she had copied from Gregorov's server. She scrolled through the photos until she found what she was looking for: the picture of Gregorov and Metelov together. She zoomed in closer, bringing Metelov's face in close.

"Son of a bitch!" she said out loud.

"What? What is going on?" Anatoly asked.

Nikki sat back in her chair as she stared into the eyes of Dr. Metelov, then said. "I know where I've seen him before." She cursed again, "Son of a bitch, that bastard is still alive?"

Anatoly was confused, and Nikki offered no help in making him understand. She contemplated her situation for a moment and then spoke. "Here is what I need from you, and I will need it before the meeting today. Both of the accounts need to be emptied. Do you still have access to my personal account?"

Anatoly answered. "I do, but,…"

Nikki cut him off again. "All of it Anny, both of the accounts, his and Metelov's today, before the meeting. Can you do it or not?"

Anatoly didn't like what she was doing. It was too fast. "You should slow down. This could backfire on you."

Nikki was getting frustrated with Anatoly's repeated cautions and dire predictions. "I am not worried about what they think. I am not afraid of Gregorov." Nikki paused for a moment. "This is only the beginning, Anny. Now, can I count on you to help me or am I going to do this entirely on my own?"

There was a long silence, then Nikki spoke quietly. "I will not rest until I have the answers. Either you are helping me, or you are not."

"Ok, ok, I will have it for you. In less than an hour you will have access to millions of Gregorov's money. I hope you know what you are doing." Anatoly sighed as he began plugging at his keyboard.

"You do realize that you have just signed my death warrant if Gregorov finds out that I helped you steal his money?" He asked not really expecting an answer.

Nikki contemplated her immediate future. She wasn't sure exactly how things were going to go, but with money at her disposal and Gregorov's account held hostage, she thought she had a definite advantage. She would get the information she desired and then figure out what to do next.

"Thank you, Anny. Meet me in an hour to go over everything." With that she hung up and all that could be heard was Nikki as she walked around her apartment. After a minute she flipped through her cell phone contacts until she found one of the two bodyguards. She remembered meeting Bryzcnec. He was a piece of shit, one of the old guard, a yes man, loyal only to Gregorov. There was no way she would be able to convince him to go against the General. And Stransky was a carbon copy of Bryzcnec, sharing the same ass-kissing mentality.

Too bad, she thought, as she placed the call to the one named Bryzncec. The conversation was short. Meet up with her at one o'clock to escort Gregorov to his two o'clock meeting with Metelov. She did the same with Stransky. There were no questions from either of them.

Nikki looked up a few other closer associates. People who worked for Gregorov and had nothing good to say about him ever. Perhaps, she thought, they would want to change things up a bit. She called each one of the three men, telling them only to meet with her and Anatoly in an hour. All three complied, agreeing to the meeting with no questions. With that she tossed her phone aside, undressed and stepped into the shower.

Ramsey looked around the room. "Everyone put on your game face. Paul, get hold of Vee and Marks. Tell them to head back to the apartment to get ready for the meeting. Make sure they are up to speed on everything that just transpired."

He turned to Rick White. "See if you can figure out what the hell she was talking about between now and the meeting. Concentrate on the meeting, though. Do not get sidetracked. If you don't have time don't mess with it."

Alan looked at the time on his watch. He hoped that Metelov wouldn't screw up. They need the information he was going to get to corroborate Gregorov's involvement in the sale of the warhead that very nearly detonated in the United States.

Ramsey was sure that Gregorov not only sold the weapon, but provided transportation and a physicist to make it useable. So far everything Metelov told them about the bomb was true. He thought about his conversation earlier and wondered if Murphy would be visiting today.

Kenneth Wash

CHAPTER 12

SHOWTIME
MERINSK ST. CAFÉ, ZELENOGRAD

RAMSEY scanned the array of flat-screen monitors that lined the wall of the temporary operations center, tapping impatiently on one. "Rick, why don't I have a video feed from inside the restaurant?"

"Working on it, Sir. It's not at this end. Something's wrong with the equipment there. I don't get it. I verified all the connections. I guess we could have a bad cable." He moved to the control panel and switched feed cables then threw a couple switches. The center video monitor suddenly flickered to life.

Nearly five thousand miles away, twelve stories below ground and at five o'clock in the morning, Secretary of State Erickson stood in the dimly lit control room known as "The Fortress," drinking a cup of coffee and watching the Air Force Special Operations Communications Officer manage the information displayed on the wall-sized monitor. The images were split up into four large screens. Each section displayed the exact information that was being seen by Alan Ramsey's teams.

The technical glitch being experienced at Rick White's location was due to the additional systems spliced directly into White's equipment on the site, secretly installed, at Erickson's request, by Gordon Maxwell's agents.

Back in the suburbs of Moscow, Ramsey looked at his monitor and could see their subject. He spoke into his headset, "Vee, you and Marks getting this?"

Approximately one half kilometer away in a hotel room overlooking the Café, Agents Villacruze and Marks had set up shop. Vee put down his binoculars, glanced at the satellite-fed monitors placed around the room, then keyed his headset, "Got it, Sir. That would be General Dmitri Gregorov. Looks like he's got his usual entourage of Russian Special Service or prior KGB operative bodyguards with him."

Marks moved the joystick left to pan through the restaurant. It was dark in the corner where Gregorov liked to sit, but thanks to the technological advances of the new equipment it looked as if he were in bright daylight. He suddenly stopped the camera, settling on the figure of Nikki Sidorova. "There's our girl."

Ramsey leaned back a bit, looking at Nikki. "Ok, in case you all haven't bothered to read the information that was dug up on her, here is a bit of info. Nikki Sidorova, Bosnian born multi-geographical operative. Muslim, we believe. Probably Sunni, based on the region. She is 33 years old, has been involved with many different groups within the Russian Mafia Syndicate and, we believe, early on, the Muslim Brotherhood, since she was seventeen or eighteen. We're still putting a file together on her, but most recently she has been involved with Dmitri Gregorov. She tends to follow the person with the most power. You can bet if she is involved, there is a major player involved."

Agent Villacruze suddenly spoke up, interrupting Ramsey's report, "Heads up folks, the doctor is in the house."

The monitor showed the image of Dr. Metelov making his way toward the entrance of the restaurant. The man looked nervously toward the building that housed the two agents. "Damn, man, don't be looking around like that," Vee said, to no one in particular.

Ramsey watched the feed and reiterated the goals for the mission. "Alright guys, here's the deal. When Metelov engages with Gregorov make sure you are getting the audio. Metelov will be talking about any new jobs that require his expertise as a bomb builder. Stay awake. We need something to hang Dmitri with, but more importantly listen for anything that could indicate any upcoming events."

Erickson glared at the monitor and the image of the Russian scientist walking toward the café as he listened to Alan Ramsey brief his people. He scowled as he sipped his coffee, thinking to himself that Alan Ramsey and Gabe Anderson were wasting time with a bullshit operation. They both knew that the three subjects in the inn less than two kilometers away were guilty. Instead of pussyfooting around with their lame investigation, they should have rigged the building to explode. They could have made it look like a hit on Gregorov. Too bad if it would have taken out the others. There wasn't a person in the inn's cafe that wasn't tied to some type of crime.

Metelov walked through the restaurant and then stopped in front of Dmitri Gregorov's table. Nikki moved around the man and yanked off his jacket searching for any sign of a wire or weapon and found his Motorola phone, opened it and saw that it was not powered on. She removed the battery cover and took out the battery. Satisfied that it was not bugged she tossed the phone in its disassembled condition onto the table.

"We lost Metelov's phone. She yanked the battery," Rick White said over his com set from Marks and Vee's location. "I still got Metelov covered and we have Nikki's phone and the restaurant bugs."

One of the bodyguards stepped in and frisked Metelov. He was about to pronounce him clean when the doctor offered the info himself. "I am not armed, I assure you."

He turned his attention fully to Gregorov. "Hello, Dmitri. How have you been?"

Dmitri Gregorov smiled and gestured for the doctor to sit. "Please, have a seat. We have much to talk about. How is your family? Are they enjoying your newfound wealth?"

Gregorov lit a cigarette and inhaled deeply. "I am concerned that one day they will say something about what happened. What do you think, Doctor? Am I worried for no reason?"

Nikki moved around the table to sit next to Gregorov and directly across from the physicist. She placed her weapon on the table and played with it, spinning it slowly and eyeing Metelov.

Metelov found himself staring at the woman. She looked familiar and he wondered had he ever met her before. He shook away his thoughts and returned his gaze to Dmitri, concentrating on what Dmitri had just said.

Metelov thought it ironic that Gregorov would express concern about his family's possible disloyalty when, in fact, it was he that was helping the Americans with their investigation. Though, again, he did not have a choice. Spending life in a Russian prison was not an option for him. He would not be able to survive there. No, his only choice was to help the Russian Investigators. He must work with the Americans under the supervision of the Russians to help implicate Dmitri or be tried for treason.

"You do not have to worry. They still believe that they were abducted and held for ransom. My wife does not know about the money yet. She thinks that I had to pay to free them. I am a modest man and my wife a modest woman. She does not need more than the love of her family to be happy."

Gregorov leaned against the back of his booth smiling. "Ah, a love story. I think I feel a tear welling up." He laughed heartily at his own joke, striking the table with his hand and then became serious again. "Speaking of money, Doctor, You are aware that your friend, Ahmed, stole from me? He did not pay me the final payment of one million dollars. That was the deal I made with his boss, Leaja, you know. One million after delivery."

Metelov wondered where the conversation was going. "Zuqawri was not a friend. He was a kidnapper and a murderer. Besides, it is of no matter now that he is dead, I would imagine."

Dmitri took another long draw on his smoke. "After he was captured I sent a...liaison to meet with Leaja to discuss the matter. They never got to meet with him. Ahmed's murderous Muslim Brotherhood killed all but one of my men."

He downed the last of his drink, set the glass down on the table, and gave it a spin. He waited for the glass to settle before continuing, "I tried to negotiate with them and all I got was their treachery. They stabbed me in the back." Gregorov smacked his left palm with the side of his fist as if he were plunging an imaginary knife through it.

"Therefore, I was determined for them to fail, so I gave the Americans a little push in the right direction."

The doctor looked inquisitively at Gregorov. "Then it was you who led them to the warehouse?"

Gregorov moved the meeting along, "Why are you here, Doctor? Why did you arrange this meeting? Is one and a half million American dollars not enough money for you to live your...modest life?" He smashed out his cigarette as if punctuating his sentence.

Metelov answered without hesitation, "On the contrary. I was paid more than agreed. I feel that my obligation for the money is not settled. I come to you to offer my services."

Agent Marks was checking the audio feed on the external camera when he noticed the first of the two black U.A.Z Hunter S.U.V.s pull down the street. "Heads up, we got company. Looks like two R.S.S. vehicles heading this way."

Ramsey turned to face the three Russian Security Service agents in the room. "What's going on here? This is *our* investigation. You gave us full authority to run this operation and capture Gregorov, if possible."

"I assure you, we do not know anything about this." The Russian pulled out his cell phone to make a call to his superior as Marks came back on the speaker.

"Look at your monitors, folks. There's some bad shit going down here."

Both vehicles were stopped and two groups of masked Russian Special Service Police formed up at the curb and entered the building.

Nikki was the first to react. She nearly jumped over the table as she pulled up her weapon pointing it in the direction of the intruders. Then suddenly, she turned and shot both of Dmitri's bodyguards before they could pull out their own weapons.

Dr. Metelov jumped up and began to plead. "Please do not kill me. I am not one of his men. I am only here because I am working with the police and the Americans!"

Nikki stepped from behind the table staring at Dmitri as she made her way to the doctor. She held her finger to his lips and told him to be quiet. Metelov dropped his arms down to his sides and stood, shaking.

Nikki suddenly stepped up to him and placed her pistol on his forehead. Metelov closed his eyes tightly and cringed.

"Are you afraid, Doctor? Is that why you help the Americans? Because you are afraid of what they might find out about you...Jovan Kovicevic?"

Metelov opened one eye slightly. He glanced at Gregorov then back at Nikki. "I do not know what you are talking about," he stammered in a low voice.

Nikki hit him hard with the pistol causing him to fall to his knees. "You are Dr. Jovan Kovicevic. You are from Bosnia and you are a traitor to the Muslim people." Nikki yelled at him as she walked around his kneeling figure.

"I am Vladimir Metelov. I don't know what you are talking about." Metelov would not look up for fear of being struck again.

Nikki screamed at him, "You are a traitor and a murderer!" She reached in her jacket pocket and removed some photos and tossed them down on the floor in front of Metelov. One of the photos showed at least a hundred lifeless bodies, or more correctly, pieces of bodies, laid out on tarps next to one another, excavated from a mass grave. Others showed rows of green fabric-covered coffins on a hillside, each waiting next to a freshly dug grave.

Metelov recognized the subjects in the photos as the remains of some of the eight thousand men and boys killed by General Ratko Mladic's Serbian army, and whose remains were recovered recently. He began to sob uncontrollably.

"Yes, yes, I am Jovan Kovicevic," he said through his sobbing. "Mladic's men forced me to help them. I had access to the names and birth records of all of Srebrenica."

He looked up at Nikki, tears welling in his eyes. He wiped away his tears and glared at her. "I recognize you now. You were there, at the busses, before the massacre, when they came to take us away."

He suddenly remembered the moment he told the Serb soldiers the true age of Nikki's brother. She had lied to them to get him on the bus with her, the bus reserved for the women and children. He could see the image of Nikki screaming at the Serbian soldiers to let go of her brother as they pulled him from her grasp and pushed her aside. Now, he stood in front of her once again. He had to make her understand, "They were going to kill me if I didn't help them."

"You sold out your own people. My father and my brother were taken from me. For fifteen years I waited for word that they had been found alive, then, as the years passed, I hoped only that their bodies might be found at last."

Nikki picked up the photos and looked at the rows of coffins. "Five hundred more bodies were recovered. The last of over seven thousand that were tortured and murdered, identified and laid to rest on that hillside. And now, they have stopped looking for any more. My father's own countrymen, the government that he stood with to help secure the freedom of the people of Bosnia, have stopped searching. And still, they have not found my father or my brother."

In the apartment, a half of a kilometer away, the Russian agents were screaming into their headsets that something had gone wrong. Ramsey was asking for information, but the Russians all but ignored him as they walked out into the hallway.

Nikki stood over the man, contemplating the photos in her hand. She took a deep breath and shoved the pictures back into her pocket. "But now, Jovan Kovicevic, I have found you." Without hesitating further, she pulled the trigger, sending the man backward to the floor.

Everyone in both apartments stopped when the sound of the gunshot punctured the tense atmosphere. Villacruze's voice came over the speakers, "Metelov is down. He's been shot."

Ramsey turned to face the lead agent. "What the hell are you waiting for? Get your men down there and stop her before she kills Gregorov."

The Russian looked stunned. "We have people on the way."

Ramsey wanted to go to the inn and capture Nikki and Gregorov, but he had no jurisdiction, no weapons and no vehicle to get there. He was fuming over losing Metelov.

"You've got three men right there. He motioned beyond the closed door into the hallway. You could walk there faster than your response team can be on site!"

He threw his hands up in exasperation. There was nothing he could do. Next time, he thought, the operation would be secret. No approval and just Americans.

Deep in the Fortress Erickson's eyes went wide as he watched what was happening. He fumbled around in his pocket and found his phone, placing a call to his Moscow contact. The phone rang twice followed by Gordon Maxwell's voice.

"I know what you're thinking, but it's not us," came the greeting from Moscow.

"No shit, not unless you hired that bitch to do your job. Now shut the hell up and listen." Erickson did not have time to screw around. He wanted to take advantage of the opportunity playing out on the screen.

"Get somebody down to that inn. Have them finish what she started. Take the whole place down if you have to."

The voice hesitated, and then spoke, "We don't have a plan for this. All I got is a couple of techies here right now. I got two guys with me and a single pistol. What the hell you want me to do about it? I'm already outgunned."

"Don't you ever plan for contingencies?" Erickson nearly yelled then added in obvious disgust, "One damned pistol?"

His contact spoke calmly, "Maybe, you should have told us there was going to be a psycho at the meeting. Maybe you're the one who needs to plan better next time." With that the phone went dead. Erickson listened to the silence of his phone for a few seconds then turned back to the scenario taking place.

Gregorov stared at Nikki not believing what he'd just witnessed, then raised his hands and stood at the table. He turned toward Nikki. "What is going on here?"

The sounds of emergency vehicles and wail of police sirens could be heard in the distance. Nikki Sidorova studied the man in front of her before speaking. "How is it that you know Jovan Kovicevic, eh, Dmitri?" Nikki walked around the table closer to Gregorov.

"I only know of him because of Zuqawri." Gregorov waved his hand through the air dismissively. "Ahmed needed someone who had knowledge of our warheads. I am a business man. I get people what they need."

Nikki motioned for two of her masked accomplices to move forward. They grabbed Gregorov and forced him to sit. Nikki moved to the corner of the table to retrieve Dmitri's satchel. She pulled his laptop from the bag and set it in front of her. Nikki looked upward with a feigned look of contemplation. "Now, let me see. What was that password?" After a few keystrokes she turned it to face him. Dmitri displayed a genuine look of surprise at her ability to defeat his password security.

"I want you to see something, Dmitri. Look at your account information. What do you see?"

Gregorov saw that he had no money in his safe account. He touched his fingers to the touchpad and scrolled through the document. Millions of dollars were gone.

"You whore bitch. You stole my money."

Nikki leaned across the desk, closed the laptop and then slid it to the side. "Money that you earned selling rifles and bullets to General Mladic for his assault on Srebrenica." She began to walk toward him. "Money that you earned by becoming partners with a war criminal and kissing the ass of Slobodan Milosevic!"

"I do not know what you are talking about," Dmitri lied, regretting that his sidearm was not within reach.

Nikki stepped forward and shoved the pistol against Gregorov's forehead. "You do not remember the chants of the Serb Nationalists? Slobo! Slobo! Slobo! You were there, Dmitri, chanting with them all, thinking about how rich you would become selling the weapons of the defunct Soviet Union to a mob of Christian madmen."

Gregorov winced from the pressure of the steel barrel against his skin. "General Mladic killed those people. He was to blame and was hung for it."

"Wrong, Dmitri. Mladic is still a fugitive. He has never paid for his crimes. The Americans had him, but let him go. You know where he is, don't you, Dmitri?"

Gregorov was sweating now. He pulled a cigarette from his pack and lit it, inhaling deeply and exhaled quickly.

"I have not seen him in years. I have no clue as to his whereabouts." Gregorov leaned his head to the side and waved his cigarette around as he spoke as if to dismiss the whole idea. He looked over his glasses, scowling at Nikki.

"Now, take the money you stole from me and leave...Consider it...reparation."

Nikki pushed hard on the pistol. "Where is Mladic? Tell me!"

The sirens were very close. The taller of the two men holding Dmitri spoke. "We must hurry. Let's go."

Dmitri recognized the voice and turned suddenly to look into his eyes. He noted the fear, the eyes flitting back and forth within the openings of the mask. He smiled nervously as he motioned toward Nikki with a sideways nod of his head, then turned back to face her.

"You must keep your eye on this one, Anatoly. She is a pathetic bitch and will surely throw you to the wolves when it benefits her."

With that Nikki Sidorova fired the shot to end Dmitri's life. She cursed for not getting the information she wanted and then yelled for her people to move. Anatoly hesitated, stunned by what he had just witnessed.

Nikki pushed him toward the door with the side of her pistol. "Move!" she yelled as she followed them out the door to the awaiting vehicles.

The sound of screeching tires and gunned engines filled Ramsey's headset. He pulled off his headphones. "Get that feed cleaned up! I want to know what just happened there."

Agent Villacruze was calling, "We need the Ruskies to get someone on their asses! We need to stop them! They are heading toward the city."

The three Russian agents were also trying to figure out what had just happened. Ramsey was furious.

"We must go now," Russo said. "I will contact you with any information about what has happened here."

He started out of the apartment, but Ramsey stepped in front of him. "Hold on a second, Russo. Who the hell is Mladic? What was Nikki talking about?"

The Russian rolled his eyes and sighed as if it was hard to muster an answer. "General Ratko Mladic was a Serbian General in charge of Slobodan Milosevic's Serbian forces. The Bosnians believe he is responsible for the genocidal attacks on the Bosnian Muslims, and the destruction of nearly all of Bosnia."

Ramsey knew little of the Balkan wars or the American efforts to end them. He only knew it had been a mess of failed diplomacy. He guessed that he would be getting a crash course on the topic.

The R.S.S Agent turned toward the door. "We will contact you with any information that arises from this. Meanwhile, you may want to look to your own government for some answers." With that he turned on his heel and left.

Ramsey picked up a microphone and keyed the transmit button. "Vee, Marks, shut it down. There's nothing more we can do. No Gregorov, no weapons. At least not for now."

The sound of emergency vehicles filled the street below Vee and Mark's position in the hotel. The two agents packed up their gear as the Russian police moved into the building across the street to assess the situation.

Ramsey looked around the room. "Let's pack it up and get it back home so we can scrub through the audio and video. Paul, we need to get some flights arranged. Looks like we got our work cut out for us when we get back home."

"You got it," Paul Jackson said as he stacked one of the components on a two-wheeled cart. "I know one thing," he began as he removed his phone from his pocket to call the international ticketing agent. "I sure as hell wouldn't want to be anybody that had anything to do with that whole Bosnian shit. That woman is on a mission."

Ramsey was thinking over what had transpired not ten minutes before.

"That's what worries me. That she is on a mission."

He looked at his watch, noting the time, and did the math in his head to figure what time he would be back home.

"I hope you can sleep on a plane, because in about fifteen hours we're going to be back in full swing trying to determine what role our government had in Bosnia and whether or not we should be worried about Nikki Sidorova."

Kenneth Wash

CHAPTER 13

ARTISTIC LICENSE
THE FORTRESS, WASHINGTON D.C.

SECRETARY Erickson was trying to turn the situation to his advantage. He was on the phone again, this time calling Ron Carlton, the President of the United States. The Secretary of State noticed that the Air Force Special Operations Officer was staring at him. He pointed toward the door. "Go take a break. Get some coffee or a pop, but don't leave the A.O."

Without a word the Lieutenant Commander headed out the door. Within seconds of his departure President Carlton was on the line.

"Ron, it's me, Jim Erickson. I'm calling from The Fortress. Are you alone?"

President Carlton looked at the two visitors he was entertaining and asked to be excused for a moment. Motioning toward the door to guide them out, but speaking to the Secretary of State he said, "No, but I will be in ten seconds." He covered his phone and promised his guests that he'd be only a moment, then turned back to his caller, dropping all pretenses. "What is it, Jim? Why are you at The Fortress?"

"I'll explain later. Sidorova just killed Gregorov and Metelov."

The President was shocked. He took a seat behind his desk before responding. "What the hell? Why would she do that?"

"I don't know for sure, Ron, but…" Erickson began.

President Carlton cut him off, thinking about why Erickson would be in the underground command center. "Damn it, Jim. What the hell are you doing getting involved with Ramsey's investigation? Didn't we just settle this shit?"

Erickson didn't have time for a lecture just now. "Ron, listen to me. She's got all of Gregorov's account information. She has his files, too. They were on a laptop that she showed him before she shot him." He repeated some of what he said so that he was sure that the President clearly understood. "She's got his files, Ron. That probably means she knows where the weapons are. That also means she may have access to other, more sensitive information."

President Carlton's tone became emotionless as the ramifications of what his Secretary of State had just told him sunk in. "Where is she now? Did anyone make an arrest?"

"She's on the run. Nobody was ready for this. They all screwed up. Ramsey, the Russians. I hate to say I told you so, but we should have taken this operation over from the start. You should have backed me more on this, Ron. We'd be a hell of a lot…"

The President interrupted, "Jim, shut the hell up. Let me think."

Erickson stopped talking immediately. President Carlton was silent for a long moment then asked, "What about those special ops that are over there? Can't they take this on?"

Jim Erickson knew that the President would not be so accepting of the special ops teams if he knew Maxwell was in charge, a detail he would leave out for the moment while Carlton was eager to commit. He explained the lack of preplanning. "Nobody anticipated this. They don't have a quick response team ready to go, but they do have access to aerial surveillance and reconnaissance drones they can send up. The damned things are controlled from Latvia, but can be patched over to us. You authorize a launch and once they are airborne we can control the ship from here in The Fortress. Hell, we could strap a couple missiles to them and once we make contact, our problems would be over."

The President thought about Erickson's plan. "Jim, how's it going to look to have one of our drones flying over Russia, let alone armed with missiles? Are you crazy? I can already hear Rashnev screaming at me over the phone. You know how sensitive the Russian President is about border incursions of any type. You go in there hot and screw up, you can kiss your political future goodbye." He paused for a second and then added, "The Russians will probably take it out the moment you send it up anyway."

"The birds are already in Russia. That's the advantage. They're close and hard to spot. These things are the Israeli copy of our RQ version. The MK150 tactical U.A.V.s. Very stealthy. The Russians officially purchased twelve of them through approved channels after the intelligence failures they suffered during their skirmish with Georgia in 2008. I was on the International Security Council, remember? Israel doesn't sell shit to anyone without a global council. Just so happens, we bought a few as well, for situations like this where we don't want 'Made in USA' stamped all over everything."

Erickson looked at his watch. "You gotta make a call, Ron. We're running out of time. Who knows what Gregorov has on that laptop. If it gets back to the Russians or Gabe Anderson's goons, it will be damaging to both our political futures.

The President didn't hesitate. "Ok, do it. Send one up, but no missiles, just reconnaissance. Are we clear?"

"Got it, no missiles. I need to make this happen. I'll call you later." Erickson disconnected and immediately scrolled through his names until he found Maxwell's number. "Gordon, I need a drone. You said you have MK150's right?"

"I do. I have a couple RQ180's too. They're more expensive, but much better than the MK's. Maxwell was all about quality.

Erickson replied, "No, can't have a U.S. signature. Get one in the air immediately aimed toward Moscow and patch it in to The Fortress. Use the same information that you used to set up the commo link."

Maxwell heard the sound of money talking. "You got it, Boss. I'll need a few minutes to get it airborne."

Erickson shot back, "There's a bonus if you can get it up in five minutes or less. Oh, and Gordon, give me two of whatever kind of missiles you got that can take out a moving vehicle on the ground, something that can't possibly miss."

CHAPTER 14

REMOTE CONTROL
NEAR THE TOWN OF KHIMKI, RUSSIA

THE two U.A.Z., Hunter S.U.V.'s sped toward Moscow, down Highway M10, a federal highway that connected Russia's two largest cities, Moscow and Saint Petersburg, and continued to the border with Finland. The M10, also known as Leningradsky Shoss or Lenin's Highway, was a four lane highway that ran through the town of Zelenograd, where the meeting was held, allowing the two vehicles quick access to the café.

The scenery changed from clusters of older houses and small businesses to farmland and back as they headed to the staging area set up in a defunct automotive garage in the town of Khimki, just on the outskirts of Moscow.

Anatoly had not spoken since they left the meeting with Gregorov. He wasn't sure what to say. He had never been involved in such a hideous crime and was both angry and terrified. He peeled off his mask and stared at Nikki who was directing the driver.

Anatoly was breathing hard. He had never experienced an adrenalin rush like the one he had just felt. The sensation was both exciting and nerve racking. His muscles were burning from the physical exertion. He was exhausted, hyped and afraid all at the same time. But mostly he was afraid, worried about what the commitment he had made meant for him and the rest of his life. He needed to discuss it with Nikki, but was not sure what to say. Finally he could not keep quiet any longer.

He turned and moved closer to Nikki, the mask, still warm, clutched in his hand. He could feel his hair was mussed from its wearing and combed his hand through it as he wiped the sweat from his forehead.

"Now what?" he asked Nikki simply.

Nikki stopped talking to Vostav, the driver, and faced Anatoly. She leaned into him and kissed him, pulling his mouth hard against hers.

"You were wonderful, Anny. Did you see the look on Gregorov's face when he figured out it was you?" She was excited. Anatoly couldn't fully understand her pleasure with what had happened.

"Nikki, stop." Anatoly pushed away from her and sat up straight. His emotions were all mixed up, but overwhelmingly he felt angry and betrayed.

"I thought you wanted information from Gregorov. It's kind of difficult to expect a man to give up his secrets when the back of his head is one big exit wound."

Nikki shot back, "He didn't know anything. Dmitri was not lying. That man was a lot of things, but he was not a liar."

"Then why did you kill him, for spite? That doesn't make any sense to me. Gregorov protected us. Unless you plan on taking over his organization, you have just removed all of your armor, making both of us vulnerable." Anatoly thought about the meeting. "Remember what Dr. Metelov said? Didn't you hear him say that he was working with the Americans and the Russians? How many enemies do you want?"

The driver of the S.U.V., Vostav, looked into the rearview mirror.

"Anatoly, how long have you been bookkeeping for the Boss? Surely you don't think all of that money you were moving around was from honesty in a days work? This is not our first cowboy show. What do you think, Nikki and I knock on customer's doors and ask politely for the Boss's money?"

Anatoly couldn't help but laugh at his attempt at western metaphors.

"You mean, an honest day's work...and, it's not a cowboy show, it's a rodeo. And yes, I do think you knock on the doors and ask nicely. Don't you? I mean, why wouldn't you?"

Vostav thought about it for a moment. "Ok, yes, we do knock at first. But if we have to go knocking then usually we kill them. It's easy. You will get used to it." He met Anatoly's eyes through the rear view mirror and shrugged away the lack of response by either of his passengers.

Nikki waved him off and pulled Anatoly's face around to look into his eyes. "Anny, you have to trust me. Yes, I am going to take over the organization. We have the money and soon we will have the weapons."

Anatoly stopped her. "Wait a minute. Don't you think that there are others in the organization that might think they should be in charge? Not everyone will be happy that Gregorov is dead."

"Who, Anny? Who do you think will challenge me?" She reached out and smacked her driver in the back of the head. "How about you, Vostav? You want some of this?"

He turned around. "I am not the squeaky wheel. Why are you asking me? I am happy to just be Vostav." He turned back around in time to see that he was about to put the car in a ditch and made a sudden correction to the vehicle.

Nikki laughed, "Anny we will have everything that we want."

Vostav looked in his rear view mirror. He was about to pick up his handheld radio to contact the driver of the second vehicle, trailing about one hundred meters behind them, when something caught his attention, a flare or reflection of some sort. He rolled his window down and wiped at the mirrored glass, adjusting it as the vehicle behind him suddenly exploded.

Nikki turned toward the fireball in time to see the swift moving aircraft not far overhead. "Drone!" she yelled to no one in particular, then moved to the side glass to find it again.

Vostav accelerated hard pushing the U.A.Z. Hunter to its limits. The vehicle picked up speed as the drone swept around, unseen, over the buildings of the small town, circling for a second strike.

Deep in The Fortress Jim Erickson stood in the shadows of the control room. He looked at the images on the floor to ceiling, high definition screen, which, at the moment, showed the color images of the clay tile rooftops of the small town of Khimki.

Data from the MK150 stealth drone flashed on the screen. A wireframe image of the delta shaped drone twisted and turned on the screen in the upper right corner. Information indicating speed, height and degree of vector control scrolled upward next to the image. The pilot, Air Force Special Operations Captain, Danny Akins, controlled the drone remotely from the subterranean control room in Washington, having been patched in from a remote site in Latvia.

"Coming around for the second sweep," the pilot called into his headset. The information read out as teletext on the large screen as the view changed from rooftop images to the view of the road below. The remains of the burning SUV could be seen as the drone zeroed in on its next target.

Nikki saw it first, pointing as the drone moved into an attack position.

"There it is! It's coming back again! Move, Vostav, hurry!"

Vostav pushed harder on a pedal that was already as far down as it would go. The U.A.Z. was a good off road vehicle, but was not much for a high-speed chase. He slid around a sweeping curve, veering to the right of the main roadway.

Anatoly watched with a sense of both excitement and fear, looking back at the aircraft that was settling on a steady path just above the roadway. The drone had just passed over the burning S.U.V., now about three miles behind them.

Vostav was not slowing down as he headed toward a more populated area. The surface of the road dipped and fell away as the M10 highway narrowed to pass through a thin corridor between older high-rise apartments and office buildings. With no room for four lanes of highway traffic to travel through the heavily congested area of older brick structures side by side, the oncoming traffic lanes were supported overhead. It was a highway on stilts with the eastbound lanes above those leading west. Vostav felt a bit more secure as his S.U.V. disappeared under the raised eastbound traffic lanes.

Back in the control room of the subterranean fortress, the pilot of the U.A.V. was concerned about the sudden urban environment that had enveloped the S.U.V. The collateral damage indicator on the screen suddenly spread from a thin green line in the middle of the screen to yellow, then quickly to red, completely filling the graph.

An audible warning sounded to warn the pilot that any weapons used would more than likely cause unintentional damage to buildings, people or other vehicles. He had to decide what to do and he had to do it quickly, but this decision was well above his pay grade and one that he was not willing to make.

"Sir, we have just gone from green to red. What are your orders?" Akins knew he should pull back from the attack and was relaxing his grip somewhat expecting the order to abort.

Secretary Erickson stepped out of the shadows. He glared at the screen.

The captain repeated his request, "Sir, I need to know what you want to do." On the screen the highway split was just ahead. The MK150 banked to the left, following the highway down. "Sir, what are your orders?"

Erickson suddenly blurted out, "Stay with them. Wait for a clear shot, but stay with them."

Akins reestablished a secure grip on the controller and pushed the stick forward. The drone dropped from the sky, diving from two-thousand feet, hurtling toward the highway.

Nikki was looking out the rear of the U.A.Z. when the drone suddenly came into view. The aircraft was inches from the asphalt surface. The MK150 settled on a course moving up quickly behind her vehicle. She couldn't believe it. The aircraft was flying under the eastbound lanes as if it was just another car on the roadway, only this one was moving extremely fast and was armed with missiles.

The driver alternated his view from the road ahead to his mirrors as the U.A.V. approached. Vostav tried again to accelerate, meeting only the resistance of the floorboard against the gas pedal. He looked at the speedometer. The vehicle was capable of 200 kilometers per hour according to the instrumentation, but he had the pedal floored and the needle was stuck at 180. He glanced in his outside rearview mirror again. The drone was closing in.

Nikki grabbed her pistol from the seat and, removing the safety, clamored over the back of the seat and into the cargo area of the S.U.V.

Anatoly saw her with the weapon and blurted, "What the hell are you doing?"

Staring at the front of the drone and wondering what to aim for, Nikki searched for a target that would possibly disable the aircraft that was now only car lengths away. There was one missile hanging under the left wing. Maybe she could take out the camera, or fire at the air intakes on either side of the fuselage to try to disable the engines. She wasn't sure what she was going to do, but she wasn't waiting for the drone to fire on her S.U.V. At the same time she wondered why the drone hadn't in fact fired. Perhaps the pilot didn't want to destroy the drone.

Whatever the reason for the hesitation. she was going to use it to her advantage. Nikki rolled onto her back, braced herself, reared back and began kicking at the rear glass.

In the control room the captain had throttled back some trying to keep the drone steady between the road surface less than two meters below, and the raised highway about five meters above. He watched the image on the screen as the drone moved closer to the S.U.V. He was sweating from the stress of maintaining the MK150 in such a strict flight pattern and was startled when the Secretary of State was suddenly standing next to him.

"What the hell is she doing?" Erickson asked to nobody in particular as he leaned on the pilot's chair. He peered at the huge monitor to get a better look. He could see the grainy image of Nikki Sidorova crawl into the back of the vehicle with a pistol in her hand.

"What the..." he began, as Nikki suddenly started kicking at the rear glass of the S.U.V. Erickson screamed at the weapons officer, "Damn it Lieutenant, what the hell are you waiting for? Lock on to that target! Fire the damned missile!"

The weapons officer, First Lieutenant Janice Adams, called out, "Going Hot!" She flipped up the red safety cover on the weapons control center and pushed the toggle switch to the on position. The left missile icon, a green outline on the wall monitor, turned red, indicating that the missile was now armed.

Adams pressed the trigger to fire the missile, expecting the rocket engine to spark to life, but nothing happened. She pressed the trigger a few more times with the same result.

When nothing happened Erickson became more agitated, "What the hell is going on, Lieutenant? Why aren't you firing?" He looked back at the screen while cussing a steady stream of expletives at the young officer as she tried to think through the problem. "What are you doing? Fire! Fire! Fire the damned missile!"

Adams could take no more. Slamming her fist down on the console she turned and screamed back at Erickson, "Mister Secretary, with all due respect... Shut the hell up!"

Erickson was stunned, and in the brief reprieve the lieutenant's thoughts refocused. The missile wouldn't fire because of the close proximity to the target. Although she armed the missile, it wouldn't launch until the minimum distance was met. She leaned across the weapons console and slammed down on the distance delay override. Now the missile was fully armed. The drone could ram the S.U.V. and it would detonate, if they needed that option.

She steadied her thumb over the fire control switch when the back glass of the S.U.V. suddenly flew outward toward the drone. As if watching a 3D movie, the weapons officer instinctively raised her hands to block the hit as the tempered rear glass caught air long enough for the drone to fly directly into it. The glass shattered across the nose of the drone, damaging the camera and causing the pilot to flinch. The aircraft dipped, scrubbing the asphalt, then banked right and left as the pilot recovered from his unexpected movement. All that Captain Akins could see now was the road surface below and the edge of the roadway to his left and right. He began to panic as he tried to maintain control.

Nikki sat upright and aimed her pistol at the drone. The aircraft was jerking side to side and getting extremely close to the ground and uncomfortably close to the back of Sidorova's S.U.V.

She fired on the aircraft, emptying her magazine into the nose and through the GPS and navigational components. Nikki reloaded quickly and then fired a second volley through both air intakes as the drone moved right and left, up and down, at times scrubbing the pavement like a stone skipping across the surface of water. Dark smoke wisped from one of the two engines, trailing behind the aircraft. Nikki heard an obvious change in engine pitch from the screaming jet motors as the drone fell back.

She took aim at the missile, not sure what the outcome would be if she hit it, but squeezed off another three rounds. One of the bullets slammed into the control head. The round broke into pieces embedding into the targeting control gyroscope and shattering smaller electronic components, but it didn't detonate.

The voice of Bitching Betty, an automated cockpit voice, present in F.A.18s, that was incorporated into the system warning program of the remote aircraft control cockpit, began to report the system malfunctions along with the alarm warning. "Port engine power loss, sixty percent. Engine temperature normal." Betty repeated the warning every few seconds in a robotic woman's voice as the power loss increased, "Port engine power loss, fifty-three percent. Engine temperature normal."

"Fire that missile now!" Erickson screamed over the automated voice and the sound of the alarm.

The weapons officer looked for a target, but still could only see the blurred image of the asphalt surface passing below the aircraft. She knew the number-one-rule of any engagement was that you had to have a solid target lock, *regardless* of who was back seat piloting. Not even the President of the United States could *make* her fire the missile without a confirmed target. She damned sure wasn't pulling the trigger for the Secretary of State. She turned, glaring at Erickson and screamed, "I don't have a target, Sir! No target. I cannot fire without a confirmed target lock!"

By now the pilot was exhausted. He had no real feel for the aircraft. Akins could tell that he had just scrubbed the pavement again. Sparks shot across the lens of the camera, filling the floor to ceiling monitor with streaks of yellow and orange. There was no tactile feedback to fall back on as with an actual aircraft, making it extremely difficult to guide the nearly blind aircraft.

He glanced left and right, then back and forth between the heads up display's virtual gauges, taking note of his speed, horizon line, and distance from the ground, then to either side of the screen, paying close attention to the image of the left and right edges of the roadway, where he could make out a guard rail here and a light, or sign post there. He had no idea where he was headed, or for that matter, how he was even still aloft. His hands were sweating and shaking on the controls. He was going to have to land soon, ditch the aircraft, something that he'd never had to do before, and he wasn't sure how, with no way to see what he was doing.

"Finally!" Vostav said loudly as the roadway widened and the raised road surface moved to his left above, opening up the sky and bathing the vehicle in bright sunlight. He was out from under the highway. An exit suddenly appeared. Without slowing Vostav veered around a tandem truck and trailer and down the exit ramp.

The MK150 moved up quickly toward the rear trailer of the tandem rig that had been lumbering up the road just ahead of

Vostav's vehicle. Without a target lock, Akins, nor his weapons officer, knew that the Hunter U.A.Z. was no longer on the road ahead of them.

The driver of the truck saw the drone as it flew out from under the overpass and into the bright daylight. He didn't know what to make of the object that was moving erratically, sparking against the roadway and leaving a trail of smoke behind. Still, he decided it was best to move to the right and let it pass. He only hoped that he would be able to get out of its way. Whatever it was that just shot out of the darkness, was moving incredibly fast. He pushed the accelerator hard to the floor and pulled as hard right as he could causing the tandem trailers to lean hard left and swing wide. Instead of moving out of the way, his rear trailer swung outward, directly into the path of the drone.

The proximity alarm suddenly began barking, indicating that his aircraft was close to a large object. Captain Akins had no time to react to a new alarm. Seeing only the looming shadow of an impending object on the road surface, he instinctively pulled the nose of the drone up and rolled hard left in an attempt to avoid colliding with an uninvolved vehicle or building. The MK150 slammed headlong into the steel skeleton of an overhanging highway road sign, damaging the right wing and engine. The unmanned Aerial Vehicle glanced off the steel structure and although still gaining altitude, began to spiral in a widening circular pattern upward. The aircraft was out of control.

Lieutenant Adams called out the danger to the pilot. "Port vector control lost, U.A.V. track is no longer stable." Bitching Betty was adding to the list of problems in a voice too calm for the circumstances, "Port engine failure, extreme engine temperature. Fire detected. Camera off line."

Captain Akins reported, yelling over the alarms and Betty's voice, "I've got a dead stick. No response. I've lost navigational control! Prepare to abort!"

The bark of alarms blared from the console speakers and Bitching Betty calmly told her story of impending doom as Lieutenant Adams attempted to deactivate the missile distance override and safe the missile. More and more warnings blared over the speaker, filling the control room with multiple indications of major system failures.

"I can't disarm the missile! Missile is still hot." She repeated her warning several times as she tried over and over to place the missile in safe status.

The huge wall sized monitor was filled with nothing more than the blurred image of the suburban skyline spinning around. The aircraft continued to climb and become more and more unstable.

Finally the weapon's officer called out, "Fifteen hundred feet! Confirm, total mission failure! Abort mission! Destroy U.A.V.. and all weapons!"

Captain Akins had never "splashed" an aircraft. An unpalatable feeling of dread settled in the pit of his stomach as he uttered the confirmation that would signal the destruction of his aircraft.

Nikki had her eyes glued to the U.A.V. as it maneuvered awkwardly, spinning and twirling, climbing higher and higher. Anatoly was leaning out of the side window, waiting for the aircraft to stop its ascent and plummet back to earth when the sky lit up in a white fireball. Milliseconds later the huge clap of the explosion engulfed them.

"Holy shit!" Vostav exclaimed as he pulled his head back in the vehicle, "Who the hell did you piss off?" He looked in his rear view mirror at Nikki while she climbed back over the seat, looking ashen. Anatoly noticed the look in her eyes and got the impression that Nikki was genuinely shaken up by what had just happened.

"Nikki, who would have access to that type of weapon system?" he asked her as he looked back toward the hanging pall of smoke above the skyline of the city.

"That had to be an American drone. Why would the Americans want to kill you bad enough to use something like that and risk such possible collateral damage?"

Nikki looked at the smoke rising from the location of the destroyed S.U.V. and thought about her other two accomplices, dead and burning on the road far behind them. She thought back to the death of Dr. Metelov and what he had said about helping the Americans, and then about what Anny had just asked. Why would the Americans want to kill her? She couldn't help but wonder the same thing.

CHAPTER 15

UNDERMINED

THE two hotel rooms were cleared in about twenty-five minutes. Marks and Villacruze had packed their bags quickly. Both men, used to traveling light, each carried only a large field pack and shared a storage tote. They were a few miles north of Ramsey's location and were preparing to head to the airport.

Villacruze had just closed the trunk of the BMW when he heard the concussion of an explosion. Marks, settled into his seat, got back out, looking over the top of the car at Villacruze. "That didn't sound good," he said, as he looked off in the direction of the explosion.

"No, that didn't sound good at all." Villacruze scanned the horizon, but saw nothing unusual.

Across town Rick White looked up from the screen of his smart phone and asked, "What was that?" directing his question to Paul Jackson.

Jackson had just finished securing all the electronic equipment in the Mercedes van when he heard the rumblings of the explosion in the distance and wondered the same thing. He was familiar with high yield explosives, and that's what it sounded like to him. He even felt it under his feet. He looked to the sky, around the apartment buildings, for any telltale sign of smoke in the distance. When he saw nothing, he turned to answer White, who was back at whatever he was doing on the phone.

"Well, it sounded and felt like a fairly large detonation, almost like an I.E.D."

Rick White didn't know what an I.E.D. was. "Is that some kind of bomb? I.E.D?"

Jackson still wasn't used to all the civilians he worked with. At times he felt like he spoke a different language, constantly having to explain. "I.E.D. is an acronym, stands for improvised explosive device. Iraqi and Afghani insurgents used captured munitions like howitzer shells to make bombs. An I.E.D. was just one type."

Alan Ramsey stepped out of the front door, interrupting White's schooling.

Jackson looked up to where Ramsey was standing and asked, "Did you hear that?"

"I heard something. Rattled the windows upstairs," Ramsey answered. He didn't seem too concerned.

Paul Jackson noted his boss' lack of concern. "I don't know. I guess it was nothing, an explosion of some sort. I was just telling young Mr. White how it sounded like an I.E.D."

Alan looked off into the distance, repeating the scan done by Jackson. He didn't see anything that would indicate a danger, or anything of interest. "Well, it's definitely not thunder. Looks clear as anything."

Jackson reached out for Alan Ramsey's luggage, collapsed the handle and packed it in the van with the rest, then asked, "You Ok?"

Ramsey sighed, "It irritates me to no end to have my hands tied the way that they've been throughout this investigation. Our main subject and lead to a possible weapons cache is dead. The guy who was helping us is dead. Nikki, and who knows who else, has disappeared, and the R.S.S. has zero information to share with us."

Jackson added to the litany of wrongs, "You'd think that after our success at stopping a terrorist attack at home, these guys would give us the support we need. Instead we get shut down. That's bullshit if you ask me. We should be able to continue the operation here, and do it without being limited by the politics at home or the secrecy of the R.S.S."

Just as Ramsey stepped up to get into the van a second explosion, louder and more pronounced, turned both men on their heels to face the opposite direction. Ramsey felt his phone buzzing in his pocket and removed it, sliding it open he saw Hector Villacruze was calling. "Hello."

Villacruze was excited, "Sir, did you hear that?" he asked.

"Yes, that was the second one in the last twenty minutes. Any idea what it was?"

Vee and Marks had a different viewpoint, traveling from the North toward the airport. Ramsey thought maybe they saw something that he and Jackson didn't.

Vee answered quickly, "No to the first one, but yes to the second."

Ramsey gave Vee his full attention, holding a hand up to Jackson and White to prevent them from interrupting. "Go ahead."

Villacruze started explaining, "First, we did hear something earlier, but decided it was probably nothing. We were sitting here in traffic staring at the brake lights ahead of us, when Marks noticed something shoot straight up from the ground."

He took a breath before continuing. "It was trailing smoke and was really easy to see. So it goes up, to maybe two thousand feet when there's this huge fireball. I mean, huge fireball, that seriously lights up the sky, and within a second, the explosion. A big explosion. We're talking Army munitions type of explosion."

"So, what do you think it was?"

"Don't know. The way it shot up from the ground doesn't make sense. I know what it wasn't. It wasn't a plane wreck. That's what the news is saying is the cause for all the damned traffic. Planes don't shoot straight up into the air like that"

Ramsey agreed. "Ok, good info. Let me know when you reach the airport. Sounds like it's going to be awhile." Vee acknowledged and signed off.

Paul Jackson stared. "What the…"

Ramsey asked, "So you heard what he said?"

Jackson followed Ramsey into the van, letting Rick White take shotgun position. "How could I not hear, he was nearly yelling."

The van's driver held up his phone as Ramsey buckled in. He motioned to the traffic map showing the Moscow ring road and all of the local routes displayed on his smart phone.

"The highway is closed ahead. There's been some sort of an accident. I don't have all the info, but first reports indicate that it may have been an airplane that crashed onto the highway."

"Well now, that explains the explosions… I guess," Jackson quipped sarcastically. "Can you find another way around using the GPS?"

The driver, Brandon Eccles, was a young intern and was supposed to be the group's translator, but Ramsey had found early in the trip that his mastery of the Russian language was as green as his experience in the field. The intern plucked the Tom-Tom from the windshield mount and began fiddling with its controls in an attempt to find an alternate route around the closed highway. Jackson watched with little patience as the route was reset. The Tom-Tom began to speak in a Russian male voice, announcing the new direction.

"I hope you can understand those directions better than you can interpret a live person. We have to be at the airport in less than an hour."

Brandon looked into his rearview mirror at Jackson. "Funny," he said, without amusement as he reset the device to speak in English.

Ramsey suddenly felt the vibration of his cell phone. He pulled the phone up and flipped it open, recognizing the number as that of the lead R.S.S. officer, Ruslan Makovich. He pressed the answer button. "Hello, this is Ramsey speaking."

With a deep voice and a strong accent Makovich attempted his best English for Ramsey's sake, "Mr. Ramsey, have you arrived at the airport?"

Ramsey replied quickly that they were just heading that direction, but had been delayed due to the highway closure.

"Good, then please, come to the Leningradskoye Shoss, sorry,...Leningrad Highway number M10, to the exit for the Vneshnyaya Storona in the town called Khimki. There is something that you need to put your eyes on. Come as quickly as you can.

"Russo, how about you tell me what's going on. Our plane leaves in less than an hour. I don't have time for puzzles."

The R.S.S. Agent replied to Ramsey's concerns in his monotone, broken English to ensure him that he was not trying to play games or waste his time. "This highway is the same way to Moscow Domodevo International Airport. You take the M10, the Leningradskoye Highway, to the M.K.A.D. Vneshnayaya Storona, the outer ring road. It is right before you cross the bridge at the Khimkinskoye Vodokranilishche." The R.S.S. agent stopped to interpret his own words for Ramsey. "That is a big lake, it means the Khimki Reservoir." He paused to give Ramsey time to relay the directions, and then continued, speaking slowly so that Alan Ramsey fully understood what he was saying.

"You will find that the location I just gave you is the place where one of the two fleeing vehicles from your operation at the Merinsk Street Café in Zelenograd was destroyed."

Ramsey's eyes went wide with surprise. He sat up straight and looked at his driver with a questioning glance as he asked about the accident site. "We were told that a plane had crashed there. Was there a plane involved?"

As soon as White got into his seat and closed the door Ramsey motioned for Brandon to drive. "That will put us right in the middle of the traffic. Twenty to thirty minutes to get there," he said to any one who was listening as he pulled away from the curb.

Russo continued with his report, giving Ramsey all the information that he had at that moment. "There has been a crash, yes, but first there was an attack on the two vehicles. Witnesses are telling us that a rocket destroyed the truck."

"Rocket? You mean, missile? Are you saying that someone fired a missile at those vehicles?" Ramsey questioned in utter disbelief and shock.

Paul Jackson stared at Ramsey as he listened to one side of the conversation. Ramsey noticed him straining to hear and pulled his phone away from his ear and placed it on speaker.

"We think there was only one...missile. There was, however a second explosion, but it was not a truck, it was a small aircraft of some type, by witness description possibly a military drone."

"Holy shit!" Ramsey blurted out, "We're on our way. We'll be there as fast as we can. Have one of your cars on standby to escort us through the traffic." He started to hang up but pulled the phone back up. "Russo, you still there?"

"Yes."

"The vehicle that was destroyed, was it Nikki Sidorova's vehicle?"

Russo answered blandly, "When you get here, possibly the fire will be extinguished. At this moment I do not even know how many people are in it."

"Thanks, Russo." Ramsey eyed the Tom-Tom. "See you in about twenty five minutes."

He looked up to see Jackson staring at him. "Did I just hear what I think I heard? Did he just say that Nikki's vehicle was destroyed by a missile?"

Ramsey's mind was racing with the thoughts of who could have destroyed the vehicle. The only countries he was aware of that freely used drones for military operations were Israel, The U.K., The U.S., and Russia. The latter being the only country with a dog in the fight.

Jackson was waiting for an answer as Ramsey came back to the moment. "Don't know if it's Nikki or not. Russo believes it's one of the two vehicles though."

Jackson sat back some. "And the Russians say they ain't got nothing to do with it?" he questioned sarcastically, "Who the hell else has that kind of firepower at their disposal?"

Alan Ramsey stared out the window not really seeing the passing farmland as they sped toward Moscow. He looked back at Paul, "Hell, who knows. Maybe the drone is Russian, but maybe it's out of Gregorov's own collection and the Mob was controlling it to kill Nikki as payback for killing their boss and stealing his money. Either that or..." He paused to collect his thoughts.

Jackson watched the expression on his boss' face go from quizzical to seriously angry in about three seconds flat.

"What? What are you thinking? ...Either that or, what?"

"...Or our investigation was hijacked. Call the airport. Cancel our flights, then call the hotel and get a couple rooms for us. If what Russo is telling us is true and that is a U.S. Military drone then we are going to need some time to sort this out."

Jackson picked up his phone. He looked out the windshield at the thick pall of black smoke ahead, then noticed the second billowing cloud about four miles distant. "I wonder how the hell they were able to get away? How do you outrun a drone or a missile in a piece of shit like a Hunter U.A.Z.?" he said out loud as he waited for the airline agent to pick up.

Ramsey replied. "I don't know, but I'm beginning to think that Nikki Sidorova must be part cat. She seems to have nine lives." He didn't say it, but he hoped like hell she'd survived.

CHAPTER 16

WOUNDED WARRIOR
ALEXANDRIA, VIRGINIA

DARIN Martin heard the sound of his phone's ringtone from the other room. Martin, one of the F.B.I. agents that had worked with Alan Ramsey on the St. Louis bombing investigation, had transferred to the C.I.A. in Langley at Ramsey's request, to serve as a member of the T2T.

He stepped out of the bathroom and into his bedroom, looking toward his alarm clock. He noted the time. It wasn't yet six o'clock.

"This can't be good," he thought as he grabbed the phone and turned it over to see who was calling, smiling when he saw Ramsey's name illuminated on the display. Martin toweled the shaving cream away and raised the phone to his ear.

"Good morning Darin. I didn't wake you, did I?"

"Hey, Alan. Good morning, and no, you didn't wake me. I've been having to get up and get started a little bit earlier these days. It'll be nice when this thing gets healed up." He rotated his shoulder a bit in the sling and felt the pain that he had been living with for the last three months, since the shoot out with Leaja bin Masri that shattered his left shoulder blade.

Grimacing, he continued, "I have another surgery at Bethesda in a couple weeks. Maybe then they can get all the pieces back in the right spot, but I'm going to bet you didn't call me this early to ask me how I'm feeling. What's going on? You still in Moscow? I figured you'd be somewhere over the Atlantic by now."

Alan answered, "No, were staying a little longer than expected." He took a moment to explain briefly the recent investigation, the killing of Gregorov and Metelov, and the escape of Nikki Sidorova. Martin listened intently as Ramsey got to the part about the mystery U.A.V.

He whistled a long tone as he leaned back against his dresser and asked the obvious question, "Well if you didn't send the U.A.V., and the Russians didn't send it, then who did?"

"That's why I'm calling. I need some help tracking down who might have sent it out, if indeed it was one of our drones. I need someone to back door into this and keep it very low key. I have a strong suspicion that someone in the administration is trying to eliminate the leads to Gregorov and keep us from finding his collection of Soviet Era toys."

"And by administration you mean..."

"I mean the current presidential Administration. Look, in a few minutes I will be getting in touch with the boss. I know that he will get people to check into it, but my gut tells me that this attack has been actioned by someone outside of the C.I.A. or the F.B.I. If that feeling is right I'm not going to be surprised if Secretary Erickson doesn't have something to do with it."

Paul Jackson couldn't help but overhear what Ramsey was saying. He put down his phone and turned his full attention to Ramsey's conversation with Martin and was ready to join in when he heard Darin Martin's voice raise a few octaves and increase in volume.

"Whoa, Secretary Erickson? As in, United States Secretary of State, Jim Erickson? That's quite a few miles outside of his lane wouldn't you say? What makes you think that he's got anything at all to do with it, or for that matter, the authority to order such an attack?"

Ramsey noted his audience had grown to everyone in the van. He glanced around at the faces staring at him in disbelief before continuing.

"Look, I don't know for sure yet that it's even one of our drones, but let's do the math. Gabe Anderson told me just two days ago, that Erickson was ready to pull the plug on our investigation, and that Erickson voiced very strong opinions that he wanted Gregorov, Metelov and Nikki Sidorova eliminated. And, I think, since she helped him with the elimination of the first two, he must be trying to return the favor. For some reason both he and President Carlton want to end this thing and want it to end quickly with no loose strings.

Here's the deal, Darin, I need someone to poke around a bit, but I'm afraid to go through my offices for the moment. Since you aren't really assigned to T2T yet, you can move around a bit more freely than Gabe or Jennifer, my aid back there."

Martin wasn't comfortable with the plan. "Don't you think they are going to get suspicious if someone notices the new guy searching databases around D.C.? I don't have the kind of access that is required for a thorough system search and my expertise of the controlled hosting network is pretty limited."

"Don't worry. Rick White can grant you access. He's the administrator for CHERI In fact the entire system is his creation. The guy is a master geek. He has access to any part of the network and will know how to keep it on the down low. I'd have him run the search, but I'm afraid they'll recognize his log-in. The fact that he's here with us on this mission could throw up a red flag. Besides it's expected to see nationally based, three letter organizations communicating. That's what it's for. I'll have him get set up tonight and give you a call. Between you two I'm sure we can get some answers on this and not get noticed."

Martin was still apprehensive. "Ok, I'll see what I can come up with, but I'll need you to back me up if this plan of yours backfires."

"Trust me Darin, if this plan backfires we'll all be needing backup?" Ramsey looked up to gauge the amount of distance they had travelled while he was talking. He realized the answer was less than a mile. He looked at Rick White who was already fast asleep and Jackson who had settled back in his seat and pulled his baseball cap over his eyes.

"I'll get you and White together tonight. He'll give you a quick tutoring on how to manipulate the world of CHERI as soon as we get settled into the hotel. It'll probably be a couple of hours."

Martin acknowledged with a quick "Roger." Then added, "let me know if there's anything else I can do from my end."

Alan ended the call. "Thanks, Darin. Talk to you later."

Jackson pushed the bill of his cap up, turning his head just enough to peer over at his boss with one eye. "So, you really think Erickson had the authority, not to mention, the gigantic balls, to put a drone in the air in the middle of Moscow? Kind of hard to hide the use of a multi-million dollar drone I would think. He'd have to be a damned fool if he thought that nobody would figure that shit out."

Ramsey looked over at Jackson's one eye showing below the cap's bill and added, "Or he knows someone's got his back, and there's only one person I know who would protect that jackass. President Carlton."

Jackson closed his eye and tugged the cap down again, sighing a deep sigh, "This is probably gonna get worse 'fore it gets better," he said.

Ramsey thought about just a few of the ramifications of the investigation and how bad it would be if the President had knowledge of what happened. "You're probably right, Paul."

Jackson, as usual, got in the last word. "Oh no, Mr. Ramsey, not probably. I *am* right." With that he crossed his arms and settled further into the seat, then called to the driver, "Hey, Brandon, wake me when we get to where we're going." He paused, then added, "In English, not that crap you've been trying to pass off as Russian."

CHAPTER 17

THEORIES

BRANDON hit the brakes again causing the van to stop for about the hundredth time in less than a kilometer. The obnoxious stopping and starting finally made Ramsey quit his attempts at note taking on a virtual keyboard. He let out a sigh as he straightened up and looked around to gauge where he might be in comparison to where he needed to go.

Both White and Paul Jackson were out cold. Neither of them had gotten much sleep in the last few days. Ramsey was sure that Paul had been awake for at least the last 30 hours. He looked past his sleeping agents to the GPS on the windshield then, in a near whisper, grunted his displeasure with the traffic.

"So much for a police escort," he said to Brandon quietly. Brandon looked back at Ramsey in his mirror and shrugged. The unmistakable sound of an emergency siren chirped and whooped through the traffic, eventually stalling two or three vehicles back as the traffic attempted to shuffle out of the way. Ramsey wondered where the cruisers were that were supposed to be escorting him into the crash site. He guessed that the stalled traffic was just too thick.

There was nothing more to do except wait. He pulled his phone out, deciding it was a good time to call his boss, Gabe Anderson. Might as well get him caught up on the mission thus far, he thought. He noted the time, making the calculations for the eight hour difference. It was nearly five-thirty in the afternoon in Russia and seven-thirty in the morning at Langley.

"Good morning, Alan. How'd the meeting with Gregorov go?"

Alan cringed a bit as he thought about his answer. He'd meant to call his boss immediately following the meeting.

"Actually, it's afternoon here, but good morning just the same." He figured he had best just tell him what happened, just to get it over with. "The meeting went to hell. Nikki Sidorova went crazy and killed Metelov and then turned on Gregorov and put a bullet in his head. Everybody screwed the pooch. Nobody was prepared. It just...happened."

Alan could tell Gabe was upset. He was quiet, but breathing heavily as Ramsey explained. He thought his boss was handling it fairly well, even after learning that Metelov was an alias, until he got to the part about the possible drone attack. That's when Gabe came unglued. Ramsey felt sorry for anyone who was in earshot of Gabe Anderson's stream of expletives.

Paul Jackson awoke from his powernap in time to hear the tirade from Ramsey's phone as Ramsey held it at nearly arms length to protect his hearing.

Jackson's eyes went wide and a faux look of fear showed on his face as he pushed his cap back and sat up fully. He mouthed the word "Gabe" in the form of a silent question. Ramsey nodded.

"I'm going to put us on speaker. I've got Paul Jackson with me." There was no pause as Gabe Anderson began asking about the possible missile attack.

"When will you be on site? How soon before you know for sure if Nikki was killed or not? What about her boyfriend?" He asked the same questions that Alan had been asking himself for more than an hour and Alan just didn't have any answers yet.

"Look Gabe, I want answers as much as you do, but I can't get shit done sitting in this traffic. I got hold of Darin Martin back home. He's on medical leave, but he's going to do a little snooping through the CHERI network with Rick White to see if he can find out where the drone came from, who was controlling it, and if it was on our side. White thinks he should be able to hack into the linked networks and programs. He says he should be able to find the control network, something about the amount of bandwidth it would use should look like a black hole in cyberspace, or something. White will work it from over here, but I need Darin to get it all set up on your end."

Gabe listened to Alan and Paul as they interjected their theory that someone on the President's staff had to have knowledge of, or control of the drone and how they were leaning toward the possibility that it had something to do with Secretary of State Erickson. What they suggested worried Gabe even more than the drone attack.

"Alan, I want you to tread lightly with this Erickson theory of yours. Frankly, I don't trust the guy either. In fact I can't stand him, but if he was able to get a hit on Sidorova, especially with the use of a drone and or missiles, there are two major things to keep in mind. First, if he did it without the knowledge of President Carlton, then that makes him rogue, and extremely dangerous. If that's the case then we must immediately notify the President." He paused to collect his thoughts.

"And if the President is involved?" Ramsey asked.

"Well, that brings me to the second possibility. If the President secretly approved this mission then we will have to be extremely careful in how we approach it. Personally, I can't imagine President Carlton letting a fool like Erickson manipulate him like that. Think about it. Carlton has done some really great things for the country in a very short time. He's sure to get a second term."

Paul Jackson added, "They have to know that the fallout from this would be political suicide. It makes you wonder what the hell they were thinking. Why in the world would they want Nikki Sidorova dead?"

Ramsey entertained the question. "Makes no sense to me. They'd have to think that they could cover it up, no ties at all, no loose ends. There's no way that someone can get a drone airborne without a staff of professionals helping them. Someone had to fly the damn thing." Alan thought for a moment and then reasoned.

"Maybe there is something else, something deeper than this investigation."

Gabe couldn't see it, but Paul Jackson could, the look that Ramsey always got when he had a feeling in his gut.

"Perhaps, whoever made the hit, and for the moment let's say it's Erickson, doesn't give a rat's ass about bringing Gregorov or Metelov to justice, or finding the weapons. In fact, what if Erickson preferred that the weapons were never found. Maybe it all has to do with the eight thousand dead Muslims in Bosnia and Milosevic and all that. Nikki has been talking non-stop about it."

Paul Jackson chimed in. "What if it was just luck that Nikki Sidorova did them a favor and took out Gregorov? And now, Nikki has Gregorov's laptop and his money. You don't suppose that Gregorov has all his files on that old Dell?"

Rick White sat up, turned around in his seat to join the conversation. "No, she has to have access to more than just his laptop, but the fact that Gregorov had the laptop with him tells me that it has some important shit on it."

White explained, "Look, the guy is a dinosaur. He's too old for Facebook, I mean seriously, all his friends are probably dead, and I highly doubt he's a gamer. If I had to guess, I'd say Gregorov's passwords and his get-out-of-jail-free information is on that piece of shit. That's why he takes it wherever he goes. Maybe it just happens to have something that the Secretary of State and the President for that matter, don't want anyone else to know. Did you ever stop to think that maybe they weren't necessarily trying to kill Nikki, maybe they were trying to destroy the laptop."

Alan snapped his fingers and turned to Jackson, "You said it, Paul. After she killed Gregorov and Metelov you said it was like Nikki was on a mission, remember? You said you would hate to be anybody who had anything to do with that Bosnian shit. You remember saying that?"

Paul sat up. "Yeah, I do. Why?"

Alan continued, "What if she is on a mission? We already know that her intent is to get her hands on Gregorov's weapons and use them to attack anybody that she considers to have been directly responsible for the massacre, and I bet that means anyone who had the power to stop it, but didn't. My guess is the names of those people are on that laptop?"

Paul jumped back in. "And you think that the President of the United States and the Secretary of State are two of the names on that list." He said more as a statement than a question.

Gabe Anderson was going to say the same thing, but after hearing Paul Jackson say it, he thought he might already have the answer.

"President Carlton was involved with the Dayton Peace Accord. He was the Secretary of State then, and a member of the unified commission that was trying to end the war in Bosnia. Some say he was responsible for the deal that eventually lost Milosevic the election and landed him in prison. He was a major player in the peace talks.

"What about Erickson," Ramsey asked, "What was his role, or was he even involved?"

"Oh, yeah, he was right in the thick of it. Erickson was the U.S. Ambassador to Germany. He worked with the Swedish Prime Minister to broker a peace agreement between the warring factions in Bosnia. In fact, there was talk of the Nobel Peace Prize for his efforts."

"Hardly sounds like a guy that would be so bent on the shoot first, ask questions later philosophy," Ramsey acknowledged.

Gabe agreed. "Something happened to him. He wasn't always the asshole that we know and love today."

Paul Jackson didn't get it. "If they were trying to stop the war then doesn't that make them good guys? I'm afraid I'm not following along very well."

Gabe Anderson tried to explain, "It's all in the perception. Look at Bin-Laden. We go into Pakistan on a secret op, take out a houseful of people and rid the world of the worst terrorist in modern history and the Pakistanis attack our embassy and jail the one person who helped lead us to him. Sometimes the choices we make are only good for one side. We can't always be winners. Maybe we made a bad deal at Dayton."

Brandon, the driver, turned to look over his shoulder and interrupted the conversation. "Sir, looks like our escort is here."

Jackson and Ramsey both looked to see the flashing lights of a blue and white cruiser and an officer on a motorcycle.

"Now were talking," Jackson quipped.

"Gabe we're getting ready to move here. I'll call you back when I can. You'll probably be hearing from Darin Martin before too long. He might need some information from you. Let Jennifer know he will be contacting her as well, and to get them whatever they need from my database."

"You got it. Be careful, Alan and keep Paul under control." Gabe joked. "Seriously, be extremely careful." With that he hung up.

CHAPTER 18

CARNAGE
M10 HIGHWAY, KHIMKI

RAMSEY'S Mercedes van exited the river of slow moving traffic, following the escort. As the vehicles came upon the detour only one lane of traffic was being allowed to move through an opening made in the disassembled center guardrail. Ramsey could see the Russian Special Services head investigator, Ruslan Makovich, standing in the road ahead. Russo was talking with the driver of the wrecker as Ramsey's vehicle pulled to a stop.

What remained of the still smoldering S.U.V. sat on the flat bed of a rollback wrecker. Long deep scars in the asphalt led from the rear of the wrecker to a blackened, cratered section of the roadway, the striations indicating the difficulty of moving a four thousand pound vehicle that was void of tires or wheels.

Ramsey peered through his window as the emergency workers swept and sprayed the debris to the edge of the highway with powerful fire hoses. Incredibly, the site of a supposed missile attack was being treated with no more care than the aftermath of a normal accident, the workers disregarding any forensic evidence, treating it all simply as debris to be discarded. It was obvious to Ramsey that the R.S.S. were not ones to agonize over the purity of a crime scene.

Ramsey jumped from his vehicle and ran up to Russo. "What the hell, Russo? I thought you were sending a car for us. We waited in that mess for over an hour." Ramsey pointed back in the direction he'd travelled at the bumper-to-bumper traffic that still went on forever into the distance.

"Yes, and as you can plainly see, there is nothing moving very fast at this moment," the tall R.S.S. officer calmly stated as he turned his palm upward and motioned to the gap in the guardrail and the inching traffic negotiating through it. "We have more than one responsibility, Mr. Ramsey. These people all feel their problem is just as important as yours. The highway has to be cleared."

Paul Jackson stepped up, and hearing the end of Russo's statement, replied sharply, "Cleared? More like *sanitized*. Did you guys even look for evidence before you let this crew in here? Why the hell did you even call us? You knew we were on our way, but by the time we can get here, you have the place all spic and span and the wrecker ready to roll out."

As if on cue the wrecker began to pull forward. Paul Jackson whistled a two fingered, high pitched whistle as Alan ran along side the truck, pounded on the door, and yelled for the driver to stop.

Ramsey eyed Russo, an angry look on his face. "Damn! You think we can have a look at the truck?" he asked sarcastically as he shook his head, agitated that the R.S.S. agent, who was supposed to be helping with the American investigation, would even think about releasing the truck before Ramsey and his team had a chance to take a look.

Russo motioned to the driver to stay put for the moment. The driver glared at Ramsey and Paul Jackson and muttered something in Russian as Russo briefed Alan on what they had found when they first arrived on the scene.

"There were two people, we think both men. Each body had a chest holster and a pistol. They were wearing their seat belts, which kept most of their body in the vehicle. Of course pieces were missing, recovered ninety meters all around."

He pointed at each location with his pen as he narrated his report. "The head of one man was found there, arms there and there. We found one AK-47 in the vehicle, it had gone through the passenger seat, through the body, and was laying on his feet. It nearly cut him in half. We found one more AK on the road over there," he said pointing near the right shoulder.

Ramsey was somewhat relieved that Nikki Sidorova was not among the dead.

"Where did you take the bodies?" Ramsey asked as he watched his partner climb atop the deck of the rollback truck to take a look for himself at the condition of the destroyed vehicle.

Russo looked at his notes, "The morgue at the Breshlov Hospital on Veshnyakovskaya street in Moscow, not far from here, about twenty five kilometers."

Jackson was leaning on the passenger door, scanning through what was left of the interior of the truck which was nearly completely burned away.

Randomly placed pieces of melted and burned exterior components, such as partially disintegrated alloy wheels, smoldering pieces of tires and steel cording, as well as asphalt, rocks, and gravel from the destroyed road surface, combined with the vehicle's melted, broken glass and burned interior materials to look like wet steaming charcoal, had been haphazardly thrown or shoveled into the vehicle by the clean up crew to be taken away with the mess.

Steaming, pungent vapors rose from inside the burned out truck, creating a stench familiar to Paul Jackson. The distinct odor of hot steel and burned rubber triggered the sudden, unexpected images of destroyed military vehicles and the faces of dead and wounded soldiers. Paul Jackson felt anxious, almost dislocated from his body. He found himself transported back in time, back to Karbala, a town about fifty miles southwest of Baghdad, Iraq, accompanied by a sudden sense of dread as the hazy images of his past came into focus.

Jackson shook his head from side to side, closing his eyes tightly, but he just could not escape his memories as the unrelenting thoughts turned to crisp images and sounds. For all practical purposes he was back in Iraq. He turned to find the Humvee's driver, Specialist Cox, to his left. "Watch it. They're stopping."

The convoy of M1151A1 Up-Armored Humvees came to an abrupt halt, stopping for a delivery truck that pulled in front of the lead vehicle. Jackson could feel the anxiety building, feel the fear return, already knowing what was about to happen. As if watching a movie that he had seen a thousand times before, he watched as the driver of the stopped delivery truck jumped down from the cab and ran out of sight.

First Sergeant Jackson wanted to warn his men, but he could only watch as the first explosively formed penetrator detonated on the right and then a second E.F.P. blasted on the left, ripping into the second and third Humvee in the convoy. He watched in agonizing slow motion the thick copper projectile, the signature component of an E.F.P., explode from the hidden canisters and impact the doors of each truck, creating a secondary spall effect, spraying the interior of the armored vehicle with molten copper, steel, and glass.

Jackson knew it was a dream, a false reality, but couldn't escape. He felt somehow transported from Moscow into the midst of a raging battle. A battle that he knew all too well the outcome, and like it or not, he was once again fully immersed in the most deadly and frightening battle he had ever experienced. He felt the weight of his A.C.H., the advanced combat helmet, as he tried again to close his eyes and shake away the images from his mind.

As if someone had just turned up the volume, the sounds of battle infiltrated his reality. He was fully immersed in the action now, a real time reenactment, his mind experiencing the battle as if he were really there. Jackson picked up his handset and called to the lead vehicle, "Foxtrot-Two-Zero, you need to hook up for extraction! Get your vehicles out of the kill zone."

"One-Six. Two-Zero. Roger," the squelch of the SINGARS radio sounded so real as he heard the lead vehicle commander, Captain Borah, acknowledge his directive. Jackson stared at the handset, doubting its existence, then looked ahead of the destroyed vehicles to Borah's Humvee as the captain directed his squad into action, responding to their new mission, to save any survivors pinned down in the vehicle behind them.

The images and sequences of the battle changed rapidly, moving from action scene to action scene as if Jackson was fast forwarding through a movie. And like an instant replay, Jackson watched as one of Foxtrot Two-Zero's squad members kicked open the left rear door of their Humvee, stood, fired several rounds forward, then rushed around the back and then to the right side of the vehicle to retrieve the end of the rear extraction strap that was mounted on the right mirror. Captain Borah's front door was open and he was up, standing behind the thick door armor and glass. He reached around the door, unhooked the strap and threw it to Sergeant Spaunhorst who had just rounded the back of the truck.

Jackson felt an eerie sense of dread, knowing what was going to happen next, watching once again, in fearful apprehension, as Sergeant Spaunhorst sprinted back, amid heavy fire, to hook up the heavy rear tow strap of the lead Humvee to the front tow strap of the first ambushed vehicle.

Jackson flinched at the false reality of hot brass raining down from the turret above him as his SAW gunner fired round after round to cover Spaunhorst's return to his vehicle. The sound of the machine gun, the attackers AK-47s and the surrounding fire from the M-4's were deafening, still, Jackson could hear his own heart beating and feel the pressure as it pounded inside his chest, his eyes locked on Sergeant Spaunhorst who was waiting for the exact moment between enemy fire to make his move.

The timing had to be perfect. Jackson heard several AK's firing, a deep resonant report, easily discernable from the pop, pop, pop of the American weapons. He timed it in his mind against the cacophony of firing weaponry when suddenly there was a change, a pause. One of the AK's was reloading. "Go, now! MOVE!" he heard himself yell at Spaunhorst, knowing full well that the soldier couldn't hear him.

As if on cue, Sergeant Spaunhorst sprang to his feet and sprinted back toward his Humvee. Jackson's heart stopped when he saw Spaunhorst get hit in the chest by two rounds from an unseen enemy, spin, and fall to the ground in a cloud of dust just as he reached the door of his vehicle.

Jackson clenched his eyes tightly trying to block out the images that were bombarding him, and hoped that when he opened his eyes he would be somewhere, anywhere else. But the images didn't go away, nor was there a reprieve from the sounds of battle.

His eyes went wide and he watched in amazement, once again, as Sergeant Spaunhorst rolled to his side, pulled up his weapon and fired several rounds at the enemy that Jackson could not see. The soldier got to his feet, yanked the door open and climbed back into the vehicle, yelling to the driver of the Humvee to go. The driver launched forward, slamming into the bullet riddled vehicle blocking his path, pushing it out of the way while towing the second, still burning vehicle out of the kill zone.

Now it was the Humvee directly in front of Jackson's that began drawing fire. They had to get away. He turned to see the two vehicles to his rear accelerate backward, leaving his vehicle and his commander's vehicle in front of him still in harm's way.

His driver threw the gear selector into reverse to move to the rear like the others, but Jackson yelled for him to stop. Rounds pinged and ricocheted from his vehicle, striking the thick armored glass, but over all the noise, Jackson heard the sound of gunfire from the vehicle in front of him. Somehow there were survivors in that vehicle, and his vehicle was in position to pull them to safety. He screamed at the machine gunner for cover fire as he opened his door.

Jackson suddenly found himself between the two vehicles. Bullets whizzed past him as the SAW belched rounds to cover his movement. He sprinted forward to the damaged vehicle and grabbed the rear tow strap hook from its mount, and then, ran back to his own Humvee. He clasped the two hooks of the tow straps together and ran to the still open door of his Humvee.

"Go! Go! Go!" he yelled at his driver, as the engine screamed to full power, the front tow strap unraveling from atop the hood of his vehicle and dropping out of view, his Humvee nearly stopping as the two straps became taut.

The tires bit hard into the dirt and asphalt of the roadway, regaining its rearward traction and dragging the commander's Humvee backward, out of the kill zone.

The scene changed again as Jackson found himself standing at the door of his Commander's vehicle, peering in the window at the dead Lieutenant Colonel, the radio handset still clutched in the hand of his severed left arm. The smell of burned flesh, plastic and rubber overwhelmed his senses. He heard one of his soldiers calling his name, but couldn't move from the window to answer.

He heard it again. "Paul! Paul!" and wondered oddly why they were calling him by his first name. Suddenly a strange feeling, like blood rushing through his body, brought him back to the present, to the sound of Alan Ramsey's voice calling his name.

Paul looked up to see Alan Ramsey looking through the driver's door opening. He looked concerned.

"You OK? You looked like you were a million miles away. You didn't answer."

Jackson stood fully, pushing away from the door, looking at his surroundings and his position five feet above the ground on the deck of the rollback. He shook his head to help clear it as the reality of the present moment rushed back at him. "Umm, yeah, I think. I was thinking about Iraq. How long you been there?"

Ramsey stood, looking just over the top of the burned vehicle, "I just got up here, ten seconds, maybe." He looked concerned. "You sure you're OK?"

Paul felt normal again. "Yeah, I'm fine. It was weird though. I saw…" His voice trailed off as he thought about what happened and whether or not he could even explain it. "..Ah, never mind. I'm fine."

Ramsey stared for a brief second, wanting to say something to console his partner, knowing how confusing having a flashback could be, but instead he got back on target. He looked around the decimated interior and broke the silence. "Looks like it was one hell of a ride."

He focused on the melted dashboard and steel ring that was once the steering wheel, hanging from the tilt steering knuckle joint and wires of the steering column components, then at the two front seats. Ramsey made an observation to Jackson about the fact that the lower back and the seat bottom leather were nearly untouched by the fire.

He pointed out that the rear seat foam padding and leather upholstery were completely burned away leaving the wire frame, hinges and release mechanisms fully exposed to the viewer, but in sharp contrast the two front seats were probably only seventy percent destroyed. Although the upper materials and the back of the seats were completely burned away, the leather and foam padding that made up the lumbar and lower seat area were still intact.

"What do you make of that," Ramsey asked Paul who was looking at the same thing.

Paul thought the answer was obvious. "There's no air between the seat and the bodies to support the flames. If there's no source of oxygen between their butts, lower back and the contact area of the leather on the seats, it won't burn. Kind of like burning a paper cup filled half with water. Every time it will only burn to the level of the liquid."

Ramsey grunted his agreement. He pulled his head and shoulders from within the vehicle and called down to Russo. "Hey, Russo. Did you guys get any identification off the bodies? From the looks of the front seats their butt's were intact."

Ramsey jumped down from the rollback and motioned to the driver that he could go. As the truck pulled away Jackson walked over to where Russo and his boss were standing as Russo looked over his notes. The R.S.S. agent scowled and shook his head.

"No, there was not any identification recovered." He let the note page fall back into place, a questioning look on his face. "I guess they didn't want to be identified."

CHAPTER 19

REDIRECTION

THE driver of the rollback carrying the Hunter U.A.Z. pulled clear of the area, entered the main lanes of the highway and picked up speed. He passed the highway exit that would have put him on a secondary route to the police station. Instead he kept driving, away from the R.S.S.' impound lot. It would probably be a day before they assembled their forensic teams and discovered that the S.U.V. wasn't in the lot. When he put about two miles behind him and the impact site he pulled up his phone and selected the first contact on his list, Gordon Maxwell.

Maxwell saw the name of the caller, his partner, Aaron James, another American Cold War relic turned dark agent. He flipped his phone open before the completion of the first ring and placed it against his cheek, being careful not to disturb the curl at the end of his handlebar mustache. "Aaron, where the hell are you?" he asked

"I'm on my way. I was stopped as I was pulling out," James said.

"Tell me it wasn't the Russian. I told that son of a bitch he better stay out of our way…" Maxwell started in.

"No, it wasn't Russo," Aaron James interjected quickly, "He didn't give me any trouble. I was loaded and ready to head to the warehouse when I was stopped by two Americans, one black guy, one white guy. They wanted a look. Russo didn't have a choice, but to let them. They asked about the bodies and identification. The Russian played it off pretty well. No matter, I will be at your location in less than an hour."

Maxwell thought about the cost of doing business in Russia. "That's good to hear, 'bout time I start getting my money's worth from the R.S.S. God knows I pay them enough."

He thought about the two men Aaron James had described. They must be the men that Erickson was bitching about, the ones who were going after Gregorov. He grunted to himself before continuing. "Alright then, good man. Glad you got out without a hitch. I'm not at the warehouse yet either, I just left the crash site. Next time I bring my own damned forklift," he said sarcastically as he picked up speed and looked in his rear view mirror to ensure that the lightweight wing panels of what remained of the drone were strapped securely to the bed of the rollback.

"There's gonna be some mad sons-of-bitches in Moscow. See you when you get back." Maxwell ended the call, slipping his phone into his pocket.

Aaron James checked on his own cargo, the burned Hunter U.A.Z., thinking that it looked ok, then folded his phone over and tossed it down next to two leather wallets on the seat beside him. "Yep, someone's gonna be pissed," he thought.

CHAPTER 20

MAXWELL
STATE DEPARTMENT, WASHINGTON, D.C

PRESIDENT Carlton was not happy with his Secretary of State. He'd known Jim Erickson for over twenty years. They served in the Senate together for ten of those years and been on one president's staff or another since. Though their qualifications as statesmen were near equal, Ron Carlton had always been the one in charge.

No matter the committee or the staff, Erickson always worked below the current President. That's just the way it had always been and that's the way it was now, until today, when Erickson decided to override the wishes of, not only his long time friend and colleague, but the President of the United States.

"What the hell were you thinking, Jim? Didn't I say no weapons? Didn't I?"

Erickson had listened to it more than he wanted to at the moment. Hadn't he called the man immediately? Woke him up to let him know? That said something about his loyalty to him.

President Carlton was not cutting him any slack. "Missiles?" he questioned loudly, "AGM Hellfire one-fourteens?" he asked, looking at his Secretary of State for any sign of remorse, but saw none.

"I specifically told you stealth tracking only. I said, nothing made in U.S.A., no American drones and absolutely no missiles!"

Carlton blazed a path as he paced the office heatedly, continuing his rant. "Not only do you disregard a direct order...my direct order, and blow off two one-fourteens, which, by the way, cost about seventy thousand dollars apiece, but you lose a damned drone as well?" He paused only to take a breath, then finished his thought. "God only knows how much that's going to cost!"

Erickson should have taken care of everything first, then briefed him after the fact, but he thought Ron Carlton deserved to know that the plan had gone bad. He expected more support than what Carlton was giving him. They were in Erickson's office, and that was a good thing because the conversation had become heated rather quickly and the President's voice was the kind that could easily be identified. Considering that he was approaching a yell it was probably best that he was in a whole different building.

President Carlton wasn't finished, still not believing that his Secretary of State could be so irresponsible... "And then you just nonchalantly tell me that you crashed a drone. Not in the desert, not in the mountains of Afghanistan, but in the middle of freaking Moscow. And, oh, by the way, you decided...YOU DECIDED...to arm the drone with missiles after all!"

Carlton's face was red as he stood less than a foot away, driving his points home to Erickson. He turned to face the wall as he dragged his hand down his face, then turned back to face Erickson. "Good God, I can hear President Rashnev already. For crying out loud! Do you have any idea how bad this can be?"

Outside the office door, Erickson's secretary, Betty Phillips, could hear quite plainly the President's side of the conversation.

Phillips had worked for so many powerful Washington figures, both Bush Presidents, The Clintons, and Obama, as well as department heads at the Department of Homeland Security and the C.I.A. at Langley.

Betty Phillips didn't anticipate her move to the State Department, a move that came less than a year after her husband's death and less than two years after buying her house in Mclean, Virginia.

Erickson had her transferred to his office during a massive reduction and relocation of staff. Although it was a testimonial to her stellar work history to have been retained, Betty wasn't happy to hear the news that she was being transferred, requesting instead to remain at Langley, but to no avail.

She didn't like Erickson. She knew him from her White House days and found him to be a power grabbing staffer who would say and do anything to get what he wanted. Once he made a decision there was no turning him back.

After so many years of service, to have him disregard her request, especially when there were so many qualified others who lived closer and would have fought for a position as the Assistant to the Secretary of State, upset her.

So when she heard Jim Erickson discussing things that hadn't anything at all to do with his duties as Secretary of State, she was all ears.

The sound of the coffee cart rattling over the tile floor in the hallway caught her attention. She looked at her watch, only then realizing the time. Eight o'clock already. Betty stood and walked to the door to intercept the cart in the hallway before the server had a chance to enter. Regardless of what she thought of Erickson, she didn't want someone like Ricardo Perez from hospitality picking up any of the conversation that was going on behind Jim Erickson's door and delivering it as gossip, along with the coffee, as he went from office to office.

"Oh, good," she said to the server, "I'm glad you are here." She noted that the cart had only one coffee pitcher left and immediately got an idea. "Ricardo, why don't you leave the cart with me and swing around in an hour or so to pick it up. I will set up the service in there when I hear a lull in the activity." She smiled as she pointed with her thumb over her shoulder, just as the raised voice of President Carlton and string of expletives emanated from beyond the inner office door.

"No problem," he said, smiling as he rolled the cart against the wall, just out of the hallway.

Wheeling the cart inside, and closing the door, she thought about what she was about to do. Secretly recording a conversation in this building could be considered a type of espionage. Still, if what she heard was true, then the recording itself would be as much her defense as it would be evidence against her. That is, if she was found out.

Betty grabbed her iPhone and placed it on silent, then pulled up her voice recorder app and set it to record. She placed it on the lower shelf of the cart, face down, behind a box of sweetener. She felt criminal as she took a deep breath and exhaled a large sigh, rationalizing her actions. She was sure that Gene Patterson and Gabe Anderson would be interested to hear the conversation. She was doing the right thing, she told herself one last time as she turned to the door, noting again the intensity of the conversation, before giving the frosted glass a knock and turning the knob to enter.

The knock on the door stopped the conversation mid sentence as the door suddenly clicked open. Betty stuck her head in. "Would you gentlemen care for some coffee? The kitchen cart is here."

The President glanced at his watch while turning to address her, "Yes Betty, that would be very nice. Thanks."

She placed the coffee carafe and two cups on the French lace placemat that protected the inlaid oak and mahogany surface of a nineteenth-century table. She poured two cups and handed them to the men. "There you go," she said. Each of them acknowledged her with a quiet thank you as she backed out of the door, leaving the cart in place.

"The steward will be back shortly for the cart. Will there be anything else?" Betty smiled, folding her hands in front of her as she waited for a reply.

"No, thank you, we are in the middle of something very important." Erickson said tersely. He raised his hand and flipped it toward the door motioning for her to leave. "Close the door behind you, please."

She turned on her heal to exit, smiling to herself as she closed the door and the conversation picked up again. She could hear the exchange as plainly as if the two were talking to her.

Betty lifted her tablet from the desk and swiped a finger across the glass surface. She selected her notepad app and glanced over the notes she had made a few minutes earlier. There were no real specifics until the last couple entries. The President and Erickson nearly talked in code. You had to read between the lines to make any sense of it. She knew that a transgression of matters of state had occurred, that an act of aggression took place in a sovereign country. Russia, if she had heard right. Missiles were fired, Erickson screwed up, and Carlton was not happy about it.

The President's passion had subsided and now the words spoken were much harder for her to discern. After a few minutes passed in which she heard nothing audible, she went back to her book. She would let her phone do the work for her. Whatever happened, she figured, Gene Patterson would thank her, take her hand and give it a pat, and that was enough for her. What he did with the information after that was not her concern and she would never ask him about it.

Inside the office the two had become more cordial to one another. Erickson was glad for the interruption. The President always thought more clearly with a hot, fresh cup of coffee in his hand. The Secretary of State decided he would take the next step to try to reassure his boss.

"Ron, I have this under control. The contractor I told you about is Gordon Maxwell."

Carlton spun around quickly, "Maxwell?" he looked surprised. "He's still on that godforsaken continent? What the hell, doesn't that guy have a real life?"

Erickson answered quickly, "Actually, he's got a wife, a kid and a ton of cash, but the best thing about Maxwell is that old ties are binding, he still works for us when we need him."

The President had mixed feelings about the operative. On the one hand he considered the guy a rogue, someone who was hard to control, a guy whose only motivation was money. Still, Maxwell could make things happen and he always stuck to the plan to see it through. The problems always came after the mission was completed. Maxwell exerted the minimum effort. If he met the basic requisites of a deal, he felt he'd earned his money. Going the extra mile was not something he did often. You would always get what you paid for using Gordon Maxwell, but nothing more.

Knowing that Erickson's "old reliable" was on location handling the details made him feel a little more confident, even though he didn't like the guy. President Carlton lowered his cup, nestling it in both hands, then spoke. "So then, I take it that you have a plan to clean up your mess?"

Erickson frowned at the question. He didn't like being called a screw up. "I got it," he said tersely. "Maxwell is on his way now. It will be expensive, but he'll fix it."

President Carlton tipped his cup to get the last swig down. He set the cup back on the serving tray, turning the handle so that it was pointing toward the center, like the other three. He moved toward the door, but stopped a few feet away and spun again to look at Erickson.

"Jim, I want this cleaned up. Do what you have to and make sure that it's done right. put Maxwell back on the payroll, but tell him no strings, no clues, and no trail back to this administration. Got it?"

Erickson stepped closer. "Don't worry. It's under control," he insisted as he reached for the crystal doorknob.

The President stopped him from turning the knob. Erickson looked up from the door. "Also, find out what's on that laptop that's so important to Sidorova. Get Maxwell on it."

With that the President pushed Erickson's hand away and turned the knob himself, stepped out and closed the door behind him.

As he stepped into the hallway Betty got to her feet, calling to him, "Have a nice day Mr. President."

Chapter 21

Baby Steps
Abandoned Yugo Dealership, khimki

Nikki sat staring at the screen on Gregorov's laptop, trying hard to concentrate. It was difficult not to think about the events of the day. She looked again at the clock. It was almost 21:30. She was finalizing her plans for her first meeting with Gregorov's dealers. She had sent out the invitation, more of a directive, for the spur of the moment meeting as soon as she found the list and was surprised that all but one had responded positively that they would be there. Tonight would be just the first step she needed to take to gain control of Gregorov's business and she was anxious to get to it.

The meeting would take place in the main shop of a long defunct Yugo dealership garage, until recently, owned by Gregorov, but now the offices of Sidorova and Associates.

Nikki assumed that many of the people who showed up would be old friends of Gregorov's. People she could lean on for answers. Those who refused to cooperate would be questioned further, in private, in a way that would make them want to help. She read over her list of names again. Some of them would know who she was through Gregorov. She had sat in many meetings with many of those listed. She looked at the checkmarks indicating those whom she had met before, about two thirds of the list.

She tried to think how Gregorov thought. What would bring *him* to a meeting like this, last minute? The answer was easy, she would have a sale. Nikki created a brochure of sorts, a quickly compiled menu of weaponry she hoped would spark an interest.

She had already made up her mind to sell most, if not all of the weapons. Other than a few items that she might need for her own personal fact finding missions, she would get rid of everything, buffer her account with the money she made, and concentrate on her main mission, locating the remains of her missing family.

She would start the second phase by chasing down a couple leads, many whom she believed had relocated to Moscow. Friends of the political structure at the time had safe haven here, but soon that would change. She would locate those Gregorov had dealt with for many years first. They would aid in her quest for information about the massacre at Srebrenica, its leaders, battle locations and burial sites, whether voluntarily or by coercion, didn't matter to her.

Eventually she hoped to find the one man who she thought was most responsible for the massacre, General Ratko Mladic. She would find him, torture him and then kill him. She dreamed about it, his face coming to her at night, and recently, in the middle of the day.

Nikki understood and accepted the psychology of her deranged passion, her relentless desire to destroy the man whom she held responsible more than any other for destroying her life. What she couldn't understand were those who didn't have the spirit for revenge, the fortitude to find the people responsible for the deaths of thousands upon thousands of people, mostly Muslims, killed because of false blame and the difference of their religious ideology. How could they forgive the murderers and not look back, not want to cause pain to the ruthless leaders whose only legacy was an overabundance of misery bestowed on a nation's worth of people?

And Mladic was the pinnacle figurehead to her, representing the loss of everyone she had ever known and loved. She knew that it was because of him that she'd became the person she was, and although there would be others who shared the burden of responsibility, and who would meet the same fate eventually, none had a higher importance than Mladic. No longer plagued by feelings of remorse, she accepted the fact that many would die before she got what she wanted, revenge on Ratko Mladic.

The door suddenly clattered against the wall as Anatoly walked into the makeshift office. "I think they are all here. Are you ready?"

Anatoly was genuinely surprised at the response to the late day request and the number of people who had complied. "I have to hand it to you, Nikki. I didn't think they would come tonight. Out there in that shop are the heads of Gregorov's business family, salesmen, and crime bosses. Nikki, I recognize some of these guys. They've been to the castle. This is a tough crowd. They are not going to like the fact that you are a woman." He looked at how tired she appeared. "You look exhausted. They will see that, too."

Nikki pushed herself up and away from the desk and stretched. She had to admit to herself that she was tired. It had been a hell of a long day. She attempted to reassure Anatoly. "It will be fine," she said waving a dismissive hand, "You worry too much, Mother." She said sarcastically.

Anatoly eyed Nikki, taking notice of her bare torso as her shirt lifted, exposing her flat stomach with its perfect six-pack. Nikki was athletic, her sleeveless shirt exposing her broad shoulders with well-defined trapezius and deltoid muscles, while hidden under her breast were the pectoral muscles of an Olympian. She was like a machine crafted by God, with painstaking attention to detail and perfection. Nikki was fast and agile and extremely smart, and she could handle a weapon better than most. Her survival in a world of sabotage and assassinations a testament to her skills. Anatoly thought, speaking of weapons…"Where is your gun? You aren't planning on going out there unarmed are you?"

"Anny, don't worry. Vostav has my back. With that she moved to the door, "and I have these." She sliced her hands through the air with a series of moves that could have been either karate or judo. Anatoly knew nothing about either, as far as he knew she could be making it up. Nikki's display ended with a light smack on Anatoly's left cheek, startling him. Nikki pushed herself against him and planted a kiss on his lips, then disappeared through the door.

The groups of men were loud as they talked amongst themselves, speculating on the reason for the meeting. Anyone not in attendance, or not represented by an associate, would be excluded from any deal.

The closing of the office door behind Nikki signaled the men to stop talking. As Nikki walked with a purposefully speedy gait, stopping to stand in the front center of the group, she barked at those who were still standing, directing them to take their seats in one of the metal folding chairs provided. A few of the associates decided to remain standing. Nikki took note of their positions in the room, whether they were obviously armed, their size and build, then glanced at Vostav to make sure he was registering the possible threats.

As Nikki was about to introduce herself the door to the lobby opened, ringing the small service bell, a relic of the shop's days as a legitimate business. The toy-like tinkling of the bell was in sharp contrast to the man standing in the doorway. He was almost the height of the doorframe with shoulders nearly as wide. He wore sunglasses and sported a scraggly beard and mustache, which from that distance, nearly made his facial features indistinguishable.

Quietly he pushed the door closed with a click of the latch and once again, the ringing of the bell.

The room erupted in hushed murmurings as the seated struggled to look behind them at the distraction. Eventually the noise quieted and the attention in the room was again directed toward Nikki.

"Good evening, gentlemen, I am glad that you could make it on such short notice. I assure you that I will not waste your time. We have business to discuss and money to be made and the first thing you should know about me is that I believe in mission first and I admire and reward loyalty and job efficiency."

From the man in the back of the room came a deep voice. "Who the hell are you?"

Nikki immediately felt the uneasy feeling that was always associated with danger. She glanced around the room and at the other two men still standing in the back, and then to Vostav, who nodded at Nikki to let her know that he had them all covered.

Nikki, satisfied with her quick assessment, directed her attention to the large figure, "Well, I was just about to introduce myself, so, if you will take your seat, I will continue."

Nikki stared back at the giant. She dropped the pleasurable tone as she motioned to an empty chair in the last row and spoke, as if to a dog, "Now, sit your ass down and let me talk."

The behemoth ripped the sunglasses from his face exposing deep-set dark eyes. He folded the glasses and pulled his jacket open to reveal a pistol in its holster as he placed them into an inside pocket of his jacket, a move noticed by everyone in the room, raising the level of tension a hundredfold. He walked to the front row of chairs where he stopped, crossed his arms across his chest, and looked down at Nikki ten feet away.

"I asked you a question. Who…the hell…are you?" He looked around the room, "and where is Dmitri? Why are you calling a meeting and ordering us around in the middle of the night?" he bellowed.

He closed the gap between him and Nikki until he was within five feet of her. Vostav moved warily to the huge man and was about to tell him to move back when the giant uncrossed his arms, and in a motion too fast for his stature, delivered an open handed punch to Vostav's chest, brutally forcing him backward. He pointed a huge finger in his direction and growled, "Get away from me!"

He turned his attention back to Nikki, and bellowed again, "I said, where is Gregorov?"

Vostav pulled his pistol, a 9MM Beretta, but stopped when Nikki stepped between him and the sinister looking giant. She was going to have to show the stranger that she was in charge.

"No, Vostav, I got this!" she said, ordering him to stand down. Vostav moved back, but stayed close with his pistol at the ready. Nikki saw his reluctance to holster his weapon.

"I said, put it away!" Then, as the pistol was returned to its holster, Nikki turned her full attention to the man, now standing directly in front of her, and poked three fingers into his chest, surprising the mammoth with the energy behind the action. She repeated, then answered his questions, drilling into his eyes with her rock steady green eyed gaze, stabbing at his sternum with the tips of her fingers after each answer.

"Who am I? I'm your boss, that's who. Where is Dmitri? Dmitri is dead, and the reason I called you here is because I have some shit to put out. Now sit your big ass down and shut the hell up!"

The towering man's black, hedge shaped eyebrows turned downward and his scowl plunged as his huge paw swatted at Nikki's hand, but Nikki was lightning quick, withdrawing her right hand, causing the man to strike at the air. Then, just as quick, Nikki planted a solid punch, ringing the man's right ear with her left hand, then took a defensive step backward outside of his reach.

The giant was pissed and getting angrier. He reached into his jacket and yanked out his pistol, raising the WWII, Soviet Era, seven round revolver to head height. Just as he stepped forward, Nikki lunged at him. She slammed her foot against her opponent's knee, a resounding crack echoing through the room as she continued her attack, driving her open palm into the center of the behemoth's face, pulverizing the cartilage in his nose.

Blood sprayed from the nostrils of the crushed appendage as he stumbled, taking several awkward steps backward as he tried to stay on his feet. His eyes narrowed and his jaw muscles tightened. "You bitch," he growled, spitting away the blood that streamed across his lips as he recovered enough to aim and fire the revolver.

Nikki bounded forward and grabbed the hot barrel of the revolver, forcing it up and back, causing the behemoth to loosen his grip on the antique firearm. She ripped the revolver from his grasp, spun around and fired off two rounds, the first slug tearing through the man's jacket, slamming into his chest, the nearly 8mm round causing him to exhale loudly as the impact forced the air from his lungs. In a split second Nikki adjusted her aim higher, the second round smashing through his forehead and exiting through the back of his skull in a cloud of spattering blood and bone fragments as the man fell against the brick wall and slid down to the floor.

Nikki stared at the settling body. She spun the revolver in her hand and held it out for Vostav to take from her. He was staring, jaw agape and eyes wide with surprise. He was mesmerized by Nikki's quick action.

She pitched her head back and to the right, throwing her short hair back into place from its errant position over her left eye, and turned to find that everyone in the room was wearing Vostav's same expression. She stepped back to the center of the group and asked simply, "So, are there any other questions?"

The two men who had been standing quickly took their seats as Nikki started over, feigning a look of contemplation. "So, where was I?" She paused for a second, then snapped her fingers. "My name is Nikki Sidorova and, to get straight to it, Dmitri Gregorov is dead and I have taken over his business." The murmuring in the room returned at the news of Gregorov's death.

"You are probably wondering, how this affects you." She glanced around the room before continuing, "First, any overdue accounts are now forgiven. So, if you owed Gregorov you are no longer indebted to him, or the company."

The announcement got the full attention of Anatoly, who was casually leaning against the wall. He stood upright at the news and glanced questioningly at Vostav who shrugged his shoulders, returning his quizzical look.

Nikki casually placed her hands behind her back and, after a brief pause, continued, "I have decided to close down the business and sell the weapons to any interested party, a sort of going out of business sale. As I have only recently acquired this position I will need time to go through the inventory. I will honor any promise of any particular merchandise or deals you may have made with the previous owner, so, if any of you have information you feel is pertinent, meet with me to discuss your concerns."

Nikki's only remorse after Gregorov's death was that she hadn't gotten the location of the weapons. She had just assumed that the man would have a map or some documents or data that could have led her to it, but she'd found no reference to the location. Her hope was that someone would take the bait and come forward, and with their interest in a deal, bring the information on the whereabouts of the storage site.

Anatoly smiled to himself as he caught on to what Nikki was doing, "Smart girl," he thought to himself as he looked around to see if anyone seemed nervous or antsy. One man, in the second to last row of chairs, was looking around as if he were looking for a means of escape. Anatoly saw the phone in his hand and it appeared he was texting someone. The man wore thick glasses with wide rims, pulling them off to wipe the sweat from his brow after every other key press. He looked up, noted Anatoly looking in his direction and dropped his phone to his lap. He returned his attention to Nikki, who was still discussing her plan.

For the next half hour Nikki answered questions and spoke about the weapons and what would come next. When it appeared that everyone was satisfied for the moment, and there were no additional questions, she allowed them to go.

A few stayed to speak with Nikki privately and asked if they could see what was available. Their questions told her that they did not know the location of the weapons. They had never been to the site and were interested in perusing.

Gregorov had basically run a mail order weapons catalog according to most of the people with whom she spoke, and did not allow visitors to the site. Evidently he would contact the salesmen and offer them systems that he thought they could use. If a purchase was made, he would deliver. He was politically savvy, paying close attention to world politics. Gregorov understood the strategies of warfare, knew who was threatening whom, what was being brought to the fight, and who would most likely win.

Gregorov would study battles as a military strategist, but he played both sides as an arms salesman, selling one regime a weapon that could eliminate the advantage of the other, and then sell another system to their enemy to defeat the first.

Anatoly watched as the bespectacled man moved purposefully to the door. He called to Vostav and motioned for him to intercept. Vostav trotted over and, like a sheep dog, redirected him toward Anatoly, who was heading his direction.

Anatoly introduced himself. "Good evening, Sir. I am Anatoly. I work for Miss Sidorova. Can I ask you a few questions?"

"I am Uri Breslev," the man replied without hesitation, surprised at Anatoly's politeness, "If you must question me, please be prompt. It is late and I have a ways to travel."

"Thank you," Anatoly said, maintaining his professionalism. "I guess I should begin by asking you what you do. Why are you here tonight?"

"I was sent here by one of the buyers. I am a liaison," he answered curtly.

"Is that who you were sending messages to, one of the buyers?"

"Yes. My employer," Uri sighed as he answered. "May I leave now? It is getting late."

"...And, I do apologize, but first, tell me please, what is the name of your employer?" Anatoly asked.

The man looked at Anatoly questioningly, "Why do you need to know this? The buyer wishes to stay anonymous. I am not at liberty to say whom I represent, you should know that, the rules have been this way for many years now."

Anatoly had no idea what the rules were. He glanced at Vostav, who was standing behind the man, shaking his head to indicate that Uri was speaking the truth.

Anatoly switched gears. "Yes, I understand. My mistake. Might you feel more comfortable telling me what it was that you were sharing with him that could not wait until the end of the meeting? Normally I would not ask, but given the current circumstances I hope you can understand my interest."

The man stayed silent for a long time and finally said, "If you must know, I was telling him about Mikhail."

"Mikhail?"

"Yes. Mikhail, the courier. The man she killed tonight." He gestured to the body of the hulking figure. Uri looked around the room, making eye contact with Nikki who was listening from a distance. He could tell by the look on all of their faces that they had no idea what he was talking about and began to laugh.

"You didn't know who he was, did you?" He was looking at Nikki as he laughed again.

"So that is why he questioned you. You had never met." Uri moved across the room to where Nikki stood. "He was only trying to protect Gregorov's interest and you killed him." The man walked to where the dead Mikhail was laying against the wall. "Well, well, you have gotten yourself into a pickle, haven't you?"

He walked back over to stand in front of Nikki, staring up into her eyes, smiling, as if he were relishing the moment. There was an awkward silence, then the little man held out his arms and said gleefully, "You shot, quite possibly, the only employee of Gregorov who knew where the weapons are kept." He laughed loudly before continuing,"...And you don't know where the weapons are stored, do you?"

Nikki answered his question honestly, with a shake of her head. With a smug look Uri replied, "This puts you at quite a disadvantage, you know. But I think I might be able to help you." Again Uri feigned deep contemplation and looked at his phone as if he were deciding whether or not to make a call.

"I should call my boss, tell him that you have killed Mikhail and are challenging him on the ownership of the business. I am sure he would think it is his to inherit from a dead Gregorov."

Breslev looked once more at the phone, then snapped it closed, put it in his pocket and then turned back to Nikki.

"But, I am not going to do that. Do you know why?" he asked, "Because I am tired of being the middleman. It is time that I am rewarded for my years of service, and, I believe tonight the opportunity has presented itself that will allow me to better myself,...if I take advantage of it."

Uri peered at Nikki over the frames of his glasses. "My employer knows the location of the weapons storage site. He has flown there with Gregorov. I know this to be so as he has mentioned Gregorov's plane, expressing a desire to own one like it one day.

Anatoly suddenly spoke up, "Gregorov has a plane? I was not aware that he was a pilot and I never saw any records of a plane in all my time working for him."

"Gregorov was no pilot. His pilot was Mikhail." He motioned again at the crumpled body of the huge Russian.

"It is no matter, we do not need a plane to see my boss. I will take you to him, but, once he gives you the location, his clients and his accounts will be mine to manage. He will be out of the picture and I will be the one you will do business with from start to finish. No middleman. Is that a deal?"

Nikki considered the development. "...And if your boss doesn't agree?"

"Agree or disagree is not a problem. It is when he tries to stop me that things will get...complicated. I will make the arrangements for you to meet with him. Be warned that he has a staff of bodyguards, prior soldiers who were loyal to him during the war."

Nikki looked at the man quizzically. "And which war is that, the Afghan War or the Cold War? I am not afraid of soldiers from either. Both wars are examples of failure as far as I am concerned."

Uri looked indifferent to her statement. He had never been a soldier and really did not care, but he knew from discussions with his boss that the man was once a soldier in Bosnia and that he'd fought under the flag of Serbia. "No, it was not Afghanistan," Uri explained. "He was a Serbian soldier.

The information sparked Nikki's interest. She glanced at Anatoly, whose attention was also piqued, then back at the aspiring little warmonger. As Nikki studied the man for a moment before speaking, she wondered where this strange looking man's loyalties lay.

"I would be very interested in meeting with your boss. Make the arrangements and give me a call at this number. I may be able to help you...ah...eliminate your competition." Nikki smiled, handing Uri a piece of paper with her number scribbled across it. "Call me as soon as you are ready. Good night Mr. Breslev."

CHAPTER 22

EVIDENCE

STATE DEPARTMENT, WASHINGTON, D.C.

GENE Patterson's office was at the far north end of the State Department's Kissinger Hall. Patterson rounded the last corner and entered through the frosted glass door into his office suite to find Betty Phillips standing at the desk talking to his office intern, Michael.

He walked toward them, closing the door behind him. "Betty, how nice to see you." He moved his bag to his left hand to take hers, shaking it, then pulled her to him for a slight hug. He backed away and looked fondly at her. "So what brings you to the far north side of the building?"

"Well, I wanted to talk to you about something," she said as she stepped a little closer to him.

Gene understood that whatever Betty wanted to talk about was important. "Ok, let's go in here and talk," he said as he opened his office door and ushered her in. Upon entering he motioned to the chair next to his desk. "Ok, shoot," he said as he took his seat behind the desk.

Betty began by asking him about the current T2T mission. "The other day, when you and Mr. Anderson met with The President and Secretary Erickson. I overheard some of the conversation." She paused to think how to legitimize her eavesdropping. "They were speaking very loudly, I wasn't *trying* to listen," she said, smiling, and then asked, "The mission that those two were arguing about that day, it's in Russia isn't it?"

"Yes, Alan Ramsey is heading up an investigation in Moscow. Why?"

Betty wasn't sure how to present her information and decided it would be best just to tell him the whole story. "Well, this morning, very early, President Carlton met with Erickson. The President was very upset when he arrived and, as soon as the door closed behind him, he started yelling. I mean really yelling, and cussing, at Secretary Erickson."

Having been in several meetings with a wide range of politicians and statesmen, Gene Patterson had heard his share of arguments. Generally though, the President was the peacemaker.

"Hmmm. That's pretty unusual for Carlton. I can see why you might pick up parts of the conversation."

Betty continued, "Exactly. And really, I tried to ignore them at first, until I heard the President mention Russian President Rashnev and Moscow. That got my attention, when the President mentioned Moscow, but then, he started talking about losing a drone and hellfire missiles."

Gene Patterson had not been briefed on the situation surrounding a mystery drone in Moscow. He sat up straight and wondered where Betty's story was going when she reached into her pocket and withdrew her iPhone.

"I placed this on the coffee cart and recorded what they said after that."

Patterson's eyes went wide. "Betty! You can't record somebody without their permission, *especially* the President of the United States." He whistled, pushing a hand through his hair.

"I know, I know, but Gene, I heard them talking about things that were definitely out of range of the duties of any Secretary of State." She paused, then added, "...and I'm sure, illegal as anything."

Gene Patterson sighed and planted his hands on the desk, pushing himself back in his chair. "So, you have that on tape?" he asked, thinking how the word *tape* seemed so antiquated, but how it fit the moment.

Betty corrected the timeline. "No, I heard him mention missiles and Moscow first, *and then* the coffee cart came by, *and then* I started recording. I did not get the first part, no."

She held up her phone, rocking it in her hand. "It wasn't until afterward, when I listened to it, that I knew for sure it had to do with Mr. Anderson's investigation."

She lowered the phone, placing it on the glass desk overlay, slid it toward Gene Patterson and then poked at the screen, hitting the play icon. The recording started with the shuffling of the phone on the cart and then the opening of the office door, immediately followed by Betty's voice. She played the recording through to the end.

Betty: "Would you Gentlemen care for some coffee? The kitchen cart is in the hall."

President Carlton: "Yes Betty, that would be very nice, thanks."

Betty: "The steward will be back shortly for the cart. Will there be anything else?"

Erickson: "No thank you, we are in the middle of something very important. Close the door behind you, please."

Erickson: "Ron, I have this under control. The contractor I told you about is Gordon Maxwell."

President Carlton: "Maxwell, he's still on that godforsaken continent? What the hell, doesn't that guy have a real life?"

Erickson: "He's got a wife and a kid and a ton of cash. The best thing about him is that old ties are binding, He'll still work for us when we need him."

President Carlton: "So then, I take it that you have a plan to clean up your mess?"

Erickson: "I got it. Maxwell is on his way now. It will be expensive, but he'll fix it."

President Carlton: "Jim, I want this cleaned up. Do what you have to and make sure it's done right. Tell Maxwell no strings, no clues, and no trail back to this administration, got it?"

Erickson: "Don't worry, it's under control,"

President Carlton: "Also, find out what's on that laptop that's so important to Sidorova. Get Maxwell on it. Put him back on the payroll."

The sound of the office door opening and closing could be heard, then Erickson cussing as he opened the door a second time and pushed the coffee cart into the outer office. The rest of the conversation was of Erickson telling Betty to get rid of the cart, the door closing and Betty retrieving the phone to turn it off.

Gene Patterson sat quietly for a moment. The look on his face revealed his thoughts, that what he had just heard was the making of an impeachment investigation. He knew that what Betty had heard, along with the recording, would easily destroy the current administration. What Betty held in her hand was the equivalent of dynamite,...no, he thought, more like a nuclear bomb for the presidency. He couldn't stop his words, "Holy shit!"

The woman across from him smirked. "That's exactly what I said after I heard it the first time." She sighed, "Now what?"

Gene Patterson thought again about what he had just heard and what betty reported hearing before she made the recording. He had no idea who Maxwell might be. Perhaps an agent, but if that was the case Patterson should have been informed. So, for now, the only truly incriminating information on the *tape*, as far as Patterson was concerned, was that the President mentioned one of the subjects of Ramsey's investigation, Nikki Sidorova.

He had the urge to call Gabe Anderson, but remembered that he was on the Hill giving testimony on the Russian invasion of the Ukraine. That would easily go into the night, then, more than likely, he would be on lock down to brainstorm any actions that might be taken by the United States. Patterson looked at his watch, contemplating the time.

"Betty, I'm going to need a statement from you. I will have to write my own about what you just told me, but your statement will be the most important."

Betty Phillips had anticipated the move and held up a silver USB drive.

"It's all on here. I wrote the statement, saved it as a PDF and digitally signed it. The same for my notes, printed, signed and scanned. I converted the recording to MP3 format. It will play on your machine here or your personal computer."

Betty put the USB Drive in front of Patterson. Gene Patterson looked at it as if it were going to explode.

Betty continued, "I emailed the file to you as well. It's a small file size. You shouldn't have any problem sending it to Mr. Anderson."

Patterson looked nervous. "Problem is, Gabe probably won't be available until tomorrow sometime. He's got a lot going on right now."

"Yes, I know, the Ukrainian thing." She leaned forward. "Gene, relax. This isn't the first time Erikson has stepped on his dick." She smiled, "Tomorrow is as good a day as any to start the process of firing that bastard."

Patterson noted the look of satisfaction on her face. "Why do I get the feeling you're enjoying this?"

"Look, Betty, I'm sure you know what you have here is very incriminating, hell, career ending. If Erickson ever finds out you recorded him he will probably grow scales and spit fire. I wouldn't let anyone else know about what you have or that you have it until I get the chance to speak with Gabe Anderson. Seriously, until then, if I were you, I wouldn't trust anyone."

"I'm trusting you." She said flatly. "Nobody else knows. It's all on you now." She saw the look of apprehension on Patterson's face. Betty smiled and said, "Call me if you need me. I have to get back to the dragon's lair."

CHAPTER 23

OLD ACQUAINTANCES

VOSTAV pulled up to the front of the house slowly. It was hardly fitting to call it a house. The structure was more like a small castle. He turned into the driveway, well manicured rows of hedges on either side. The engine labored slightly as he crested the last rolling hill, the low early morning sun greeting him as he drove out of the slight haze now on the roadway behind him.

The hedges stopped abruptly and the mansion came into full view. Three stories of rough cut granite and red and gray brick made up the façade. Several buildings dotted the immediate landscape. Vostav identified one building as a carriage house, dating the structure to the turn of the century at least.

Nikki squinted, straining to see through the glare on the windshield. Pointing to the vehicle parked ahead she said, "There, pull behind them, but leave room to maneuver around."

As he pulled to a stop the driver's door of the vehicle ahead of him opened and Uri, the man they had met the night before, stepped out under the canopy of several large trees.

"Good morning Miss Sidorova," Uri said as Nikki got out of the car, extending his hand.

Nikki met his hand with hers giving it a shake, surprising the man with the strength she displayed in the simple gesture.

"Just you and your driver this morning, I see." Uri looked around and back toward the road to see if there was any sign of others.

Nikki saw Uri's quick search, "That is Vostav. He is much more than my driver, but he will stay out here. You said on the phone that your boss wanted a private meeting, so..." Nikki faced both palms upward, indicating that she was indeed alone.

Uri laughed a little and placed one hand around Nikki, pointed toward the walkway with the other and ushered her in the direction of the huge covered entrance of the mansion. As he stood close he spoke quietly, "It is not your men I am looking for. I tasked the guards on two separate missions. I was just looking to see that they had followed my orders. It would appear that they are both gone."

The passenger door of Uri's car opened and a tall armed man stood as if he were going to join the stroll to the house. Uri held up his hand and told the man to stay with the vehicle. He nodded his understanding at Uri, then glanced over his shoulder to Nikki's car where Vostav stood pulling hard on a cigarette, trying unsuccessfully to light it in the wind gusts that blew from the valley. Vostav caught the man glaring and gave him a quick nod, acknowledging his presence.

At the entrance of the mansion they were greeted by a thick arched wooden door. The rough hewn wood merely a frame to ornate stained glass artwork, depicting a skirmish on some battlefield, a fitting decoration for a man who peddled the wares of death. The release of the latch and a slight squeak echoed in a huge foyer decorated with antiques of all kinds, but themed with the art of war. It was more a museum than a home. The centerpiece of the room was a cannon, the type that would be pulled behind a horse and dated to around the turn of the 20th century, Nikki guessed, yet, looked as though it could still function.

Nikki stepped to the side marveling at the marble and granite mosaic floor, painstakingly crafted from thousands of meticulously carved bits of polished stone depicting a map of a battlefield. The cannon pointed north, matching a north facing arrow made of pure white marble, embedded among a circle of dark green Brazilian granite. The design, a graphic representation of a compass, served as the base for the cannon.

The compass and cannon were the centerpiece of the map that Nikki immediately recognized as the land mass of Greater Serbia before World War One. At the northern most edge of the mosaic, embedded in brightly polished black granite, was a gold star, marking the position of Belgrade, the northern city and capitol of the country. To the East were the bordering countries of Romania and Bulgaria, known then as the Ottoman Empire. To the south, Greece, then Albania and Montenegro. To the left, was the Austrian controlled country of Bosnia, formed from a pie shaped, ivory colored marble. At its center, another gold star. A jagged line of gold snaked from the star of Belgrade to several points across the map, eventually ending at the star within the border of Bosnia.

"That is Sarajevo, if you were wondering." Nikki was somewhat startled at the sudden words that echoed in the large foyer. A tall man with reddish hair and patch over his left eye walked with a slight limp from a large double doorway, silently at first, until he stepped from the carpeted room onto the marble floor. His heavy footsteps resounded loudly as he moved to Nikki's side, stepping around her to her left so that his uncovered eye could have full view of her stark beauty. He eyed her down then up as he pointed to the marble floor.

"The star there is Sarajevo, the site of the assassination of Archduke Ferdinand of Austria and that line represents the route of the assassins from Belgrade." He traced the line with an outstretched hand then turned again to face Nikki. "Quite a story of intrigue and suspense, I assure you," he said as he smiled.

"But forgive me, I have not introduced myself, I am Vojislav Princip and you must be Miss Sidorova. Uri has told me quite a bit about you, and your ability to handle yourself when put on the spot." He offered his hand to Nikki. She grasped it briefly, giving a curt shake, then let the man's hand fall away. She noted that his hand was damp with sweat.

"So, you are a collector." Nikki said as she motioned around the room. "Are you a historian as well? You seem to know some interesting details about obscure people."

Princip was taken aback by her statement. "Oh, I assure you, the story of the assassination of Ferdinand may contain some unknowns, but to the true Serbian the story of the mission to drive Austrian control from Bosnia, and the names of the men who embarked on such a mission, are held in high regard among the officers of the Serbian War Colleges." He smiled before continuing, "I do however have a deeper interest in the history of the event. You see, my Grandfather was Gavrillo Princip, the man who shot Archduke Franz Ferdinand on the Latin Bridge overlooking the Dvina River."

Nikki stared at the man, scornfully. Nikki knew the story of the assassination. She knew that not only was Ferdinand shot in the neck and bled to death on the way to the hospital, but his wife was also killed, shot in the stomach, orphaning their three children.

"So, your grandfather was responsible for the start of World War One," she said, her disdain for the man growing. She laughed and shook her head in disgust, "Almost a hundred years have passed and the Serbs still believe they should own Bosnia."

The man glared at Nikki with his one eye. "My grandfather was a Hero. His execution showed the world that he was ready to die for his beliefs."

Nikki turned to face Princip. He was slightly taller than she. She knew the history of Serbia. She had studied it, as a true leader would study the history of an enemy. She knew all the actors, all the intricate details of what made them the madmen they were.

"Your grandfather was a self serving zealot," Nikki growled. "He was too small for the army, and his own government turned him away when he volunteered for the Serbian Military Intelligence."

Nikki saw that she had struck a nerve with her host. She moved within inches of Princip. "You can spin your web of intrigue and martyrdom all you want, but everyone knows that Gavrillo Princip died a shamed man, in a prison cell of cancer, not a hangman's noose. I find it Ironic that they had to amputate the arm he used to draw the weapon that killed Ferdinand, yet still failed to save his life."

She spun away from him and walked toward one of his displays of World War One weapons locked behind glass.

"I am not interested in your historical fantasy. I am interested only in the location of Gregorov's weapons cache. It is my understanding that you know where it is. Are you ready to talk business or do you insist on bloviating about your rich history?"

Vojislav Princip was not used to being talked to in this way. "I am not going to do any business with you. How dare you come into my home and disrespect my family history. Who do you think you are? Get out of my house!" He screamed.

Nikki leaned against the glass cabinet. "Tell me, where are the weapons? I know that you know."

To Princip's horror Nikki bent down and picked up one of the eight pound, six inch diameter cannon balls and smashed it through the glass of the cabinet. The weighted relic broke through the bottom glass causing several items and the cannon ball to land on the marble below with a clattering thud, cracking the Brazilian marble.

Nikki picked up another of the cast iron spheres and prepared to lunge it through the art glass of the front door. "Where are the weapons?" She screamed.

Princip yelled down the hall to his guards. "Illic, Djuro, Come here!" "Illic, Djuro!" He screamed at Uri. "Don't just stand there. Go find Illic and Djuro!"

Outside the house Vostav sat in his vehicle out of the wind so that he could smoke his cigarette. He knew that Nikki would not be happy that he was smoking in the car with the windows up.

Suddenly the guard who had been leaning against Uri's car raced across the yard toward the house, getting Vostov's full attention. Vostav leaned forward, turned the radio down and looked toward the shattered glass of the front door as the cannon ball bounced down the two stairs to the walkway and into the grass. "Shit!," he mumbled as he struggled to open the car door.

The guard got to the door, weapon drawn, and prepared to step inside when he heard Nikki yell at Princip. "Where are the weapons?" He looked through the door and could see Vojislav Princip furious at the sight of his broken door.

Princip lunged at Nikki, but in a move that he didn't see coming, Nikki moved aside and launched into a spinning back kick that landed at the back of Princip's neck causing him to fall forward. Nikki's kick drove him headlong into the barrel of the cannon, opening a gash on his brow above his eye patch, nearly knocking him unconscious. He crumpled to the floor under the cannon as his gunman entered with his weapon drawn. Princip saw the opportunity to gain the advantage over this crazed female and yelled to the guard, "Don't just stand there, Kill that little bitch!"

His words hung in the air, echoing through the room, thrashing through years of memories in Nikki's brain. She had heard those words before, that voice. In a split second the image of Nikki's father being beaten, fighting with one of the Serbian soldiers as she stood too paralyzed to move, came to the forefront of her mind. She could hear her father yelling to her, "Nikki, go! Run!"

She could see the face of the soldier as he looked up, distracted by her father's orders as she ran past him and up the stairs. It was Princip staring at her from deep inside her mind. The scene replayed itself in slow motion, her father pulling the man around by his face, Princip screaming as his eye and flesh were torn away.

She remembered running at full force with her brother in tow and kicking the bleeding soldier down the steps backward. She could see now, in her memory, his twisted, broken leg as he lay at the bottom of the staircase, and again heard him yell, "There is a boy upstairs. Get him, and kill that little bitch!"

Nikki returned to the present as the large bodyguard stepped through the unopened door amid the broken stained glass and into the path of an angry Nikki Sidorova who was moving toward him with lightning speed. She kicked his knees out from under him causing him to slip sideways on the broken glass, slamming down onto his left side against the marble floor. Nikki reached down and plucked the pistol from his hand. She racked the Beretta, ejecting one round, but ensuring that the pistol had a round chambered, and moved toward Princip, who was just getting to his feet.

Vostav stepped through the door over the guard who was trying to figure out what had happened. Vostav grabbed him and pulled him to the side, weapon trained at his face. The guard looked up, raised his hands and shook his head to let Vostav know there would be no trouble from him. Vostav turned in time to see Nikki cold cock the redhead with the eye patch who immediately went back down onto his knees.

Nikki pulled at him, making him stand up, and then immediately nailed him again, this time with the butt of the pistol. Vojislav Princip was afraid for his life now. He had no idea what triggered such a wrath from this woman or why he was the target of her sudden, severe attack, but his guard was down and Uri appeared to be enjoying the show.

"What the hell do you want from me?" he said as he leaned on his knees, one hand on the floor, the other covering his bloody face. He was shaking as he attempted once again to get to his feet.

Nikki was breathing hard as she thought about what to do next. She could not kill him, not yet. She needed information, more than just the weapons now. This man, she was sure, would have information about Ratko Mladic. He would probably know where he was, where General Radislav Krstic was, and hopefully, the location of her father and brother's remains. She would have to interrogate him.

She walked a half circle around the bloodied man to face him on his right. She wanted to be sure he could see her. "You don't remember me, do you?" she asked, getting not only his attention but Vostav's interest as well.

"Remember you? I don't know you. I'm sorry, Have we met before?" he said sarcastically as he spit blood from his mouth. He tried to recognize her. There was some resemblance, some memory of her face, maybe because of her eyes. Green eyes are always memorable. He spat again, "I don't know who you are."

She grabbed him by the hair and shoved the pistol against his neck driving it so hard into the bottom of his jaw that he could barely swallow. "I'll give you a hint. Srebrenica 1995, My father ripped out your eye just before you were kicked down a flight of stairs."

Princip suddenly looked astounded, then angry. "You, you're Sidorova's girl."

She wanted to pull the trigger, wanted to kill him just for saying her father's name. She thought about the fact that he would have known his name at all, then smacked him hard with her free left hand.

"Why do you know my father's name?" She hit him again. "Why? Tell me why, before I kill you right now." Princip put his hand up trying to block the throws.

"You're kidding right? Everyone knew your father. He was our enemy. He killed many of our men before his capture. Sure, he was a hero to your people, but to the Serbs he was a scourge, a target of high value." Nikki relaxed a little to let him talk.

Princip continued to explain. "That day we separated the men and boys from the women. My orders were to take the men to the village, to have them collect belongings in preparation for the move to the Muslim territory. I was only twenty four and newly promoted. I didn't kill one person, I swear." Princip's one eye began to water at the memory of the atrocity. "I didn't kill anyone." He paused for a minute to collect himself, then went on. "There was no order to do so, not then, just, go to the village, collect the belongings."

Nikki pushed him a little, a flat handed chest punch, forcing him against the cannon's wheel. "I saw you fighting my father. I watched him do that to your face." Nikki pointed to the exposed scars and sewed closed, grown together eyelid that formed a reddish sunken, skin-covered, empty eye socket. Princip tried to put the patch back in place, wanting to cover it, himself uncomfortable with the image.

Nikki yelled, "Leave it!"

Princip reluctantly dropped his hands back down to his sides. "We were next door supervising the collection there when one of my men saw someone run from the woods toward the back of the next house over. The first soldier kicked the door open and was killed when your father threw him to the floor and stabbed him. I stepped in only to be disarmed and kicked. I fell backward and, as I did, that's when I found out that the man we were fighting was Nikkolai Sidorova, the second most wanted man in all of Bosnia. There I was fighting with Masa Orlich's second in command. For me it was like capturing a General."

Nikki, as well as the others were listening intently. She had never heard first hand accounts of her father's war experience and the powerful force her father must have been.

Princip continued his story. "When your father had managed to free himself a second time I knew that I had to stop him or he would kill us all. I was so afraid. I had to force myself to move, but when I did, I suddenly found myself with the advantage and felt, for a moment, that we might actually bring him down."

He suddenly looked sullen as he wiped some of the drying blood from the gash on his head. He pulled both of his hands across his face, then staring at some unseen point, continued. "It was at that instant I saw you staring, just standing there, frozen. I saw you jump when your father told you to run. I remember thinking, why is there a girl here?" He snorted at his own foolish thoughts, the thoughts that had distracted him allowing Nikki's father to attack him.

"That is when the great Nikolai Sidorova blinded me. The pain was incredible. I let go of him and fell back out of the way to let the others take him down. That's when I ran up the steps after you."

He leaned a bit forward, looking into Nikki's eyes, his one eye darting to and from each of hers. "I really don't know how I could have forgotten those green eyes of yours. I remember now seeing the anger in them. When I reached the top step and you kicked me and as I fell backward down the stairs, I could only think that I was about to die, killed by a girl."

"I broke my leg in three places. The Serbian military doctors were not the most skilled. I thought I would lose it to their ineptitude. I half expected a bottle of whisky and a saw would be the fix, but, well, at least I still have it."

His one eye welled with tears. "I've lived with the pain and my shameful appearance since that day. The only reason I did not end up in prison was that my injuries were so severe, my ability to serve my country so diminished, that I was discharged."

The man stood up straight. "A blessing in disguise really. I can only imagine what atrocities I would have committed had I been allowed to stay in."

Nikki was actually surprised to hear his side of the story. She had always assumed that he would have recovered and continued on, lived to fight another day and all that.

"Where did they take my father and brother?" Nikki was still trying to sound forceful and in charge.

There was no fight left in Vojislav Princip, he had nothing to hide any longer.

"I was put on one of the trucks that was full of the wounded. They were not in the vehicle I was in. My vehicle went on to a field hospital. The other trucks and busses drove to several different locations such as Cerska Valley, Kravica Warehouse, Oravac, Branjevo Farm, Ptrkovci Dam and Kozluk. I was not there, but I heard the stories from many other soldiers. The prisoners were blindfolded and executed.

Still, no one ever told me what happened to Nikkolai Sidorova. I had asked on several occasions, mainly to see if I was given credit for his capture, but either nobody knew, or at least, said they didn't know. I was told by General Radislav Krstic himself, who came to visit the wounded, that I should not want to find out. It was none of my business and to let it drop. It was Krstic who introduced me to Gregorov, sort of introduced I should say. He gave me Gregorov's contact information. He called him, 'an old friend' and told me that he might have some business for me. He said Gregorov looked after heroes like me. After I recovered I left Serbia and came here to Moscow. I haven't been back since. As you can see, I have made my life here as a collector." Princip held his hands up and spun side to side acknowledging his surroundings.

"And what happened to Krstic?" Nikki asked. "I was told he was released from prison. Where is he?"

Vojislav Princip was tired of being held at gunpoint. He placed his hand on the pistol and lightly pushed it aside. "There is no longer a need for your threats Miss Sidorova. I have nothing to hide."

He began to loosen up a bit, walking gingerly through the bits of glass. "I will tell you what you want to know, then, you must leave me be. Though, I do not think that we will be business partners as I once was with Dmitri." He had managed to hobble over to the liquor and glasses that were on display. He removed the top of the crystal decanter and poured a small amount in two glasses.

"This scotch is over one hundred years old. My grandfather reportedly drank this same scotch from this same decanter the night before he and three others left from Belgrade. One of those men was my namesake, Major Vojislav Tankosic." He hoisted the glasses offering one to Nikki who stood unmoving, weapon in her hand.

Princip shrugged once then threw back the first glass, followed by the second. "General Radislav Krstic was tried at the U.N. War Crimes Tribunal in The Hague. He was convicted of conspiring to commit genocide and sentenced to 35 years in prison."

Nikki was appalled at the short sentence. Her surprise and disagreement showed, but before she could say anything Princip continued, holding up his hand, still holding the glass and gesturing for Nikki to wait until he was finished.

"It, would seem that investigators gleaned a lot of information from Krstic. In fact, the American Secretary of State, their current President, made a deal with him for information that would prove that Slobodan Milosevic, Radovan Karadzic and General Mladic were the masterminds of a plan to eliminate the Muslims, to rid the country of Serbia and Bosnia from what they considered a plague. Because the information he gave was reliable information he was sentenced to a minimum thirty five years."

Nikki pondered the time spent in jail. "It has been only seventeen years. Why was he released?"

Princip narrowed his one eye and shook a finger, "Good question, Miss Sidorova. There is a U.N. charter that forces the country members to house the war criminals, share the burden of their institutional care, so to speak. On his fifteenth year of incarceration General Krstic was moved to Wakefield Prison in the UK. Some of the Muslim prisoners held there found out who he was and decided that they would administer their own form of punishment. They crafted shanks and knives and stabbed and beat him. He managed to save his own life, but only barely, by defending himself with his prosthetic right leg."

Vostav, who was quietly listening to the story, snorted, trying not to laugh. Nikki shot him an impatient glance.

Princip tried to explain, "Some years before the Serbian war, Krstic stepped on a land mine while inspecting a battle field, nearly ending his career in the military. His right leg below the knee was amputated and, after several months of care, he returned to duty, resuming his task as the Commander of the Drina Corps. I was told that during the fight in prison he removed his right leg and began to beat the Muslim prisoners with it until he passed out from loss of blood."

Vostav could not control his laughter. Nikki stared him down, trying hard herself not to laugh due to the contagion of Vostav's loud, spontaneous outburst and yelled, "Vostav, shut up!"

Princip continued, "Because of his injuries, the commission decided that he could be released, his debt to society paid in full."

He paused and looked around at all he owned, sighed and said, "Maybe it is time that I retire. You know, I will be forty in a few months, perhaps I should consider padding my retirement savings. Tell me, Miss Sidorova, is there a reward for the information of the location of General Radislav Krstic?"

Nikki looked at Princip for a long minute before answering. Uri looked on, watching what was transpiring. *She had to kill him,* he thought to himself. *They had a deal.*

Nikki thought that Vojislav Princip was honorable enough. She felt that he harbored true remorse for his actions as a young Serbian Lieutenant. He had obviously paid a price for his choice to follow those who eventually would destroy the country. Finally, she spoke.

"Tell me where the weapons are, and give me Krstic's location and I will let you live."

With That Uri pulled his own pistol and pointed it at Princip, but faced Nikki as he walked the few steps toward Princip to be sure of a kill shot.

"No! This is bullshit, we had a deal. I am taking over his business. He needs to die, remember?" He glanced at Princip. "Tell her what she wants to know!" he screamed.

Nikki raised her pistol, pointing it directly at Uri's temple. She couldn't miss. Vostav was no longer laughing as he covered the guard making sure that he was not a threat.

All three men jumped at the sound of the gunshot as Nikki fired one round through Uri's brain destroying his skull and spraying blood over the wall. *Stupid little man*, she thought, as his lifeless body fell to the marble floor. Suddenly the room grew dark as the light coming from the broken front door was blocked by one of the guards sent on errand; Illic had returned to see the events unfolding.

Nikki spun around, pulling her pistol up to face the man in the opening and began to move to the side, but wasn't fast enough to outrun the successive three rounds fired by Illic. The first round from Illic's nine-mil drilled through Nikki's trapezius just under her raised right arm. The second and third rounds missed their mark and burrowed into the chest of Vojislav Princip, sending him backward.

The other guard, the one who stood in front of Vostav, lunged toward him, but had no chance, as Vostav fired only once, straight into the man's forehead at very close range causing the back of his skull to disintegrate.

Nikki roared as the round passed through her body and, in what seemed a slow motion chain of events, watched as the other two rounds drove deep into Princip's chest. She continued her spinning move, disregarding the pain, as her brain recorded the flash from Vostav's weapon and the sight of the second guard's head exploding causing a huge wave of bone, blood and brain matter to spray directly across the line of sight of her target. Nikki pointed at her attacker and fired, repeatedly pulling the trigger, sending as many nine millimeter rounds in his direction as quickly as she could, seven shots through the still expanding spray of blood and into the chest and abdomen of the guard in the doorway, sending him backward through the opening from which he came.

Nikki settled into a crouch and lifted her arm to look at the damage inflicted. She ordered Vostav to cover the door for the last guard in case he should return. She had a clean in-out wound through her skin and muscle. One hole in and one hole out. She was lucky that the round missed her chest or scapula. The wound burned like hell, but her blood loss was minimal.

She turned her attention to Princip who was still alive, but from the sound of his wheezing and the amount of blood that was oozing out of one of his wounds, he wouldn't be alive much longer.

Nikki knelt down close to inspect his wound. She could hear air as it whistled inward through one of the gunshot wounds. Nikki grabbed Princip's left hand and pushed it against the sucking wound offering some immediate relief to the dying man. "Hold this here, keep it on the hole," she told him. Within seconds bubbles appeared in the oozing bloodstream exiting from the wound closer to the center of his chest.

"Princip, listen to me, we don't have much time." His eye was rolling upward then settling back onto Nikki's as he tried to hang on. "Where is Krstic? You said you would tell me."

Princip managed a smile, "You said you would let me live," he wheezed. "Guess I made a bad deal this time." He said quietly, grimacing from the pressure of the blood filling his chest. He was drowning and he knew it.

"As…I said…Krstic…and Gregorov…are old…friends. Krstic lives…in Kiev. Still…uses…his…real…name." He gasped, trying to fill his lungs with air, but choked, coughing and forcing the blood to fountain out of his chest. He was pale and could no longer keep his hand on the chest wound. The gurgling, sucking sound returned as well as more pain and his inability to breathe.

He was whispering with each shallow breath, determined to hold up his part of the bargain. "Gregorov owns…a house…and a farm… in…the Ukraine." He struggled to take another breath. His chest felt heavy and he wasn't sure he could continue. "In the barn…on his farm…the weapons…near…Kiev…" Princip inhaled one more gurgling breath, trying to ignore the pain and pressure and whispered, "Find the farm…and…you will…" He coughed weakly, spitting blood, but managed to continue, "find…the weapons…and…Krstic." Princip exhaled a raspy breath and fell silent.

"Vojislav?" Nikki shook him, "Princip?" There was no more noise.

She called Vostav back into the house. Instead of entering, he stood by the door still wanting to keep watch. Nikki pulled Princip's eye patch around and placed it back over his missing eye, then reached over to close the right eye fully. She stood, then pulled out her phone and called Anatoly.

Anatoly answered on the first ring, noting the caller I.D. "So, how did your meeting go?"

Nikki looked around at the carnage as she assessed the last hour and twenty minutes of her life. "It went better than I'd hoped. A few surprises is all. I need you to get a few things from the apartment. Get my laptop and some clothes. Just grab what you can, quickly, and meet me at the shop. Looks like we'll be taking a trip." She started to hang up, but thought of one more detail. "…And, find me a pilot."

CHAPTER 24

BACK ON LINE

RICK White was putting the final touches on his latest application. He had tested it with Matthews, Vee and Paul Jackson's phones and, so far, it appeared to be functioning perfectly. Each time one of them called anywhere, the longitude and latitude of their location populated a list on his screen. By selecting the phone number he could pinpoint their locations on a map.

The system was a hack of the find-my-phone feature that was installed on almost every phone produced in the last year or so. As long as the phone was new enough his application could access another phone's data. The information could then be used with one of the turn by turn driving direction programs, such as Google Maps, and traced from one position another.

He had already programmed Nikki's phone into the list and was just finishing updating the list of "friendly" phones when his phone vibrated and chimed.

He looked at his screen to see who was calling, expecting it to be Matthews, letting him know that he was parked outside the hotel waiting for him, but he realized quickly that he wasn't receiving a phone call, though Nikki's phone number had just popped up on his screen.

White stood up quickly. His eyes were wide with excitement. "Hey! You guys. Look! Nikki's back on the grid!" He looked around the hotel room, remembering that nobody else was there. "Shit!" he said as he selected the map to see if her location would populate. Instead the phone chimed again and he realized he was getting a push notification from the re-engineering program indicating that Nikki's phone was operating again and ready for the trace call to install the bugging virus.

He poked the screen a few more times, going back and forth between the two programs making adjustments to each to see which app was actually working fully and found that neither of the programs were doing anything right, other than indicating that Nikki's phone was working again.

White decided that the apps must be conflicting with each other. The best way to resolve the conflict was to remove one of the two programs, but which one? Even if he got the virus spun up and was able to turn on Nikki's microphone, there was nobody close to her to pick up the Voice Over Blue Tooth Signal. He remembered how Marks' BMW was losing the signal before as the distance between his and Anatoly's vehicle increased. There's no way they could get the signal if she were even a mile away, and without knowing where Nikki was, they couldn't get close enough to track her. However, the new program would show her location. White decided that knowing where she was would be best. If they located her, they could start tracking again. Besides, he thought, the new program would allow his team to keep tabs on each other. He decided to keep the GPS program and lose the V.O.B.T.S., at least until he could correct the conflict issue.

He returned his phone to the home screen, then hooked the phone to his laptop. Within seconds his App manager opened up for him to deselect the V.O.B.T.S app. He hit *apply* and his phone restarted. When the system was fully operational he scrolled to the GPS app and selected the icon. Now, Nikki's phone number, along with the grid coordinates of her phone, populated the screen.

White selected the map overlay. The Google Map appeared for a moment then disappeared leaving a pin dropped into place showing her exact location, or at least, the location of her last phone call. White refreshed the page hoping for the map to reset. Again the Google Map appeared then went off. "Shit!" White uttered, acknowledging that he still had some work to do to perfect the app.

Still, he was excited. He had to call his boss. He didn't want to take a chance of losing the info on his phone, so he placed the call to Ramsey from the hotel room phone. He couldn't wait to tell him the news.

CHAPTER 25

NIKKI'S APARTMENT

RAMSEY parked on the street about a half block from the entrance to Nikki Sidorova's apartment. He and Paul Jackson walked the short distance, rounding the corner of the complex into the corridor that led to the parking area behind the apartment building. Agent Villacruze walked toward Alan Ramsey and Jackson. Marks was following close behind, scanning the area as if he were on patrol through a Middle Eastern village, a habit that he couldn't seem to shake and one that he developed covering Villacruze throughout the Iraq war and then again on a second tour in Afghanistan.

Two Russian officers of the R.S.S., Agent Russo and one other whom Ramsey recognized from the R.S.S. arms vault where they had signed for their weapons, R.S.S. radios and protective vest that morning, stepped from their sedan and moved quickly toward Ramsey.

Vee stepped up to give his report. "Doesn't look like anyone is inside. I don't think Sidorova has been back here since the meeting with Gregorov." He glanced side to side and held his lock pick tool set in full view for Ramsey and Jackson to see. "The door's open," he said, with a slightly crooked grin.

Ramsey pushed his earpiece in place, its coil of cording nearly undetectable, disappearing into his jacket. He motioned to where Marks had stopped about fifty meters away. "Tell Marks that just because he's armed now doesn't mean he has to shoot anybody."

Ramsey heard Marks' voice come over the headset. "Just so you are aware, Sir, coms are working." He smiled and gave Ramsey a thumbs up.

Russo stepped up, hand outstretched, "Mr. Ramsey, this is Iliev. He will be joining us for the look inside."

Ramsey shook the man's hand. "Right, we met briefly this morning," He turned to introduce Paul Jackson, but found he was no longer standing beside him.

Ramsey instead turned toward Vee. "You've already met Villacruze and Marks, I take it." The Russian nodded that he had.

Vee nodded slightly also, looking a bit uneasy with the two Russians. "We've met," he stated somewhat flatly.

Ramsey noticed Vee's cautiousness, the same feeling of apprehension that he assumed was shared by his partner, Marks. He turned and started walking, while pointing toward Jackson.

"The guy looking like he's ready to kick some ass is Paul Jackson. Don't mind his attitude, he's actually a nice guy."

Jackson was at the door with his pistol at the ready. The weapon felt good in his hands, giving him the feeling that he had some level of control over his own situation. Jackson spoke into his mike so that only his team could hear in their earpieces, "I heard that."

Iliev stepped around Ramsey and moved to the opposite side of the door, across from Jackson. He pulled a small automatic weapon from where it hung under his jacket, raised it and nodded to Paul that he was ready to go.

Jackson looked at Russian agent's Uzi, then at his own pistol in comparison. He glanced at Ramsey who was viewing the exchange and could see Paul's dismay that the Russian had a better weapon. With a look of defeat and shaking his head in disgust, Paul uttered, "Really?" as he pushed the door open carefully.

Villacruze was right, the apartment did not looked lived in and, given Nikki's recent return, that made sense to Ramsey's team and the Russians. There was no food in the refrigerator, only bottled water. The bed had been slept in, the shower used, and in the dining room on the table was Nikki's computer, some papers, a few printed pictures and a cell phone.

Paul Jackson pushed the phone around noting the battery had been removed, exposing the empty SIM card slot. "Well, now we know why we couldn't get any info from her phone. I bet Rick the Geek didn't count on someone removing the battery."

Ramsey poked at the keys on her laptop causing it to come out of sleep mode. "We can reinitiate the virus when he gets back. Should be easy if she still has the SIM card. She probably thought the battery was bad given that it wouldn't hold a charge very well."

He turned to Russo to explain a little about Rick White, his resident surveillance technician and the re-engineering virus and it's tendency for the hacked phones to have a degraded battery life.

"Oh, speaking of gadgetry, I sent White and one of our other agents, Bob Matthews, to the Merinsk Street Cafe. They're meeting with a couple officers from the local precinct to sanitize the site, you know, remove the electronic surveillance equipment they had installed."

Russo suddenly looked worried. "You should have told me this. I would have sent an agent with them." The Russian agent didn't like the matter of fact tone of the American, Ramsey. He lifted his radio and speaking in Russian told his dispatcher to send a team to the cafe to meet Ramsey's men. He looked back at Ramsey, "I do not trust the local police," he said simply.

Ramsey took the opportunity to express his own concerns. He spoke quietly, but sternly to the tall Russian officer. "Frankly Russo, I'm concerned that you have a leak in your department. So far we haven't had the best experience with trust."

"What are you saying Mr. Ramsey, that you do not think my men are capable of..." Ramsey cut him off mid sentence, raising his voice a little to match the increased pitch of Russo's voice, "What I'm saying is, so far, every effort we have made in this investigation has been hijacked in some way or another."

Russo countered Ramsey's statement. "And you think we have something to do with those events?" His voice was approaching a yell and his face reddening. "It is obvious that the woman, Sidorova, is behind all of this. She's the one who set up Gregorov's hit, she's the one who killed your physicist..."

Ramsey interrupted again. "And your people, in fact, you, didn't even try to stop her! You didn't have anybody there for back up, and the ones that you had with you did nothing as she drove off!" He turned away to see his and Russo's men staring at them.

Ramsey regained his composure before continuing. "What the hell am I supposed to think? The meeting with Gregorov goes bad, a drone chases down our lead suspect and destroys one of the two vehicles, and then, not only does the destroyed getaway car disappear, so does the identification of the two crispy critters in it. Oh, and let's not even mention the fact that your people let the remnants of a crashed aerial drone get out of your sight."

Ramsey was interrupted suddenly when the radio on Russo's belt started squawking. He couldn't understand what was being said, but could tell by the look on the Russian officer's face that something serious had happened.

Russo barked some commands to the dispatcher, then to his men who where moving toward the door having understood the radio conversation. "I am sorry Mr. Ramsey, but I have to leave.

My presence is requested at another site. I will leave you one of my men as an observer, to keep my boss…happy."

Russo could see the distrust building in the American. Too bad, he thought. He knew that his boss would not allow the American teams to just do what they wanted. Not here in his country. He would hate to see anything happen that would put Ramsey and his team in danger, but events were beginning to unfold quickly and he could no longer promise the safety of the Americans. They were armed now and could at least fend for themselves. Russo waved two of his three men out the door then turned once more toward Ramsey. "I will call you shortly." He stepped out, got into an unmarked sedan and drove away.

Four blocks away Anatoly Vecjevic was checking for new messages from Nikki and Vostav. He wished he was the one who had gone with Nikki that morning rather than Vostav. He felt like a simple errand boy going to gather things for his boss. He mused over his involvement with Nikki and how he was no longer the husband of the daughter of one of the richest, most influential people in Russia, but instead, the boyfriend of the sexiest, deadliest woman in Russia.

His mind raced through the decision process that had placed him in the passenger seat of the Ford Expedition on the way to her apartment. It wasn't too late to change his mind. *I could step out of this vehicle and simply walk away from this whole James Bond shit*, he thought.

He looked over at the driver, Stasa, a burly bodyguard type, repatriated for Nikki's growing organization, and wondered if the man would allow him to walk away, questioning whether Nikki had given her bodyguard the order to kill him if he ever decided to run. Could he *choose* to return to his life with Elena now that he knew of Nikki's plans, or at least, some of her plans? He waved off the thought that Nikki would warrant his death in the event of a change of heart. Still, at the back of his mind the thought lingered.

He contemplated if he was being used. What if she was playing him like the many others she had used before, a pawn to move at her whim, a tool? Too many thoughts were swimming around in his head. He closed his eyes for a moment and relished the lack of stimulus as the Expedition rounded the last turn to the apartment. He was too deep in thought to notice Russo's sedan leaving as the expedition pulled through the entrance of the parking lot.

Inside the apartment Ramsey turned his attention to Nikki's computer, sliding three fingers across the track-pad to scroll through the desktop, switching from one workspace to another. Each one displayed information about some person of interest, an electronic dossier with video clips, notes and photos. The last desktop was a collection of American personnel including, Secretary of State, Carlton, now President Carlton. He called over his shoulder to Jackson, "Paul, come look at this."

"That ain't a good sign," Paul said as he walked to where Ramsey stood in front of Nikki's laptop.

"It may just be residual fodder from her internet search, but just the same, we'll get this info back to Langley and let the teams there run it to ground."

Paul scratched at his growing facial hair. He hadn't shaved lately and couldn't stop raking through the stubble. "This chick is getting scary," he said, reaching across the table to the track pad.

He selected the internet browser icon, then selected history from the file drop-down menu. There was some search history, but the private browsing option was selected and the history was limited. Still, there were links that showed a trail of browsing. Mostly about Ratko Mladic, but there was also info about other key people: Slobodan Milosevic, a Dutch General, United Nations officials.

Ramsey was beginning to see the pattern. He turned to Jackson, "Paul, get with the N.S.A. and the F.B.I., give them a WARNO that we are starting to see a lot of the same names being thrown around. All people who were involved with the war in Bosnia. Tell them to stand by for more info from us, but to stay alert."

"You got it." Paul acknowledged. He pulled up his phone to place the call as Alan spun the laptop, displaying the image of Secretary of State Erikson, then a U.N. Ambassador.

"Paul, check it out." Paul Jackson looked at the screen and simply said sarcastically, "Surprise!"

There were maps of Bosnia, Russia, Western Europe, America and South America. Locations marked on the map displayed information about mass graves and excavations, names of the dead, even tags that led to on-line videos about the repatriation of those who either died fighting or were slaughtered during the war.

Ramsey zoomed in on the Russian map with a click, then placed the cursor on a small photo and clicked.

"Gregorov," Paul said as he pointed to the date below the picture and stepped back up to the desk, "Look, that was the day of the meeting."

Ramsey looked up and said, "Or is it the date Gregorov was killed?" He clicked again on the picture causing it to resize, then clicked on the icon next to it. Dr. Metelov's photo, a clipping from some online newsletter populated the desktop. The caption under the photo read "*Dr. Vladimir Metelov receives the Fundamental Physics Prize for his work in the field theory and string theory.*"

Paul Jackson made note of the date. "Same date as on Gregorov's."

Ramsey circled the name under the icon with the cursor after he minimized it. "Notice the name." Instead of Metelov, the name under the icon read *Jovan Kovicevic.*

Ramsey suddenly made a face and reached into his pocket for his phone. He looked at the screen, recognizing the Russian phone number as their hotel suite. He put the phone to his ear. "Hello?"

"Sir, it's me, Rick White. I have some great news. I know where Nikki is!" White was excited, talking fast.

"Whoa, slow down, Rick. I can hardly understand you. Where are you?"

Rick White took a deep breath and exhaled. "I'm at the hotel, waiting for Matthews. He's on his way, but stuck in traffic. Anyway, I was finishing up an app that I was working on and it works! I know where Nikki is, or at least, I know where her phone is. I have it on my phone. Hang on, I'll give you the grid coordinates."

"It's White. He says he knows where Nikki is." Ramsey shrugged his shoulders.

White came back on the receiver. "OK, you have a pen?"

Ramsey motioned to Paul that he needed something to write with and was immediately handed the pen and notepad that Paul carried, a habit developed from his days as a non commissioned officer. Ramsey flipped open the notepad. "Ok, ready to copy."

White relayed the information from the screen of his phone. "55 degrees, 25 minutes North by 37 degrees, 32 minutes East. The map feature isn't working or I could give you the name of the location. Sorry, but I think the configuration of the Google Map link is off somehow, I'll try to reset the parameters in the car when Matthews gets here."

Ramsey had no clue what White was talking about. "Mr. White, you're losing me. Stop. I won't ask how you know, but are you sure that Nikki is at that location?"

White looked at the time. Several minutes had passed since the notification. "Well, she *was* there. I mean, that's where she used her phone last."

Ramsey tried to get some clarification, "So you got her phone back in the tracking app or whatever?"

"No, not the V.O.B.T.S., this is a different program. Kind of hard to explain quickly. It's the new app I've been testing over the last couple days."

Bob Matthews walked in the hotel room door to find White on the phone. "You ready to go? I tried calling you several times."

Rick White glanced at his phone. For each of Bob Matthews' failed phone calls there was a set of coordinates to match, each different as he made his way through the downtown traffic to the hotel. The app was definitely working for tracking the location, the map feature was the only glitch.

He turned his attention back to Ramsey. "Sir, all I can tell you is that she was at that location about eight minutes ago. Until I get the app working one hundred percent, I can't tell you any more. Sorry."

Ramsey thanked his youngest agent. "Ok, thanks, that's great. Let me know when you guys are finished removing the electronics from the inn." With that he hung up, turning his attention back to Nikki's computer.

Paul had already put the grid coordinates into a Google search and, although he didn't read Russian, he could read a map. The town at the coordinates Rick White gave them was named Podolsk.

Paul stood back up, motioning to his work. "Well, there you go."

Ramsey slid the web page off the screen to look at Nikki's map, then selected another icon on the Russian map. The icon didn't have a picture, but instead a star with the label, "*Podolsk 900.*"

Ramsey gave a confirming look at Paul. "Yeah. There you go."

Paul pointed with the cursor. "What about this?" He was circling the number with the cursor. "I guess 900 could be a time. It's definitely not a date" He looked at his watch. "…and if it was nine o'clock today we missed it. It's almost noon." Jackson put his arm down and suddenly looked as if he'd just had an epiphany, "Shit!" he blurted out.

He spun around and called to the remaining R.S.S Agent. "Hey, big Russian dude." The agent didn't respond. Jackson noted that the tall blonde agent looked a lot like the actor Dolph Lungren, who played the Russian boxer, Ivan Drago in Rocky Four. He called again, this time louder. "Yo, Ivan."

The huge Russian agent turned to face a smug Jackson, who was now waving him over, in case he didn't speak English. "That's right, big boy, come on over here." Jackson chided, knowing the big Russian didn't understand what he was saying.

Ramsey wondered where Jackson was going, watching as the R.S.S. agent maneuvered the three meters to the desk in a little more than two steps, ending up directly in front of, and towering over Paul Jackson with a scowl. The Russian agent was easily six foot, four. Paul asked, "Hey Ivan, you speak English?"

The agent glared at Paul Jackson who was staring up at him as he answered in very broken English, "Better at listening than to speak English."

Jackson swallowed, wondering if the huge human knew he was teasing him. "Good enough," Paul said as he placed a hand on the giant's arm and guided him between the two Americans to stand in front of the laptop. Alan took almost two steps aside to allow enough room for the man to move in.

Paul Jackson pointed at the laptop screen, pushing it back some to change the angle for the taller of the three. "This place right here. Podolsk," He tapped the laptop screen at the star, "is that where Russo is going? Is that why he had to leave, to go to that place?"

The Agent stooped to get a closer look at the map. He looked at everything displayed realizing that it correlated with Russo's call and subsequent departure. He stood fully, looking somewhat surprised and grunted, "Da."

Jackson celebrated with a fist pull and a loud, gloating, "Yessss!"

Ramsey, rolled his eyes at Jackson's response to being right while closing the laptop when Agent Villacruze's voice came over his headset. "We got company. A black S.U.V. just pulled into the parking lot."

Anatoly told the driver to wait for him as he opened the door and stepped out of the truck. Stasa grunted his understanding. He was already out of the truck, leaning with his back against it, lighting a cigarette.

Anatoly waved a hand to clear the air as he walked around the front of the vehicle through the wafting smoke and stopped at the apartment door. He pulled his key out and slipped it in the deadbolt.

As the door opened the sunlight moved across the floor and illuminated the figure of Paul Jackson. "Good Morning, Anny." Jackson said to Anatoly sarcastically, startling him to a sudden stop just inside the door.

Anatoly hadn't yet released the door lever as he looked around the room at each of the men staring back at him. There was a brief silence as the command to flee transformed from his thoughts into action. Anatoly turned and lunged back through the door, toward the parked S.U.V.

The bodyguard saw what was happening and quickly drew his weapon, aiming it in the direction of the open door. Marks and Villacruze stood, weapons aimed at the gunman and yelled simultaneously for him to drop his weapon, only to be answered by several shots fired in their direction. The rounds slammed into the brick and wood surrounding the door or whistled past, speeding through the apartment to impact the wall at the far end, narrowly missing Ramsey and the Russian agent.

Marks fired back without hesitation. He fired three shots in quick succession. Two of the nine millimeter rounds passed through the guard's neck, the final round spinning through the bodyguard's forehead just above the eye socket. The bodyguard crumpled to his knees and then fell face first to the asphalt, unmoving.

Anatoly's eyes were wide with fear as he watched the bodyguard's head explode. He changed direction, running as fast as he could away from the S.U.V. and through the corridor that led to the main street, disappearing around the corner.

"I got it," Marks yelled as he bolted after Anatoly, followed closely by Villacruze.

Anatoly never ran so fast. He was in good physical condition, but he was no athlete and quickly could feel the burn in his lungs as he gasped for air with nearly every step. He had no idea what to do other than run. Glancing over his shoulder he could see the two agents closing in. He was no match for their physical agility, but he knew the streets better than they did. He had to lose them in the alleys and backstreets. It was his only chance.

He spun around a corner into an alley that ran behind a row of shops, dodging and weaving between parked delivery trucks and carts. He ran out into the main boulevard and toward the bus depot.

Marks saw Anatoly duck down the alley. He motioned for Vee to move to the front of the market and try to head him off. Vee was a good runner but not as fast as Marks.

The alley opened to a large central market place where there were rows of street venders, carts and temporary structures. The cobblestone open air market was packed with customers enough to keep Anatoly hidden. He slowed some to catch his breath, hiding near a vegetable stand. He looked through the crowd and spotted the person chasing him. He was American. "Shit" Anatoly cursed between gulped breaths.

Anatoly looked around, peering through the crowd for any glimpse of the second one. He didn't get a very good look at that one either, but his dark skin pegged him as Mexican or something. Probably American too, he thought. Dark hair was not unusual in this part of the world, but dark skin was. He purchased a bottle of water, keeping his eyes on Marks who was closing in. The agent hadn't spotted him yet and had migrated to the other side of the street, heading toward the center of the square.

Marks scanned the crowd, but couldn't see through the thick mass of people and feared he had lost his subject. He had to get above the throngs of shoppers that were milling about in every direction. His eyes continuously swept through the crowd, looking through every gap that opened and closed with their movements when his gaze fell on a concrete fountain in the center of the square.

To his right Vee had continued to follow the main road around the square and was heading into the crowd from a cross street when Marks' voice came over his headset. "Hey. You see him anywhere?" Marks asked.

Villacruze looked around, but still saw only the vendors and old women with baskets of bread and fruit. "Nope. Lost him. I got nothin'. Where are you."

Marks took a few seconds to answer, "Right now I'm at the fountain on the middle of the square." Vee looked through the crowd, scanning above the bobbing, moving heads. His search stopped at the figure of a lone soldier on horseback. The sculpture was massive. More than 20 feet tall, depicting the horse rearing up on its muscular rear legs, tail swung to the side. The figure on its back waved an outstretched sword forward, the face of the soldier frozen in the act of bawling out some military command. At the base of the statue was Marks, pulling himself up on an stone outcropping some six feet above the crowd.

Vee wasn't the only one watching Marks' ascent to a higher vantage point. Anatoly was watching from across the sea of people, swearing, as the American clambered up the fountain and onto the large basin.

Marks found his final footing and stood. He scanned the grounds and, within seconds, spotted Anatoly near a covered vegetables stand. "I got him," Marks called to Vee over the head set. "At the far end of the market, opposite where we came in! My twelve o'clock!"

Vee looked in the direction of Mark's pointing, following it to the sign above the stand. He couldn't read the Russian words, but he could plainly see the crates of vegetables displayed side by side on the angled shelving. Next to them he saw the figure of Anatoly. Vee pushed into the crowd, zigzagging around and through groups of people, keeping the sign in sight as he headed toward the stand.

Anatoly could almost feel Marks' glare as he pointed in his direction. Nervously, Anatoly looked through the crowd for the dark haired agent as Marks jumped down from the fountain and started heading his way. He looked left and right, but could not see Villacruze. That's when he spotted the red Metro Transit round the corner and stop to release its passengers, more people heading toward the market's center. He saw two police officers patrolling through the crowd and began yelling in Russian as he pointed to Marks who was on a direct path toward him.

"Help! Police! That man has a gun!"

The officers looked in the direction he was pointing. Marks looked at the officers who were now moving to intercept him, yelling orders that he could not understand, but assumed were orders to stop. He quit moving and stood waiting for the officers as he removed his I.D. in preparation for their questions and was not prepared when they immediately disarmed him, forcing him to the ground.

Villacruze had made it to within a few meters of Anatoly. His weapon was drawn and he was about to confront him when Anatoly started yelling to the Russian police. Vee stopped in his tracks and looked toward Marks just as the Russian officers took him down to the ground. When he looked back to where Anatoly was standing, Anatoly was gone.

Vee scanned the area, but couldn't see Anatoly through the thickening crowd. A light drizzle had begun. Across the market place umbrellas were opening up, spreading out across his field of view and removing any hope of spotting Anatoly in the crowd. Vee looked up at the overcast sky as the drizzle developed into a steady light rain. He moved to Marks' last known location, holstering his weapon to go to the aid of his partner.

Villacruze had suggested to his partner that he learn at least some Russian for the mission and spent the fourteen hour flight listening to Rosetta Stone downloads. Marks laughed at him and spent his time on the plane catching up on movies he wanted to see. Marks wasn't laughing when Vee stepped up to the first of the two officers and introduced himself in a near-perfect Russian greeting. Instead Marks looked up at him in surprise and relief from his handcuffed position kneeling on the wet cobblestone pavement.

In the distance the chime of the door-closing bell could almost be heard over the crowd of shoppers as Anatoly stepped in against the outward flow of passengers exiting the Metro Transit vehicle.

Nikki was going to be furious, Anatoly thought, as he replayed the scene of the confrontation at the apartment over in his mind. He was sure Stasa was dead. He saw again, in slow motion, the guard's head pitch back as the force of the last shot destroyed his face and skull, the cigarette still hanging from his lips as he crumpled to the ground. A scene he was sure would haunt him till his end days.

He cursed at leaving the vehicle behind, but then remembered that it was one of Gregorov's fleet. The Americans would be surprised to find out the S.U.V. belonged to a dead man. The thought made him feel a bit better until he thought about how much more upset Nikki was going to be knowing that both American and Russian agents were in her apartment. Not to mention that Anatoly failed to get the items she requested, especially her laptop. He was screwed either way.

Oh well, he thought, panting, still breathing hard from the chase, this would not be the last of his woman problems. That he knew for sure.

CHAPTER 26

SANITATION CREW

ACROSS town the high pitched metallic sound of wet brakes squealing sharply punctured the mid morning silence as a small work van splashed through the water to a stop in front of the Merinsk Street Cafe. The sound caused Oleg Lenonev, one of two R.S.S. officers sent over by Russo to meet with Ramsey's men at the inn, to get up from the bench he had been sitting on for the last hour.

He yawned and stretched as he got to his feet. Lenonev was tired of this type of duty. He yearned for field work, wanting to be where the action was, not babysitting a crime scene. He was in good shape, physically fit, he thought to himself. Babysitting should be reserved for officers about to retire, the ones with families. It was safe he supposed, but to him safe was just boring. Groggily he stepped outside the yellow cordoning, shaking the accumulated water droplets away and walked toward the work van avoiding stepping in the pools of water collected along the uneven sidewalk.

"It is about time you got here," he said to the passenger in the van, "We were told you were supposed to be here two hours ago."

The driver of the van had already gotten out and walked to the back of the vehicle. Opening one of the rear doors, he leaned around the van to look at the officer.

"We are very sorry. There was some confusion as to which crime scene we were supposed to clean up. There are so many in Moscow." The driver, Gordon Maxwell, said in perfect Russian as he smiled and pulled at the curl on his mustache before continuing, "How bad is it?"

Lenonev tipped his hat back some, "Now, not bad. No bodies. Just blood and brains to clean up. You should have been here yesterday," he shuddered a bit then added, "Disgusting."

A second person got out of the van, stood, shook a cigarette out of a pack from his pocket. As he lit the cigarette he noticed a second R.S.S. officer step through the doorway of the inn.

Maxwell pulled a bucket from the back of the van and held it out, motioning to the officer to take it. "Here, please set this over there for me."

Lenonev didn't want to help. *What did this guy think he was, a janitor?* he thought to himself and was going to say something, but really had nothing else to do at the moment. He gave a scornful look as he held out a hand to take the bucket. Just as he reached out to take the handle, the driver let it drop. Lenonev wasn't fast enough to grab it and was left with an empty outstretched hand and a questioning look on his face.

Before he could complain, Maxwell grabbed Lenonev's arm and yanked him around to the back of the van. In one smooth motion he wrapped his arm around the officers neck, cutting off the blood flow to his brain. Lenonev struggled briefly before slipping into unconsciousness as Maxwell guided his falling body into the back of the open van.

The second officer spun around at the sound of the bucket hitting the ground just in time to see his partner's sudden move out of his peripheral sight. He reached for his pistol, but before he could react Aaron James clubbed the man with a solid pistol whip at the base of the back of his skull knocking him out cold. He dragged the limp officer to the back of the van, folding him in next to the other Russian.

Maxwell secured the hands and feet of the officers with plastic zip ties while his partner gagged them both. He slammed the doors closed and looked around, eying the windows and doors up and down the street for any possible witnesses. It was a quiet morning, he thought as he smoothed his hair and placed a work cap from his pocket onto his head.

"Let's go. Get the ladder. I want to be out of here in twenty minutes or less. Take only what equipment is ours." With that the man pulled the ladder from on top of the van and followed him into the restaurant. The two men split up once inside the building as Maxwell stepped to the bar and pulled at a wire running up its base, hidden among the decorative trim. At the end of the wire was a microphone about the size of a pencil eraser. He coiled the wire and placed it in his pocket, moving on to the next microphone located in the darkest corner of the inn.

"How're you coming with the cameras?" he asked his partner as he stepped over to where the man stood on a ladder disassembling a smoke detector.

"Last one," he stated in a low voice, motioning to the light fixture that was a few feet away. "I had to snip the wire on that one. Not sure how but the leads to the wireless transmitter got tangled with the one the others put in. I'm surprised it hadn't shorted together where the cover crimped it."

Maxwell didn't really care as long as the systems were removed and couldn't be traced. Within minutes Maxwell and James cleared the building of the four electronics they had installed. He pulled his phone out while the second man removed the ladder and walked back toward the van. He dialed the number and waited. The ringing stopped abruptly as Secretary of State Erickson picked up.

"This is Erickson, go ahead."

Maxwell hated the way he answered his phone, acting like he was on a radio. He rolled his eyes as he spoke. "All clear," Maxwell said simply then closed his phone and placed it back in his pocket.

Rick White had his eyes on either his laptop or his smart phone since leaving the hotel, furiously trying to correct the glitches with his app. He was poking at his screen when it chimed a few times indicating another phone call had been picked up. A message popped up on the screen causing a questioning grunt from White. Bob Matthews looked over from his position behind the wheel and asked what was going on.

White explained, "Well, I created an algorithm to track phone calls. It tracks any of the phone numbers I put in. Since we've had so many different theories as to who is involved with whom, I set it up to track calls made anywhere in Europe and plugged in about seven different cell phone numbers from back home. Secretary of State Erickson's is one of them, and guess what? I just got a hit."

He pinched at the screen and pulled up the log on the signal tracker showing the point of origin and the end point of transmission in latitude and longitude. 38.8900 North by 77.0300 West he knew was Washington D.C.. and he was near positive 55.7517North by 37.6178 East was Moscow since he had input the ranges for several cities in Europe. White touched the second set of numbers causing a map with phone numbers to populate on his phone.

"Ha, success! Look at that!," he exclaimed, holding the phone up for Matthews, who really had no idea what he was looking at.

Matthews asked for clarification. "Not all of us are dweebs. You mind explaining what you find so exciting?"

"I just told you, I programmed my application to track any phone calls going to the Secretary of State's cell phone. I put some other folks' numbers in as well, Ramsey's, that Russian cop's, the President..." Again he was stopped by Matthews.

"The President? You can't be bugging the President's phone. Are you insane? Does Ramsey know about this?"

White rolled his eyes, as if explaining the program to Matthews was too difficult. "I didn't 'bug' their phone. Not in the traditional sense anyway." He made the universal sign for quotations to stress the word "bug," then explained.

He sighed. "Look, all the app does is tell me when the programmed number gets a call, what number called, where the call originated and ended, by latitude and longitude. It doesn't listen in, or record anything, other than the position of the caller. I was having problems with the maps, but I think I got it fixed now."

Matthews made the last turn before arriving at their destination. White was back to fiddling with his phone. He thought about what White had just told him. "So...are you going to tell me where the call came from, or what?"

"I'm working on it." Rick white pinched at the map enlarging the detail. He looked around outside the vehicle as if he were trying to get his bearings. He compared the location on the map of the dot representing the cell call made to Erickson against two other dots indicating his and Matthews' cell phone GPS signal. As Matthews pulled against the curb in front of the Merinsk Street Cafe and Inn, and after a couple seconds of bewilderment, White shot a confused look toward Matthews, answering his question.

"According to this, the call came from right here."

Matthews stared at the device and then at White, "That program you made has to be jacked up...Why would it show...?"

White cut him off, "Nope, it's not wrong. Can't be. I've checked it over and over, tested it myself. Whoever called the Secretary of State called from here. Probably from the inn."

Matthews thought about who would be calling the Secretary of State and why. He pulled his sidearm from its holster, pulling back the receiver to place a round in the chamber. He looked at White. "You ever have to draw your weapon before?"

White suddenly realized that the moment had just gone to hell. He answered reluctantly, "They don't issue guns to techies."

"That's probably a good thing," Matthews quipped. "It's best if you stay here."

The look on White's face argued that point, but White knew Matthews was right.

Matthews stepped out of the car into the cold drizzle. He moved cautiously toward the van, wiping the raindrops from the back glass and peering in. He saw two people in the van, dead he suspected. White, was staring from inside the sedan, mouth open, eyes wide, watching his every movement through the intermittent swipe of the wipers as Matthews looked at him, raised a free hand to his ear and mouth, making the sign for a phone receiver, and mouthed the words, "Call Ramsey."

Matthews had stepped out from behind the van when the leading end of a ladder, and then Maxwell's partner, Aaron James, appeared in the door opening. James stopped half in and half out of the doorway at the site of Bob Matthews' raised pistol.

"United States C.I.A. Special Operations Officer! Put the ladder down and get on your knees, hands behind your head," Matthews barked.

The man moved slowly as to keep from startling Matthews. He moved toward the van raising the ladder to set it in place on top of the van. Matthews eyed the man cautiously as he lifted the ladder toward the rooftop rack, but then, suddenly, heaved the aluminum ladder at him.

The ladder crashed against the agent forcing him backward and onto the wet hood of his vehicle and causing him to drop his weapon. Matthews tried to recover, but his attacker jumped on him as soon as he was free of the ladder. He yanked Matthews off the hood and delivered a sharp blow to his throat and a knee to the groin.

Matthews was unable to protect himself as the burly figure grabbed him by his jacket, slamming him into the corner of the van, sending him quickly to his knees. Just as the man reared back to hit Matthews with a roundabout kick, he heard Rick White yell for him to stop and looked up to find the techie standing in the rain next to the car, pointing Matthews' pistol at him.

Maxwell stepped out of the building with his pistol pointed at White. With one more sudden move, Aaron James landed a final blow, sending Matthews down to the curb with a splash.

He was moaning, so he wasn't dead, White thought, as he stood shaking, moving his aim from the man who knocked Matthews out to Maxwell and back, not sure who to cover, surprised when Maxwell spoke and it was in perfect English.

"It's OK, we're American." Maxwell motioned to himself and his partner. Why don't you put that down. I don't want to get shot and I don't want to kill either of you two, but I will if you leave me no other choice." Maxwell was calm as he moved toward White, weapon rock steady.

"Seriously, Mister…," Maxwell paused not knowing the agent's name and expecting him to provide it at that moment. White didn't take the cue. Maxwell looked at the agent with a quizzical look on his face.

Rick White weighed his odds. He knew that if he shot one, he would have to shoot the other, very quickly. He wasn't sure he could manage that. He took a deep breath, wiping the back of his free hand against his cheek to brush the rain away, then said his name as he exhaled, still alternating between the two targets, both of whom where getting closer.

"My name is Rick White, I'm an American too, so don't shoot. Who are you?"

Maxwell ignored White's questioning and in a nearly imperceptible move, reached out, put his hand over and pushed back the upper receiver on White's nine millimeter, released the detent with his thumb and yanked the receiver from the pistol and tossed it down to the wet pavement, rendering it ineffective.

White was astonished. "Ok, that was about the coolest move I ever saw. I know you could theoretically kill me now, because I am totally disarmed, but still, that was pretty awesome, seriously."

Maxwell looked at White curiously, then at the object in his left hand, motioning to it with his eyes and a slight nod. "What have you got there?" He could see the small LCD screen illuminated with a grid and two pulsing markers.

White tried to play it off. "Oh, nothing, a game, you know, a game app."

Maxwell stepped forward, snatching the iPhone from Rick White, who cringed a little, "Dude, don't break that, really I don't make a lot of money working for these guys. Not yet anyway."

Maxwell again looked at the geek quizzically, then at the image on White's phone. He compared the grid's location and street illustration, obviously a Google map image, with his surroundings and a list of grid coordinates, one that he recognized as Washington D.C., and phone numbers, including his and the number he'd just called, Secretary of State Erickson's. "What is this?" he asked again.

White looked like he'd been caught stealing, "It's just a little program that I made. Kind of tracks who's calling who and gives the GPS coordinates. Pretty awesome actually, if I do say so myself. I could tell that whoever made that last call made it from right here somewhere." He smiled a gloating smile. "I'm guessing that was you."

Gordon Maxwell was surprised at White's openness. "You're not a *real* agent are you?"

White shook his head a little. "No, just the computer guy."

With that Maxwell pocketed White's iPhone. White was shocked, "Awe man, serious? What the heck? I thought you were cool." He raised his hands in a gesture of exasperation then slumped his shoulders as if giving up on the world.

Maxwell looked at his partner and motioned for him to get in the van, then turned back to White. "Tell your boss, Ramsey, to leave it alone, let the Russians deal with it."

He turned, moving toward the van, pistol still aimed at Rick White, opening his door. "There's no need for us to be enemies. Tell him that."

"Well, yeah, there is. You took my phone." White said, rather matter-of-factly.

Maxwell smirked at Rick White's geekiness, tossed his pistol onto the seat and dug out his own phone. He popped the back off, pulled the SIM card out and tossed the phone to Rick White.

"Be a good man and pay the bill on that for me." He smiled, tugged at his mustache and slid into the seat, closing the door as the van sped off down the street.

CHAPTER 27

SALT IN THE WOUND

NIKKI rounded the last corner on the way to the bus station. It had been raining for several hours, but in the last twenty minutes the hard rain had become a drizzle. Just enough to need the wipers but not enough to keep the rubber of the wiper blades on her BMW 328i from ratcheting across the glass. She pulled to the curb, stopping at the wet figure of Anatoly who took only a second to get in, out of the constant rain he had been waiting in for more than an hour.

"What happened?" Nikki asked immediately, noting how miserable the man looked.

"They were in the apartment, that's what happened. Americans and the R.S.S.. There were more in the parking lot. I barely got away." Anatoly explained without looking at Nikki. He paused to take a breath and then added solemnly, "They killed Stasa."

Nikki stared at him as she thought about the loss of a third man. Her silence only lasted a second or two. She got back to questioning. "How do you know they are Americans? What did they look like?"

Anatoly looked up, "The ones in the apartment or the ones who chased me?" he asked, a sarcastic edge to his voice.

Nikki countered sharply, "The ones who were in charge."

Anatoly sighed, then answered, "Well, there was a black guy, tall, older looking, and a white guy, tall, wide shoulders, dark hair with a military cut. They spoke English when they told me to stop or they would shoot me. I don't know if they were in charge or the Russians. It was a redhead and Mexican looking guy, both also with short cropped military haircuts, that chased me through town cussing at me and yelling in English for me to stop running or *they* would shoot me. Everybody wanted to shoot me. They were definitely American."

He stopped and glared at Nikki, obviously upset. Suddenly he looked as though he had an epiphany, "Wait a minute, they knew my name," he said incredulously. "How did they know to call me Anny?"

Nikki ignored his last question, looking at the road ahead, thinking back to the mission she had just worked for Gregorov in the U.S.

"Ramsey," Nikki said almost to herself. "Ramsey is the white guy and Jackson is the black guy. They are the ones who stopped the terrorist attack in the U.S."

Anatoly looked surprised, "That's who's trying to kill you?"

Nikki waved a hand at Anatoly, "No, it doesn't make sense. Gregorov helped him. They had some kind of deal." She thought for a moment before continuing. "No, I do not believe Ramsey wants us dead. He wants Gregorov's weapons."

"Yeah, well, I'm sure he wasn't happy about you killing Gregorov and Metelov." Anatoly tried to prove his point. "What about that drone? I'll bet you that drone was American, had to be. They are the only ones who fly that kind of shit and..."

Nikki interrupted him. "No, not Ramsey. He doesn't want us dead because he wants us to lead him to the weapons. He has no choice now that Gregorov is dead."

Anatoly thought that what Nikki said made sense. "Then, who sent the drones. Who fired those missiles?"

"I don't know, but they obviously *don't* want us to get to the weapons." Nikki answered.

He thought for a second then added, "...and there is no doubt that the Americans and the R.S.S. have your laptop, all of the papers, pictures and information you gathered. They saw me there. They know I'm involved now and soon will find out that you were looking in the archives and that I am the one who set it up."

"I have news for you, Anny. They knew you were involved since you picked me up at the airport. That's who drove by in that car you saw, not someone sent by your Elena to spy on you. They have been watching me since I got off that plane and probably before that."

The drizzle had become a downpour and the melodic thump of the windshield wipers suddenly became noticeable as Nikki thought for a moment, then added, "All the more reason for us to get to the weapons first. Find them, find a buyer and sell them."

Anatoly looked at her strangely, "No Nikki, you don't need that money. If you stop now you have Gregorov's and Metelov's money. That is about twelve million dollars combined. Leave the weapons for the Americans to find. Let's get out of this city, out of Russia, go somewhere and just stop all the bullshit. You have enough."

"It's not about the money!" Nikki nearly screamed. "You of all people should know that. I only need the money to find my father and my brother. I have to find them. I have to know who gave the order to kill them. I can't just walk away from the people who did this. It is not right and I am going to make it right."

She paused for a moment. She didn't need anybody to hold her back. If Anatoly didn't want to be a part of her future, a future that would get more chaotic before getting better, then she felt that he could leave at any time. The sooner the better for her to stay on track. She looked through the rain streaked windshield contemplating what she was about to say. She didn't want to lose Anatoly again, but she was driven to move forward with her plan.

"If you want out, then go! Go back to your wife and your quiet life with your little sporty cars and be happy." Nikki threw her arms up in a gesture to punctuate her words and grimaced, not thinking about her injury.

Anatoly saw her cringe and then grab across her chest and under her arm on her right side, then noticed the bandage that was protruding above the edge of the sleeveless shirt Nikki wore.

"What happened?" He asked, trying to look more closely at her bandaged wound.

Nikki brushed away his concern. "It is nothing."

"Let me see," Anatoly insisted. Nikki raised her arm. A bit of blood stained her shirt having soaked through the bandage.

"When did this happen? This morning at your meeting? This is what you meant by a few surprises?" He lifted her shirt exposing the obviously self applied bandage. Anatoly lifted the bandage away to reveal the gunshot centered within a two inch circle of bruised skin. He continued to fold the bandage back to look at the exit wound that was basically the same size and had the same appearance as the entry wound. It would have been so much worse had the bullet struck bone.

"It's a clean shot in and out," Nikki said dismissively.

"You were lucky," he said flatly. "Tomorrow you must see a doctor."

Nikki pulled the bandage back around and smoothed the tape down against her ribs. Pulling her shirt back she explained, "I am not going to the doctor tomorrow. We are leaving tonight for Kiev. Once we locate Gregorov's farm and the cave where the weapons are stored you will inventory everything in the cave while Vostav and I talk to Krstic. He will know where to find Ratko Mladic. Vostav is with the pilot you contacted now, negotiating the terms of our new contract. He will be back in the morning to pick us up. We will leave as soon as the pilot plots the course and gets the plane cleared."

Anatoly simply stared at Nikki for a few seconds before speaking. "Talk? Is that what you call a bullet through the head? Talking? How many more are you going to kill Nikki? How many more until you are satisfied that everyone responsible has paid the price? Eight, ten, fifty? It took an army to murder all of those people. You can't possibly think that you will find every soldier and make them pay."

Nikki turned to face Anatoly, a fierce look of anger contorting her face. She slammed the accelerator to the floor and picked up speed, barreling around a rain slick curve, sliding across the road, barely in control. After a minute she applied the brakes. The BMW's antilock system clicked and chattered, slowing, then stopping the car on the right shoulder of the road.

She unbuckled her seat belt and got out of the car. Anatoly stared in amazement as she walked through the pouring rain, around the front of the car, through the haze of the headlights and steaming radiator and hood, then to his door, yanking it open.

The rain blew into the car as she looked down at him, soaked, hair dripping, hanging straight down and clinging to her cheeks. Nikki spoke loud enough for him to hear over the rain beating against the roof of the car and the constant noise of the wipers.

"There are those who were followers, and those who were leaders. It is the leaders I am interested in." She stepped closer and spoke louder. "I do not need you telling me what is right and what is wrong. Either you are on board with me and you are going to support and help me, or you are not, but you are not going to convince me that the path I have chosen is the wrong one, not now, not ever!"

Nikki stood over him, her right arm raised and outstretched, as if inviting Anatoly to join her outside. "If you do not want to be involved, then, as I told you before, go home!"

Anatoly stepped out of the vehicle into the bludgeoning rain. Nikki backed up some, her chest heaving from the passion of the anger flaring inside her. She thought that this was it. Her relationship with the only man she ever truly loved was going to end here, on the side of the road, in the pouring rain.

Anny stood in front of her for a moment. He grabbed her arms and looked into her eyes. He knew that what was burning in her soul could not be quenched with his words or even salvation from the heavens. He watched the anger and the desire for revenge grow, encompassing all of whom she had become. In mere days his life had taken a drastic turn and he could see no other future than one with the woman standing in front of him. The noise of the rain was extremely loud, and because of it Anatoly had to yell to reply to her.

"I don't have a home anymore!" Anatoly began, "I can't go back. Like it or not, this is my life now." He stretched his arms wide as if to encompass everything around him. He stepped forward and pulled Nikki against him. Her body was warm, a stark contrast to the chill of the pummeling rain.

Nikki embraced him as his lips met hers and he gave her a passionate kiss. For the briefest moment she felt comforted, almost calm. The feeling was inviting, warming.

Anatoly moved back, sliding his arms from around her as she released him back to the rain that fell between them. He brushed the lock of wet hair from in front of her eye, pushing it back over her ear. Even here in the rain, soaked to the skin, she was beautiful to him.

Speaking loudly, he stared into her green eyes and said, "You *are* my life now. I am here to stay."

Chapter 28

Crime Scene

Russo stood staring at the remains of the stained glass front door of Vojislav Princip's mansion as the first body, one of Princip's personal body guards, was whisked away after being analyzed and photographed by the forensics team. The shattered pieces of colored glass and distorted leaded framework was mired in a pool of blood.

He noted that there were more blood droplets leading away from the house and three partial footprints through the blood and down the walkway. He bent down to examine the smaller of the footprints. It appeared to be a woman's boot print Twenty-three centimeters, maybe. The arch was high and the heel was small compared to the other set of prints that were wide with a typical military tread design. There was no doubt that at least two people had left the scene, one man, one woman, and one of them was bleeding.

He stepped through the door opening into the large foyer. He had stopped directly in the path of his lead investigator, Zsolt

Vrebinsek's pointing finger. Zsolt was standing as if pointing a pistol. Russo leaned back a little as if to get out of the finger's path then looked in the direction it was pointing, across the room to a massive blood stain on the wall.

Vrebinsek dropped his stance and pointed to the dead body laying on it's side in the middle of the room. "That guy right there was shot at near point blank range. Looks like maybe he was running, given the distance between where his head was destroyed and where he ended up."

He motioned to where he was standing.. "The guy who shot him was standing right about here."

Russo looked at the body, then back at the blood spattered on the wall, head high. "Ambush?"

"I don't think so. Here's why." He stepped over to the body and lifted the jacket to expose the empty holster strapped to the dead man's chest. "He's got a holster, but no weapon."

He carefully stepped over to where Princip's body was leaning against the wall. "Now over here, next to this guy, there is a pistol, but no owner."

He stood up and pointed at Uri, "That guy had a pistol and a holster, not that it did him much good." He spun in the direction of the door, "The guy we found outside had a pistol and a holster." He turned back, moving toward Princip. "This guy, obviously the master of the house, didn't have a holster, but there is that pistol laying there. I think that pistol belongs to that dead guy." He pointed again at the dead bodyguard in the middle of the room.

Before Russo could say anything, the investigator had moved back to Princip's body, which sat in a slumped position against the wall. "This guy right here, I'll call him One-Eye. Take a look at his face. He appears to have been roughed up before he was killed."

He stood up and looked back toward the door, again pointing. "I think the guy out there, the one we just carted off, shot this guy." He pointed at Princip, "and, I think this guy," he pointed at Uri's body, "was shot by whoever was standing here." He planted his feet at a spot between all three of the other bodies and turned to face Uri's position and the blood spatter on the wall. "Two people. One here and one over there by the door."

Russo, looked around and nodded. "That would explain the two sets of footprints outside."

"And it explains the blood down the walkway." Zsolt was excited about the investigation, he felt that he had it pegged and it showed on his face.

"Here's what I think happened. Mr. one-eye was standing about right here, he had just finished off a shot of whiskey when for some reason, this guy, who, I'll call, Baldy, pulled out his pistol, which is still in his hand by the way, to shoot One-Eye, over there.

Zsolt pointed in the direction of Princip. "But then, for some reason, the person standing here, notably, one of the two people who are not dead in this room, shot Baldy and did it at extremely close range. And, I think whoever shot Baldy then came under fire by someone on that side of the room, maybe by the dead guy we hauled away."

Zsolt moved to the wall, pointing above Princip. "They were a moving target, see here?" he pointed at the blood stains caused by the exit of the bullets that passed through Princip's body, "BAM! Misses whoever is moving across this way, but shoots One-Eye, then BAM! Shoots again, misses again, but One-Eye gets a second round. Then, one more shot, BAM! That one nails him. It ends up here."

Zsolt pulled his pen and pointed to a hole in the wall, a slight trace of blood surrounding it.

"This is the bullet that wounded one of the two who are missing. It's there all by itself and there is blood to match. Whoever shot that guy," He pointed at Princip laying against the wall, "was trying to shoot someone else, and it looks like they got whoever they were aiming for. It may not be the only bullet that hit them. They may have left with more, I don't know, but we dig that out of there, test for DNA, and, I would bet, you will have the one that got away, or at least, one of the ones who got away."

Russo stood up fully and looked around the room, nodding his head in agreement. Everything that his inspector said made sense. "Good job, very good analysis. Get that bullet out of there, like you said, also pull prints on that weapon. I would add to your theory that whoever did all of this," he motioned at the carnage around the room, "left their fingerprints on that pistol." He pointed at the lone weapon laying on the floor closest to Princip. "I'm sure you will find more than one set, as it was not their weapon. If it was they wouldn't have left it behind, wouldn't you agree?" Zsolt nodded in agreement.

Russo continued. "Let's find out who all these people are. I want an update when anything at all becomes solid." He patted Zsolt on the back, "nice work."

He looked around once more then stepped outside, avoiding the glass, blood and bullet casings. He knew who'd committed this crime, or at least had a strong suspicion. He pulled his phone up as he moved away from the front of the mansion, standing under the eve of the porch roof trying to avoid the sudden light rain and thought about the rain washing some of the evidence away. After several rings the phone went to voicemail. He scrolled to the secondary number and dialed.

Across town the phone on the seat of the small work truck sounded loud enough to be heard outside the truck where two men were unloading two unconscious police officers. Maxwell sprinted to the cab of the truck and answered the phone, noting it was the Russian detective. "Good afternoon, Detective. I was just about to give you a call to let you know that you can come pick up your men. We are leaving them in good health, albeit with a headache or two. They are resting at the truck stop on the outer ring road and highway 720, but it is beginning to rain here so you might hurry.

They'll be out for another hour probably." Maxwell took the opportunity to light up a cigarette.

Russo didn't like Maxwell. "They better not be injured in any way..." he began.

"Other than their pride they will be fine. Now, why did you call me?" Maxwell asked.

"The Americans are getting suspicious. I can't keep covering your tracks. This Ramsey is not stupid. He has resources that are far reaching and has much information. They have been at Sidorova's house."

"I told you to keep them out of there until I got there first. I pay you a lot of rubles to do what I ask."

Russo was agitated with Maxwell. "I could not keep them from going. They are still authorized. It is still their investigation, at least for a couple more days. I've done everything I could to keep them from getting too close. I nearly had them on the plane until you sent that drone up. If there is anyone to blame that they are still here, it is you."

He took a deep breath before continuing. "Now I must go, I got a call twenty minutes ago from one of my men that they are back at the hotel. I have to go there now to pick him up," Russo explained.

Maxwell took a deep drag and exhaled. "I met two of Ramsey's men back at the inn. We were there at the same time and ...bumped into each other. I sent them back with a message for Ramsey to pack it up."

Russo laughed. "Ramsey will not just walk away. He is determined to find Sidorova, and the weapons. You should consider finding a new location for the weapons. He *will* find them. Our government will have no choice but to take control of them if that happens. There goes your livelihood."

Russo had no love for Maxwell. He wished he had never gotten involved with him. His career was moving forward, but he just knew that Maxwell, the man who helped him move up the ladder of success, would also be the reason he came tumbling down.

"You're kidding right? It would take weeks to move all that shit. You're talking about warehouse amounts of weapons, not a couple crates of grenades." He pulled hard on his smoke then exhaled forcefully, thinking about the consequences of an attempt to relocate the older stocks of artillery shells and tank rounds. "Some of it can't be moved. Too dangerous. Some of that crap is sixty years old. We try to move that shit and the whole hillside will disappear. I don't even let the forklifts get close to that shit. It hasn't moved since Gregorov put it there."

He took one last drag and tossed the cigarette out the lowered window. "No, it's time to get Ramsey and his men off Sidorova's tail. Before they find what they are looking for and end *both* our careers."

CHAPTER 29

HEADACHE

SKYPOINT SHEREMETEVO HOTEL, MOSCOW

"ARE you sure he said Ramsey?" Alan Ramsey asked Rick White.

Jackson jumped in before White could say anything. "I'm telling you, there's something going on that we aren't fully aware of. How is it that some Russian mafia guy knows who we are?"

White looked at Jackson. "I told you, this guy wasn't Russian. The other guy maybe, he didn't say much. But the guy with the mustache was American, I'm pretty sure. And, sorry, but he didn't mention you, only Mr. Ramsey. He said for Ramsey to leave it alone, not Jackson and Ramsey." White smiled knowing that Jackson liked the fame surrounding his last mission, or as Jackson liked to tell it, his act of saving the world.

Jackson frowned, "Whatever. How would he know who *any* of us are?"

"No, the question is how did they know that we were set up at the inn? They bugged our bugs. They were watching what was going down at the meeting. I found the reason for the crossed up video signal at the camera in the vent. They cut the wires to remove their bug. Not sure what they did, but somehow, I think, they installed wireless transmitters from our equipment. I'm going to guess that they were parked outside monitoring. It's pretty obvious by the fact that he was in direct contact with the Secretary of State. He called him. I saw it and so did Matthews."

Matthews grunted in agreement from the couch where he was lying, resting after his fight with Maxwell's partner.

Ramsey turned back to where White was setting up his new phone. "I guess we'll know for sure once you get the app back on line."

White sighed. "It won't have the save data. I won't be able to show you who called who. It doesn't save anything. It's not that kind of program. I don't get why you guys are questioning the number. I programmed Erickson's number in the phone. It was his number that popped up on the screen, simple as that. It's obvious that's why the guy took my phone. He recognized the number."

Ramsey looked at Paul, "I called Gabe Anderson as soon as we got the meeting time and place. He must have reported to Patterson who reported it to Erickson."

He turned to Rick White. "Rick, I want you to get CHERI into Erickson's system. Get with Darin Martin at Langley and get him set up. He'll do the legwork from his end."

Rick White was about to acknowledge Ramsey's request, when the program sent a push message to his replacement phone. He had just picked up another call from Maxwell. Everyone in the room heard the chime and looked toward White. "Oh Shit! How about that? Am I good or what? It's that guy again. Same number that Erickson called. Look."

Ramsey and Jackson looked at the screen. Two phone numbers were displayed along with their locations on the map. Ramsey recognized one of the numbers. "That's Russo's number!"

He stepped over to the laptop and punched in the coordinates of the number he recognized into the on line map program. The map filled the screen populating the surface with buildings and streets, a red pin marking the phone's location. Ramsey yelled to Jackson, "Call Vee, give him the other grid numbers. Tell him to track the location, see what he can find out. Do it now before our company arrives."

Jackson was already calling, but looked confused as Alan Ramsey sprinted to the window. He pulled the curtain aside and looked the 15 stories down to the street where he saw an R.S.S. quick response vehicle and Russo's sedan, lights flashing, parked in front of the hotel. A group of R.S.S. agents were gathered on the street preparing to enter the building. He recognized Russo by his leather jacket and nearly bald head. "The R.S.S. is heading up here. Russo is with them."

Jackson suddenly understood the urgency. The American that had confronted White and Matthews was in contact with Russo. "Damned Russians!" he said out loud as he dialed. *Come on, pick up,* he thought impatiently as he waited for Vee to answer.

"Vee. What's up Jackson?"

"Shut up and listen!" Jackson barked, then relayed the coordinates. "We got some shit going down here, can't explain now. Go to that coordinates I just sent you and take a look around. Be careful, not sure what your going to find. Send me a text when you get there."

Vee read the coordinates back and said simply, "Roger."

Jackson walked over to where Ramsey was standing near the window. Ramsey let the curtain fall back in place and said, "They're in the hotel. Probably on their way up to see us. My guess is Russo's been ordered to shut down our operation."

Jackson looked at Ramsey, "What exactly do you mean, shut down?"

"Well if I had to guess, Russo is going to disarm us, escort us to the airport and make sure we get on a plane." He got Rick

White's attention. "Rick, take the laptop and go in the other room. Get word to Darin Martin back home about what's going on here. Get him set up to start the CHERI search. We are more than likely not going to be able to do it ourselves. Also send him all the information that you transferred from Nikki's computer."

White looked confused as he gathered the power supply and Dell laptop from the table. "What's going on?"

"Just go," Ramsey barked, "Before we lose the opportunity. We'll keep them busy as long as we can while you get Martin set up."

With that White started toward one of the bedrooms. He stopped short at the counter where two magazines and a pistol sat, supposedly for him. He gathered the weapon and rounds and added it to his collection, noting that Jackson was watching. He called to Jackson. "If you get a moment, come show me how to load this thing."

CHAPTER 30

MOVING TARGET

VEE pulled the GPS off the windshield mount and plugged in the coordinates, barking orders to Marks. "Follow these directions!" he nearly yelled as he hit go and the voice of the Garmin directed them to the destination. They were less than five miles from the location on the map. The problem was that Vee didn't know what or who was at the location.

"Where we going?" Marks asked as he sped along the first street highlighted on the map.

"I got no clue." Vee replied, "All I know is it sounded like some kind of shit was happening."

"What kind of shit?" Marks asked.

Vee raised his voice. "Like I'm supposed to know? Just drive!"

Marks They drove for about ten minutes. White pulled down a quiet street, rows of grey steel buildings and concrete warehouses lined both sides of the street. He slowed to a stop. "We're here,…wherever here is."

They looked around at the business district's warehouses and storefronts. Parked under a streetlamp, in front of one of the steel structures, Vee spotted a grey work van with ladders mounted on roof racks. He hit Marks in the arm. "What color did White say was the truck at the inn?" he pointed at the work van.

"Pretty sure he said Grey." Marks pulled his pistol from its holster. "Let's go check it out."

Vee was more cautious. "No, let's not, numb-nuts. Jackson said to let him know when we got here." He pulled his phone up and texted Jackson's number, typing in a simple message, *we're on site*. His phone buzzed, acknowledging the message was sent.

CHAPTER 31

AMBUSH

MAXWELL peered at the carefully chosen equipment laid out on the floor. He pulled open the canvas bags and began placing the weapons in the bag. Erickson had sent him the signal that he was tired of the problems, basically telling Maxwell to solve the meddling from Ramsey any way he could.

Maxwell knew what that meant and hated the idea that he would have to kill his fellow countrymen, but then again, he was far removed from his American citizenship and, in reality, was as much a foreigner in the U.S. as Ramsey and his team were foreigners here.

His choice of weaponry was based on what the R.S.S. used. Nothing more. He would make it look like Ramsey and his men had resisted arrest and the R.S.S. had no choice but to use deadly force. It was unfortunate for Russo that he would get the blame and doubly so that his citation for gallantry and dedication to duty would be awarded posthumously. Maxwell reminded himself that it was business, nothing more. His conscience would not keep him awake tonight.

An unfamiliar chime sounded. Then sounded a second time. Maxwell's attention was drawn to Rick White's phone. He noticed that the screen was illuminated. He walked over and picked up the phone. The same app that he had seen at the inn was open, a notification with the words *signal acquired* was centered on the screen.

Maxwell selected the *view group message* option and the screen changed from the push notification to the map. A pin marked a location on the map and the words *we're on site* was displayed. He looked closely, zooming in on the location, expanding the street name, *Vitchy*.

Maxwell called to his partner and motioned for him to move. He grabbed one of the assault rifles from the floor. He stopped at the edge of a large multi-paned window and rubbed away the grime. A black BMW had slowed to a stop at the work van parked directly in front of the steel door. The light from the sun that was now moving toward the horizon shone on Villacruze's face, illuminating it for Maxwell, who thought how convenient it was that they had come to him.

"Pull up over here," Vee directed Marks with a pointing finger to a spot along the curb in front of the truck. He looked at his phone, but there was still no reply from Jackson.

"Now what?" Marks asked.

Vee looked at the surrounding area. He wanted to go check out the van, but Jackson told him to let him know when he got there. He glanced one more time at his phone. Nothing. He turned to Marks and said simply. "Let's go check things out, but be careful. Jackson seemed freaked out when he called." With that, both men stepped from the BMW, weapons holstered, but hands at the ready just in case. As they neared the van Marks drew his pistol and held it down to his side. Upon seeing his move, Vee did the same. They each walked to opposite sides of the van looking in the front windows and checking the doors, finally rounding the back to meet at the double doors of the cargo area.

Vee reached for the handle. Marks looked him in the eye and said, "Ten bucks says it's locked."

Villacruze gave him a strange look as he attempted, but failed to turn the handle. "I ain't paying you shit," he said to his smiling partner as the sudden sound of rifle fire erupted behind Marks. Two of the rounds struck the van as several others drilled into Marks' back, puncturing his right lung, ripping through his heart and exploding from his chest. Blood sprayed against the rear van door as Marks slumped to the ground behind the van.

Villacruze immediately dove for cover. He could hear Marks moaning and gurgling and moved closer to the corner of the van to try to help his partner, only to see Marks fall fully to the ground, his arm outstretched above his head, weapon still in his hand. Villacruze yelled for him to hang on. "Don't die on me! You hear me? Don't do it!"

Marks could hear his partner yelling at him. He was feeling no pain and knew that was probably not good. His breathing was becoming more and more shallow and with each breath he heard the rasping sound of blood being sucked into his lungs. Between gasps and even over Vee's voice he could hear his own heart beating. Like his lungs, his heart just didn't sound right. Thump, pause, thump, instead of the normal thump-thump, thump-thump, that he had heard all his life.

Thump...pause...thump…pause...thump...pause.

Marks recognized that he was dying, the odd heartbeat getting slower and growing more faint. He looked at Vee who was hunched down, back against the van, yelling at him, telling him it was going to be ok, ordering him to stay alive, but today he would not be able to do what his partner asked of him. It was the first time in his life that he could remember not following Vee's orders as he lost consciousness.

Vee saw that Marks was no longer moving, his eyes fixed in a lifeless stare. Blood pooled under his body, wicking a red stain on his clothing. Vee shut his eyes for a second in an attempt to shake the image from his mind and tried to think about what was going on around him. He thought about how much time had passed and realized it'd been only a few seconds. He got his breathing under control and assessed his situation, taking a chance to peer around the corner of the back of the van where the shots had been fired.

The late afternoon sun cast glaring white light across the windows and he thought he saw movement behind the glass, possibly two people, but definitely one guy with a moustache. He ducked back behind the safety of the truck, wishing he had his headset radio with him so he could call back to the others his current situation. Instead he pulled his phone up and selected the last number called, hoping that this time Jackson would answer.

CHAPTER 32

DETAINED

SKYPOINT SHEREMETEVO HOTEL, MOSCOW

RAMSEY waited by the door for Russo and his men to reach the room. Matthews was on his feet covering the opposite side of the door, his weapon in ready position, lowered, but locked and loaded. He was ready for whatever was going to happen.

Jackson stepped over to Ramsey. "What do you think, really? I don't have a good feeling about all that hardware coming up the steps. If Russo wanted us to stand down he would have just come here with the usual suspects."

Paul Jackson looked over at Matthews, then at the tall Russian and could see that the man was tense. Although he hadn't drawn his weapon his eyes were locked on Matthews. "Hey, Ivan." Jackson called out.

The Russian was startled. Jackson held out a hand, "Steady there, big man. Let's all just keep calm." Jackson turned to Matthews. "Matthews, you're making Ivan nervous. You might want to relax some." Suddenly Jackson felt his phone vibrate in his pocket and reached in, pulling it out halfway, noticed it was Vee.

He pressed the talk button and said, "Yeah, Vee. Go ahead." He didn't expect the frantic words that followed.

"Marks is down! We're on site at a warehouse. Marks is dead! We were ambushed!"

Jackson's eyes went wide as he relayed the message, getting the everyone in the room's attention. Jackson yelled into the phone, "Who ambushed you? Vee, who…"

Vee was still giving his report, obviously not listening to Jackson, but to what was going on around him. "I'm out in the open. I got a pistol, sounds like they got AKs. We're at the coordinates you sent me. Gotta go." With that the phone went dead.

"Damn it! Marks is down. Vee's in trouble! We gotta go! Screw this shit!" He walked forward and yanked the door open only to be met by Russo and his men. He immediately pulled his pistol and stuck it in the Russian police officer's face, while pushing him backward across the hallway and against the opposite wall. The sound of additional weapons being pulled tight in their slings and the clicking off of the safeties answered his actions.

Alan Ramsey stepped between two of the AK-47s and the officers ready to use them. "Whoa! Whoa! Paul, what are you doing? Ramsey motioned with his hands for everybody to lower their weapons. "Everybody, calm down!"

Paul Jackson was breathing hard as he spoke to Russo. "Who you got ambushing our people?" The question was ambiguous. Russo had no idea what the American was asking and grunted, "I don't understand what you are talking about."

Jackson leaned in with the pistol, and nearly spit as he yelled at Russo. "One of our men is dead. You were in contact with someone at that warehouse. Who did you send after our guys?"

Suddenly, the tall Russian rushed in. He grabbed Jackson in a choke hold with one arm and pulled his hand backward into an awkward position, forcing it open to release the pistol to his control. Ivan pulled the pistol out of Jackson's hand and shoved him out of the way and against the wall next to Ramsey. Within seconds Jackson was covered by Russo's three man tactical squad.

Russo stood away from the wall, straightening his jacket. "How does it feel to be at the end of a gun barrel, Mr. Jackson?" He asked as Ivan handed him Jackson's pistol. "Now everybody, please, back in the hotel room."

Jackson got to his feet, scowling at the big Russian, who was scowling in return. "Way to go, Ivan," he mumbled as they trudged through the doorway.

—

Kenneth Wash

CHAPTER 33

NEAR DEATH EXPERIENCE

VEE had to move. He reached over and grabbed Marks' pistol and sprung to his feet firing several rounds in the direction the enemy fire had come from, then sprinted back toward the BMW. He took only two steps and realized that Marks still had the keys.

Maxwell had barely gotten out of view when the bullets from Villacruze's offense rocketed through the window shattering several panes of glass. He saw the agent disappear behind the van. "He's heading to his car. Move! Cut him off! Don't let him get away!"

Aaron James threw himself through the door and raced to where the BMW was parked. He held the AK-47 at the ready and looked in the vehicle, but nobody was in the car. He scanned the area as he stepped around the front of the truck cautiously, expecting one of the two agents to suddenly jump from the other side of the car.

Villacruze held one of the pistols out, again facing the front of the warehouse, pistol raised waiting for the slightest movement from behind the shattered glass. Without looking he placed his phone and Marks' pistol on the bumper of the work van and began searching Marks for the keys, finding them in his right front pants pocket, luckily the pocket that was accessible with Marks lying on his left side.

With the car key in hand he retrieved the second pistol and stood, back against the van, both pistols facing opposite directions out to his side, and cautiously, slowly, moved back toward the Beemer.

Maxwell's partner suddenly appeared around the front of the truck and fired. The first round slammed into Villacruze's upper arm near his right shoulder, ripping through muscle tissue, tendon, and slamming into bone causing sudden, excruciating pain. Villacruze immediately spun his left arm forward and fired on the gunman, his rounds finding their mark center mass, driving James backward and to the ground next to the BMW.

Aaron James writhed in pain from the rounds embedded in his chest and stomach. He struggled up off his back, turning onto his side trying to get in a position to return fire.

Villacruze didn't hesitate, firing another round from Mark's borrowed pistol.

The last thing Aaron James saw was the flash from the round that ended his life and a glimpse of the ejected shell casing arcing upward from the pistol as the round sped toward its destination and slammed into his face, just below his left eye..

The gunman fell limp as Vee dropped the pistol and clutched his right shoulder in pain. He lunged over the dead body to the driver's door of the BMW, placed the key in the ignition, fired up the engine and painfully pulled the gear selector out of park and into drive.

Villacruze looked up to see a dark haired, mustached man running toward him, weapon raised.

Vee quickly assessed his situation, glancing in the rear view mirror at Marks' body, then at dead man on the ground outside the car door, then back at Maxwell, now standing just to the front left of the Beemer. He floored the accelerator, causing the BMW to move sideways, then jump forward as the spinning, smoking right rear tire gained traction with the asphalt. For the briefest of seconds he thought about the pistol in his right hand and whether he could even lift it, let alone pull the trigger as he yanked the wheel to the left and the Beemer responded, spinning the car in the roadway in a cloud of burning rubber.

Vee raised his pistol and squeezed the trigger, the action of the pistol sending painful shockwaves through his body as several rounds crashed through the right front passenger door glass and screamed within inches of their target.

Maxwell had jumped back to evade the swinging rear end of the BMW. He stumbled backward then steadied himself, firing the AK at the fleeing agent. The seven point six two, high velocity rounds drilled through steel and shattered the rear and left side glass as they zipped past Villacruze and through the front windshield or slammed into the on board GPS LCD screen, narrowly missing him.

Villacruze pushed the Beemer for all it was worth. He could barely control the car, fishtailing side to side as he painfully spun the steering wheel back and forth. The last Maxwell saw of the BMW was as it slid around the corner and disappeared from view.

Time to finish this, Maxwell thought as he dragged the two bodies out of view and into the warehouse. He threw the AK in with the rest of the weapons and then loaded the oversized tactical bag into the passenger side seat of the work truck. He pulled away from the curb and sped toward Russo's location.

CHAPTER 34

PROBE

SKYPOINT SHEREMETEVO HOTEL, MOSCOW

RICK White heard some of what was going on outside the bedroom door. He had to hurry before he was discovered. Most of the data from Nikki's computer, saved on his government laptop, had been successfully transferred to Martin's computer at Langley. All that was left was to set up Darin Martin's computer using a remote interface to get CHERI up and running. White pushed his glasses another half inch up the bridge of his nose and leaned back.

"There, you should have full access to all three CHERI databases and the senior level backup drives. I don't have much time to go through the whole thing so I'm going to help get it started as I go," he said, speaking quietly to Darin Martin.

Martin asked, "What's going on there? Are you guys in trouble?"

White replied, "I don't know for sure. Ramsey thinks the Russians are closing us down. They're already here so pay attention." White moved the cursor on Martin's screen. He had already accessed the system.

"Here's how I set this up," he said as he scrolled through the network list and picked an icon that represented the State Department's system. The icon opened up to a mapped representation of the connected drives within the State department building.

"To do a manual specific search look for files that have an asterisk for personal historical information. Those tags indicate files that were collected from emails, scanned documents and faxes for any one person in the system. The archives go back to the eighties. The further back the less asterisks. Anything in the eighties has one, nineties, two, up to two thousand ten, three..."

Martin stopped him, staring at the screen. "Ok I got it. I think I'm good to go."

White continued, "CHERI is developed to take advantage of an automated system-wide, linked, algorithmic search engine. Once you get it started it's automatic."

"Rick, you need to know something about me. I'm kind of a dinosaur when it comes to modern technology. I have an iPad mini and a laptop. I can use Word and email, and I can Skype. I have no idea what you're talking about," Martin confessed.

White sighed and looked at the door. He didn't have time to give the GEEK 101 class to Martin, not now. "Ok, surely you have searched using Google or Bing or something like that. This is the same thing. The difference is that it will *keep* digging through archives at every level by itself. Once it gets a match, it will set another search parameter based on the match. I call it 'snowballing'. It just keeps on gathering more and more info and gleans that info for the search criteria that is entered in the original search. In the case of your search, I set the parameters to search email, notes, even chat messaging for whatever key words you input. The only thing it won't allow you access to is medical files. Those are restricted in accordance with H.I.P.A.A. regulations. Don't want to be breaking any laws. Other than that, it's wide open."

Martin's comfort level plummeted. "Ok, how is that not eavesdropping?"

White sighed again as if teaching Martin was exasperating him, "Because the PATRIOT act says it's not in instances of national security. Internal or external, doesn't matter, everybody is accessible for the most part." He paused for a moment then said, "Welcome to the age of transparency."

Martin rolled his eyes, unseen by White, "Somehow, I don't think that's what the administration meant." He poised his hands over the keyboard. "Ok, I got it, I think. Just type what I want in the search window and hit go?"

"So easy even a dinosaur can do it." White said, smiling. White couldn't help himself and continued to show Martin how the system worked.

"Ok, watch, I'm going to go through the first steps and get a search started for you." He manipulated the mouse to place a check mark in each of the database icons that represented the State Department, the White House, C.I.A., F.B.I, and Homeland Defense. "Once you make your selection go to the top and type a word from the list Ramsey provided, into the search box." He typed in JAMES DONALD ERICKSON.

The sounds of Jackson yelling at someone and noise of a scuffle in the other room told White that his time was running out. He cussed and turned back to what he was doing and started speaking faster. "Now, watch what happens when I select 'search'."

Martin watched the search bar with the entry as it moved into a cue that listed the search time, which data base the search was currently perusing, the amount of data searched in kilobytes and the amount of matching data in kilobytes. The resulting information was stored as an alias in list form in a search folder.

A new search bar populated the center of his screen. He typed in the next search entry, JAMES LINCOLN CARLTON, then repeated the process for DMITRI GREGOROV and NIKKI SIDOROVA.

Martin watched as the last entry settled into the cue. Already the search bars indicating the percentage-searched data were filling up, a blue bar moving from left to right. "So when it gets to the end of the bar that means it has searched all the applicable sources?" he asked.

White replied. Once the bar is full it will place a tag for the database it finished searching, then will automatically move to the next. In this case, State department first, then White house, then…"

Martin stopped him again. "Got it," he said and wondered if the system could ever actually run out of things to search, or if the program would actually be overwhelmed and stop churning at some point. He dwelt on that thought when a musical chime sounded. He noticed the word *"Match"* in the search folder for both the President and Secretary of State.

White's eyes lit up, "There, see that. They have data that is shared." He listened for any more activity outside his door. It was quiet. He wondered what that meant as a third chime sounded then a fourth. *"Match"* was again displayed for three of the four entries.

"Shit," White said as curiosity got the best of him. He needed to log out before he was discovered, but he wanted to see what was being tagged.

"Ok, now watch this part." As Martin took note, he moved the cursor to the search bar titled, *James Donald Erickson.* "At any time you can double click on the blue progress bar. It will open the related search results folder. Look for the word *"match."* It will be highlighted. If you see it you know that that information is shared by more than one of your entries."

He opened the *Erickson* search folder. The list of documents pertaining to Jim Erickson scrolled off the screen. Rick White scrolled down to a highlighted entry, noticing two others close by. He clicked on the word *"Match"* on the first highlighted entry.

A small window opened up showing a single word and the instances that it had been found during the search. There were easily fifteen references, each with asterisks indicating recent activity. Some with only two but others with six or seven. He clicked on one of the seven asterisked entries. It was contact information for someone named Maxwell. White recognized the phone number. "No way!" he blurted out.

Darin Martin saw his sudden change of expression. "What? What did you find?" He saw the name highlighted. "What's Maxwell?"

White was looking at his phone, pulling up his tracking application. He corrected Martin's phrasing of his question, "Not what, who," he said, then cussed again as he matched the phone number on the contact info on Martin's computer with the entry on his GPS locator grid on the tracking application. "Hell yeah, another match!" he nearly yelled wagging the phone in front of the built in camera on his government laptop for Darin Martin to see. White continued to gloat about the information, "I cant believe it. I know who he is!" he exclaimed excitedly.

Without explaining further he moved back to the main window and selected the *James Lincoln Carlton* folder and found the same name about as many times, the number steadily growing. He opened *Gregorov*, the third folder indicating a match. Again the single name was highlighted and indicated by the word *match*.

"Shit. I can't believe it!"

Martin was lost. "What? Tell me! What's going on?" he asked.

White opened another "match" in *Erikson's* and *Gregorov's* search results folder and saw the name again. "Gordon Maxwell! Gordon Maxwell, that's what's up! Holy shit!"

Darin Martin still didn't understand. "I don't get what…"

Rick White heard loud talking and people moving around loudly on the other side of his door. He grabbed both magazines and the pistol and placed them in his laptop backpack, then made a couple key commands. The screen flashed on his and Martin's computer as he restored control of the desktop back to Darin Martin. Martin could hear someone banging on Whites door.

"Sorry to keep you hanging. Gotta go." And with that Rick White's picture disappeared from Darin Martin's desktop.

Martin stared at the screen in front of him. "What the heck..?" he said out loud, sighing as he began inputting the rest of the names into the search windows. He would just have to wait to find out who Gordon Maxwell was.

Chapter 35

Getting Your Money's Worth
Domodevo Airport, Moscow

MAXWELL had just driven away from the warehouse after dragging both of the dead bodies inside when his phone rang. He struggled to dig the phone out of his pocket noting the number and recognizing it as one of his many informants.

"Hello Kyle, it's been a while since I heard from you." Kyle London was another American that worked for Maxwell. He was an Aviation Safety Inspector for Airworthiness, Avionics and Maintenance Safety at the Domodevo International Airport in Moscow.

A nasally voice returned the greeting. "What's up, Gordon? I don't have much time, but I thought you might like to know that I just got the order for a flight safety check on that Learjet 25 of Gregorov's."

Maxwell knew that the plane wasn't normally kept at Domodevo and was curious about when it came in. "Do you have access to the last flight record? When did it arrive and what's the destination?"

Kyle London answered, "It's interesting you should ask. It came in day before yesterday, really late. The pilot didn't file a flight plan either. Just came in unannounced out of Kiev Local. The guy's got balls is all I can say. With everything as tense as it is on that border, it's a wonder it didn't get blown out of the sky by the Russians or N.A.T.O. They've got the airspace all sliced up into different no fly zones down there. If you ain't legit, they don't give a shit. They'll drop you. The guy had balls, that's for sure."

Kyle London always gave Maxwell his money's worth. Maxwell kept him on payroll to monitor the coming and going of Gregorov's plane as well as others. "Where's it headed, and when?" Maxwell asked.

"Looks like it's heading straight back, flight plan says six this evening, but here's the interesting thing. They changed out pilots." London looked at his info. "Used to be a guy named Gerdenko, Mikhail Gerdenko. They just turned in all the documentation for the new guy. His name is Arkady Dernov, used to be a fighter pilot. Retired from the soviet Air Force. This guy has flown everything from Ilyushin II Tankers to MIG-29's. Good pilot to have for flying in and out of the Ukraine at the moment."

"Is there any way to keep them from leaving till I get there. Might save me some flight time and fuel cost if I can meet with the owner there." Maxwell asked.

Kyle London worked as the American safety liaison for Domodevo. He didn't have any real authority, more reporting and inspections than anything else, but sometimes he could convince the Russians to ground aircraft, depending on the safety concern.

"Let me see what I can do." He looked at the information on the screen in front of him, "That's a Canadian Built Bombardier Learjet 25. Depending on the manufacturer's date and the maintenance records, I might be able to do something. Let me see what I've got to work with. I won't promise anything just yet, not unless you are willing to throw some cash this way. Money always seems to make the Russians more safety conscious."

Maxwell didn't mind paying as long as he got what he paid for. "Ok, but lowball them first. Just see what you can do to keep that plane from taking off."

The American inspector reaffirmed his abilities. "Don't worry. I'll find something that will stick them to the tarmac like gum on a shoe." He heard the phone click as Maxwell hung up, then reached for his bible, The International Flight Safety Regulations and flipped it open. Given the thickness of the book, a testament of the thorough reporting of the I.F.S., he should be able to find something that he could use to hold the plane until Gordon Maxwell could arrive.

CHAPTER 36

-

ALL HELL

SKYPOINT SHEREMETEVO HOTEL, MOSCOW

TWO of Russo's men moved methodically through Ramsey's office/hotel suite as the other stood by, covering Ramsey and Jackson. Russo, still standing just inside the open doorway, spoke slowly so as to be understood. "I have been sent here to tell you that this mission is no longer being supported by our government. I must retrieve your weapons and escort you to the airport."

Paul Jackson looked at Russo with contempt. "Who are you working with?"

Russo looked toward Jackson. "I told you, I have no idea what you are talking about." He motioned to one of the R.S.S. tactical officers and spoke quietly to him in Russian. The officer turned around as Russo explained. "T.S. Renkski will now collect your weapons."

Not having any other choice, Ramsey ejected the clip from his pistol, racked the nine mil to remove the round, locked the chamber open and turned it over to the Tactical Officer, Renkski, who moved to Matthews by taking a side step to the right. Matthews followed Ramsey's lead, clearing the pistol then handing it over.

Jackson was still staring angrily at Russo. He didn't think the Russian was being truthful in the least. He wasn't satisfied with the non-answer given by Russo and pushed it a bit farther, "Oh, I think you do know what I am talking about. As a matter of fact, I think you're on the take. Who's paying you?"

Ramsey had also been losing faith in his Russian counterpart, and although he was less apt to consider Jackson's constant conspiracy theories about the Russians, he too thought that Russo was hiding something, and this time backed up his partner, prodding Russo to talk. "Come on Russo, Jackson's right. Somebody got to you. Was it our guys or yours?"

Russo looked back at Ramsey. "There are people in your government who are closing you down. I don't know who. It is not my job to question my superiors."

"Well, I got at least one man down and possibly another, so you need to find out who the hell is making these calls." Jackson said as he moved toward Russo again only to be stopped by one of the R.S.S. tactical police. Jackson looked the Russian in the eye and put his face inches away. "I think you need to get out of my way. I'm trying to have a conversation with your boss."

The Tactical Officer had no idea what Jackson had said, but he understood his tone and backed away slightly. "That's right son. Move out." Jackson chided.

He moved past the officer and over to where Russo was standing. He glanced over at Ivan, not sure how the biggest Russian in the room was taking his actions, then back to Russo. "I was asking you a question. You can deny it, but we were tracking your phone Russo. We know you were in contact with someone at a location not too far from here."

Jackson stepped in close as Russo watched him warily. "That person that you were in contact with, the one you say you don't know nothin' about, that guy is an American. He killed our guy, Marks. You remember Marks? About this tall, red hair. Could kick your white Russian ass, yeah, that guy."

"No. Your information is wrong. I do not know what you are talking about."

Rick White, extricated from his room by one of the two R.S.S. tactical officers, replied from across the room. "I do. His name is Gordon Maxwell."

White knew better than to prove his point by showing them his phone and thought it best not to approach the subject of his mobile tracking application. He looked at Alan Ramsey.

"Sir, CHERI matched him up by phone number to the track we had on Russo's phone. There is no question, Russo was in direct contact with that number. The number belongs to somebody named Gordon Maxwell. This is the same guy that confronted Matthews and me. The guy who took my phone.

Based on the phone number match to the grid coordinate at the warehouse, Maxwell is for sure the guy that ambushed Villacruze. What's worse is that Maxwell has had contact in the past with Dmitri Gregorov and with Secretary Erickson."

"Erickson! I knew it!" Jackson blurted out. He turned to face Russo. "And you, lying piece of shit! You're working for Maxwell, aren't you?" He moved even closer to Russo. This time when the R.S.S. tactical officers started to move, the large Russian, Ivan, stepped in.

"*Wait. Stop!*" He said in Russian, ordering the tactical team to stand down.

He stepped through the two tactical officers to confront his boss and in very broken English joined Jackson in questioning Russo.

"What they are saying...is it true?" Ivan could see that Russo was nervous about what was going on. He pushed Jackson out of the way and stepped closer, hovering over Russo and asked again, this time in Russian, "*is this true?*"

Russo didn't answer. Ivan screamed at him. *"I asked you a question!"*

Russo stepped backward away from Ivan and nearly yelled. *"You have no right to question me!"*

One of the tactical officers demanded to know what was going on and confronted Ivan. The tall Russian told them that Russo's integrity had been compromised. Russo could no longer be trusted. He made it clear that Russo was no longer in charge. He looked around at the tactical team and said, *"I am in charge now."*

Ramsey had no idea what was being said, but could tell by Ivan's actions that Russo was being ostracized. As if choreographed, they each took a step or two backward, away from the growing tension of the power struggle being played out in front of their eyes. Ramsey turned to his driver, who had stayed remarkably calm thus far, and quietly told him to run to the van and pull it around at the first opportunity, in case they had to make a break for it.

Ivan saw Russo reach for his pistol and reacted, pulling his own service pistol from its holster. Both men stood tense, weapons aimed at each other. Russo spoke sternly, *"You have no authority to arrest me. I have done nothing wrong."* He ordered the lead tactical officer to disarm Ivan, but the officer just stood there, not sure what to do.

"Arrest him!" Russo screamed at the tactical officer.

The R.S.S. agent moved toward Ivan, slinging his weapon and reaching for Ivan's. *"I must take your weapon. I have no choice but to do what he says."*

Suddenly Russo's phone buzzed in his pocket. While still covering his tall Russian partner he reached his free hand up to his Bluetooth headset to answer. *"This is Russlav."*

Maxwell's voice filled his earpiece. "It's me. I'm on my way. One of their guys got away."

Russo's eyes met Ramsey's as he reported to the caller that all the Americans were detained.

Erik White's phone chimed in his pocket. White looked at Ramsey. "It's gotta be Maxwell. Vee's number is set to vibrate only."

Ivan heard the sound as well and saw the exchange between Ramsey and White. He knew about the tracking application and what the chime implied. Ivan suddenly head-butted the tactical officer now standing in front of him, sending him stumbling backward.

Russo's eyes went wide and he tensed up on the trigger of his pistol as Ivan reached out with his left hand, grabbing at Russo's pistol. Russo fired. The round screamed within inches of Ramsey, unintentionally hitting Russo's lead tactical sergeant in the throat just above the protective vest.

The officer grabbed at his throat and stumbled backward, spurting blood through his clasped fingers, knees folding as he crumpled to the floor. One of the other officers immediately went to his aid while the other pulled his weapon up and began screaming in Russian at Ivan to stand down.

Ramsey seized the chaotic moment, lunged forward and grabbed the screaming officer from behind. He yanked the weapon up hard, slamming the surprised tactical officer in the face with the short stock submachine gun, stunning the officer as he pulled the weapon around, tugging the strap tight around the tactical officer's neck.

Matthews quickly moved to where the other tactical officer was working to save his wounded comrade. He reached down to recover his pistol. Before the officer could react, Matthews placed the barrel of his pistol to the man's temple.

The officer was too busy trying to control the blood oozing from the injured officer's neck to resist in any way. He looked up at Matthews and said in broken English, "I cannot stop what I'm doing or this man will die." Matthews kicked at the weapon laying on the floor next to him, sliding it toward Rick White and away from the others.

Ramsey looked over at Brandon. "You still here? Now's your chance, Brandon, Move! Now!"

The stunned young man burst past Jackson and out the door, picking up speed as he ran past the two fighting Russians. He would take the elevator all the way down. Had to be faster than running the stairs, he thought.

CHAPTER 37

EXHAUSTED

VEE pulled into a parking spot across the street from the Sheremetevo hotel. He yelled as he tried to move the shifter from drive to park. The pain was extreme, causing him to stop his attempt. He settled back into his seat, breathed deeply, knowing that the round from the AK had broken or shattered one or more bones in his shoulder. The pain wasn't the biggest problem. What worried him most was that he hadn't yet stopped bleeding.

Vee looked at the blood covered selector lever as he gathered his strength, gritted his teeth and pushed the gearshift forward to place the vehicle in park. He leaned back in the seat breathing hard. "That sucked," he said loudly to himself, as he looked for his phone.

He needed medical attention, but had no idea where the local hospital was. After a quick assessment of his wound and an attempt to dress it himself he drove himself back to the hotel, figuring that if he made it there somebody would call an ambulance for him. If he could just find his phone he could call Jackson or Ramsey. They could come to him. He realized finally that the last time he had it was when he went back to retrieve the keys from Marks' body. He had set it on the truck's rear bumper along with his pistol. He must have left it there.

He was just going to have to go in, he thought as he pulled the latch to pop the door, stepping out into the street and standing upright. "Shit," he said out loud as he steadied himself, stabbing his nine mil as best he could into his left pocket rather than the holster he wore on his right side.

Villacruze looked across the four lanes of steady traffic he would have to cross, cursing the distance. He let the door of the BMW close and took a step toward the traffic when he suddenly froze in place, staring at the mustached face of a man walking toward the entrance of the hotel. It was the man who had killed Marks.

Vee growled, wishing he could call to warn his team. He took a deep breath, mustered all his energy and jumped out into the lanes of traffic.

CHAPTER 38

FILE DIVING
STATE DEPARTMENT, WASHINGTON, D.C.

JIM Erickson was going over his daily routines, matching his calendar with his morning's schedule changes, when the sound of a digital chime rang and a small window appeared on his desktop.

"Controlled Hosting Session In Progress. Do not shut down your computer. Do not disconnect any external drives at this time. Indexing operation in progress."

The prompt, was followed by a large blue banner with the symbol for the Director of Homeland Security and another warning statement.

It is a federal offense to remove, disconnect or disable any authorized external drive, internal optical disk or drives, empty emails or relocate files during indexing of the controlled hosting network, punishable by fines and/or imprisonment.

He glowered at the screen. "Great," he said out loud, knowing that the network would slow to a crawl. For all the money the government spent on networking and IT management, they were always at least two iterations of software and hardware development behind the civilian sector, he mused. The systems were so bloated with security protocol that time-outs due to programs not responding had become the number one reason for work non-productivity, relegating coffee and cigarette breaks to second place.

Erickson didn't like that CHERI, the most thorough search program in the history of the N.S.A., was designed and maintained by a newly expanded division of geeks under the control of the T2T director, Gabe Anderson.

He thought briefly about his last encounter with Anderson. They never had really seen eye to eye on anything. To Erickson, Gabe Anderson was a do-gooder that refused to bend on even the slightest rule. God forbid that the administration put the needs of the country above those of *his* organization. Anderson pushed back on every request that came from Erickson's office, even those directly from Erickson himself. His only success was the recent changes in the way the Gregorov case was being handled. And that was due to the President's personal involvement. He smiled at the thought of Anderson being shot down by President Carlton and thought it was good to have friends in high places.

Erickson's thoughts were interrupted by the hum of fans and the clicking and whirring hard drives of his external RAID drive. The device, a six gigabyte storage array that housed the political files that spanned his entire career, was, he thought, the most complete record of any government office in the history of the United States.

He and his staff had painstakingly scanned thousands of paper documents to build it. Some of those documents he'd personally scanned, due to the sensitive nature of the contents. There were files that could not be seen by people other than himself or those with higher authority. Even though it would have been against protocol, the fact that he had not disconnected it when the index warning came on pissed him off. The small LED indicator was blinking rapidly now. There was no doubt that it was being accessed by the system. Erickson thought about immediately unplugging it, but knew that would send up a huge red flag.

Erickson watched as the LED light flickered from drive bay to drive bay. This was not a normal index. Why would it be jumping around like that? he thought. Somebody was looking for something specific and using the CHERI scan program to find it.

He got the sinking feeling that it was about the Gregorov mission and the Drone Operation. "Shit," He cursed loudly, worrying that CHERI might find and access his personal file, a backup of his personal laptop drive and information that made up his "Get-Out-Of-Jail-Free Card." He had placed the file on the RAID for safe keeping, realizing at this moment that the plan to store them as a backup on the RAID drive was a foolish one.

He quickly negotiated through layer after layer of his records to a single file, titled simply, "Armor," a security blanket of scanned files and documents, built from bits of information that he could use to protect himself. In it were the personal records of hotel stays from all over the world, photographs that showed high ranking officials in unflattering light, hand written notes, mp3 records of phone recordings, archived emails, and anything else that seemed weighted in his favor.

Most influential people in Erickson's circle knew the file existed. Erickson himself alluded to it on occasion, saying that it was for his biography when he retired. During state functions Erikson's guests and acquaintances would sourly quip to others to mind their p's and q's, "lest they become a note in Erickson's memoirs."

He right clicked on the file to select it to move it to the trash, but a prompt came up saying that the indexing was in progress and that files were locked until indexing was complete.

He reached for the computer's power button and held it down, only to get another prompt that the shutdown command was disabled during indexing and that shutting the computer down by any other means could cause loss of data and could result in fines or imprisonment.

Erickson was frantic. He dove under the desk and pulled the power cord to shut down the computer hoping it would look like a system failure, but the docked laptop's battery kept the computer on. Finally he reached around to the back of the dock and unplugged the power to the RAID drive. The LED lights quit flashing and the sound of the whirring disks stopped.

Erickson stood back, wondering what CHERI was looking for, and worse, what information it had collected. He collapsed back into his chair and ran his hand through his hair, pushing it back in place while he wondered what to do next. He thought for a moment, then reached for his desk phone. Peering at his computer's desktop screen he took note of the phone number for the IT section, known as the S6 shop, and dialed the extension for the IT Help Desk.

"Harry Thomas, help desk. What can I do you for?" came the greeting.

"Harry, this is Secretary Erickson. I hope you can help me. Looks like my system may have crashed during an index. My system locked up and now I've got some important stuff I was working on missing. Tried recovering the files but it's a no-go. Thought maybe if I knew who pulled it I could see if possibly they have a copy of what's missing."

"Hmmm, Ok, Mr. Secretary, if you would give me the I.P. address there on your desktop tag I will sure see what I can do."

Erickson read him the numbers. "Call me back as soon as you have the info."

"No need to hang up, Sir. This will take about..." Erickson could hear the working of the I.T. specialist's keys clicking madly in the background. "There. Got it," Thomas said smugly. "Yes sir, it was an authorized CHERI run with authorization number 151 Alpha."

Erickson wanted to sound helpful. "Any idea which agency made the request? I might be able to assist with whatever they are looking for. Seems like people don't like to talk anymore, especially to ask us higher ups, when we probably have the answers they need right in front of us."

After a couple more key clicks Thomas answered. "C.I.A., looks like, T2SCI, Authorization: R. White. Rick's a good guy. I could get you his number if you..." He stopped for a minute then came back. "No, wait, he authorized it, but the search was initiated from Langley, from a different computer than White's."

Thomas was mumbling, reading information that Erickson couldn't see. He read the name of Erickson's external drive, "Datastor Diamond USB 3.0 drive. Is that your external?"

"Yes, it was churning away and then my system froze up," Erickson answered, lying. "Three days of work on several documents, and they're just gone. I'm hoping I can recover at least some of it."

Harry Thomas clicked away at his keyboard. "The collection point is one of the newer laptops. It's assigned to a D Martin at Langley. The router shows he's in suite 301 room 301-22. His machine is T2SCI-14, but the guy must have logged off. The network is no longer active from that address. I've got his phone number at that desk if you want it."

Erickson sighed. "Nah, that's ok. I'm heading that direction anyway," he said, convincingly, "I'll stop by. I got my fingers crossed. Thanks for the help."

Erickson placed the handset in the receiver as he thought about who might be available to pay a visit to Darin Martin's office on his behalf.

CHAPTER 39

STANDOFF

SKYPOINT SHEREMETEVO HOTEL, MOSCOW

BRANDON ran quickly down the hotel corridor, rounded the last corner and stopped abruptly in the middle of the elevator lobby. As soon as he had come to a complete stop the chime of an arriving car sounded. Before the doors could open fully, Brandon was squeezing through.

"Excuse me," he said in English, a language not spoken all that commonly in the Moscow suburbs. The plead for pardon garnered the full attention of the car's rider, Gordon Maxwell.

Maxwell held the doors and, in such a way that suggested he was just another American and part of the investigating team, asked in English, "Is Ramsey still up here?"

Without thinking Brandon answered. "Yeah, he's up to his ears in alligators though." As soon as he spoke he regretted his words and suddenly looked as though he were guilty of a crime.

Maxwell smiled smugly, "Got you," he said in a childlike, chiding voice while bringing his pistol into full view, causing Brandon to freeze.

Still holding off the closure of the elevator doors, Maxwell motioned with his pistol for Brandon to move. "Well, come on then," he said, almost too nonchalantly. When Brandon didn't move quickly enough Maxwell's facial expression suddenly changed, showing his impatience. His eyebrows dropped closer to his narrowing eyes, but most noticeably was the drooping of the curled tips of his thick, dark, mustache as a brooding scowl appeared. He stepped toward Brandon, gave him a prodding shove and growled menacingly, "Move!"

Ivan and Russo were still locked in a desperate battle. The two had managed to move back into the hallway, Russo countering Ivan's every attack, each knowing the moves of the other, as if they were still in training. Ivan pinned Russo's pistol hand, slamming it against the wall trying to force him to drop the pistol, but Russo's grip was unrelenting through blow after blow from Ivan's powerful right fist to Russo's face, gashing his forehead and working the same area over and over trying to get his boss to give up.

Russo suddenly landed several hard blows with his free left hand. He forced Ivan back, kicking him hard in the groin then gained some distance from his new enemy and freed his pistol hand. When Ivan came at him again, Russo was waiting and, in a sudden, unexpected move, slammed the butt of his pistol hard against Ivan's temple. It was a striking blow that caused the huge Russian agent to stagger backward, then drop, first to one knee and then, face first, with a thud, to the floor.

Russo pointed his pistol at his unmoving partner, his finger resting on the trigger, blood streaming down his face from the cut on his brow. He should finish it, he thought, but did not want to kill him.

The sound of Alan Ramsey's voice broke his concentration. "Drop it, Russo."

Suddenly there was more than just he and Ivan in the world. Russo was somewhat startled by the voice of Alan Ramsey. He turned his head to look at the American, blinking away the blood that had run down his eyelid.

"I said, drop the pistol." Ramsey was holding one of the police Kedr PP-91 Submachine guns. "Don't even think about doing anything stupid."

Russo raised his gaze to look beyond Ramsey and into the room. All of his men were immobilized. He stood, breathing hard and bleeding from his lip, nose and eyebrow, still pointing his pistol at Ivan.

He thought about the dramatic turn of events that had just transpired. His plan was only to deliver Ramsey and his men to Maxwell, but now…Now what? he thought, as he tried to figure a way out.

Suddenly there was movement down the hall, capturing the attention of both men. Ramsey looked away to see Brandon step from around the corner of the hallway, immediately followed by the man that Ramsey now knew to be Gordon Maxwell.

"Well, it looks as though we've gotten ourselves into a bit of a conundrum." Maxwell said, as he halted Brandon and pushed his own pistol closer to the young driver's skull.

Brandon looked at Ramsey. "Sorry, Sir. He was coming up as I was going down."

Maxwell added, "Yes, it was quite serendipitous." He sighed, then continued, "I was hoping it wouldn't come to this, Mr. Ramsey. Now, *you* drop *your* weapons and stand down."

He pulled Brandon in closer and increased the pressure of the pistol barrel on his temple, causing him to wince. "Now, Mr. Ramsey. Now!"

Ramsey looked at Maxwell and the pistol pointing at Brandon and attempted to diffuse the situation, "Look Maxwell, none of this…"

Maxwell cut him off mid sentence. "Don't test me, Ramsey. I *will* kill him. Now, drop your weapon, All of you, drop them now or I will blow this kid's brains across the hall."

Ramsey was the only one with a shot and knew that if he tried to take out Maxwell, Russo would surely kill him.

Suddenly Maxwell pushed Brandon against the wall, "Time's up." Brandon's eyes went wide as he settled against the wall and stared at Maxwell's pistol, realizing that in the next instant he would be dead.

"No! Wait!" Ramsey yelled, then, as he lowered his assault rifle to the floor, barked over his shoulder to the others, "Do as he says."

Matthews followed Ramsey's lead and lowered his weapon, as did Paul Jackson, grumbling, "That's the second damned time today."

Maxwell recognized Matthews and then, seeing White behind him, said, "Well, well, if it isn't the nutty professor. I must say that phone app invention of yours has come in very handy. Well done."

Maxwell released Brandon to stand with the rest of the disarmed crew, then stepped through the door and looked around the room, stopping at the wounded R.S.S. tactical officer. Without warning or hesitation he pointed his pistol at the bleeding agent and with a scowl, pulled the trigger, killing the wounded man and sending the soldier tending his wound scurrying.

The young agent grabbed one of the Kedr submachine guns from the floor and spun around, bringing the weapon to bear on the mustached American, but Maxwell was too fast and fired again, dead center of the R.S.S. tactical officer's forehead, stopping his forward momentum and propelling him backward to land on the floor next to his patient.

Russo couldn't believe what he was witnessing and raised his pistol, pointing it at Maxwell then back at Ramsey and back again at Maxwell and yelled, "What are you doing?"

Maxwell explained. "Don't you see? It's perfect. The Americans caught you off guard. They killed your men. You tried to stop them, but they just kept coming," He scanned the room and zeroed in on the last of Russo's tactical team.

Russo pointed his pistol at Maxwell and yelled frantically, "I said stop! Stop!"

Maxwell stopped at the last tactical officer, paused for a moment, then pulled the trigger, killing him too. Without a second look, he turned to Russo and slapped his pistol away, then pointed with his pistol in the direction of Ramsey and his men. "Are you really that stupid Russo, What don't you understand?"

Maxwell spoke to Russo as he stepped further into the room, pistol raised and pointed at Ramsey. "You need an alibi, Russo. You're the last man standing...the big hero. It was this guy, right here, Alan Ramsey, who caused it. He was desperate. He was running out of time and you and your men were standing in his way."

Ramsey was watching his every move as Maxwell spun his tale, wondering where he was going with the story and waiting for an opportunity. Maxwell's eyes were wide and his gaze intense as he continued rambling, pointing the pistol at each one of the men still standing in the apartment.

"You ordered them to stand down, to pack up and go home after they lost control of the meeting that allowed Sidorova to kill a Russian citizen, and not just any citizen, a World War Two Soviet hero." Maxwell stepped over to stand once again in front of Alan Ramsey before continuing. "But Ramsey refused. He disobeyed your orders and, when you tried to arrest them, they turned to weapons to settle the argument and a battle raged, right here, in this hotel room, where you and your men fought gloriously to protect the citizens of Moscow from the rogue American C.I.A."

Maxwell pointed a finger at Russo, stepped backward a step and feigned a look of reverence, "You, Russo, you were the lone survivor. One by one you killed the Americans, and when the battle was over you managed to get to the airport just in time to keep Nikki Sidorova, a wanted fugitive, from leaving for Kiev to sell weapons to the Ukrainian resistance. You will be a national hero for capturing and killing a Ukrainian spy and preventing her from supplying weapons to the enemy of your precious Russian motherland."

Ramsey looked at Paul Jackson at the mention of the location of Gregorov's hidden weapons. Maxwell saw the exchange.

"That's right Mr. Ramsey, you have been trying so hard to get your hands on those weapons, and you let a girl beat you to the punch. She is preparing to fly there as we speak." He smiled a broad grin, "But, don't you worry, I doubt she will survive long enough to use them. As you know, it is very tense in the Ukraine right now. The chance that she will even be allowed over the border without being shot down is very, very, low." he said, his smile diminishing as he retrained his pistol at the forehead of Alan Ramsey.

The sound of a pistol being fired cracked loudly as the round from Villacruze's pistol slammed the steel door casing of the hotel room, sending shards of lead and metal to impact the side of Maxwell's face as a second nine millimeter round narrowly missed him. The bullet zipped through the door opening, past White and Matthews, and embedded into the wall behind them. Rick White dove for the floor, slamming down on his laptop bag and spilling his laptop, the pistol, and two magazines, across the floor in front of him.

Maxwell stumbled backward, growling and holding the side of his face, feeling the jagged metal splinters and the fresh warm blood. He turned, grimacing, in the direction of the gunfire, to see Villacruze stooped just behind the corner

"You forgot about the surprise ending, Bitch," Villacruze yelled from down the hall. He was shaky and unsteady, firing with his left hand.

Ramsey scrambled for one of the police submachine guns on the floor, but Maxwell, spotting his movement, quickly spun around and fired, narrowly missing Ramsey and sending the message that what he was doing was not a good idea.

He turned back toward the kneeling agent, firing wildly, rounds peppering the wall causing large chunks of plaster to shatter directly in front of Villacruze. Suddenly Vee felt an impact to his chest. He was hit. The round driving through his chest, shattering his sternum, the force of the impact knocking the wind out of him. He collapsed to his side against the wall, still kneeling but with no strength remaining in his body.

Russo had to stick with Maxwell now. If not he would be in prison the rest of his life. His only chance was to stick to the script as Maxwell outlined it. Amid the firefight between Maxwell and Villacruze he pulled his weapon up and aimed it at the one he disliked most, Paul Jackson, but before he could pull the trigger he felt his leg being kicked from underneath him. He screamed in agony as a round from Rick White's pistol slammed into his leg, shattering his shin bone.

Russo fell to his knee and looked up to see Rick White holding the pistol out, still aimed at him. White was shaking. "Don't make me kill you."

Russo knew it was over for him. There was nothing left. Either he won this fight or he died trying. He steadied himself on one knee and took a deep breath. The pain was incredible. He looked at White with intense anger as he brought the pistol into position, but he wasn't fast enough.

White literally closed his eyes and pulled the trigger multiple times, sending a stream of nine millimeter rounds to impact Russo's chest, neck, and face and sending the agent backward to the floor.

Maxwell saw Russo go down and realized that there was no way he could prevent Ramsey and his agents from reforming and taking the offensive. He weighed his options. Without Russo, he had neither the means to fight effectively, or for that matter, a real reason to stay and fight, other than to ensure his escape. With Russo dead he simply had no commitment here and soon would be fighting more than he could possibly handle. He had to move, get out while he could. Live to fight another day and all that, he thought.

Taking his chances, he fired randomly into the hotel room, then turned and sprinted down the hallway, past Villacruze as he rounded the corner. The agent wasn't moving. He had slid to the bottom of the wall, a huge streak of blood from his wounds marking the wall above him.

Villacruze heard the footsteps as Maxwell made the turn. He had no energy to do anything more than lift his eyelids enough to see someone run by. He hoped it was his guys getting away. He was slipping away. He could feel his life ebbing as the loss of blood took hold.

CHAPTER 40

GETTING THE BALL TO ROLL
C.I.A. HEADQUARTERS, LANGLEY, VA.

DARIN Martin opened the outer door of Alan Ramsey's office. He had just finished burning the information to a disk for Ramsey's page and was dropping it off before heading to Gabe Anderson's office to fill him in on what he gleaned from the CHERI database search. He stopped at the desk, noting the name placard, Jennifer Wilkins, on the front edge of a tidy desk when the inner door of Ramsey's office opened and the shapely figure of Jennifer Wilkins stepped out.

Jennifer spun on her heel, startled to see Darin Martin in his blue arm sling standing at her desk. "Oh, I wasn't expecting anyone this morning." she said, smiling with a hand on her heart as if to still it.

"Sorry, I didn't mean to startle you. My name is Darin Martin, I work for Mr. Ramsey, or I guess I should say, I will soon be working for him, once I get this healed up." He smiled as he patted the sling with his right hand, then reached out to shake Jennifer Wilkin's outstretched hand.

"So, *you're* Darin Martin. Alan told me you were coming. I didn't know you were already being tasked out. Can I get you some coffee, Mr. Martin. It only takes a moment," Jennifer offered, as she turned on the machine.

Martin waved away the offer, "No, thank you. I have to head to the Director's office. I came by to drop this off." He held the clear plastic CD case out for Jennifer.

"Mr. Ramsey asked that I give you this information to transcribe. This is some very sensitive information. Once transcribed onto the secret side, shred the disk. There are some audio files and photos on there as well. Make sure to encrypt everything with the highest security encryption."

Jennifer took the disk from his hand. "Alan called me. He said I would be getting something and gave me specific instructions on how to deal with it. He gave me the security lecture and iterated, same as you, the seriousness of the content."

She looked at the portrait of the President of the United States on the wall next to the flag and sighed deeply, "It's too bad. And to think, I voted for him."

There was a bit of a silence as they both contemplated the ramifications of the release of the information when it came. Darin Martin broke the silence.

"Ok, well then, I guess I'm finished here. It's been very nice to meet you. Any idea when the boss is coming back?"

Well, I expected him back over the weekend, but here it is Friday and he hasn't got a flight back arranged, or, if he does he didn't share the itinerary with me."

She grabbed her own coffee cup and stepped over to the machine. As she inserted the coffee and closed the lid Jennifer turned back to Darin Martin and closed the conversation.

"I'm sure he's more than ready to get back. It's terrible what happened over there, but without Gregorov to investigate, I can only imagine those boys are all bored to death and chomping at the bit to get back home."

CHAPTER 41

INFORMATION TECHNOLOGY
C.I.A. HEADQUARTERS, LANGLEY, VA.

FRANK REED stepped out of the elevator on the third floor and made the sharp right turn that led to the 300 series suites. Suite 301 was a vast collection of offices and team rooms with hundreds of networked data centers, printers and video conferencing equipment.

Reed was familiar with the telecommunications set up, having been a telecommunications information system officer assigned to this suite as well as the 400 series suites for the duration of his five year contract. He knew the systems inside and out; he and his teams installed the majority of the high speed networking and videoconferencing systems throughout the two floors, including the recent refit done to support the CHERI program.

He wondered why he'd been given this task at the end of his contract, in fact, on the last day of his contract, and one that was not being renewed. He figured it was either extremely top secret, extremely illegal, or both, and if he had learned anything in the five years working I.T. issues for the C.I.A., it was best not to ask questions. Regardless of the legalities, the fifty thousand dollar bonus he was being paid for such quick work was just the cushion he needed to help him stay on his feet as he looked for a new job in the National Capitol region.

Reed used his controlled access card, or CAC, to enter the office suite and moved along the outer corridor behind the main work areas. 301-22 was an office consisting of mostly team rooms, a telecommunications lab, and a free open office area that was used mainly when groups visiting for a conference needed a place to pull emails or print. The area was also used for in-processing personnel to have a place to work temporarily, until they had gone through all of the information assurance training and were assigned their own individual desk and system.

Finding T2SCI-14, the numbered name given the government laptop, was as easy as finding the CAT5 connector wall plate and reading the numbers. Reed knew that the lowest numbers were closest to the door and there were two lines to a cubicle. There were two rows of six cubicles for twenty-four laptops, and the numbers alternated left and right, one and two starting on the left, three four on the right, and so on. Reed counted by twos as he walked through the empty guest area, finding connector 14 and laptop T2SCI-14 in the fourth cubicle on the left. "Simple enough," he thought to himself.

He lifted his canvas tool kit, unzipping it and opening it like a book across the office chair. Reed removed a device that looked like an external optical drive bay and set the six by six inch, square, plate like device on the desk next to the laptop.

Reed pulled the chair under him, adjusted the height a little and raised the screen of the laptop. He tapped the keyboard to bring the computer out of sleep mode and inserted his CAC into the reader on the side of the laptop. He noted that the CD tray was open, and without thinking much about it, slid it back in place. Then Reed pressed the control alt and delete keys simultaneously, prompting the computer to ask him for his personal identification number. Once the P.I.N. was entered the desktop loaded with Reed as the administrator, giving him full access to Darin Martin's desktop and files.

On the desktop was an open folder labeled "Burn Folder." Reed looked through the file quickly, noting that the files all had the prefix CH indicating CHERI search content. After the prefix was the folder's name. He recognized *CHErickson* and *CHCarlton*, but wondered about *CHGregorov*, *CHSidorova* and *CHMaxwell*. The fact that they were all aliases within the burn folder told Reed that the last action on the computer was to burn the files to a DVD or CD.

The last user had initiated a CHERI search. Whatever information had been downloaded must have been some sensitive shit, considering both the President and the Secretary of State were listed in the search folders.

Must have been too sensitive, he thought, as he negotiated to the computer tab and opened the hard drive image, verifying that the CH files were indeed on the C drive before proceeding.

Lifting the laptop, he found the access cover for the internal hard drive and memory and slid the six by six inch device under the laptop, then set the laptop onto the device. Reed extended the cord to the power supply and plugged it in an available outlet, then, without hesitation, he switched on the device.

The laptop screen suddenly distorted as if all of the pixels were being pulled downward. The desktop icons and open hard drive image flickered and changed shape as the device emitted a huge electromagnetic pulse, pulling against the magnetized disk of the hard drive, scrambling the information. The unit clicked off and the screen returned to its normal shape, but with no icons or files, then, back on with a hum, contorting and twisting the image on the screen similar to the way a degaussing process worked to clear ghosting images when computer monitors were large bulky cathode ray tubes.

The device Reed used was part of a decommissioning kit, designed to wipe hard drives and RAM of all data. Put in use during the drawdown of equipment from Iraq, the electromagnetic pulse generator saved hours of time that it normally took physically removing the hard disks and RAM modules from the laptops, leaving even some of the newest computer systems unserviceable, and still requiring the destruction of the drives and RAM through shredding.

The E.P.G. saved millions of dollars in equipment cost by electromagnetically resetting a hard drive to a non formatted condition and could do it in a very short time. Additionally by allowing the cycle to complete several times, all data on the disk became non recoverable and the computer could be reformatted and put back into use, making it a recoverable asset. It was a great way to ensure good stewardship of the taxpayer's dollar and a quick fix for rendering T2SCI-14 useless to anyone who used it until it was reformatted and reimaged.

He thought about the money he had just made and the little effort and time that it took. *Not bad, and, done well before lunch*, he thought, as he packed up his tool kit for the last time. He glanced at the blank, blue screen on the laptop before holding the power button down long enough for it to shut down, then pressed the button again and waited. After a few minutes the command prompt illuminated and the words, *"NO OPERATING SYSTEM PRESENT, PRESS C TO BOOT FROM DISK. PRESS ANY KEY TO SHUT DOWN."* appeared on the screen with a flashing cursor, prompting the next command.

He, hit the return key as he got up, and then stepped out and down the hall, secure in the knowledge that he'd done what he'd been asked and, as usual, in an efficient manner. He wondered about the information that had been burned to a disk and whether to say anything about it. Maybe he would have, if his contract had not been cancelled, but really, this was his last day and he didn't give a shit one way or the other.

CHAPTER 42

BORED TO DEATH

SKYPOINT SHEREMETEVO HOTEL, MOSCOW

RAMSEY grabbed the police Kedr PP-91 submachine gun from the floor at his feet and jumped out of the door. Paul Jackson ran out the door after his boss and sprinted past him only to stop where Villacruze was slumped on the floor. He felt for a pulse, which was there, but weak. Ramsey looked on.

"Go on, I got this. Get Maxwell! Brandon, you stay with me."

Ramsey didn't move. Jackson barked. "Go, go, get Maxwell. Don't let him get away."

Ramsey looked back at Matthews and White. "Let's go."

Paul Jackson called for an ambulance as he carefully lowered Villacruze onto his back and found the chest wound. "Brandon, get over here and make yourself useful. Put pressure on that chest wound."

Brandon had never seen a real live wound. He was not an agent in the typical sense of the C.I.A. or F.B.I. He was more like Rick White, he was a support personnel, a behind the scenes guy, with minimal training on first aid and absolutely no training in the trauma inflicted by a gunshot to the chest.

"I'm not sure what to do," he replied as he knelt next to Vee. That was when he saw that Vee's shoulder was also soaked with blood. "We got a second wound. Right shoulder."

Jackson was checking his vitals. Vee's pulse was extremely weak. "Stay with me, Vee, damn it, stay with me." Vee wasn't moving at all and worse, barely bleeding. Jackson only hoped he could keep him alive until the ambulance arrived.

Ramsey reached the bank of elevators and barked orders for White to take the elevator down, while he and Matthew's took the stairs the fifteen stories to the ground floor.

Ramsey's military training took over as he motioned for Matthews to fall in directly behind him, forming a two man stack, "You cover high, I'll cover low." Ramsey barked, before pushing the stairwell door open.

As the door slammed open Ramsey quickly moved to the staircase leading down. Matthews raised his weapon high and looked upward. "Clear." he said quietly, to let Ramsey know he was ready for the next move. Ramsey cautiously leaned over the rail, holding his finger up to his lips and motioning for them to listen as well as look. Alan couldn't see any sign of Maxwell, but could hear the sound of his footsteps as he ran down toward the bottom floor. It sounded as if he were bounding the ten or so stairs to each landing that made up the twenty sets of steps between each floor. "Go," he said as he and Matthews began the descent.

Gordon Maxwell used the handrail to his advantage, sliding the length of the last five of so staircases, riding the rail to each landing then repeating the process until he finally reached the lobby exit. He caught his breath and while listening to the footsteps of his pursuers, wiped the sweat from his brow and straightened his hair.

He opened the door slowly, peering across the lobby. It was fairly empty allowing for an easy walk across the lobby and out the front door. Instead, however, Maxwell turned to his left, walking less than twenty meters to the next corridor and turned left again, heading toward the back of the hotel.

As Maxwell exited the hotel Ramsey and Matthews came to a halt inside the stairwell. "Hold it. I can't go out there with this machine gun in my hands. Sure as hell, I'll get arrested." Ramsey was breathing extremely hard. He pulled open his jacket and stuffed the submachine gun into his jacket as best he could, then stepped through the stairwell door into the quiet open lobby. Maxwell was nowhere to be seen.

Matthews immediately asked, "Which way?" scanning the lobby to the front doors, then noting the doors at the end of the hallway on the left and right side. Ramsey ran over to the desk and asked the clerk, "Do you speak English?" to which the clerk only shrugged his shoulders. "Shit," Ramsey cussed, as he spun around looking for any sign of Maxwell.

Matthews raised his hands in defeat. "He could have gone out any one of the exits."

Ramsey took one last look around just as the whoop of a siren sounded and an ambulance pulled to a stop under the entrance. "Let's head back up. We'll check on Vee, gather our things, then make a plan to head to the airport. Hopefully we can stop Nikki there, before she takes off or before Maxwell gets to her."

CHAPTER 43

SAYING GOODBYE

VILLACRUZE was out of it. He had been in and out of conscious-ness and his mind was in a state of confusion. The last thing he remembered was his position slumped over in the hallway after being shot, but where was he now? He looked around trying to understand the change in his surroundings when he felt a hand on his shoulder. He spun, surprised to see Nathan Marks standing there.

"C'mon let's go. We gotta get back. You did your best." Marks said quietly.

Villacruze squinted his eyes and shook his head, confused by the sudden appearance of Marks, dressed for combat, complete with gloves and knee pads. "How...what...I watched you die," he said stammering the words and not believing what he was seeing.

"I'm ok, Battle. I'm here to show you the way." Marks' words were reassuring, calming.

Villacruze looked at the weapon in his hands. He was no longer holding a nine mil. He stepped backward, dropping his M4 to let it hang from the combat sling, suddenly realizing how he was dressed, and feeling the weight of the battle armor and the improved combat helmet on his head.

He looked at his right arm and grabbed at his chest, feeling only the hybrid ceramic plates of his battle armor. There was no pain. No wounds. No blood. He was confused and it showed.

Villacruze looked at the barren landscape around him, a cold wind blowing down from the mountains where he had been so many times before. He turned back to face Marks. "How'd we do? Is everybody ok?"

Marks grabbed his arm, pulling him along, while reassuring him. "Everybody's fine, you did great, Battle. The war is over. We gotta go now."

Vee felt reluctant to leave, feeling as if his job wasn't done. He pulled away from his partner's grasp.

"I'm not ready." He stopped walking. "You're gonna have to go by yourself."

Nathan Marks looked relieved. "That's ok, Vee. Are you sure? It's ok if you're not ready, I just thought I'd come get you. I figured you'd want to head back with me."

Vee didn't want his Battle to be alone, but he knew he just couldn't leave yet. "Thanks for coming back for me, Bro, but I don't think I'm ready. Now, go on, numb nuts. Get out of here. I got this."

Marks thrust out a gloved hand that Villacruze took, then pulled him close, hugging him as best he could with the amount of gear they were wearing. Marks whispered, "Take care of yourself Hector. Thanks for being my Battle. I'm gonna miss you."

With that Marks pulled away, turned on his heel and began walking over the rough rocks and chad that littered the landscape, heading back toward the jagged mountains in the distance.

Vee didn't want to let go, but he had to get back in the fight. He turned to face the opposite direction and started moving when a sudden wave of pain overwhelmed him and he found he was having trouble breathing.

The pain was getting worse. He doubled over as another surge of intense pain racked his body. He stopped, grasping at the velcro, ripping open the flaps and buckles to remove his gear and let it fall to his feet, relieved at the sudden loss of the weight. He pulled at his shirt, tearing it open, exposing his bare chest to the wind and heat from the desert sun, agonizingly peeling it back, off his shoulder, where it was stuck with thick, drying blood.

He grabbed at his chest as another wave of pain caused him to drop to his knees. He looked down at the blood streaming down his chest as he wondered what the hell was happening. He fell to his side and rolled onto his back. He felt the hot sand and rough, jagged stones underneath him when the pain in his chest increased sharply, causing him to shudder uncontrollably. Suddenly the shrill pitch of a warning siren permeated his consciousness.

He opened his eyes to find Paul Jackson and a paramedic leaning over him. Jackson was yelling over the blaring siren, "You just scared the shit out of me. Don't do that again. At least, wait until we get to the hospital," Jackson said, forcing a smile to hide his underlying concern.

Villacruze looked around to regain his bearings, his sense of reality returning as he recognized his location as the inside of a moving ambulance. Even though he was in tremendous pain, he felt as though a huge weight had been lifted somehow. He felt peaceful. He closed his eyes once again, but saw only blackness.

"Goodbye, Battle." Vee said quietly. Jackson thought to respond, but this time let Villacruze have the last word.

CHAPTER 44

CONVERGENCE

DOMODEVO AIRPORT EAST. MOSCOW

ANATOLY followed the road as it looped around the longest of the commercial runways of Moscow's Domodevo airport. An Irkut MS-21 200 passenger Super Jet was lifting off, engines screaming overhead as the huge aircraft used the last meters of runway, barely twenty meters above the ground, as it zoomed skyward.

The road ended abruptly at a chain link, motor driven gate and a numeric key pad. Anatoly lowered the window, preparing to enter the numeric passcode.

Nikki read from a small piece of paper the four digits that would gain them access. The electric motor came to life, rattling the chain, pulling the gate open, and when adequate room was provided, Anatoly continued through.

The tarmac was a parking lot of mostly Lear, Gulfstream and Beechcraft planes, parked with limousines or corporate shuttle busses at their sides, interspersed among civilian and military cargo aircraft. Rows of huge corporate owned hangers lined the parking lot, swallowing Nikki's BMW in the long evening shadows that reached from the parked aircraft to the hangers.

Nikki pointed ahead to the open hanger and the Learjet 25 about midway down a row of newly built hangers. She could see Vostav standing with another man, presumably the new pilot, Mikael's replacement. "There, pull over there. That is Vostav."

Anatoly veered to the right, stopping near the two men. As he pulled up Nikki saw the pilot in a defiant pose, arms crossed over his chest and a scowl on his face. Vostav closed the gap between the pilot and the BMW, walking quickly to Nikki's door as her head appeared above the roofline. "What is going on?" she asked.

Vostav answered quickly, exasperation showing on his face, "It's the pilot. He is refusing to fly into the Ukraine. He says it is too dangerous."

Nikki looked at the pilot who was staring hard back at her. She pushed against Vostav and headed for the pilot, Anatoly and Vostav following, "What is the problem? Why are you delaying this trip? We are paying you twice the normal pay for a pilot. The reason you are receiving that pay is because of the dangers associated with the border crossing and travel through the flight restricted area. Now, I suggest you get over what it is you fear and prepare to fly this plane as you are being paid to do."

The pilot uncrossed his arms, stepped closer to Nikki and looked her directly in the eyes, still scowling. "I am not afraid of the Ukrainians or N.A.T.O. I was a MIG pilot. They do not scare me."

"Then what is the problem?" Nikki asked, looking from the pilot to Vostav and back.

The pilot crossed his arms again. "Ask him," he said, nodding toward Vostav. "I have only explained it a hundred times." He became quiet, pursing his lips, returning to his childish stance of defiance.

Vostav rolled his eyes and sighed, "Mr. Dernov here says the plane is not safe to fly. Evidently, there was an inspection that showed that the tires need to be replaced before the plane can take off again."

Nikki glanced at the tires. She noted an "X" drawn in yellow on the side of the tire facing her, a mark, she assumed, placed on the tire during the inspection marking it as bad, but to her, they looked to be in perfect condition. She turned back to the pilot. "What is wrong with the tires?"

The pilot looked as though he was dealing with children who couldn't possibly understand. He sighed a deep sigh. "They are too old. As old as the plane, according to the American who inspected it."

Nikki immediately became suspicious. "American? What American?"

Again the pilot sighed, as if explaining was too difficult a task. He reached in his pocket, removed an inspection checklist and pointed to the failure annotated on the paper as he handed it to Nikki.

"This is a Canadian Built Bombardier Learjet 25 built in 2008. There have been some planes like this that have crashed during takeoff due to tires that come apart. The American Federal Aviation Administration and the Canadian Air Safety Federation has convinced our politicians that the planes must be inspected. They offered to perform the service with Russian personnel at no charge, so now, we have to have our tires inspected every four days for proper pressure. During this inspection they noticed the date on the tires, some code there." The pilot pointed to where the "X" was scribbled on the sidewall.

"According to the American, it shows that the tires are as old as the plane, installed in 2008 when the plane was built."

Anatoly saw the look on Nikki's face. She was suspecting that it was a trick, a setup by the American C.I.A. to keep her from leaving. Anatoly joined the conversation. "What he's saying is true. There were several crashes a few years back. The tires were disintegrating on takeoff. It was actually due to an under-inflation issue, not necessarily because of the age of the tires."

He walked over to the plane and looked near the "X" and found the date stamp, a four digit code embedded in the rubber during manufacturing, in accordance with the United States Department of Transportation and The Canadian Air Safety Federation.

Anatoly pointed at the date stamp. "The D.O.T. stamp and tire manufacturing date was required on all tires made in or imported to the U.S. and Canada."

He read the code out loud, "forty-six-zero-eight. These tires were manufactured in the forty-sixth week of 2008. If this plane is a 2008 model, then the information on the safety inspection is correct. Regardless, the tires are supposed to be replaced every three to four years. It's been more than seven years."

Nikki looked at Anatoly strangely, handing him the inspection checklist. "How do you know about such things?"

Anatoly replied, "I can fly. I do not have a license and have never flown anything other than propeller driven aircraft, Cessna single engine, and a twin engine Beechcraft G58, and only have flown a little, but I read a lot about them. Maybe one day…"

Nikki stopped him from talking. She turned back to the pilot. "When can the tires be replaced?"

"At the earliest tomorrow afternoon." The pilot felt triumphant, but the feeling didn't last long.

"Why don't you just sign the waiver?" Anatoly asked both the pilot and Nikki. "The plane isn't grounded. It's an American rule. I guarantee you that most of the passenger liners in Russia have tires older than those. I seriously doubt that any Russian aviation office really gives a crap about the age of those tires. That is, unless they have been paid to give a shit." Anatoly was being sarcastic, but the words he spoke rang like church bells to both Nikki and the pilot.

Suddenly the pilot looked nervous. Nikki pulled the Makarov from its holster under her left breast and stepped up to the pilot, glaring at him. The pilot's eyes went wide as Nikki pointed the pistol directly at his face and slipped her phone out of her pocket. "Anny, there is a phone number on that piece of paper. Near the bottom, where the American signed. Read it to me." She made the call as Anatoly read off the numbers.

In an office on the commercial side of the airport, Ryan London was just about to leave for the night when the phone on his desk rattled to life. At first he thought about ignoring it and nearly closed the door with it ringing, but he couldn't do that. As hard as it was for him to push away from his desk, and actually enjoy time for himself, it was even harder to ignore a plea for help, and that is what he considered every phone call and every email, a plea from some poor soul needing his assistance. He dropped his jacket on a chair and headed back to his desk, grabbing the receiver and interrupting it's fourth ring. "London, flight safety," he said in his official tone.

At the Czerecec Hospital, in Moscow, not far from the Domodevo Airport, Rick White sat listening to Alan Ramsey, Paul Jackson and Bob Matthews as they discussed what to do next. He was not one of them, he thought, not the kind of guy to understand all there was to know about the ramifications of Maxwell and Nikki's existence. He was a tech guy. A computer geek, not a gun toting C.I.A. operative.

He couldn't stop thinking about the shoot-out with Russo. He was actually ok with his part in killing the Russian agent. It was obvious he was a bad guy and it was, after all, self defense, but he couldn't shake the images of Maxwell indiscriminately killing the Russian officers. He looked at his fingernails, realizing again that he was gnawing on the little he could actually get a bite on. He was going to need counseling, he thought, staring at his destroyed thumbnail, when an chime sounded on his phone and the screen lit up showing one notification.

White sat straight up, lifted his phone from the table and interrupted Alan Ramsey in mid sentence, "Hey, guys, I just got a hit. Nikki's back on the grid."

Gordon Maxwell was overseeing the loading of weapons and equipment onto the a C-130 cargo plane when he felt the buzz of his phone. He pulled the stolen phone from his pocket, noting Rick White's locator app was active, and stared at the number on the screen. Adjacent to the phone number was the grid coordinate of the caller. He had seen the number before. Although he hadn't programmed the phone, he assumed that Ramsey's tech specialist would surely have had a track on Nikki's phone and assumed it was her number.

Maxwell tapped on the glass over the grid coordinates and the screen changed, bringing up the map. The outline of Domodevo Airport appeared with a marker denoting the location of the caller. With a pinch Maxwell zoomed in on the marker location. It was at the east end of the airport. He selected *satellite* from the menu and the outlined map suddenly became a snapshot of the east end of Domodevo. Maxwell's location was highlighted by a green dot and Nikki's by the red marker. Maxwell looked past the hanger door, beyond the lowered ramp of the C-130 and smiled at his luck and at the Learjet 25 parked at the hanger a little less than a mile away, well within range of any number of weapons he had at his disposal, weapons that were being loaded on the C-130 at that moment.

Nikki yelled into the phone as another low flying aircraft passed by overhead. "Hello, is this..." Nikki paused for a moment, leaning over to glance at the inspection sheet...Mr. Ryan London?"

"Yes. How can I help you?" London asked, taking his seat behind his desk.

Nikki looked at the pilot, but spoke into her phone. "Mr. London, my name is Nikki Sidorova and I am here with a..." She looked again at the paper, "...Mr. Arkady Dernov, my pilot. He tells me that you are responsible for delaying my flight tonight. Is that true, Mr. London? Are we restricted from flying?"

Ryan London suddenly tensed up. "Shit," he cussed in a whisper as he pushed away from his desk and moved toward the window, dragging the phone across his desk as he attempted to raise the blinds. The evening sun cast long shadows across the tarmac, but illuminated the front of the row of hangers at the far end of the runway.

London grabbed the high powered binoculars and adjusted the focus. He could see the image of a woman and three men. The woman appeared to be holding a gun on the pilot. "Shit," he said to himself again.

He wasn't sure what to do. This was the woman that Maxwell had told him about. He needed to contact Maxwell, that was for sure. His heart was beating inside his chest so loud he was sure that the sound could be heard by the woman on the phone. Nervously he stared at the phone's receiver wondering what to say.

"Uh...Ma'am, is it ok to put you on hold for one second. I have another call...one that...I...uh, have been expecting. Sorry." He placed the phone on hold, pressed a second line and called the number he had scribbled on his desk calendar.

Maxwell's phone vibrated, spinning just a little on the removed lid of an open weapons case. He recognized the number as Ryan London's and carefully set the components of the M107 fifty caliber rifle back in the bottom of the case. "Yeah," he said, with no introduction or greeting, as he unlocked his screen and lifted the phone to his ear.

"There's trouble," London began, "That woman you talked about, she's here, on the phone, down at hanger five with the pilot. She has a gun and she's asking questions."

"Yes, I know. Don't worry. Just tell her something she wants to hear. Keep her busy. I will be heading over her way shortly." Maxwell said with no emotion at all, ending the call abruptly and leaving the aircraft safety representative holding the receiver and thinking of something to say as he took the phone off hold.

Brandon weaved the Mercedes van through the traffic on the M10 as if he had been commuting on it for years. He was speeding toward the airport to Nikki's location pinpointed by the tracking app on her phone.

The road had just cleared of traffic when he saw the sign for the Domodevo exit. He accelerated, taking advantage of the last stretch of open highway when he saw Rick White fidgeting around in the seat behind him, another tone emanating from his phone app. White knew the sound, it was the ring tone he had set for his own number, the phone taken from him by Gordon Maxwell.

Alan Ramsey heard the chime as well and was staring in White's direction.

Rick White fumbled with his phone to get the map back up on the screen. "Shit!" he said, looking ashen.

"What is it?" Ramsey asked, watching his techie's reaction.

"It's my phone,…well, Maxwell's phone. According to this he's at the airport too!" He yelled, holding the phone out, first to Ramsey, and then Jackson.

Paul Jackson noted the close proximity of the two tear-drop-shaped markers on the screen, "They look damn close to one another. How far is that? How far away is he from Nikki?"

White looked at the map, scrolling up to find a legend. "Maybe a mile at the most." he said as he switched to the satellite mode. Suddenly the aerial photos of the map program appeared, showing the hangers and runways in great clarity and confirming the fact that Maxwell was indeed at the airport. White gasped. Again he held the phone so that Ramsey and Jackson could study the image. then said, "The red marker is Nikki's location, the green marker is Maxwell's. He's definitely at the airport."

Ramsey was the first to notice that neither of the two points were moving, but the blue dot, indicating White's position, and that of Ramsey and the others, was steadily getting closer to the east end of the airport. "Those points are in real time, right?" Ramsey asked, garnering an affirming nod from White. He followed up with another question, "Then, why aren't they moving?"

Paul Jackson snatched the phone from White to take a look. "They definitely aren't moving. Maybe they don't know the other is there." He handed the phone back to White.

Ramsey sat up fully in his seat, "Exactly! That's why we need to get there before they each figure that out. Brandon, pedal to the metal please."

Ryan London came back on the phone, not seeing the scowling redhead's face, but peering at her through the binoculars. He could tell by her body language she was not happy. "Sorry about that. Where were we?"

Nikki wasted no time, "I need you to tell the pilot that he can still fly the plane, that the rule is only to ensure the inflation is correct. I'm handing him the phone. Tell him." She held her phone out to the pilot.

The pilot didn't care what the safety coordinator was about to say. He had already earned his money two-fold, three if he counted the money Vostav paid him. After all it was not his fault the plane had been grounded. He placed the phone to his ear.

"Act like you are talking. We're to keep her busy," Ryan said as soon as he saw the man was holding the phone. The pilot only scowled more.

Nikki was impatient. "Well, what did he say?"

The pilot handed the phone back to Nikki. "He said it is my call. We are not flying." Nikki's eyes went wide, then narrowed as her anger flared. She screamed into the phone. "I told you to tell him to fly the plane. Why didn't you tell him?"

Ryan was glad he was not on site. "Ma'am, I cannot order him to fly the plane. As a representative of the Moscow Air Safety Administration I can only let him know that the plane *can* be flown. It is entirely his decision to weigh the odds. I'm sorry if he chose against your wishes."

Nikki was steaming. She shoved her phone in her pocket "You son of a bitch. Who's paying you to keep us from leaving?" She cocked the pistol and stepped closer to the small Russian.

He didn't flinch. "We are not flying. If you shoot me the result will be no different."

As Brandon neared the gate he saw the security kiosk. He looked in his rear view mirror to Ramsey and asked, "Anybody here have the code for the gate?"

Ramsey, along with the others, strained to see what the driver was talking about, but didn't answer.

"Nope, didn't think so.," Brandon said as he adjusted the trajectory toward the center of the gate.

Paul Jackson saw the gears turning and braced himself against the seat in front of him. "Uh, hold on there, stuntman. This ain't Hollywood and you ain't Steve McQueen."

Brandon slammed the pedal to the floor, pushing the four cylinder powered Mercedes van for all it was worth. He yelled back at Jackson as the Vito van crashed into the gate, "Who's Steve McQueen?"

CHAPTER 45

THE OTHER SHOE
C.I.A. HEADQUARTERS, LANGLEY, VA.

GENE Patterson stood quietly, waiting for Gabe Anderson to look over the information prepared by Betty Rogers. The look on his face showed his growing anger. The more he read the more furrowed his brow became.

He dropped the report on his desk and pulled away his glasses, staring at the papers and then at the now quiet Mp3 file on his desktop monitor. After a moment he sat down, sighing a deep sigh. "Have a seat, Gene."

Patterson parked in one of the two chairs directly in front of Anderson's desk. "Well, now what?" Gene Patterson asked, leaning forward.

"Well, this is pretty incriminating stuff, but I'm afraid that there will be more attention given to the way it was attained, without both men's knowledge, and less attention to what it represents."

He pushed his chair back, "This is a hell of a mess. The laws regarding senior statesmen preclude their prosecution, so guess who's actually going to go on trial here before the word impeachment is even uttered? We will. You, me, Ramsey, all of us, will be run through the political wringer."

Anderson saw that Gene Patterson looked worried. "Gene, you have to understand that it's going to be a hard road ahead. A long, hard road. The worse part is that unless the President or the SECSTATE voluntarily step down, they can finish out their terms before any indictment can be leveled against them. That means at least another 30 months. Unless, of course, the petition to impeach is upheld. Given all the good Carlton has done since he took office, I can't see that happening."

Patterson finally spoke, "Even if they are caught with a smoking gun?"

Gabe retorted quickly, "A smoking gun and blood on their hands won't take them out of office, unless the House Speaker can convince the House that an impeachment is in order. About the only way the process is trumped is when a foreign power is involved. And that is where we hold all the aces at the moment. If the drone attack is proven beyond a doubt, especially if Rashnev makes a formal appeal to the UN, then we've got Erickson by the balls.

Anderson paused, drumming his fingers on his desk, thinking, as he stared off into the distance. "All we need now is for the other shoe to drop. If it does then they will have no choice but to petition charges."

Gabe Anderson's phone buzzed on his desk, startling Patterson and effectively ending the conversation.

The voice of Gabe Anderson's secretary crackled over the speaker. "Sir. There's a Darin Martin here to see you. He says it's imperative that he speak with you."

"Thanks, send him in."

Gabe Anderson got up from his chair and moved toward the office door. Patterson followed his lead, asking after a moment, "Should I know who Darin Martin is?"

Gabe Anderson had met Darin Martin while he was still in the hospital. "Well, if you had read the report on the bombing attacks in St. Louis you would know that Darin is one of the St. Louis F.B.I. fellas that jumped ship and came on board."

Gene Patterson apologized. "Sorry, didn't know. They keep me pretty tied down as the State Department liaison. I'm always playing catch-up. What role did Martin play in the investigation?"

Gabe Anderson looked at Patterson sternly, "He was with Ramsey when the shoot out at the hospital took place. Took a slug from bin Masri that shattered his shoulder blade."

He paused for a second, "You really didn't read the report through, did you?" he asked, a disbelieving look on his face.

Patterson shrugged with an apologetic look on his face. "Sorry, I didn't, but it is on my desk, for when I have the time."

"Consider it required reading. This guy's a damn hero, Gene. Make sure you treat him as such."

The inner office door swung open and the figure of the wounded man entered, ushered in by Anderson's secretary.

"Good Morning, Dan. Welcome." Gabe Anderson turned, motioning to his right. "This is Gene Patterson, he is the C.I.A. liaison to the State Department."

Patterson smiled and offered a hand to shake. "Nice to meet you."

Martin turned to Anderson, "Sir, I have some information for you. Alan Ramsey asked that I get it to you this morning A.S.A.P. It is very urgent and sensitive information regarding the Secretary of State. Martin glanced at the C.I.A. Liaison wondering if he should continue.

Gabe Anderson prodded him, "Go on, Mr. Patterson is one of the white hats," a reference from the days of playing cowboys and

Indians, one that showed Gabe Anderson's age and one that flew directly over Darin Martin's head.

Anderson sighed, "It's ok, son. Please, continue."

Darin Martin began cautiously, "This information was extracted during a CHERI scan yesterday." Martin handed Gabe Anderson a duplicate copy of the disk he had just given to Jennifer Wilkins before continuing.

"There is information that shows that Secretary Erickson and the President have been in direct contact with a person of interest that Mr. Ramsey has learned may be involved in some way with Dmitri Gregorov's weapon sales, a guy named Gordon Maxwell."

"There it is. That's what we were looking for. What kind of information is it?" Patterson said, looking hopeful.

Martin explained how the CHERI search worked. "But here's the thing. It looks like Erickson may have shut down his system to prevent data collection. We got a match on several names: Erickson, the President's and Maxwell's, even Gregorov. All from Erickson's external drive, but no real substance. Very few files. As CHERI was indexing and starting to copy the files, it was shut down.

We think Erickson figured it out and pulled the plug. If that's the case, and the Secretary has ties with this guy, Maxwell, then you can bet Erickson has already tipped Maxwell off, and that could be dangerous for Ramsey and his team."

Anderson mulled over the information. "Ok, does anybody else know about the files on the disk?"

I just gave a copy to Ramsey's page, Jennifer. She's supposed to analyze the data, but I can tell you, what files we did get are from his government assigned laptop and I doubt that he stores any of the really incriminating stuff on a government device."

Patterson turned to the C.I.A.'s Director, "So we're back at square one then?"

Anderson looked confident, "Yes and no, there may not be enough hard evidence to go full bore, but there is definitely enough between these two pieces of information to request a lock-down on their systems, suspend the highest security authorizations, and pave the way for an authorized system information search."

He thought about his options for only a minute. "Gentlemen, We need a search warrant and a seizure affidavit to pull Erickson's and President Carlson's systems off the grid. I can get them locked out, but we need what is on their hard drives, including Erickson's external, and that's going to take some help from the Justice Department."

He turned to Darin Martin, "Where do you have this information stored? Tell me you backed it up to the network drives."

"Wherever CHERI stores information, I guess." Anderson could see that he really wasn't sure..

"CHERI doesn't store information, it's a search engine. Supposedly that's what keeps it legal, somehow. It's like a Golden Retriever, you tell it to fetch and it brings the info that it gathers back to you and only you. It would probably be wise for you to go back and upload the info to the network drive. You should have access to the J Drive. Put it there, Erickson can't get in that drive."

Darin Martin understood and turned to leave, "I'm on it, Call me if you need anything more," he offered, before stepping out of the office and closing the door.

Gene Patterson looked more worried than usual. "We should shut down the investigation and get Ramsey and his men back before it gets out of control."

Anderson replied, "That's my next step. We're going to need a flight out for them. I'll call Ramsey, you get with transportation and get a flight scheduled. Pull a favor from Erin Shields of the 31st Fighter Wing at Aviano. She's the U.S.A.F. Brigadier General there. They've got a V.I.P. Learjet with all the bells and whistles. Have her place it on standby. If she balks, tell her Gabe Anderson is asking."

CHAPTER 46

FLIGHT OUT

DOMODEVO AIRPORT EAST. MOSCOW

MAXWELL squinted as he placed his right eye just behind the eyepiece of the Leupold Vary-X optic sight and scanned the length of the runway to the Learjet and the four people standing next to it. He made his calculations for a guess of fifteen-hundred meters, or just under one mile from where he had set up the Barrett fifty caliber sniper rifle.

Traveling at eight-hundred-fifty meters per second, it would take about two seconds for the fifty caliber projectile to reach its target. By the time the first round struck, Maxwell could acquire a new target and squeeze off a second round.

He set the crosshairs on the auburn hair of Nikki Sidorova and, without hesitation, pulled the trigger. The half inch diameter round jumped from the end of the barrel as the gas and flame propelling it spit sideway from the muzzle brake like the flames of a dragon.

The short-spring-recoil-action cushioned the bolt as it moved to the rear of the carrier. The bolt mechanism slid past the accelerator assembly and the cocking lever while the extractor pulled the expended casing from the firing chamber, clearing the rear of the barrel extension and ejecting the empty brass cartridge from the ejection port.

Before the casing could ping against the concrete floor, a second round sprung upward from the ten round magazine and slid into position, driven forward into the firing chamber by the bolt's forward movement, awaiting the operator's next trigger pull. Maxwell counted to himself the seconds between the trigger pulls.

One-thousand-one.

He aligned the sight picture, moving it slightly right and up, to place the crosshairs on the forehead of Anatoly Vodjosic. Again he squeezed the trigger, releasing the eleven-thousand-five-hundred foot pounds of energy, sending a second round toward Nikki's position.

At the far end of the runway, Arkady Dernov, the pilot of the Learjet, had grown tired of the woman who was confronting him and blocking him from leaving. He had come face to face with weapons before, in much worse scenarios and was not intimidated by the redhead in front of him, nor was he concerned by the others in her group.

"Either shoot me or get the hell out of my way!" he growled, pushing Nikki's pistol aside with a sweeping backhanded motion. His action took Nikki off guard as he continued to move past her, thrusting his right hand forward, forcefully shoving her backward to collide with Anatoly.

Vostav took a step forward in an attempt to stop him from leaving when the barely audible zipping sound of the half inch diameter round, moving at nearly two and a half times the speed of sound, impacted the pilot's skull just behind his right ear.

One-thousand-two.

With a noise that sounded like a watermelon being smashed to the ground, the pilot's head exploded. The force of the impact lifted his lifeless, headless corpse, flinging it against Nikki and Anatoly as the second round buzzed overhead and ricocheted off the frame of the aircraft's cargo door, where, a second earlier Anatoly had stood.

Brandon had just looked up after bursting through the gate. He watched the scene unfold as the van rocketed toward the Learjet. Nikki had her pistol pointed at one of the men standing with her. He saw the man shove Nikki and then saw the man's head burst.

"Holy shit. She just shot him!" he yelled, thinking that Nikki had just literally blown his brains out.

Ramsey saw it too, but he knew that the damage inflicted was not caused by Nikki's pistol. He saw Vostav look left as he dove for cover. Ramsey wondered what he was looking at as he too then glanced to his left, to the far end of the runway, and thought about the coordinates on the locating app. The shot had to come from Maxwell's location. And that could only mean one thing; Maxwell had some heavy firepower. The first weapon that came to Ramsey's mind that had the range, accuracy, and the force to throw a man like a rag doll, was a fifty cal.

Ramsey yelled to Brandon, pointing at a location near the front of the plane. "Stop there, block them in! Everyone stay as low as you can. They are being fired on from across the runway."

Jackson heard Ramsey's words and immediately understood their meaning. Almost automatically the word came to him and he yelled out the warning that he had heard and said so many times in his past.

"Sniper!"

He grabbed the handle of the sliding door, preparing for a quick escape, knowing that by blocking Nikki Sidorova and her people with the van, they had just placed themselves in harm's way. "Move people. Get out and take cover!"

Maxwell watched the van pull to a screeching stop. "What the hell," he muttered as he put his eye back against the scope just in time to see the driver bound from the van and run to the other side. Nobody else was visible, but he knew it had to be Ramsey and the Americans.

Jackson was the first one out, crouching near the right rear tire as Brandon ran past the van to Nikki's BMW and crouched by its opposite side.

Ramsey jumped out of the van, also crouching, and ran closer to the dead man. Nikki and Anatoly were behind an auxiliary power unit that was attached to the Lear. Ramsey ducked as low as he could to stay behind the van, still in the elongated shadow. He had his pistol out, but not pointed at anyone. He looked at Nikki, who had a look of total surprise on her face, then at Anatoly, noting that he was not armed. "Nikki Sidorova, I'm Alan Ramsey. I am…"

Nikki cut him off. "I know who you are." She collected herself, pushing away the hair hanging over one of her eyes. She thrust out her pistol, pointing it at him, and asked angrily, "Why are you trying to kill me?"

She stood up defiantly, thinking that it was Ramsey and his men that had tried to kill her, not understanding that the deadly shots came from a different direction. All she knew was that her pilot was dead and the ones responsible were now only meters away. She walked quickly toward Ramsey, her eyes bouncing left to right as she scanned the location of each of his men. She stopped, positioning herself with her back to the Mercedes van and glanced warily at the black C.I.A. operative, all the while her pistol trained on Ramsey.

She glared at him, nostrils flaring and nearly screamed, "Why are you trying to kill me?"

Jackson reached for his pistol, but Nikki saw the peripheral movement and swung her pistol in his direction. Ramsey yelled to her not to shoot, then he turned to glare at Jackson. "Damn it, Paul! Put it away."

Nikki stepped closer to Ramsey, bringing the pistol back to face him and asked again as Ramsey tried to warn her, "Nikki, you need to get down. Now!"

Across the runway, Maxwell saw Nikki Sidorova stand up. She was talking to someone, pistol raised, but he couldn't see who. He scanned the area as best he could, looking for Ramsey or Jackson, and then brought the weapon back and placed the crosshairs of the telescopic sight on Nikki. He had a clear shot through the front windows of the van.

The target reticle settled on the back of Nikki's head as Maxwell steadied himself squarely behind the rifle. He began to control his breathing while pulling the rear grip back toward him with his left hand to drive the recoil pad firmly into his shoulder pocket. All Maxwell heard was the sound of his heartbeat, and even that seemed slow, relaxed. He was set. "Stupid bitch." He mumbled, as he squeezed the trigger.

Ramsey was really getting worried, she'd been standing way too long. He told her again to get down, but Nikki ignored him.

"Look," he said forcefully, I'm not the one trying to kill you…"
Ramsey stopped mid sentence when he saw the flash of a weapon
firing from the darkness of an open hanger across the airport. He
sprung from his crouched position and slammed into Nikki, forcing
her backward and down against the right front tire of the Mercedes
van.

Maxwell cursed as Nikki suddenly dropped from view. The
round crashed through first the left, and then the right windows of
both front doors on the van, shattering the heat treated tempered
glass, but again, missing his target completely.

Nikki and Ramsey hadn't fully settled into their position on
the ground as the glass rained down on them. The high velocity
round continued on, boring through the laminated front glass of the
BMW's windshield and shattering the back glass. The obstacles
barely a speed bump to the speeding projectile, as the copper and
steel round continued into the tree line beyond the hanger.

She pushed away from Ramsey, pulling herself up to sit with
her back against the right front wheel, immediately retraining the
muzzle of her Makarov on Ramsey.

Leaning up on his elbows, Ramsey reached over and pushed
Nikki's pistol away so that it was not pointing at him. He was
breathing hard as he spoke, "Like I said, I'm not the one who's
trying to kill you. Save your ammo, and your attitude, for
Maxwell."

Nikki looked over at Anatoly, then back at Ramsey, obvious
confusion showing in her eyes. She lowered her pistol. "Who the
hell is Maxwell?"

This time it was Paul Jackson who replied, "He's the one on
the other side of the airport trying to kill you." He paused, looked

at the shattered glass of the van, then added, "...and evidently, us too."

As if on cue another round zipped through the left tire of the van, slamming into the aluminum housing of the transaxle assembly with a resoundingly loud crack, shattering the aluminum casing. The van rocked as it dipped down suddenly, the air escaping explosively from the holes drilled through the tire as crimson transmission fluid poured out of the fractured transaxle case and onto the pavement, making a gurgling, splattering sound.

Jackson, dropped down low and peered under the van. "Great! There goes my rental deposit."

Rick White suddenly jumped up from his position and, in a crouched run, sprinted to the front of the van. He fell in next to Nikki, avoiding the windows and the open sliding door, having realized with the last round that it was safer to put the engine block and transmission between him and Maxwell.

He had his phone out with the tracking application open. He leaned over in front of Nikki who gave him a steely gaze. The young technician couldn't help but notice the striking green eyes.

White politely excused himself for invading her personal space as he leaned over her, holding his phone for Ramsey to see the screen, zooming in on the satellite photo to the number four hanger.

"Sir, take a look at this. Here's our location." He pointed at an empty area on the screen. "If this map was real-time-imagery, this is where Nikki's plane would be." He tried to convey a better picture, "We are here, and she would be about here."

He looked to see that Ramsey was following along and then scrolled the map straight down. "I saw that last muzzle blast. As best I can tell it came from here." He stopped scrolling, zooming in on a much larger hanger that was nearly directly across from them.

"I think that's Maxwell's position. He tapped the "info" icon and the latitude and longitude populated a small banner at the top of the screen. "They're the same numbers as before," he said, somewhat nonchalantly.

Ramsey took the phone from White and looked at the screen, pulling back the image to get a wider view as Nikki looked on. She stared at the device noting the green marker, coordinates, and phone number, indicating Maxwell's position. As the view broadened to encompass her position as well, she recognized her own phone number and the red marker, and coordinates to match. She grabbed the phone from Ramsey, nearly knocking it to the ground as White grimaced.

Nikki held the phone up. "So, this is how you knew where I was?" She asked, a scowl forming on her face. You bugged my phone?"

White immediately began to explain. "It's not a bug, really. It's more like a tracking device, only instead of actually applying any type of electronics, I used a program that…"

Nikki looked at White as if he was alien and interrupting his technical explanation, told him to stop talking.

Ramsey turned back to Nikki Sidorova. "Long story short, yes, we've been tailing you with that. It only works when you make a call, we get the signal and it starts tracking. He paused as he looked at White, "Unfortunately Maxwell got his hands on one of our phones and has been using it to track you as well."

Nikki looked strangely at Ramsey. She was surprised at his candor. She handed the phone back to him.

Ramsey continued, "We don't have much time before Maxwell stops trying to reach us long distance and sends his men for us. Each one of those rounds takes about a second to get to us. Add some time to adjust fire and aim and you're talking, two to three seconds of maneuver time between shots. We need to work our way out of here on foot. Around the back of the hangers, then out the gate. Every time, we move for two seconds or so, then take cover, until we get further out of range and then out the gate."

Paul Jackson interjected, following along with Ramsey's plan, "and we can't use the vehicles. The van is dead and besides, it's much easier for a sniper to judge the movement, travel distance and speed of a moving vehicle, than a group of people popping in and out of range."

Nikki interrupted, "I am not going with you. I am getting on that plane." She pointed at the Learjet over her shoulder.

Ramsey looked over at Nikki. "I thought you said your pilot was dead."

Nikki safed her weapon and threw it to Vostav, calling his name as she did. "I have another pilot," she said as she looked to where Anatoly was still crouched behind the auxiliary power unit.

"Whoa. Wait a second, Nikki," Anatoly began, speaking loudly his disagreement with her plan, "I said I flew a little. I never actually took off or landed, that is a totally different thing."

Nikki looked at him fiercely, "But, you know how. I mean, you can do it if you had to, right? Well, you have to."

Anatoly was not giving in on such a crazy idea. "If I could practice, not just jumping in, firing up the engines and taking off. No I…"

Nikki turned back to Ramsey, cutting Anatoly off mid sentence, "There. As I said, I have a pilot."

"Nikki, did you hear what I said? I said, I am not really a pilot."

Vostav tried to console Anatoly, "Don't worry, first we have to get to the plane. We will probably get shot anyway." He smiled, then added, "Six of a dozen, half of the other dozen."

Anatoly rolled his eyes at Vostav's attempt at yet another American metaphor. "Just stop, ok?"

Vostav looked perplexed, "What? It is true."

Maxwell looked off and on through the sight. Every now and then there was movement, but nothing to get a shot at. He called one of his men over. "Back one of the Rovers out of the plane. Grab a couple more guys and something to shoot with. Were going across the way to take care of some business."

The man looked unhappy, "We just set a pallet behind them and tied it down."

Maxwell, stepped away from the fifty cal. "Do you see anything else to drive around here? I don't. Now, get the Rover out of the plane, Whatever is in the way, move it. I need to end this. Now, go."

Ramsey thought about Nikki's plan to fly out. "You realize that all it would take is one well placed shot through either of those two engines and those things would come apart. And, like your guy said, you have to get in the plane first. Right now the only thing between you and the door of that aircraft and Maxwell's fifty is this van and that A.P.U. over there." Ramsey, pointed at the generator behind which Anatoly and Vostav were crouched.

"And that." Paul Jackson was pointing at Nikki's BMW. "We could use that, use it as a distraction. While Maxwell is taking his shots at it, we could get on the plane and take off."

Ramsey and Nikki both exclaimed. "We?"

"I don't recall inviting you to go with me," Nikki said.

Paul Jackson patted his pistol. "Well, maybe you ain't got a choice. Damn-it woman, we done saved your ass twice, do we gotta spell it out any better than that? We're the good guys."

"Paul, who's gonna drive the car to draw fire? I don't believe anybody here wants that job."

"Nobody will drive it. Look at the space here." Jackson motioned to the open expanse of asphalt that lay between their position and Maxwell's.

"I'll jamb something down on the accelerator and let it go. It's already pointed the right way, all we gotta do is move this piece of junk backward about five feet and the Beemer is on its way across the airport runway." Jackson slapped on the door of the Mercedes.

"Maxwell, will think we're trying to make a break for it and shoot the shit out of it." He pointed in Anatoly's direction, "Meanwhile, ol' lover boy over there can get us in the air and out of here."

Alan could see that Jackson was serious, and the plan really did have merit. Still, Nikki hadn't agreed to taking them with her. She looked at Jackson and Ramsey as if they were crazy. "No. You can take the BMW and get out of here. Drive out the way you came busting in. You are not going with me."

Jackson was quick to respond. "Look, Woman. You want us to draw fire while you and your boyfriend fly off into the sunset? Save your ass again, while we get the shit shot out of us crossing sideways across the airport? Like some C.I.A. shooting gallery? Not just no, but hell no!"

Jackson yanked his pistol out and pointed it past Ramsey at Nikki's face. "You don't have to be on the plane when it takes off," he growled menacingly.

Rick White slid down to the asphalt.

Bob Matthews, who had been absolutely silent up until now, yanked his weapon up and pointed it at Vostav who was pointing his pistol at Paul Jackson. "Ok, everyone, why don't we all just calm down. If we kill each other, Maxwell will be out of work. I don't want to make his job any easier, but I will if I have to."

He glanced over at Jackson, then back at Vostav. "Paul, how about you put yours away first, then Mr. Ruskie over there, and then me, same way as they all came out."

Ramsey didn't hold back, "Everybody put your guns down. We are not the enemy here." He turned to Nikki. "Let's get the hell out of here. Nikki, we're going with you. You have no choice. Let's work this plan and get out of here."

Jackson holstered his weapon. "I need a belt and the keys to the van."

Brandon tossed Jackson the keys. "I hope this thing will be able to move just a little. On second thought, Brandon, come over here."

He handed the keys back and explained what he wanted to happen, realizing that he couldn't "*drive*" the BMW and the van, too.

"When I tell you, stay low, start the van and put it in reverse. All you gotta do is move it back enough for the Beemer to clear, then throw it back in park and get the hell out, then run to the plane."

He looked at everyone using the van for cover. "That Beemer is coming right through here, so move when the van moves, but stay low."

Bob Matthews tossed Jackson his belt as Paul grabbed one of the police machine guns, unfolded the stock and crawled to the side of the BMW. He yelled to Anatoly on the other side of the car at the A.P.U. "Hey, Lover Boy, When you see this BMW move past the front of the plane, get your ass up, get the door of the plane open and get it fired up. Got it?"

Anatoly was unsure of himself, but answered loudly, "Yes, I got it." Anatoly turned to Vostav. "Once you hear the engines fire up, disconnect the A.P.U. You only have to wait for one engine to start." Vostav nodded his reply.

Paul Jackson opened the door of the BMW and, leaning over the seat, placed the key in the ignition and started the car. He straightened the steering wheel, sighting the tires down the sidewalls to the position of the hangers and the C130 aircraft at the far end of the runway. Then he looped the belt around the rim of the steering wheel and placed the loose end over the door hinge letting it hang between where the front edge of the door met the back edge of the fender. Once closed, the door would hold the belt in place, in turn locking the steering wheel in position.

Next, he moved the seat as far back as possible, unfolded the stock of the submachine gun, placed the weapon's muzzle on the brake pedal and the stock against the front frame of the seat, then repositioned the seat forward, causing the weapon's barrel to apply pressure to the brake.

Carefully, trying to stay low, he reached across the seat and placed the transmission selector lever into drive. The car bumped forward as the transmission engaged, but didn't move due to the brake pressure being applied by the submachine gun and the seat on the brake pedal. He slid off his own belt and looped it around the stock of the weapon, then threaded it through the window opening.

All he had to do now was force the accelerator down, release the brake and close the door and the car would be on its way. Paul looked for something to jam the pedal down, a stick or something. He spotted the plastic sill plate at the bottom of the door opening, grasped the edge of the plastic trim, and yanked it up and off completely.

He jammed the plastic trim piece against the accelerator, bending the piece to adjust it to a proper length. The engine revved and the rear wheels strained against the brakes.

Paul Jackson carefully closed the door, pulling the steering wheel's tether tight and ensuring that the other belt, the one attached to the submachine gun, remained hanging from the open window. Just as the door closed the machine gun slipped. The Beemer suddenly lurched forward with a grunt as some of the pressure on the brake pedal was released, enough for one of the rear tires to spin against the pavement, creating a huge cloud of white smoke.

The smoke became increasingly thick as the speed of the spinning tire increased, wafting around the car and into the air, up and over the Mercedes van. Jackson screamed over the sound of the BMW's squealing tire and racing engine,

"Now Brandon!"

Kenneth Wash

CHAPTER 47

DIVERSION

GORDON Maxwell saw the cloud of white smoke billowing at Nikki's end of the runway and wondered what was going on. The first thing that entered his mind was that Ramsey was deploying some type of smoke screen to cover their movement. What movement though? He looked through the scope, scanning from the van to the plane to the hanger, but saw nothing that would indicate some sort of maneuver, either forward or in retreat.

He eyed his people unloading the Rovers and picked up his hand held radio. "Charlie, you need to hurry. Something's going on down there."

He watched the tall, burley figure stop what he was doing and look down the length of the runway. Charlie pulled up his radio, "We're about ready, first Rover is out. The other one is ready to back out. I'll send a couple guys over in the one that's loose to pick you up." He waved to the two men in the Rover, pointing to Maxwell just inside the hanger door.

Maxwell couldn't hear what he said, but watched as the rover pulled around and headed his way. He started to tear down the rifle, but decided to take one more look at what was going on. The smoke was hanging heavy, growing to encompass the van and the front of the plane, drifting slowly in his direction, obscuring his view.

Brandon was inside the Mercedes van, kneeling between the front seats, having entered from the open sliding door. The smoke from the BMW's tire was filling the van making it hard to see anything outside the van more than a few feet away. The engine was running, but Brandon couldn't put the shift lever in reverse without first depressing the brake, and he couldn't do that easily crawling on all fours, staying low to avoid a sniper round to the head. He reached as far forward as he could, pushing the brake pedal with his left hand, but was in no position to pull the shift selector lever into reverse.

Jackson was screaming at Brandon to hurry. With one final attempt Brandon managed to grab the selector lever and pull it into reverse. The van moved only slightly and made a loud popping noise that sounded terrible to Brandon. He pushed the accelerator pedal further down. The four cylinder turbo diesel groaned against the inability of the transmission to move, then with another series of popping and snapping noises, the van jerked and lurched about a foot backward and then stopped.

Ramsey stuck his head in the door. "What's the matter?"

Brandon released the pedal, turned back to face Ramsey, "It won't move. I think because of the hit."

Alan Ramsey looked at the length they had to move, then at the developing thick white smoke. He couldn't see more than a couple feet in front of him, the unintended consequence of the spinning tire.

"White, Matthews, come here, help me push!" he yelled over the noise of the revving 2.1 liter diesel engine of the Mercedes, the BMW's roaring engine, and spinning, squealing tire.

Nikki, seeing the slow progress and realizing the ability to move about unseen in the dense, white smoke, yelled to Anatoly. "Anny, get the door open now, fire up the engines while the smoke is covering you."

Anatoly turned to Vostav, "Get ready to disconnect as soon as you hear the engine start," he yelled.

Vostav simply nodded, gave a thumbs up sign, and grasped the locking ring of the auxiliary power unit's umbilical power cable. Within seconds Anatoly was inside the cockpit flipping switches.

He was not familiar with the newer aircraft layout, having flown only a few different types of aircraft, and never from the point of start up, but he remembered his training, and more so the simulators and computer programs that walked a budding pilot through the start up and shut down procedures of the different types of aircraft. It would take him a minute, but he would get it started.

Brandon screamed to be heard. "Everybody back off, let me try something else." He yanked the shift lever into drive and accelerated. The van shot forward about three feet. He applied the brakes and immediately slammed the selector lever into reverse, accelerating hard.

The Mercedes van rocketed backward. The torque of the cracked and leaking transaxle forced the differential gears past the internal debris, shattering the weakened aluminum transmission case, but with enough inertial energy to move the van out of the path of the BMW.

Paul Jackson yanked hard on the belt dislodging the submachine gun from the brake pedal. The weapon clattered against the framework of the door glass opening, flinging up and out of the window opening and releasing the brakes. The BMW launched like a rocket, disappearing into the cloud of smoke and down the runway toward Maxwell's position.

Maxwell searched for a target. He placed the tip of his index finger on the trigger as he scanned the billowing cloud. He could make out the silhouette of the Vito van and set the cross hairs at the center of the driver's side window when the dark blue BMW burst into the open. White clouds of smoke rolled along the sides of the car, spinning and swirling in the turbulence of the vehicle's forward movement as the Beemer came into full view.

Maxwell squinted as he set his site reticle on the driver's side of the windshield and squeezed the trigger. The round leapt from the barrel and zoomed down the runway colliding with the windshield of the oncoming vehicle. There was no change in the vehicle's momentum or direction. He adjusted his aim and pulled the trigger again. The second round slammed through the windshield, passing through the interior and continuing on to some unseen destination. Maxwell saw the impact through the high powered scope, but there was still no change. In fact, the BMW seemed to be picking up speed and closing the distance, now less than a mile away, and on a straight line trajectory to his position.

Vostav heard the whine of the first of the two turbojet engines as it fired up and came up to speed. He grasped the ring of the receptacle connector and spun it left, causing the A.P.U. umbilical to back out. He let it drop to the ground as the silhouettes of Ramsey, Nikki, Jackson, Matthews and Rick White moved quickly through the lingering white cloud and up the two steps.

Brandon was still scrambling out of the van when the first round from Maxwell's M107 slammed into the port wingtip fuel tank with a thud, followed by the second round that hit the leading edge of the port wingtip and ricocheted with a bright flash.

Brandon saw the spark from the ricocheting round and yelled at Vostav. "They're shooting at us!"

Vostav heard Brandon but couldn't make out what he said until he had cleared the distance from the van and was at the door. Vostav was waiting, ready to close the door. Brandon saw liquid gurgling from the round thing at the end of the wing and immediately put the picture of imminent disaster together in his mind. He pointed to what he figured was fuel leaking from the end of the wing and screamed for Vostav to look.

This time Vostav heard what he said and followed Brandon's pointing to the subject of his concern. His eyes went wide at the sight of the leaking fuel as he ushered Brandon up the steps and inside the plane. Vostav stopped just inside the door and began speaking in fast Russian at Anatoly and pointing out the still open door.

Anatoly turned to look out the cockpit glass at the leaking wingtip tank and then at the center pedestal panel fuel gauge, flipping the selector from total pounds, through each position, starting with the starboard or right wingtip fuel cell.

All five of the tanks were full according to the gauge. He searched for any shutoff, but found only the fuel jettison switches for each tank. There was no way to control the fuel loss. Anatoly turned to Nikki, "All we can do is let it drain until it reaches the level of the leak, until it gets below the halfway point, then I can turn on the transfer pump and pull what is left into the fuselage tank. He turned back to Vostav, "Close the door, let's get the hell out of here."

The BMW was moving at about 80 miles an hour when it passed the halfway point to Maxwell's position. Maxwell aimed at the left front tire of the BMW and took his shot. The round screamed down the runway colliding with the tire that immediately disintegrated, causing a sudden slowdown. The BMW veered to the left away from Maxwell's hanger as the first of the two Range Rovers stopped and Maxwell jumped in.

The driver pushed the accelerator to the floor heading directly toward the Beemer, approaching the car from the right side in a sweeping arc that matched the BMW's sudden change of trajectory. The SUV's tires protested the maneuver and the top heavy vehicle pitched left, threatening to roll onto its side, as the driver pulled alongside the BMW, matching its speed and glancing over through the tinted side glass.

The rear passenger in the Rover pulled up his pistol and let loose a volley of rounds that penetrated the skin of the door and slammed into first the right rear door glass and then the right front. The glass shattered, falling away in tiny bits, raining down on the runway. The absence of the darkly tinted glass revealed the surprising reason why Maxwell's accurate shooting through the windshield caused no change in the vehicle's movement. The BMW was empty.

The hanging smoke from the launching of the BMW formed two large spiraling vortexes, drawing through the two screaming jet engines as Anatoly shoved the throttles forward, propelling the Learjet down the length of the runway with amazing acceleration. Anatoly calculated his speed and thrust trying to remember his training and the specifics of Learjet aircraft.

Information of all sorts rattled through Anatoly's brain as he tried to remember the procedures for takeoff: percent throttle, aircraft weight, minimum length of runway needed, and when to pull the nose up. He checked off his mental list, glad for the extra long runway that Domodevo offered.

The twin turbine jet engines reached full throttle in about four seconds. Anatoly cursed, waiting for the flaps extension indicator to illuminate. His eyes were glued to the far end of the runway when, in his peripheral view, the indicator illuminated signaling the full extension of the flaps rearward as the Learjet blasted down the asphalt and reached takeoff speed at about the three quarter runway mark.

Anatoly pulled back on the wheel as the fifty-nine-hundred pounds of thrust pushed the plane forward to begin the climb. The performance was impressive to Anatoly as he felt first the nose wheel, then the rear landing gear escape the tarmac, sending the aircraft skyward at more than seventeen-hundred feet per second.

Maxwell saw the Learjet burst through the spiraling smoke, but there was nothing he could do to stop it at this point.

The driver of the Range Rover turned the vehicle back toward the waiting C-130 as the BMW ambled on, smashing into the airport's crosswind barrier, driving off the edge of the asphalt and going airborne for only a second before plowing, nose first into the grassy hillside.

Maxwell was quiet for the return trip to the hanger and up the loading ramp into the cargo bay. He opened his door and stepped out of the vehicle before it had fully stopped, walking away toward the diminishing light. He stepped out onto the ramp, turning back to face the driver of the Range Rover.

"Get this crap reloaded and tied down. I want to be out of here before nightfall." He glanced at the waning daylight then looked at his watch. "That means you've got about forty minutes. See if you can get it done in half that."

The tall driver saluted a poor rendition of a military salute, "You got it, Boss," and then turned and began directing the efforts for the reload.

CHAPTER 48

GAME ON

C.I.A. HEADQUARTERS, LANGLEY, VA.

DARIN Martin held his identification card against the number pad and waited for the metallic click of the magnetic release, then pulled the door open to step into the outer corridor. He listened to the sound of silence as he made his way to his temporary work area. It was always so quiet here during the lunch hour, he thought.

He preferred the quiet and found he could get more work done when everyone was out of the office. Martin stepped over to the desk and pulled at the chair, dismayed to find the right armrest lodged under the edge of the desktop. He didn't give it much thought at first as he placed a knee in the chair to push it down enough to roll free, but once sitting he noticed the chair height was different. "I was only gone an hour," he thought. "So many stations in the room and somebody had to use mine."

He muttered a quiet expletive when he noticed the machine was shut down. "Really," he mused as he pressed the power button to bring the system on-line, sighing, knowing that it could take forever to get logged back on. Instead of the usual C.I.A. image startup screen, the laptop monitor stayed dark for a moment then displayed a prompt in white lettering and a flashing cursor.

NO OPERATING SYSTEM PRESENT, PRESS C TO BOOT FROM DISK. PRESS ANY KEY TO SHUT DOWN.

"Uh oh," Martin tried pressing control-alt-delete, but to no avail. He held the power button down to shut off the laptop then attempted to restart it. The hard drive whirred and clicked for a moment then halted, the monitor displaying the same prompt.

NO OPERATING SYSTEM PRESENT, PRESS C TO BOOT FROM DISK. PRESS ANY KEY TO SHUT DOWN.

He thought about his last actions on the machine. He burned the disks. He remembered pulling out his CAC card, lifting the disk from the tray and...he'd left the CD tray open, but now it was closed.

Somebody had definitely been at his work station. Temporary or not, this was his system and he had information on the laptop that was not saved anywhere else. He cussed again as he pulled out his phone to call Gabe Anderson.

CHAPTER 49

THE FRIENDLY SKIES

ANATOLY relaxed as the plane settled out at twenty-six-thousand feet. They had been aloft for about twenty minutes. So far so good, he thought, as he searched around the cockpit, getting familiar with the controls. He found the jet's navigational computer, powered it on and scrolled through the destination log. There were only two entries, Domodevo International Airport, where they had departed, and Sviatoshyn Airfield.

He selected Sviatoshyn from the list. Information about the airport, its latitude and longitude, length of the runway and information about accessibility, city demographics and ownership populated the screen. It was an industrial airport in the middle of a large industrial complex, part of Antonov's Aircraft production facility, about eleven kilometers northwest of Kiev's city center. The airport had a single runway, just over 1.8 kilometers long, nearly three times the length he needed to land, and a good thing too, considering he may need all of it, given his skill level.

Anatoly programmed the flight calculator, selecting UKKT, the abbreviation for Sviatoshyn, from the list as the end point and UUDD, Domodivo Airport, as his start point. The flight calculator took only a moment to present the distance of 401 Nautical Miles and a time of one hour and thirty minute flight time at thirty-four-thousand feet.

Information about weather, wind speed, height above sea level and landing crosswind averages flashed on the screen. Sviatoshyn looked like the perfect airport, both to accommodate Anatoly's lack of skill during his landing, and, as was the case of Gregorov and the flights he took with his plane that would have been packed with weapons systems, very private, with no international security. Yes, it was perfect, he thought again, as he set the autopilot for the flight.

Nikki sat in the copilot's seat, her chair spun nearly 180 degrees. She stared at Alan Ramsey, wondering who he was and what he really wanted. The thought that her adversary was on the same plane and had helped her to get away from her new enemy, Maxwell, amused her somewhat.

Ramsey looked up just in time to see Nikki looking in his direction. He wondered what she was thinking as he gave her a slight nod, acknowledging her glance. Still staring, Nikki got to her feet and headed toward him, a look of mistrust on her face, her head back, her green eyes squinted, and her lips pursed.

She stopped at the seat Vostav was sitting in and leaned on the back of the seat. She snapped her fingers, getting his attention and pointing to the seat next to him. Vostav's hand disappeared behind the seat back and reappeared with Nikki's Makarov pistol.

Bob Matthews looked on from his seat not far behind that of his boss, wary of Nikki as she slid the magazine out, inspected the number of rounds, and then slid the magazine back in. Matthews heard the click of the magazine lock in place. He was ready to react in the event he was needed, but knew that she could easily take any one of them out before they could even leave their seat.

Ramsey was watching too. He noted how Nikki moved, graceful, sure footed, like a predator, eyes locked on her target, as if stalking. He stared at her emerald green eyes and her glistening auburn hair. Nikki was sexy for sure, her shapely body like a tool of the trade that she used to get what she wanted, when she wanted it.

She stepped within a foot of Ramsey and stopped, stroking the pistol as if deciding whether or not to rack it. "So…Alan," she said his name almost playfully, "I guess it is true that the enemy of my enemy is my friend. Or so it seems at this moment."

Nikki stepped directly in front of him. She stepped one leg over his, straddling his legs as she leaned on the back of the seat behind her. She held the pistol lightly in her right hand, then pointed it directly at him.

Ramsey was surprised when she threw first one knee, then the other into his seat, straddling his lap with her legs on either side of his.

Nikki leaned in closer, forcing herself on him. She put her hands above his shoulders, resting her forearms across the top of the seat and leaned down to within inches of his face. She whispered, "The enemy of my enemy," this time not completing the phrase. The way she said it was so seductive, so alluring. Ramsey could see how she so easily manipulated the men whom she had used as necessity demanded.

"Ok, that's enough, Nikki. You can get off of me now." Alan Ramsey blurted out as he grabbed Nikki at the waist. She planted herself tightly, resisting his efforts to move her away. Suddenly the sound of Nikki racking the nine mil could be heard behind his head. He stopped at the sound, dropping his hands from her waist.

Nikki sat back, bringing the pistol forward to place the barrel against Ramsey's left temple. She again leaned to within inches of his face.

Ramsey tilted his head to the side, but the action only brought more pressure of the barrel against his head.

"Uh, uh, Mr. Ramsey, put them back," she ordered, grabbing his left hand and placing it on her waist. "Now the other," she said, "like before."

She could tell he was not happy with what she was doing. "What's the matter, don't you like girls, Mr. Ramsey?" she teased, her lips close to his, whispering the words.

Ramsey pushed her away from him, "I do, but my wife, the one who gave me this ring," He held up his left hand, "she doesn't like girls, especially good looking girls. She really wouldn't like you." He answered, sliding her toward his knees.

Nikki's eyes lit up some as she contemplated his seemingly unintentional compliment. She relaxed her stance, lowered the pistol and leaned against the chair back behind her. Still sitting on him she asked, "What do you want from me, Alan Ramsey? If you are not my enemy and you are not my friend, then, who are you? What do you want?"

"What we *wanted* was to arrest Gregorov and find out more about his involvement with the terrorists that were in the U.S. We had hoped to get information that would lead us to his weapons, find any accomplices and arrest them. You know, the way the law is *supposed* to work,…"

Ramsey poked her in the chest, jabbing a finger against her breastbone. "But *you* screwed up our plans when *you* put a bullet in his head."

"Ah, the best laid plans of mice and men…," Nikki said, again not finishing the quote, as she moved into the chair directly in front of Ramsey, releasing it to spin and face him.

"So, you figured you would just follow me to the weapons, and then what, I would just let you take them?" she spun the chair side to side, as a fidgety child would. "Somehow, I do not see that happening." She patted the pistol.

"Well, not exactly. We expected to follow you to Gregorov and then follow Gregorov to the weapons. Without him we have no choice but to follow you."

Ramsey leaned forward in his seat, "You have more problems than me and my team. Even if you threw us off the plane this very instant you will still have to deal with people a hell of a lot more hell bent on getting those weapons than a few C.I.A. agents. Think about those missiles, fired from a drone. You lost two of your men because of it. More than likely that drone was sent up by Maxwell. We don't control that guy. He's rogue and, evidently, he has worked for Gregorov in the past."

Nikki's curiosity was piqued. "Who does this Maxwell work for now then? He surely doesn't seem to discriminate between you and me." She leaned forward in her chair, "Seems to me that *you* are just as much a target as I am."

Ramsey thought about the answer. The truth was he didn't know, but he knew who he suspected, additionally he didn't think he should be discussing matters of national security with a Russian assassin, or whatever she was. "We don't know for sure. There are people in the U.S. trying to figure that out as we speak. For whatever reason, the closer we've gotten to you, the more we've become targets of Maxwell's."

"Well, it's pretty obvious your own government is trying to stop you," Nikki surmised. "Perhaps you are about to uncover a deep, dark secret. One that would shake the very foundation of your country." Nikki said the words with a flair of intrigue.

She was smiling, but Ramsey was not. Depending on what they discovered here, and back home, it was possible that Nikki had just hit the nail on the head.

"That's why we need to see what's on Gregorov's laptop. Let us analyze the data. We can help you, but you have to trust us."

"Trust you?" Nikki got up from her chair and handed Vostav the pistol. She turned back to Ramsey. "Trust you?"

"When I was seventeen I trusted you. I trusted America to stop the killing of my people. I trusted America to come to the rescue." Nikki's eyes narrowed and her scowl deepened as she glared at Ramsey.

"Instead, your soldiers might just as well have killed the people they were trying to *protect*, for all the good they did. America failed then, and your country is failing today. I can not trust that America will do anything to help, not without a cost, a cost that your country will not pay and others will have to bear."

"Damn it, Nikki, look around you. We didn't have to come find you. We didn't have to put ourselves between you and Maxwell. I lost one of my men just two days ago, killed by that bastard Maxwell. Another is lying in a hospital at this very moment. Those are my guys. Not yours, not the Russian police's, mine. Just like these guys here."

He swept a hand across the cabin to encompass his team before continuing.

"Think about it. We wouldn't be on this plane if you couldn't place your trust in us." He locked onto her green eyes, "You might not be able to trust my government, but you *can* trust me and you can trust these guys."

Alan Ramsey wondered what Nikki was thinking. She was smart enough to figure out who the real enemy was, and it wasn't him. He pushed ahead with his questions.

"Nikki, tell me, what are you going to do with the weapons? We've got your personal laptop and frankly, it's scary to see some of the information you have. We saw your list of names. Krstic, Mladic, Kofi Anon, U.N. commanders and leaders from around the world. Looks like one big hit list to me. Is that what it is, a hit list? If so, maybe we should go line through Gregorov, Metelov and that guy, Princip..."

Nikki cut him off, "I did not kill Princip, His own people killed him." She yelled, stepping forward as if challenging Ramsey.

Ramsey kept at it. "Are you planning to use Gregorov's weapons to assassinate all those people? 'Cause if that's your plan, then add my agent's name, Nathan Marks, to your list, because, guess what, Nikki, he died just the same as if you pulled the trigger, and there will be many more. You will be no better than Mladic himself, wiping out people who had nothing to do with what happened then, innocent people, just like your people. You have to know, I can't allow that to happen."

Nikki let his words sink in, and then scoffed at his attempted guilt trip. She looked away briefly and, when her eyes snapped back to his, she growled, "You cannot stop me. I could kill you right now."

Ramsey sighed, sensing his words were lost on her. "Yes, yes you can, but as I said before, you've got more problems than just me and these guys. Help us help you. Let us look at Gregorov's laptop, so we can at least take any WMD off the store's shelves. The last thing America needs, or any country for that matter, is some rogue assholes getting their hands on chemical, biological, radiological or nuclear weapons."

He made Nikki an offer. "You give us access to the WMD and I will make every effort to convince my boss to help you find the people responsible for the deaths in Bosnia, That's what this is all about isn't it, revenge for the massacres, the execution and murders of the people you knew?" He paused for a second, "Revenge for your own family?"

The look on Nikki's face softened as Ramsey attempted to close the deal.

"The C.I.A. has teams of forensic investigators. You help me stop Maxwell, help us get rid of those weapons and, I promise you, the U.S. government will reinvigorate the effort to find those murdered by the Serbians. We will help you find your family. That's what *you* really want anyway, isn't it, to find your father and brother?"

Nikki was quiet for a long time. She looked away, thinking about her answer and wondering if Ramsey could actually help.

Nikki was just about to speak when something outside the window flashed by, catching Alan Ramsey's attention. He leaned over to get a better look, counting first two, and then a third, military aircraft falling in alongside the Learjet. He moved quickly past Nikki and into the cockpit to see the vapor trail from the fast moving Russian Sukhoi-PAK-FA T50 stealth fighter that shot past his window and was now in front of their aircraft.

The Learjet shuddered from the turbulence created by the close proximity of the screaming fighter jet. "MIGs," Anatoly reported. "They just came out of nowhere! That one nearly hit us." He pointed forward into the western twilight. Ramsey looked to where he was pointing and could see a gray speck turn right and begin to come about, settling in on a wide arc to eventually circle the Learjet in flight.

Paul Jackson awoke to Anatoly's yelling, got to his feet and ran across the cabin to look out the window to the Learjet's port side. He could plainly see the red star on the tail of the Russian gray and white aircraft, as well as several missiles hanging below the wing. The plane moved up slowly, matching the speed of Anatoly's Learjet. Jackson yelled so as to be heard in the cockpit as he stepped away from the window, "That's not a MIG, that's an SU-T50, and you've got one coming up on the left."

"How close are we to the Ukrainian border?" Ramsey asked, searching the horizon for any sign of more aircraft, or worse the trail of vapor indicating a missile.

Anatoly pointed at the ground map on the display in front of them, tapping the screen. The heavy outline of the north-eastern border of the Ukraine and Russia was flickering closer to the image of the Learjet. "Maybe one-hundred and sixty kilometers away."

Anatoly suddenly held his hand up to the headset he was wearing, "Quiet, everybody, quiet!"

The pilot of one of the aircraft on his left was speaking to Anatoly over his headset.

"Ukrainian aircraft TX240, you have entered a Russian controlled, restricted airspace. Turn your aircraft around,

heading, 55.4086 degrees north, 37.9061 degrees east. Acknowledge your receipt of this message. Over."

Anatoly looked to his left. The lead aircraft was flying next to him, the pilot, visor raised, was looking in his direction. Anatoly saw the lips of the pilot move as the voice in his headset returned, repeating verbatim what was just said.

The coordinates were the latitude and longitude of Domodevo Airport. He was nearly positive. Anatoly looked at the flight navigation menu at the departure information. 55.4086N, 37.9061E was displayed in the upper left hand corner.

"He wants us to turn around. Go back to Moscow." Anatoly said.

The pilot repeated his order.

"Ukrainian aircraft TX240, you have entered a Russian controlled airspace. Turn your aircraft..."

Before he could finish Anatoly answered, "Roger, I acknowledge, Wait one. Over."

He turned to Nikki, "We have to turn around. I don't have a choice."

Nikki moved into the cockpit. "No, we are not turning around. Tell him we are requesting an emergency, tell him the pilot is dead and you have to land at the nearest airport. That is why you are going this direction."

Anatoly looked afraid as he toggled his headset back on. He relayed the information. The pilot only repeated his previous statement, then added, "All Ukrainian aircraft must land for inspection."

The circling SU-T50 was finishing it's first full circle around the Learjet at a distance of about ten kilometers. The fighter jet suddenly yanked hard to the left, a stream of chaff flares spouting from both sides of his aircraft.

"Oh, shit." Jackson exclaimed, seeing the stream of flares and knowing the reason for their deployment was more than likely an inbound missile. "Bank right, Lover boy!" he yelled, pointing directly ahead to the chaff and at a barely visible vapor trail.

Anatoly had traversed the ten kilometers and was about to fly through the fountain of chaff when the R-27T infrared homing missile, fired from a Ukrainian MIG-29 from over a mile away, curved downward, collided with the super heated air and burning phosphorous and exploded, creating a huge ball of flame and concussive force.

The screaming Learjet banked right, pitching its wings in a nearly vertical position and placing the belly of the plane toward the explosion. The force of the blast hit the non tactical aircraft hard, its light skin no match for the hundreds of particles blasted outward from the center of the detonation, peppering the lower section of the aircraft with shrapnel, continuing through the fuselage fuel tank, up through the floor, barely missing Rick White and Bob Matthews and embedding in the plastic trim panels of the interior.

Matthews smelled fuel immediately, noticing several places where debris from the missile tore through the aircraft, liquid bubbling through holes in the floor and carpeting.

"Uh, we got a problem back here," he yelled, "There's fuel leaking into the cabin."

Ahead of the Learjet, two Ukrainian MIG-29s pierced the clouds and arced outward in pursuit of the flanking SU-T50's that had broken from their formation. A third MIG was heading straight toward Anatoly, pulling away within seconds of a collision.

Two K-77M missiles ejected from the Russian SU-T50's wing mounts, ignited and shot past the Learjet as the screaming T50 peeled off and out of sight. Within seconds another explosion could be felt as the Ukrainian MIG-29 disintegrated in mid air behind Anatoly's Learjet-25.

Amid the chaos the fuel in the fuselage tank had dropped to a level that caused a low fuel light and an audible, ear piercing alarm to sound. Anatoly's head swiveled from the controls to the gauges and back as he set the selector switch to the center position and then to each of the other four selections to get a reading on each of the five fuel tanks. He had lost over half of the remaining fuel in his main tank. He calculated his airspeed and the distance.

Except for the port wing-tip fuel tank that had easily lost half of the fuel early on in the flight, all the other tanks miraculously survived, but he could not draw from them unless he manually transferred the fuel into the rapidly leaking main tank first. At the present rate of depletion he could run out of fuel before reaching the airport that was now only minutes away.

Anatoly set the transfer pump for the right wing tank first. The Learjet dropped from the sky as Anatoly pushed forward on the controls, gaining distance from the dogfight above him, the pilots too engaged in their battle to notice or even care.

"You better buckle in," he exclaimed to the two standing in the doorway, and Nikki to his right, "I may not make it to the airport."

CHAPTER 50

BEGINNING OF THE END
C.I.A. HEADQUARTERS, LANGLEY, VA.

"ARE you sure about this Gabe?" The Director of National Intelligence, James Grouper, asked, but before Gabe Anderson could answer, added, "You DO realize that locking down the President's and the SECSTATE's systems is not something that is going to be taken lightly. Carlton will go on the rampage, and Erickson will have a field day with it. That son of a bitch will actually be worse than the POTUS if we shut him down."

Anderson handed the disk over to Grouper. "Sir, I'm positive. If we don't take control of their systems I'm afraid that the information will disappear. The President's is not so much my concern, but frankly, I don't trust Erickson at all. He has been neck deep into my business with the Gregorov investigation. He knows Maxwell. They have some kind of history. We have proof on that disk. What's worse, according to Ramsey's man, Agent White, Erickson has had direct phone communication with Maxwell as recent as a couple days ago. And now, to find out that Maxwell may be responsible for the death of one of our agents and at least three Russians, not to mention an attempt on Ramsey's life at their hotel…" His words tapered off as he took a breath and then sighed deeply before continuing. "It can't be coincidence. Too much is pointing back at Erickson."

The C.I.A. Director, Dean Burton waited for Gabe Anderson to finish before taking the lead. "James, I've listened to the recording made by Erickson's secretary. I know it will more than likely be inadmissible in court since they weren't aware, but to me it's proof. Hell, If it was anybody else I could possibly doubt it's legitimacy, but the recording was made by Betty Rogers. She's a dinosaur here in D.C., and she signed a statement. You know Betty. She never, ever goes off half cocked. I agree with Gabe on this. We need to lock them down and get the Justice Department to write up a piece to pull their systems for evidence."

He paused for a moment and then added, "James, you know I respect the President. He and I go way back. The guy has saved our asses many times over the last twenty years, but if he's given leash to Erickson, and Erickson has done something like this, with his knowledge, and it's obvious he knows, you'll see when you listen to the recording, then by God, we need to act against him. I hate to say it, but that's why your office has congressional oversight."

Director Grouper stared at the disk in his hand, shaking it to feel the weight as it got figuratively heavier by the moment. He looked across his desk and sighed deeply. "I don't need to listen to the disk to move forward with this. I will, but I have two of the most trusted souls I have ever met telling me I don't have a choice, and frankly, that's good enough for me. I'll save the disk for evidence."

Grouper frowned as he picked up his phone and dialed the direct line for U.S. Attorney General, Michael Faraday. Grouper dispensed the pleasantries and got straight to the point, explaining the situation and the source of the information. "Son of a bitch,"

Faraday exclaimed. "Whatever you need from me you've got. Guess I better start thinking about retirement, I just started getting used to this job. If we get rid of Carlton I'll be out within weeks." He laughed, "Oh well, gotta do what's right."

"Thanks Mike," Grouper replied. "We appreciate your support. So that you are aware my next stop is the I.T. office. I'm going to have them remove the President's and Erickson's system from the network. That's going to happen as soon as I hang up with you. Biggest thing I'll be needing from you right away is the OK to physically remove the boxes, including the external drives and any other back-up systems that are in place, so be prepared to back me up."

"Sounds like a coup when you say it like that." Faraday said in jest.

Director Grouper wasn't smiling. "Well, you know, it sort of is. A high-tech coup. Probably be one for the history books. And that's how we'll be remembered, the guys that took down the best President this country has had in the last twenty years." He paused, then said, "Damned unfortunate that good men get caught up in this kind of crap." He began to wrap up the call. "I'll send you an email to cover everything we just talked about. All I'll need is a reply that says we're good to go on shutting them down."

Michael Faraday had the last word. "James, tell your guys to be careful. Dot the I's, cross the T's and all that, but also watch their backs. I have never trusted Erickson and from what you're telling me he may be out of control. Send me that email to get the ball rolling. See you when the dust settles."

Grouper lowered the phone slowly, placing it back in the receiver and keeping his hand on it as if he were using it to steady himself. He looked at Gabe Anderson and the C.I.A. director, Dean Burton, both of whom appeared to be holding their breath. "Well, Faraday is on board."

The two men let out a collective sigh. Burton expressed his gratitude to his long time friend, "Thanks Dan, That's good news for the team." He thrust a hand toward the Director of National Intelligence who walked around the desk to grasp it and walk them toward his door.

Gabe Anderson stopped and fidgeted within his pocket, then pulled his phone out. It was Darin Martin. "Excuse me, Gentlemen, but I should probably take this."

The two men nodded their approval as Anderson pulled the phone to his ear. "Gabe Anderson speaking."

"Sir, we've got a problem. I just sat down at my government laptop to back up the information to the server and discovered that somebody has wiped my hard drive."

Suddenly the look on Gabe Anderson's face took a turn, like the darkening of the sky before a sudden storm. "Are you sure?"

Martin assured him he was. "There's no question that the data is gone. The entire operating system has been wiped."

"There's no way that it is a technical issue? That something failed mechanically or that…"

Darin Martin jumped back in. "Sir, there were other things about my work area that showed someone was here screwing around: the way my chair was adjusted, stuck under the edge of the desk because it had been raised, the CD tray was closed, when I know I left it open, the computer was off and I could see that it had been moved. Whatever happened to give this thing the blue screen of death, happened on purpose."

Anderson grimaced. "Shit. Good thing you managed to save the info to a disk. You still have the thumb drive too, right?"

Martin answered, "Yes sir, and Jennifer Wilkins has a duplicate of the disk I gave you."

Anderson was quiet for a moment as he thought about what to do. "Dan, go to my office. Bring that laptop with you. You can work from one of the systems in my office. Get someone from forensics to dust that thing for prints. I'll be back in the office shortly. See you there."

Gabe ended the conversation and slid his phone in his pocket. "Gentlemen, put on your game face."

CHAPTER 51

EMERGENCY LANDING

ANATOLY kept his eye on the center tank's fuel gauge as he brought the plane down to about two thousand feet. His concern wasn't so much running out of fuel, he was more concerned about what would happen if his landing attempt failed. What if he came in too hard and scrubbed the ground? The resulting fireball would be spectacular for sure, for people watching from outside the plane anyway.

He stared at the fuel dump switch. Perhaps he could dump what was left in the tanks just before touchdown, jettison the remaining fuel to lessen the possibility of burning to death, only to crash land anyway because of a lack of fuel. He didn't have enough experience in the seat to understand everything there was to know about flying a prop driven plane, let alone a high performance Learjet.

He could see the runway of the Sviatoshyn Airfield ahead and below. He was maybe two kilometers out, as he dropped the plane another thousand feet and toggled the switch on his headset.

"Sviatoshyn tower this is UKTX Two Four Zero. Emergency conditions, I am leaking fuel and running low. Requesting emergency equipment be on hand for an emergency landing."

A female voice replied. *Two four zero, we have you on a good heading. I.L.S. is a category one. You are cleared for landing.*

Anatoly strained to remember what he had learned. I.L.S. was the abbreviation for the Instrument Landing System. Category one, that was the best for landing, he remembered. Visibility was good and he had until the minimal height of resolution of 60 meters above the runway to make his decision to land or abort and repeat an attempt. Of course, that was under normal conditions. He was leaking fuel at a rapid pace. There would be no second attempt. He would have to get it right the first time.

The plane was at twenty-five-hundred feet now. Still too high to line up the I.L.S., but he could see the runway easily enough. He was on a proper glide path vertically.

"Tower, what is the runway frequency for I.L.S.? This is my first landing here."

The woman's voice came back. *UKTX Two Four Zero, I.L.S. runway frequency should be set to 127.125.*

Anatoly set the frequency, quickly selecting the NAV-1 controls and inputting the numbers. He then switched the NAV hold on the autopilot panel and set the navigation from GPS to NAV mode. His actions were almost automatic as his training started to kick in.

"Shit. The flaps!" Anatoly said out loud. He should have extended them well before now. He cursed at his lack of skill as he set the flaps. The drag on the plane was immediate.

"Learjet UKTX two four zero, maintain present heading. Reduce height to two-thousand feet. Maintain two-thousand until your aircraft is established on the localizer," the female voice in his headset said calmly. Anatoly was anything but calm. His heart was beating wildly and his breathing was rapid as he adjusted his speed to comply with the tower.

Suddenly the heading of the autopilot panel switched off as the I.L.S. auto pilot took control of the plane. For the moment the Learjet was under control. Anatoly hit the fuel transfer pumps switch for both wing tanks and added more fuel to the fuselage tank. He thought that he might not have to dump any fuel. At the present rate of consumption and depletion due to loss, he'd be lucky if they would even have any fuel for the reverse thrust to slow the engine. He searched for the emergency drag chute release, just in case he would need to deploy it.

The plane made slight course corrections as the autopilot lined it up with the runway ahead. Anatoly watched the airspeed dip below 200 knots to 190. The number triggered another response from him. "Lower the landing gear," he said to himself out loud.

The hydraulic sound of the mechanical equipment whined a muffled sound as the equipment lowered into position. The sound of the wind noise was a welcome sound to Anatoly, who was worried that the gear may have been damaged by the missile explosion. He watched the lower/lock indicator lights, waiting for them to illuminate indicating the landing gear was down fully and locked. The nose wheel light illuminated first, then the left wheel indicator, and after another second, the right landing gear locked into place.

Nikki stared at the three lights from her copilot seat. "That's a good thing, right?" she asked.

Anatoly smiled nervously. "Yes, that was supposed to happen."

The voice over his head set confirmed his landing was clear. *"Learjet UKTX two four zero, you are cleared to land. Emergency equipment is on hand. Good luck."*

Anatoly repeated the words, "Tower, confirmed, cleared to land."

Anatoly prepared to switch off the autopilot. Although the plane could fly itself, the Learjet 25 could not auto land. Anatoly would have to take the controls. He looked over at Nikki as he switched the autopilot off. "Well, here we go." He let out a heavy sigh as he took control of the plane for landing and descended to a landing approach altitude.

Nikki yelled to everyone in the cabin as she buckled herself in. "Hold on to your asses, we are going to land."

Jackson looked over at Ramsey. "She may be good looking, but she sucks as a flight attendant."

Ramsey couldn't help but laugh.

Anatoly was watching his fuel, concentrating on whether or not to dump the fuel and try to glide the plane in. He stared at the remaining pounds of fuel. If he was going to dump it he had to do it soon.

The outer marker signal tone sounded in Anatoly's headset indicating that he was about ten kilometers from the runway's threshold and about 425 meters above it. *This was it*, he thought, as the Morse code signal, a group of two dots per second, sounded and the "O" light illuminated on the onboard O-M-I indicator, a device that briefs the pilot about the distance to the runway. He looked at his vertical gauge. He was perfectly centered between the left and right markers. The horizontal gauge showed he was a little low, but well within the height range for a proper glide path. So far so good.

Just less than six minutes later the amber "M" lit up on the O-M-I, indicating that Anatoly had just reached the point where instrument flying ended and visual flying began. The six dot per second, thirteen-hundred hertz tone indicated that he was less than a thousand meters to the edge of the runway, or threshold. Anatoly looked at his height of 80 meters above the ground and then glanced outside the windows to the asphalt rushing up to meet him, when the final tone, the rapid high pitched beep of the inner marker signal sounded in his headset. He looked at the O-M-I noticing the white light illuminating the "I." By the time Anatoly shifted his view back to the runway from the O-M-I indicator, the plane passed the sixty meter inner marker and was directly over the white striped threshold of the runway. Anatoly held the controls steady keeping the Learjet at the three degree glide slope as the rear landing gear made contact with the runway with a thud, then the sound of rolling wheels on the asphalt.

The Learjet sped down the runway at 160 kilometers an hour for another three hundred meters with the nose wheel still in the air. Anatoly pulled the throttle back causing the nose wheel to slam downward onto the runway hard. The landing gear took the brunt of the hit, cushioning the final downward movement of the plane as Anatoly set the throttle to reverse thrust to slow the plane quickly.

The sound of everyone on board taking a collective breath emanated through the cabin as the pressure of the rearward thrust pressed the passengers against the restraining seat belts.

Jackson looked out the window as the Learjet slowed and the emergency equipment surrounded the plane, the Learjet passing them even as it was slowing to a stop. "Son of a bitch," Jackson said loudly as he turned to face Ramsey. "Lover boy gets my M.V.P. vote," he said, shaking his head.

Nikki unbuckled her seat and fell onto Anatoly to embrace him. "Hey, I am still driving here," Anatoly said, watching as an airport service tug took its place in front of the plane, amber light flashing. "I guess I'm supposed to follow him."

Anatoly moved the plane forward, following the flashing light ahead. He noted his fuel gauge reading. They had better get him parked soon or they would have to tow him, he thought, as the tug peeled away, turning the plane over to a ground crew. A ground guide motioned for him to move ahead and then turned him to the right, leading him to a hanger. He wondered, if this was

Gregorov's too, as he positioned the plane to move through the fifty foot wide doors, easily accommodating the plane's thirty five foot wingspan. He noted the huge rubberized basin that was laid out on the floor of the hanger. The device, a huge drip pan, so to speak, would allow the remaining fuel to leak into the retaining basin. Three sections in all. One large fuselage-length system, and two smaller systems, one for each wing tank.

The ground guide crossed his cones, indicating that the plane was in place. Anatoly began the shut down procedures as the ground crew placed two large ventilation fans in place. One at the front and rear door of the hanger. Anatoly went to the door, opened it and lowered the stairs, allowing the bright yellowish light of the hanger to flood into the cabin.

Nikki stood at the door behind her pilot, but facing into the cabin. "You will all follow me to the hanger office." She said pointing to a room at the far end of the hanger near the door. "You are not allowed to leave this building until we have assessed the situation and have decided on a plan." She started to step out of the aircraft, but stopped. "By we, I mean me and my people, not you." She said, pointing at Ramsey.

Anatoly was met by the head of the emergency team and stepped off with the man to assess the Learjet's damage.

Nikki led them across the hanger floor with Vostav bringing up the rear. Ramsey stepped off quickly to catch up with Nikki. "We can't stay here. Maxwell will be right behind us."

"No, Mr. Ramsey. I cannot stay here. You and your people, however, will be restricted to this hanger. That is non-negotiable."

"That's bullshit and you know it. If Maxwell shows up, this will be the first place he will look!" Ramsey stepped around in front of her, walking backward as he spoke. He put a hand out to stop her.

Nikki reached out, grabbed Ramsey's hand and spun behind him, forcing his arm behind him and shoving it hard into the center of his back, then kicked behind his legs causing him to drop to his knees.

Paul Jackson lunged forward, stopping suddenly as Nikki pulled up her pistol and pointed it straight at his face.

Jackson held his hands up, "Whoa, Bitch. What the hell is your problem now?"

"Shut up, Mr. Jackson. You talk too much." Vostav covered the rest of Alan Ramsey's team as Nikki spoke to them.

She pointed her pistol at Ramsey, then back at Jackson. "You will not be leaving this hanger. I will kill all of you if you do not listen to me." She pushed Ramsey forward, releasing his arm and allowing him to get back to his feet.

"I am not your friend. You are only here because there was no other choice but to bring you, but we are not partners. Do you understand?"

She called Vostav to her side and spoke quietly, "You will stay here with these people until I get back. Anatoly and I are going to find Gregorov's place and check it out. Find a way to secure them."

Alan Ramsey saw Nikki motioning to his group. "C'mon, Nikki. Let me go with you." He stepped toward her disregarding Vostav's orders to the contrary. Nikki threw a flat handed punch toward Ramsey's chest, but this time he would not be taken off guard. Ramsey deflected her punch, forcing her left arm down, grabbing it in a twisting, motion, wrapping it with his right arm and pulling it, and her, closer to his side.

With his free left hand Ramsey grabbed Nikki's pistol hand, wrapping his hand around hers and placing his finger in the open trigger guard and on the trigger. He aimed the pistol at Vostav.

"Back off, Vostav!" Ramsey yelled at the surprised Russian. Vostav held his weapon on Ramsey, but took a step back, keeping one wary eye on Paul Jackson.

Ramsey put more pressure on Nikki's left arm. The pain he was inflicting was incredible.

Ramsey growled, "You are going to take Paul and me with you. I don't know how many times I have to say this, but you can trust us. Besides, you're going to need help if Maxwell shows up."

With that Ramsey pulled the 9 millimeter pistol from her hand and released his painful grip on her, shoving her away, toward Vostav.

Nikki took only a couple steps and turned back, ready for a fight, but instead, when she turned to face Ramsey again, she found him standing calmly, holding the nine mil out for her to take from him.

She looked at him oddly as she stepped toward him to take the weapon back. Cautiously she reached out, taking hold of the weapon as Ramsey released it to her as a sign that she could trust him.

"You are a strange man, Mr. Ramsey," she said as she handed the pistol to Vostav. Then in a move too fast for anyone to see coming, she punched Ramsey hard with her right hand to the side of his face. Ramsey took the hit well, moving only slightly, then shuffled his feet to regain his stance. He grabbed his jaw, staring angrily at the woman who had just sucker-punched him. "What the hell was that for?"

"That is to let you know, I am not your friend." She turned to Vostav, "You are coming with me. Give Anatoly a weapon and help him secure the rest of Ramsey's people. Tell him that we will be back in the morning."

Nikki turned to Ramsey, "I will have Anatoly kill your men if you do anything stupid. Tell your friend Paul to get his ass over here. That is, if you two are going with me."

Chapter 52

Surprise Lunch Meeting
State Department, Washington, D.C.

BETTY Rogers was standing at her desk. A large stack of files and documents sat in the center of her work area. Gone were her laptop and additional storage device. She looked up just as James Erickson stepped in from the hallway, returning from a quick lunch.

Erickson scanned Betty Rogers' desk, noting the missing computer system and clutter. He looked at her strangely, "What's going on? Did you just resign or something?"

She fought to hold back a smile, then simply said, "The C.I.A. is here. They are taking away our systems."

A sudden look of alarm showed in Erickson's widening eyes. He pushed the door inward to find Gabe Anderson, Gene Patterson, ten agents of the C.I.A., and two State Department security personnel waiting for him.

He glanced at his desk, then, at one of the agents who was placing his computer into a clear plastic bag, the word "evidence" scrawled across it.

Erickson stepped in front of Gene Patterson. "What the hell is going on here?"

For a moment everyone stopped working, looking unsure. "I don't know who the hell you people think you are, or what the hell you are doing in my office, but I suggest you stop what you are doing and get out!"

All of them looked to Gabe Anderson. Gabe took a step away from Erickson, motioned to the materials around the office and calmly stated, "Continue what you were doing. Get it packed up."

Erickson was livid. "What? Get what packed up? What the hell are you talking about?"

Anderson remained calm as he pulled the supporting documents out of a folder and handed them over to Erickson. "Your equipment is being confiscated. Here is a list of the equipment that these men require you turn over to them."

Erickson was red faced as he snatched the paperwork and glanced at it, quickly scanning through the list. He nearly spat, "You can't do this. There are rules that prohibit this action."

Gabe Anderson pulled a second document. He handed it to Erickson, explaining, "Yes, Sir, there are rules that prohibit any confiscation of documents and files. Unfortunately for you those rules are fairly outdated. It would appear that it was enacted before computer systems became mobile. Laptops and external storage devices, such as floppies, DVDs, flash drives, and USB storage drives are exempt, as it was never written into the law." He stared at Erickson as the Secretary of the State scanned the document. "Basically, Mr. Secretary, if it's considered mobile it's fair game."

Erickson turned to Patterson and screamed at him, "Make this shit stop or you will be sorry. You will never work in D.C. again, Patterson. Stop them, now!"

Gene Patterson looked unsure of himself. He swallowed hard as he handed another file folder to Erickson. As the SECSTATE opened the folder Patterson explained. "It's a subpoena to revoke all network privileges. The second page there...," He began, as he tried to thumb to the next page, but Erickson angrily yanked the file out of his reach, turning the page for himself. Patterson continued, pointing, "That second page explains the reason for the process being served." Patterson was trying to be helpful, but Erickson screamed at him. "I can read. Get away from me."

"Suspected of undermining an operation, suspected of aiding and abetting a foreign national,…what the, are you insane?" He continued to read, "Conspiring to stop an active operation? Knowingly putting the security of the United States of America at risk?"

Erickson closed the file and shoved it back at Gene Patterson. "You have just screwed up royal, Gentlemen," he said as he pulled the phone from his pocket and positioned it to make a call.

Gabe Anderson reacted quickly, snatching the government issued Blackberry from his hand. "I'm afraid you can no longer use this." He held the phone up, wiggling it back and forth, "Mobile device. It's covered in the subpoena." He couldn't help but smile.

Erickson spit more expletives as he pulled a second phone from his pocket. He attempted to keep a safe distance from Gabe Anderson, but his attempt was stymied by one of the two State Department Security agents. The S.D.S. agent stepped in, grabbing the phone from Erickson.

"That's my personal cell!"

Gabe Anderson replied to his appeals. "Sir, you of all people should know that personal mobile devices are not allowed on the State Department premises. They can only be stored in the locker at the security desk downstairs. Any personal devices not turned over to security are subject to inspection and or seizure, as per State Department Security guidelines. I believe it's your own policy."

He pulled another document from his arsenal, handing it to Erickson who again pulled it from his grasp.

Erickson breezed through the contents before looking up at Gabe Anderson and shaking his head. "No, this is bullshit. What is in that safe is my business." The Secretary of State slapped at the document with the back of his hand. "This document is asking for an external drive." He spun around, sweeping a hand in the direction of his desk. "I don't see an external drive here. I'm afraid you are out of luck," he said smugly.

Anderson spouted the documents verbiage from memory, "The document says that you are required to turn over the personal external mobile hard drive *that is stored in your safe.* That requires us to inspect the inside of the safe for the drive. You don't have a choice."

He moved closer to Erickson, glaring down at him. "Open the safe, Mr. Secretary. The subpoena supports it."

The Secretary of State knew that he was out of options. His life was over. Once they found what was on the drive, let alone his computer, it was all over. He thought about the President and how he would be affected. He would be investigated as well. More than likely, he would be impeached.

Erickson's breathing slowed and he appeared to relax, his shoulders drooping. He stepped close to Gabe Anderson and spoke almost in a whisper.

"Don't do this, Gabe. You know what is on that drive will destroy Carlton. If I open that safe, it will open the gates of hell for America. The information on that drive has less to do with Ramsey's investigation and more to do with the survival of the country."

Gabe Anderson knew that the outcome would mean another black eye for America, but he wasn't to blame. The person in front of him was responsible for what happened next. There was no stopping it now.

"Open the safe Mr. Secretary."

Erickson glared at Gabe Anderson as he stepped over to the safe. He stood with his back to the people in the room as he spun the tumblers, clicking through the combination robotically. He turned back to Anderson and Patterson, his hand on the handle of the safe. "Last chance to save the republic, Fellas." When there was no reply he turned back to the safe.

Unsure what was inside, the two S.D.S. agents had unholstered their pistols and brought them up to the ready as Erickson turned the handle down and opened the door. Aside from the external drive and several documents was a personal gift that he had received from the outgoing Attorney General. There in front of him was one of the last of the recovered guns of Operation Fast and Furious, the gun-walking scandal that had rocked the last presidency, a fully loaded Smith and Wesson, model 586, thirty eight caliber revolver.

It was a reminder of yet another decision that Erickson had made in the name of keeping America strong. Another file on the hard drive that would be found and do just the opposite, weaken the country through yet another scandal. Erickson looked past the pistol at the hard drive array. "To hell with it," Erickson said to himself as he reached into the safe.

The two S.D.S. agents saw what was happening as Erickson spun to face Gabe Anderson. They brought their weapons up fully into a position ready to engage and shouted to Erickson to drop the pistol.

Erickson watched Gene Patterson's face contort as the Secretary of State placed the barrel of the loaded three-fifty-seven to his own temple.

Gabe Anderson lunged toward him as the S.D.S. agents yelled again for Erickson to put the pistol down, but was too slow to stop the pressure of Erickson's finger on the trigger.

CHAPTER 53

THE FARMHOUSE
GREGOROV'S FARM, BERESTOVO, UKRAINE

THE road turned abruptly left, the headlights shining on an ancient stone wall. Nikki slowed the car to make the turn. Gregorov's farm wasn't far from the airfield, but the rutted, gravel and dirt road made it seem as though the distance was far greater. It had taken nearly an hour to drive the twenty mile distance.

Alan Ramsey looked ahead at the lights of a sprawling city on the eastern side of a wide river. Dark stone buildings rose into the night sky, blocking the light from newer glass and steel structures. As the road straightened and the car changed direction again, the well lit span of a long bridge jutted from the eastern shore of the river.

Paul Jackson saw him gazing. "That's the Dnieper river," he offered, "and that is ancient Kiev," he added, motioning to the lights of the city. "This place is over fifteen-hundred years old and has been attacked by pretty much everybody, Mongols, Poles, Russians, and the Nazis."

Ramsey looked inquisitively at Paul. It seemed as though Paul Jackson knew a little about everything. Alan nodded and added, "...And it looks like the Russians want it back," his remarks in reference to Russia's recent incursion into the Ukraine to secure the Sevastopol Naval Base on the Crimean peninsula.

Jackson pointed to the right at the spires of a large church on a hill, its gold dome shining brightly in the night, lit by huge lights from the hills above it.

"And that," Paul said, a wondrous tone in his voice, "is Kiev Pechersk Lavra. It's one of the largest and most unique monastery complexes in the world." He stared at it in amazement as he tried to explain its importance to his boss. "What you see there is only a small part of the complex. There are huge underground networks of monks' quarters carved out underground, burial sites, and two or three underground churches."

"How the hell do you know all that stuff?" Ramsey asked, amazed at his partner's vast wealth of information.

"The History Channel, man," he said as he looked off in the distance, "You really should watch more TV." Paul Jackson smiled his trademark grin, noticing then the visible signs of fatigue that showed in the dark rings around Ramsey's eyes. "Man, you look tired."

Ramsey scoffed at the thought of getting any sleep. He glanced at his watch. It was nearly nine pm. "Yeah, I'm feeling it now. Thought I was going to nod off there for a moment, till we turned onto this road." A sudden jolt caused by a huge pothole rocked the vehicle, punctuating his statement.

"Tell me about it," Jackson said in disgust as he began fiddling with his phone, trying to get a signal to take a moment to call his wife. He hadn't had the opportunity to talk, mainly due to the eight hour difference in time, and now when he had a free moment he couldn't connect.

Jackson's wife of twenty three years, Ming-Lee, was not happy with her husband's new line of work. She liked his old security job better. His shift used to end at noon, he was home early in the day, and they had plenty of time to walk or just sit together and relax.

Paul thought back and reflected on the tempo of his new job with Alan Ramsey's department. It had been non-stop since the first mission.

Ramsey saw his partners exasperation as Jackson sighed and shoved the phone back in his pocket. "No luck getting a signal?" he asked.

"No," Jackson answered, "I think we must have slipped into a time warp or something. Maybe a black hole that sent us back to the middle ages." He grimaced as the wheels of the sedan fell into successive potholes, rattling his jaw. "If I closed my eyes I'd swear we were in some sort of horse drawn carriage."

He looked at Nikki's green eyes in the rear-view mirror and joked, "I think you missed one. You might want to go back and try again." The statement was lost on Nikki and Vostav, a look of confusion showed on both their faces. Jackson glanced over at Ramsey who was smiling and shaking his head, then back at Nikki "Oh, never mind."

Nikki accelerated up and over a crest in the road. As the road leveled out, Nikki suddenly hit the brakes, causing a cloud of dust from the gravel road to float across the path of the headlights, obscuring their view in front of the car.

As the dust settled a small cottage appeared. Nikki thought back to her battle at the mansion of Vojislav Princip and what he told her as he was dying. "Find the farm and you will find the weapons and Krstic."

Nikki leaned forward, peering over the steering wheel. "This is it," she said as she threw the gearshift into park, grabbed her pistol and opened her door.

Jackson looked over at Ramsey as he unholstered his pistol. "This chick don't mess around," he quipped as he popped his door to follow Nikki.

The four gathered outside the vehicle. Ramsey was the first to speak. In a hushed tone he asked, "Now what?"

Nikki thought for a moment as she looked around in the darkness trying to see her surroundings. She could make out the tree line in the distance, but not much more. The moon was a waning crescent, low in the sky, the only light coming from the city of Kiev in the distance that created an arc of light that illuminated the horizon.

Then she saw it. The unmistakable shape of a large structure in the dark outline of the trees. "There," she said as she pointed, "There is the barn that houses the weapons." She turned and placed a hand on Ramsey's shoulder. "You two head to the barn. Vostav and I will join you there momentarily. I may have some business to attend to here."

Alan Ramsey was unconcerned with the possibility of finding anyone in the farmhouse. He was concerned with the weapons and the weapons only. He wondered what, or who, Nikki hoped to find, but didn't question her. Instead he turned to his partner and prodded him to move. "Let's go," he said to Paul Jackson, then looked back at Nikki. "Be careful," he said, sounding genuinely concerned for her safety. With that he and Jackson stepped off quietly.

Nikki grasped the door handle and tried the latch. To her surprise the thumb latch depressed and the door swung inward. She was met with the red light of a digital clock, so, not only did the house have electricity, but the bill must be current. She felt around on the wall and found the light switch. Suddenly the room was bathed in light, illuminating a bucolic interior, filled with rustic furniture. A stone fireplace dominated the outside wall, remnants of its last fire littering its hearth and next to it, standing in a brass base was the red, blue and white flag of Serbia.

Nikki motioned to Vostav to move toward the darkness of the hallway as she stepped carefully forward. She noted a sliver of light at the bottom of a nearly closed door. Nikki peered through the door opening, catching a glimpse of a man sitting in an uncomfortable looking chair, a pile of books on one side, and shelves filled with books behind him and along the wall. She reached out and pushed the door open with a slight creek.

The man looked up, surprised, but not startled. "Who are you? What are you doing here?" he asked, as he grasped the chair's arms and pushed himself up to stand and face the trespassers. The light from the single lamp washed over the man's face as he lumbered toward Nikki, his large, stocky frame wobbling slightly each time his right foot struck the floor.

Nikki looked at him, trying to remember him from her photographs and news reports. Overall his features were the same, chiseled jaw, blue eyes and the remnants of blonde hair. His face was mottled with scars, distorted, looking as though the pieces didn't match up exactly. A long slashing trail of scar tissue started at the top left of his forehead, slicing through his brow, continuing down his cheek and ending at the square corner of his blocky jawbone. A slight scar on his left eyelid told the story of how lucky he was to have his eyesight. Still, regardless of the damage to his scowling face, Nikki recognized the man in front of her as Radislav Krstic.

Without warning Nikki punched Krstic hard in the face. She moved forward, kicked his feet out from under him and shoved him backward. Krstic, unable with his prosthetic leg to counter Nikki's move, fell back into the antique chair.

For as large and seemingly healthy as the man appeared, he was feeble, his body damaged from the attack in prison. He sat, crumpled low in the chair, his nose bleeding profusely. For the first time in many years Krstic felt the uneasy sensation of dread. He struggled to push himself up from the chair when Nikki kicked him in the chest, knocking the wind out of him.

"What do you want from me? If it is money that you want, you have come to the wrong place."

Nikki put her face close to his and seethed, "I am not interested in your money, General Krstic."

Krstic sat unmoving. "Who are you? How do you know me?"

"My father was Colonel Nikolai Sidorova," Nikki hissed.

The older man looked surprised as his memories of her father came back to him. "Yes, I remember him. He was a thorn in the side of the Serbian Army." He paused for a moment, "He was a traitor to side with the Muslims who were destroying our country."

Nikki screamed at him. "He was no traitor. He supported you against the Serbs and only turned against you when you and your forces turned against all he stood for. It was your Christian, Croatian army that was traitorous! It was your government that joined with Serbia, not his. Your army that surrendered to Radovan Karadzic and that murdering Serb general of his, General Mladic."

A blazing fire of hatred flared in Nikki's eyes as she continued to lament on the actions of his past. "You had the opportunity to end the fighting, to stop the madness, but you, like Karadzic and Milosevic did not stand up against General Mladic."

Krstic tried to reason, wanting to set the story straight and remove any perception of his guilt. He interrupted Nikki. "We stood to lose too much, Mladic seemed wise. He convinced us all that we would lose more than we gained. Thousands of Serbian and Croatian soldiers would have died for nothing had we accepted the U.N. sponsored treaty."

Nikki leveled her pistol at Krstic's face, his eyes opening wide upon seeing the weapon. "You could have saved countless lives, your own soldiers and civilians included. Instead, you chose to do nothing to stop the madmen. Your lack of action makes you a traitor to your country, an accomplice to the murder and slaughter of thousands of people. You should have never been released from prison."

Krstic stared for a moment before speaking. "So, you are here to…what? Bring me to justice? Take me back to prison? I do not have to go anywhere with you." His words were defiant.

"I have served my sentence. Look at me! Look at my face!" He leaned toward the single table lamp, "Look at it. Sliced up while I was in prison. My chest and arms have much the same scars and I am feeble because of it. Hardly a man that can be a threat to anyone. I have paid the price for my actions."

"I have no intention of returning you to prison," Nikki replied.

Krstic looked at her quizzically before responding, "Then, you are here to execute me for actions I committed in defense of my country? There was a war going on then. All involved in war are killers Miss Sidorova. To find me guilty is the same as to find your father guilty."

Nikki punched him again, causing a fresh flow of blood from his now broken nose. The general covered his face with his hands as he doubled over in pain. Nikki pulled his head back by his blonde hair, slamming it hard against the carved wooden chair back and held it there.

Krstic struggled, trying to pull free from her grasp, swatting at her.

"Yes, I am going to kill you. The question is how much pain are you willing to take before I do? Now, tell me, where can I find Ratko Mladic?"

CHAPTER 54

ALL FOR ONE

GORDON Maxwell pulled out a cigarette and fired it up as he walked off the ramp of the C130 and onto the pavement of the Kiev Bryspil airport only to be met by Russian soldiers.

Without reservation Maxwell stepped up to the commanding officer of the group, saluted, and in perfect Russian, greeted him. "Good evening, Colonel. I am Gordon Maxwell. Please, tell your men to relax. I know you've got a lot going on here, but I assure you, my plane is legitimate."

"I have already checked out your credentials, Mr. Maxwell. You must understand, however, that we can not take chances. The Ukrainians have been testing our defenses since we took over the airport last week. One cannot be too careful." The Colonel maintained his military bearing while extending a professional politeness. "Now, if you don't mind, I will proceed with the inspection."

Maxwell was concerned about the equipment the Russians would find. He thought it best to let the commanding officer know.

"Look, Colonel, the equipment that I have on board is for a special mission here. You aren't going to like what you find in there." Maxwell motioned to the cargo area of the plane before continuing.

"I need to know what it's going to take to keep your men from confiscating my equipment." He smiled and scratched at his palm giving the Russian officer the signal that he was ready to deal.

The Colonel grinned. "That depends on what we find, now doesn't it, Mr. Maxwell?" He motioned for his men to move into the plane while Maxwell motioned for his men to stand down fully.

As the Russian troops moved up the ramp the Colonel looked back at Maxwell. "What is this mission you talked about? What kind of mission can an American be on, here in the Ukraine?"

Maxwell pulled hard on his smoke. "I'm no American, Colonel. Well, I was, but that was long ago." Maxwell grinned as he exhaled. "No, you see, I'm as loyal to Russia as you are. My business is here." He opened his arms wide. "The way I see it, Boss, you guys taking over the Ukraine has just expanded my territory." His grin grew wider as he tossed the cigarette down on the rough textured paint of the aluminum ramp.

The Colonel wasn't satisfied with his answer. "But what is your mission here?"

Maxwell knew that if the Colonel understood why he was there and who he was after, as long as he left Nikki out of the equation, more than likely they would let him pass. After, of course, putting a little money in the till. So, he explained his mission as a special operation to find and eliminate C.I.A. personnel working in the Ukrainian area of operations against Pro Russian separatist. After a brief conversation, the Colonel would see that they were on the same team.

One of the Russian Soldiers ran down the ramp and stopped at the Colonel. Maxwell listened intently, the soldier not knowing of his ability to speak the language as the Russian described the items he had found in the short time on board the aircraft.

The Russian Colonel turned, glaring at Maxwell, then to Maxwell's amazement spoke in English. "Is what he is saying true?"

Maxwell sighed, "Colonel, I am a businessman. People ask for things and it's my business to get them what they desire."

The Russian responded questioningly, "Things like missiles and drones, perhaps?" He smiled a toothy grin.

Maxwell didn't look at all surprised. "Maybe," he said simply.

The Colonel displayed an inquisitive look, turning his head to the side and thinking for a moment before dismissing his soldier back to the group. When he was sure he was out of earshot he turned to Maxwell.

"It just so happens that I am looking for such a person. It seems I have acquired some equipment. I don't suppose you would be interested in surplus Ukrainian armaments, would you? If so, I think our inspection here is done and you are free to go." The Russian officer looked slyly at his new business partner.

Maxwell was sure that he would be able to take whatever he had off of his hands, and at a good price. There was money to be made. He thrust out his hand. "Damned Skippy, Colonel, I know just the guy," he said as the Russian grabbed his hand and shook it. "Why don't you just give me a number where I can reach you and I'll give you a call right now to set up our contacts.

CHAPTER 55

INTERCEPT
SVIATOSHYN AIRFIELD, HANGER 9

RICK White walked around the hanger for about the fifth time. The airport safety inspectors were there going over the airplane damage. White noted that the fuel had stopped flowing from the underside of the Learjet and had slowed to occasional drips as the last of the fuel from the fuselage tank and the left wing tank was allowed to drain into the containment bladder. Crews had already pulled what fuel remained from the right wingtip, and both intact wing tanks.

He pondered their situation, wondering what was going on with Ramsey and Jackson, and how they would all get out of the Ukraine and back into Russia when his phone buzzed and chimed. He yanked it out of his pocket, expecting to find a call or text from the others and instead found his phone tracking app had popped open and Maxwell's number was displayed.

"Oh, shit," he said to himself, noting the location of Maxwell's marker on the map. He could see it was an airport, but not *his* airport. He read the name out loud, "Kiev Bryspil," selecting the location pin. The app switched to show the information for the marker, the grid coordinates and location name. White selected "directions" and "from current location" and waited. The map showed the path between the two airports and a travel time of about one hour.

He wondered where Ramsey and Jackson would end up with Nikki and whether it was close to the other airport. The Farm was all he'd been told. He ran around the plane to where Bob Matthews and Brandon were sitting inside the office. "Hey, Maxwell's pin just showed up about an hour away from here."

Matthews cussed, "We gotta warn the boss." Matthews reached for his phone, but Rick White stopped him. "No, don't. Remember, Ramsey's number is in the app and Maxwell has the same app. If Ramsey picks up or calls, Maxwell can pinpoint him."

Matthews cringed again. "We've got to warn them, somehow. He looked around White and targeted Anatoly. "He knows where they went. We're just going to have to go to them."

He got up and made a beeline for Anatoly. "Hey, where'd Nikki take those guys?"

Anatoly stared at Bob Matthews. "I can't tell you. She told me not to tell…"

Before he finished his sentence Matthews had him by the throat. The safety officer backed away, holding his clipboard as a shield between him and the two men. Matthews stared at him while holding Anatoly at arms length. "Don't even think about going anywhere."

He turned back to Anatoly, "Look, dipshit, Maxwell is in town. We need to let them know before he surprises them. My guess is he knows where the Farm is. I'd lay odds that he's been there before."

Anatoly's eyes were wide as he struggled to breathe. Matthews reached around Anatoly's back and removed the pistol from his waist, then released him to breathe again.

Anatoly leaned forward, gasping. "You can't call her. I have her phone."

Matthews had the pistol trained on him. "We can't call her anyway. Maxwell can track her phone same as we can."

He looked at the safety officer, and then beyond him to the vehicle parked outside the hanger door and demanded, "Give me your keys."

The man didn't respond, but just stood there. Matthews pointed the gun at him. "Give me your car keys!" Still there was no reply.

Anatoly cleared his throat and asked the man in Russian for the keys. Shaking and wide eyed, the man complied. Matthews grabbed the keys and tossed them to Brandon. He racked the pistol and pointed it at Anatoly's face and screamed at him. "Where did Nikki take them?"

Anatoly yelled back, "Berestovo. To Gregorov's farm."

Matthews barked, "Everybody get in the car." He shoved Anatoly with the side of the pistol. "That means you too."

CHAPTER 56

GREGOROV'S BARN

ALAN Ramsey and Paul Jackson moved silently toward the dark structure. Jackson pointed to the brightly lit spire of a three tiered tower off in the distance. He hissed the name of the campanile, "The Great Lavra Bell Tower." Then the realization of what that meant hit him. "Holy shit, Gregorov's farm is on the grounds of the Pechersk Lavra Monastery!" He spun to the right to look for the gold dome of the Refectory Church that they had seen from the road and saw just the tips of the six spires of the Assumption Cathedral. They were somewhere at the southern end of the upper Monastery Complex.

"That's it." He said in a sudden outburst. "Son of a bitch," he said and laughed.

"You mind filling me in?"

"Kieve-Perchersk Lavra." He began, still looking around as if trying to get his bearings. "It's called the Church of Caves, or the

Cave Monastery. This farm is on the grounds of one of the oldest Christian religious sites in history, dates back to like 800 AD.

Under us right now are tunnels and caverns that make up part of the Pechersk Lavra. I can't believe it. Gregorov hid his weapons in the caves of the monks." He spun around pointing toward the east. "Let's see, the Dnieper river is that way, and the cathedrals are that way," he said, turning to face north and pointing at the visible bell tower lit up in the distance, "That puts us somewhere between the upper Laurel, or the Near Caves, and the lower Lavra, the Far Caves. "Damn, I can't believe it."

He shone the light from his phone onto the thick wooden doors of the barn, finding the wrought iron latch. The door moved with a creak to swing wide enough for them to get through.

The two men stood in the darkness, each holding their cell phones out, using them as flashlights. "Over there!" Ramsey said, pointing to what appeared to be a workbench and above it, a fluorescent light fixture. "Ok, there's gotta be electricity." Jackson located a light switch and clicked it on. The glow of fluorescent bulbs brightened and flickered to life.

The barn was not empty, there were several older military trucks parked along one wall and parts of all types, from aircraft parts to wheels, tires and even track sections for a number of different types of military tracked vehicles. But there were no weapons. Ramsey grunted. "Not the big inventory we hoped for," he said sarcastically, as he looked at a box of several components, none of which was familiar to him.

Paul added, "True, but we're only on the first floor," he said smiling as he pointed to an archway at the far end of the barn. He and Ramsey rushed across the distance, Jackson reaching the opening first.

The entrance was barred with a heavy wrought iron gate, the hinges made of thick steel, embedded deeply into the stone and mortar. The gate was then secured with two heavy, square wrought iron bars, attached on the left to similarly embedded steel loops.

The bars had been swung downward and secured with thick modern padlocks to circular locking bales.

Jackson pulled at the upper lock then let it fall back. "We either need the keys or some explosives to get through that."

Jackson pulled out his phone and held it through the bars illuminating the passage beyond. A tunnel, carved through the natural sandstone, led down into darkness. A metal conduit snaked its way along the corridor, carrying the electricity, he supposed, disappearing into the depths of the shadowy distance. Jackson withdrew his arm from the bars and turned to Ramsey. "Now what?"

Alan Ramsey walked away toward the barn's entrance. "Now we go find our hostess and see what she's found out. Maybe she located the keys inside the farmhouse."

CHAPTER 57

KRSTIC

VOSTAV was on a mission to find something with which to work. He hated punching people. His hands showed the damage associated with years of abuse, broken, then crookedly healed fingers and knuckles, the result of many an impromptu beating. He much preferred the use of tools, rather than the bones of his hands, to inflict the pain that made people talk.

He rummaged through the kitchen drawers. There he found a well used, wooden handled knife. He spotted a wooden tool caddy in the back of the kitchen. Kneeling down, he picked through the mixed assortment of home and garden tools: pliers, a pipe wrench, pruning shears, a hammer and nails. Perfect, he thought, as he tossed the eight inch long knife in the tote and picked it up, heading back to where Nikki was still interrogating the Russian General, Krstic.

Nikki released Krstic's hair, allowing his head to fall forward. She stepped away as the man slumped over the arm of the chair.

Vostav's shoulders drooped when he saw the unmoving figure in the chair. "Is he dead?" he asked, seemingly disappointed that he'd missed it.

Nikki rubbed her bloodied hand, "No, he passed out. Asshole can't take a hit."

Vostav set the tote down and pulled up the pair of pruning shears. "These will scare the shit out of him," he said as he worked the handles to open and close the curved cutters.

He set them on the floor and dug through the box, lifting each item to show Nikki. Holding the hammer and testing the weight he continued to describe the tote's contents, "Hammer, duct tape, screwdrivers, ooh, look, a hacksaw." He smiled through the gleaming steel frame as he held it up for Nikki to see.

Nikki bent down, grabbing the duct tape from the floor and immediately started securing the unconscious Krstic to the chair. As she secured his arm to the chair, Krstic came to.

He lifted his head slowly, feeling his saliva and the blood from his nose on his lip. He opened his eyes to find one swollen enough that he could only see from it a little.

Krstic heard the familiar sound of duct tape tearing, but it took several minutes for him to recover his senses. By the time he fully came-to, he realized his arms and legs were bound to the chair. He shook away his groggy feeling, snapping his head upright, defiantly tugging at his arms and legs before relaxing his attempts to free himself. He looked up at Nikki, scowling, and growled, "What do you want from me?"

"I told you what I want. You to tell me about Mladic, who supported him, and where he is."

Krstic yanked at his bound arms some more, contemplating his situation, then turned to see his captor's accomplice and the tools. Vostav was holding the hacksaw in one hand and the pruning shears in the other. He glanced from the tools to Vostav's eyes, to Nikki, and back several times as the picture of his immediate future became apparent. "OK. OK. What if I tell you what you want? Will you leave me alone?"

Nikki leaned down to put her face in front of his. She could see the damage already inflicted and thought about the throbbing pain that the man must be enduring. She wondered how much more he could take. "Tell me everything, then, maybe, you will die less painfully."

Krstic could see the hatred in her eyes. This woman did not care about hurting him. She would not stop until she got what she wanted. He nodded his head in agreement.

"Good. When was the last time you spoke to Mladic?"

"The last time I spoke with him was at the arraignment, before the trials, in The Hague, Netherlands. Mladic told me that the trials were fixed, that he would be set free. He bragged that he had made a deal with the Americans to bring down Slobodan. That was when I found out that I was part of the deal he made." Krstic's eyes narrowed as he thought back to that day, that moment in time when his life took such a dramatic turn, "...and then he apologized to me. Do you believe that? The bastard betrayed me and then apologized."

"Who made the deal? Tell me!" She glanced toward Vostav.

Krstic's eyes locked on to the figure of Vostav as he stepped toward him, hacksaw raised. "What are you going to do?" Krstic stammered, making a fist with both hands in a vain attempt to protect his fingers. His eyes were wide with fear.

"It's your fingers or your wrist, makes no difference to me," Vostav chided, raising the hacksaw to gleam in the dim light, "Hacksaw for the hand, pruners for the fingers." He raised the pruners, working them to make a *shclick, schlick* noise as the curved blades slid past one another.

Vostav smiled and leaned down, whispering in Krstic's ear, "I'd go for the fingers. Snip and it's done, otherwise...," he dragged the hacksaw blade backward across Krstic's wrist preparing for the first hacking cut forward, "...Your choice."

Krstic suddenly spat the words that answered Nikki's question, "The Secretary of State, now the American President, Carlton."

Vostav looked up at Nikki who motioned for him to withdraw. Krstic felt the hacksaw blade lift from his skin. He could hear his heart beating, he was sweating profusely and breathing hard. He closed his eyes and sighed trying hard to regain his composure, then continued,

"He and the U.N. Envoi, the one who is now the U.S. Secretary of State...can't think of his name, went against the wishes of the United Nations and the U.N. Secretary, Kofi Anon, agreeing to leave Mladic alone in return for his information and assistance. They made the deal that set Mladic free."

Krstic looked at Nikki then at Vostav. "That is all I know. I swear. I went to prison while he went free. I have not seen him since and have no idea where he is now."

Nikki walked around the room, her eyes settling on the crown and shield, set against the red, blue and white background of the Serbian flag. She stared at the white eagle with it's double head, to her, representing the two faced government that exists still. Next to the flag, on the mantle, was a flask of Slivovitz, a type of plum brandy that made in Croatia and sold in many parts of Serbia. She looked back at Krstic, "Do you drink, General?"

Krstic was thrown off by the sudden change in questioning. Nikki spoke more sternly. "I said, do you drink?"

Krstic shook his head. "No, not for over fifteen years."

Nikki looked at the man warily as she continued, "...and do you live alone, General?"

Krstic's eyes narrowed at the line of questioning, "Yes, I do. I had a cat, but I think the wolves..." Suddenly Krstic's eyes went wide at the sight of Nikki holding the flask of Slivovitz.

She pulled out her pistol, and placed it at the center of Krstic's chest. He began heaving, breathing hard as Nikki yelled at him.

"Mladic was living here, wasn't he?" She cocked the pistol and pushed harder into his chest, "Well?"

"Yes, he was here, but not for several years. Gregorov asked him to leave. Mladic wasn't the easiest person to get along with."

"Where is he now? Where did he go?" she increased the pressure again.

"He went back to Serbia, He is living in Lazarvo near Zrenjanin, in the Northern Province. I have not seen or heard of him since, except for the news reports of the manhunt and his ability to evade capture." Krstic was hyperventilating due to the pressure of the pistol and the woman's stare. She was going to kill him. He should have told her the truth to begin with, he thought.

"All I know, and I swear to you, this is everything I know…He was working for Gregorov, managing his business affairs, but he and Dmitri had a falling out. I thought Gregorov was going to kill him. Instead he asked him to leave. Evidently he an Dmitri have a long past."

Krstic looked at Vostav and back to Nikki, both seemed intent on his story, "Gregorov replaced him with another, someone named…" He thought for a moment but couldn't think of the name.

Nikki knew the name, it was the courier that she had met and killed two days before. "Mikhail," she offered.

Krstic look surprised, "Yes, Mikhail," He smiled nervously. "That's it, you know of him. Well, life has come full circle then."

Suddenly the front door burst open. Ramsey and Jackson stepped in to the welcoming of Nikki's pistol, now pointed in their direction. Ramsey looked surprised to see what was going on, the man taped to the chair, Nikki holding what appeared to be liquor and Vostav with a hacksaw.

Ramsey blurted out, "Sorry to break up your party, but we found the entrance to the cave. We know where the weapons are."

Krstic looked up at Nikki. "So then, you know of Gregorov's weapons? His weapons farm?" Krstic felt his fortune changing for the better. "The entrance is, as he said, in the barn, among some relics that he stores there. You must go down several stories. Not so easy with a prosthetic leg."

"How does he get the weapons in and out of the cave," Nikki asked.

"The cavern is vast. There is access to the cave about two kilometers from the highway, which as you may or may not know runs parallel to the Dnieper River. There is a port for the barges that travel the river and the equipment could come in by barge or over the road by truck. If you go back down the road you would go right at the highway. It is not far."

"There. I have no more information to give. Now, release me. You promised to let me go. You said I would live longer If I told you everything," he said nervously, looking up at Nikki. "I have told you everything I know."

Nikki stood, looking down at him. She pointed the berretta at Krstic. "I did not promise you any such thing. I said, if you told me, you might die less painfully. I am a woman of my word."

Ramsey saw what was about to happen. "Wait! He's told you the truth. You can't just kill him like that."

Nikki yelled over her shoulder at Ramsey. "He is a murderer, he deserves no less a fate." She pressed the berretta against his forehead, "This is not your fight, Ramsey. Stay out of it!"

Ramsey pulled his pistol and aimed it at Nikki. "No, Nikki. I won't let you kill the man like that." The move started a chain reaction around the room as Vostav dropped the pruning shears and reached for his own pistol and Jackson raised his, pointing it at Vostav, beating him to the draw.

"I don't think so. Let it go!…and you can drop your hacksaw, too," Jackson ordered. Vostav relaxed and did as he was told.

Nikki growled, looking over her shoulder at Ramsey. "I knew I should have killed you."

"First off, the entrance is locked and we need the keys to get to the weapons. Secondly, you would really kill a guy who is taped to a chair? He told you the truth. Look at him. You've already beat the shit out of him. He told you what you want...."

Nikki screamed, "He deserves to die." She leaned down, grabbed Krstic by the hair, yanked his head back and pressed the pistol against Krstic's forehead."

Ramsey yelled at her, "Nikki! I *will* shoot you! Now, back down!" He pulled his stance tighter as he prepared to do what was necessary.

For a moment there was silence, then Nikki let out a long exasperated growl, releasing Krstic's hair. She pulled the pistol away from his forehead and stared at Ramsey, seething. Suddenly she spun and nailed Krstic hard with the pistol, causing a huge gash above his left ear. She leaned down and screamed at him, "Where are the keys?"

Krstic stammered, "I'm wearing them...around my neck,...on a chain....I will give them..."

Nikki reached down and pulled the chain with two keys from around his neck, breaking the chain. She lowered the pistol and held the keys out to Ramsey, who willingly accepted them. Nikki slapped them into his hand.

The tension suddenly lifted. Krstic sighed, thankful for the American's intervention. Nikki stood, looking defeated, pistol hanging at her side.

Krstic looked around the room as everybody started to move toward the door. "Wait, please, somebody, cut me loose."

Ramsey stopped briefly at the door. He waited to see what Nikki was going to do.

Nikki growled to Vostav, "Go ahead. Release him."

Krstic was rambling on, thanking Nikki for her mercy. Nikki stepped toward the door to follow Ramsey out, but stopped short, watching as Ramsey sprinted toward the barn and Jackson who was waiting. She turned back to look at Krstic, watching as Vostav sliced away the duct tape. "I am not the one to thank. You are lucky that the Americans had pity for you. Pack your things. Leave this place before I change my mind." With that, she turned and headed out the door, Vostav at her side.

Krstic got to his feet, pulling the tape from his arms. He had survived. After all he had been through he had survived. War, a land mine explosion, prison, and now this. He was amazed at his luck and thankful for the Americans.

He called after Nikki. "Wait! When you find Mladic, and I know that you will, do not show the kindness you have shown me just now."

Nikki, stopped and turned to look at Krstic. So disfigured was his face, that even the dried and caked blood could not cover the scars. He took a couple steps in her direction before continuing. "He is the responsible one. He destroyed the country, killed all those people, and is why I was sent to prison. He does not deserve your mercy."

Krstic closed his eyes and held his arms out to his sides, then cried out, "Look at what he did to me!"

As he looked back toward the woman standing in the doorway, his remorseful look was suddenly replaced by one of surprise.

Nikki had her pistol raised again, pointed at Krstic. "It's not about you," she said, pulling the trigger, putting two rounds into his heart.

Krstic felt the rounds as they destroyed his chest, his eyes wide, mouth agape. He stumbled backward and before he could drop his arms to his sides, Nikki fired once more.

Three rounds in the blink of an eye. One for each member of her family whose deaths she could attribute to his actions.

Krstic fell backward to the floor, arms still outstretched. Nikki mumbled to herself, responding to something the man had said earlier.

"*Now*... life has come full circle."

CHAPTER 58

FINDING THEIR WAY

BOB Matthews turned to face Anatoly in the rear seat and yelled, "Are you sure this is the right road?" Matthews slowed to take the next turn, a right, putting them on a divided two lane stretch of highway.

Anatoly looked over Rick White's shoulder at the map on his phone, then, looked into the darkness. On his left was the Naberezhne Highway that ran along the banks of the Dnieper River. He slid across the seat to look to the right. That was when he saw it.

"Yes, look." He pointed to the well lit spires of The Great Lavra Bell Tower. "There is the monastery. The road should be up ahead, around this next curve, to the right."

Matthews grunted as the headlights of two vehicles ahead disappeared from the highway, crossing the road about two miles ahead of them to make a left into the stand of trees along Matthew's right side. "Uh-oh, That can't be coincidence."

Rick White saw it, too. "No way. We can't be *that* unlucky."

"You're kidding, right?" Matthews asked sarcastically, "All we've had is bad luck. Why should this be any different?" He slowed the car and turned off the headlights as he came up on the entrance. Turning in, he could see the tail lights of both cars some distance ahead. He kept back, driving slowly, staying as far to the right of the gravel road as he could, watching for any change ahead. He came to a stop when he saw the brake lights of both vehicles illuminate brightly, the second car pulling to the right of the first and stopping alongside.

Anatoly and Brandon leaned forward between the two American agents and peered through the darkness. The headlights of the S.U.V.s illuminated a manmade, concrete wall that conformed to the shape of a tunnel-sized opening in the rocky outcropping.

The monolithic wall was covered with green moss and algae, a natural camouflage. Vines and long bent grass flowed over the side like a waterfall, framing the edges of a huge, metal door. There was no doubt that what they were seeing was the entrance to Gregorov's cave.

CHAPTER 59

DISCOVERY

ALAN Ramsey glanced back at Nikki and Vostav as he followed on the heels of Paul Jackson. They had gone about a hundred feet through a meandering tunnel, lit by a string of incandescent bulbs hung from the carved stone walls.

Jackson moved ahead slowly, examining the walls of the tunnel, noting that some of the textured stone appeared to have been naturally eroded. He looked back at Ramsey, excited at the prospect of walking through such an ancient structure, man-made or not.

"These passages were carved from the Dnieper river hundreds of thousands of years ago," Jackson said, as he slid a palm over the wall's sandstone surface, some areas damp from the ground water that seeped in from above. "The river must have changed course over time. Then as the water seeped back out, it left behind these natural tunnels. Eventually, the monks would dig them out, creating what would become the Great Lavra Cave Monastery. It's hard to think that all this was started by one man, Saint Anthony of Kiev." Jackson sounded as though he were narrating a documentary.

"I'll be sure to watch the National Geographic Special," Ramsey said, grinning. "Can we move a little faster and look at the details of the cave's formation later? I'd sure like to get this wrapped up."

The passage turned to the left, the lighting ending abruptly at a final fixture hanging above an electrical panel. Russian lettering on masking tape tags bore the names of each fused lever.

Nikki and Vostav moved ahead of the other two and peered at the panel of mechanical bale type breakers. After reading the Russian word for lights, Vostav reached forward and pushed three of the marked breaker bales upward. The clack of the circuit breakers snapping shut echoed in succession throughout the darkness as first one row, then a second and third row of lights began to glow, illuminating the interior of the cave and bringing the vastness of the cavernous storage facility into focus. Rows and rows of wooden and metal crates, wheeled vehicles, missiles, rockets, and tracked vehicles, placed end to end starting from where they were standing to the dimly lit far end of the cave, were revealed.

Jackson was the first to speak. "Holy crap," he said, in a long, drawn out exclamation. With that, he set off to look at the first open crate and called back to the group. "Mortar rounds over here. Enough for several platoons." He stepped to the next crate, looking at the Russian writing, unable to read it, but he could see it said the same as the other crate. "More of the same. You could arm a small army with this stuff."

He flipped a tag on another container to reveal the symbol for radioactive materials. Jackson stepped back. "Oh shit. Not sure what's in this one, but I ain't opening it to find out."

Vostav stepped over to read the words printed on the metal container. "Depleted Uranium," he said simply, then added, "They are tank rounds. Safe to handle as long as they are not banged around. I used to drive a tank. I could load, and fire as well. It's easy. Very safe."

Jackson muttered, "I do believe you're the first tanker that ever told me his job was easy." Vostav looked confused. Jackson waved him off, "Never mind, that's Ok, I'll still keep my distance," he said, still unconvinced about the safety of the tank rounds.

Paul turned to Ramsey and spoke quietly. "You know, there's going to be some super nasty stuff down here. It's bad enough that Gregorov had access to nuclear warheads, but I will bet there is biological and chemical shit down here as well." He looked at Nikki and then at Vostav ensuring that he was out of earshot before continuing, "Look, Boss, I know you made a deal with her, but we have to be sure not to let that vengeful bitch get her hands on any of this kind of shit." He flipped the radioactive tag to punctuate his remarks.

Jackson glanced again toward Nikki. She was glaring at him. "I can hear you, you know."

Jackson stopped talking for a moment, then responded, but not to Nikki directly. He looked at Ramsey, "Was I talking that loud? How the hell did she...." His words tapered off as he shook his head in a feigned look of defeat.

Nikki stepped closer, still staring at Paul Jackson. Her gait was that of a cat, he thought, as she moved toward them, her eyes locked on his.

"Mr. Jackson. I may be a vengeful bitch, as you have pointed out, but I assure you, I do not have any use for such weapons."

Alan Ramsey glanced at his partner. He couldn't help but grin at Jackson's discomfort, but Ramsey quickly put on his game face when Nikki suddenly turned to face him.

She walked a circle around Ramsey, rubbing her left shoulder on his as she moved behind him, her arm trailing behind, tracing up his arm, her hand coming to rest on his left shoulder.

Nikki stood behind them both as she reached out with her right hand, still holding her pistol, and placed it and the weapon on Jackson's right shoulder. She leaned in between them both and spoke quietly.

"So, gentlemen, I suggest that we continue looking for what it is *you* want to find. The sooner we find what you are looking for, the sooner I get rid of you, and the sooner I can get back to what I was doing before you interrupted."

She stepped back, releasing them both, then checked Jackson hard with her shoulder, causing him to take a step forward to maintain his balance. She spoke over her shoulder as she walked away, "Now, please, let's keep moving."

Jackson looked at Ramsey, a scowl painting his emotion on his face. In a low voice, so as not to be heard, he growled, "Can she be any more annoying?"

A slight smirk grew into a huge grin on Ramsey's face when Nikki's voice rang out, "I heard that, Mr. Jackson." causing Paul Jackson's eyes to go wide. Ramsey patted the shoulder of his partner and prodded him to move, still smiling at the exchange.

They continued moving along the stacked and shelved crates, boxes, and parked equipment, reaching the end of the first row. The shelving suddenly ended, giving way to a wide open area. Across the wide expanse were more warehouse shelves and more military equipment.

Beyond that the roof of the cave dipped downward creating the curved opening of the cave and the point where the natural stone met the thick concrete wall. From his vantage point about center of the structure Ramsey saw a single service entrance door at the far left and a large steel garage door that rose nearly to the cave's ceiling.

He pointed toward the end of the cave and spoke so that everyone could hear, "That must be how Gregorov got the equipment in and out."

To the far right, four-foot square container boxes held hundreds of pieces of small arms, clothing, helmets and other protective gear. To the left was a collection of stacked ammo boxes, and more crates cordoned off with common yellow hazard tape.

Ramsey looked at Paul, "Wonder what that is," he said, as he led the group across the concrete floor toward the first dilapidated crate. The gray painted wooden box was broken open exposing WWII era German grenades, packed in hay, laid side by side. The stenciling on the loose wooden lids confirmed in Deutsch the origin of at least half of the boxed equipment. Other, taller crates had been pried open as well. Inside were tank shells. The stenciling showed them to be of Russian manufacture.

Vostav read the information on the crate. "Seventy-six millimeter. These are for the F-34 tank gun on the T-34. From The Great Patriotic War." He glanced at the other twenty or so crates that each held six of the three inch diameter high energy rounds. They are all from the Great War."

"That's probably why he has it separated from the rest." Ramsey added.

Paul Jackson turned to Nikki. "As soon as you move in, if I were you, I'd be getting rid of this shit right here."

Vostav suddenly said something in Russian and sprinted off, running toward a Soviet Era T80 tank on the deck of a lowboy trailer at the far end of the cave, near the entrance door. He stopped, motioned to the tank on the trailer and explained excitedly that it was the exact kind of tank that he had operated as a young soldier in the Soviet tank corps.

He walked around the tank, climbing up on the trailer to inspect it more closely. He pointed to the open battery cover and yelled down to Nikki. "Somebody was working on this. There is a charger on the batteries."

Vostav clamored up the front of the tank. His head and shoulders disappeared into the driver's hatch as he leaned headfirst into the opening. The sound of a warning buzzer emanated from within the hatch as Vostav selected from memory the switches to start the engine.

The telltale sound of the whir of the gasoline turbine engine spinning to life, echoed through the cavern as a huge pall of exhaust smoke filled the air. The turbine engine sputtered and whistled as the compressed fuel ignited in the cold chamber.

Vostav adjusted the engine idle lever, pressing the release button to move the lever to its lowest position as the engine speed slowed and settled down to a smooth idle. After about a minute he leaned back in the hatch and shut off the engine. Pulling himself upright and out of the driver's compartment to kneel in front of the hatch, he sat back, sighing loudly, "Ah, the memories."

He climbed off the tank and walked to the end of the trailer where Nikki stood at the rear wheels of the tractor. "Can I keep it, ...please?" he asked jokingly."

The sound of Alan Ramsey's voice echoed through the cavern, drawing Nikki's attention away from Vostav. Ramsey and Jackson were standing in front of, what Ramsey guessed, was some sort of steel blast protection door. "Nikki, Vostav, need you both over here."

Vostav had no problem following Ramsey's directive, but Nikki didn't care to be ordered around by either of the Americans. Her look of disdain showed as she moved slowly, weapon still drawn, to their position. As she approached the three men she saw what had captured their attention.

Vostav was standing at a control panel. It was mounted on a pedestal about three feet high. Cables and conduits rose upward, then across the rock ceiling, curving downward slightly then abruptly ending at a small electrical box where the wiring disappeared into the concrete wall.

Nikki examined the door, looking for a handle or lock, but found none. She stopped two feet from the door when she had the feeling that someone had grabbed her arm. With a clang that caught the attention of the others, Nikki's Makarov was drawn to the metal of the door. The pull was strong enough to pin her hand between the pistol and the door's metal surface. Nikki winced as she struggled to pull free, slipping her hand out from between the two metal objects. She stood back and glanced over at the three men, all with jaws agape staring at her pistol that was held in place as if it was mounted and on display.

Vostav was the first to speak, "It's magnetic!" he said as he turned his attention back to the console, touching the screen, causing it to light up. He expected a keyboard and the necessity to input a password, but found that the screen offered little in the way of security. The touch display was simply an on and off control.

There were two main selections, "*Na*" or "*Ot*," the words for on and off, and a second selection of "*Otkrytym*" or "*Zakryto*," for "open" or "closed."

Vostav selected "*otkrytym,*" but nothing happened other than another prompt, a flashing light next to the word for "off." Without hesitating, Vostav selected "Ot." The console immediately displayed the words *"Zamok otklyuchayetsya,"* for "lock disengaged."

Nikki's pistol suddenly clattered to the concrete floor as a loud clacking sound and an audible thump emanated from the direction of the doors, along with the momentary sound of rushing air.

Vostav's eyes lit up. "Dzhekpot!," he exclaimed in a manner that needed no translation as he touched the next selection to open the doors.

Suddenly there was a hum of electric motors as the door cracked open, dividing in half and sliding along two upper and two lower guide rails.

Alan Ramsey eyed up the doors, noting their thickness. The doors were at least eight inches thick with layered lumber, bolted together and laminated with five eighths inch thick plate steel. Obviously designed to withstand a massive explosion. As the doors completed their travel outward Alan Ramsey eyed a sign hanging from the ceiling of the room. He recognized the exclamation mark at the end of the sentence. He pointed to the sign and asked Nikki for a translation.

Nikki had just retrieved her pistol, examining it for any damage. She looked up at the sign, a slightly amused look on her face. "It says, Warning, keep metal objects clear when magnetic seals are energized."

Paul Jackson had entered the bunker and was staring at the crated warheads on the concrete shelving.

"Isn't that the same kind of crate as what was found in the back of the box truck in Texas?" he pointed out the green and red painted steel casing of the warhead. "And I will bet any money that if we had the photos of the shell casing found at the warehouse in St. Louis, this would match it also." He peered at the flat tip of the foot and a half diameter warhead. "This doesn't appear to be complete, there's no trigger mechanism."

"No, but the matching components are probably right here." Alan Ramsey interjected. He motioned to a dozen smaller containers on other shelves, steel boxes painted flat black. 5 of the six sides were welded together, the sixth, the top, was bolted. The boxes were tall and thin, maybe six by six inches square and about the same length as the warheads.

Jackson pointed at the crates, counting them, then at the square boxes. "Twelve of each. That is probably not coincidental and, wouldn't you know it, I forgot my radiation suit and Geiger counter."

Ramsey turned back to look at Paul Jackson, "Well, that answers the question on the thickness of those doors. At least Gregorov was smart enough to keep them locked up in here. He slapped the face of the thick steel door as he took one more look. "This whole cave could come down and this vault would still be standing. I've seen all I want to see. Let's get the hell out of here and close this thing back up."

Ramsey pulled out his phone, waving it to get Jackson's attention. He pointed toward the service door. "C'mon, we've got to get outside. I have no signal in here. We need to get hold of Gabe and let him know to get a recovery team moving."

Suddenly Nikki was standing in front of Ramsey, her pistol in his face. "I don't think so. If you call your boss, I will lose everything."

Ramsey was getting used to having Nikki point a pistol at him, He sighed and moved forward, pushing the pistol out of the way. "Damn it, Nikki, we don't have time for this shit. We had a deal."

Nikki fired, stopping them both in their tracks. The noise was deafening, echoing through the huge chamber as the round buzzed between the two men, slammed into the steel casing of one of the stacked tank rounds and ricocheted off with a spark.

"Are you crazy?" Jackson yelled as he lunged forward only to be stopped again when Nikki moved her aim to the center of his forehead.

"Do not make me kill you," Nikki yelled.

She stared at the two men as she barked at Vostav in Russian to close the doors of the bunker and get a truck started to begin loading some of the weapons systems.

Nikki turned her full attention back to Ramsey and Jackson. "You two can help load the truck. Once I have what I want, then you can call your boss. She held out her free left hand and gestured to the men,

"Guns, please."

CHAPTER 60
MIDNIGHT ENCOUNTER

OUTSIDE the service door Gordon Maxwell was contemplating whether to find another entrance to the cave when the
sound of Nikki's gunshot reverberated against the steel of the huge
bay door. He looked at the structure and wondered about it's
vulnerabilities.

The door was massive and made of interlocking steel panels
that looked strong enough to withstand a ramming impact from any
of his vehicles. The service door was also steel, shaped similarly to
that of an ocean vessel's compartment hatch door. There was no
lever or handle on the outside.

Maxwell stood back to get a better view. He tugged on his
moustache, twirling the tip between a thumb and forefinger as he
stared. After a brief moment he turned to the man next to him,
thumping the man's chest with the back of a half closed fist.

"Tell me you packed the explosives."

"Of course. More than enough." With that he stepped to the
back of the Rover and removed a canvas satchel containing cakes

of C4, detonation wire and the triggering mechanisms. He lay the canvas on the hood of the truck and removed enough C4 for each of the latches and formed the material into four mounds. Maxwell grabbed the first one and pressed it in place at the top of the door, covering the pattern of steel rivets, then added the next amount for each similar location on the steel structure.

He set the detonation cord and blasting caps in place, embedding each of the four caps deep into the formed explosive shape charge then rolled the cord out and around the back of the Rover where he attached the triggering mechanism. "Well then, let's make some noise."

Vostav was just about to select the "close doors" option when the cave shuddered from a deafening explosion, signaling Maxwell's successful breach.

Nikki spun at the sound in time to see the service door tumble end over end and clang to a grinding halt on the floor of the cavern, a huge pall of smoke rising from the doorway, illuminated by the lights of the two vehicles on the other side, and the silhouettes of armed men entering through the dissipating vapors.

With Nikki's concentration broken, Ramsey and Jackson took the opportunity to flee, ducking behind the first row of steel cargo containers. Vostav was also moving, running toward Nikki at full speed, weapon drawn and aimed at the first of the dark shapes to clear the smoke. He put his arm around Nikki, sweeping her away, yelling at her in Russian to take cover.

Gordon Maxwell was the first to clear the doorway. As he stepped in he heard Vostav's order and could see the hazy image of two people, both armed, heading for cover. Without hesitation he fired in their direction. Charlie and the others followed suit, sending a volley of rounds toward the quickly moving figures of Nikki and Vostav as they ducked behind the steel containers.

Bob Matthews yelled at the other two men in the car to move just as the explosion lit up the cave's entrance. "Let's go. Follow me!"

White, Matthews and Anatoly quickly exited their vehicle and rushed toward the opening as Maxwell and his men disappeared through the smoke. Matthews looked over at Rick White who had his weapon drawn. White looked nervous, again in a situation for which he had not been trained. His eyes were wide, lips drawn in a thin straight line as the adrenaline powered his movements toward the door opening.

Matthews took the role of team leader, automatically assessing the information around him, making a plan and ensuring that his team was ready. Matthews pointed to White's pistol, calmly telling him to remove the safety. He looked over his shoulder at Anatoly who was mimicking the movements of the two agents and signaled for him to stay behind them. Lastly he told Brandon to stay with the vehicle. Brandon had no problem with the directive and jumped into the driver's seat. "I'll be right here when you're ready to go," he said as he checked that the keys were still in the ignition and watched the others move toward the still smoking entrance.

As they approached the door Matthews signaled for white to move to the right side. "You cover everything on the left as you look in, I've got the right and center," Matthews barked quietly to the acknowledging nod of White's head, then added, "Don't shoot me, aim *inside* the door." Rick White again nodded nervously as he took his position and waited for the signal to enter.

Inside, Gordon Maxwell ordered his men to split up, sending three left, toward the shipping containers and the remaining four to the right, along the wall to where the entrance door had clanked and slid to a stop. He looked around the cavernous space at the amount of equipment. His odds were best if he could lure Ramsey and the others out into the open.

"Well, here we are again," he said, his words echoing through the room as he directed his lead man, Charlie, and two of his men to sweep the left side.

"Look around you. This is not the place to be shooting at one another. One round hits the wrong thing and we're all dead." He aimed his pistol at a steel upright support for the warehouse shelving and fired. The round slammed hard into the steel with a bright spark and a ping and tumbled off in a random direction. "See, it's not good to be shooting at each other in here."

Maxwell watched as three of his men disappeared around the edge of a row of containers. The first of the three spun to the right expecting to find the woman and her accomplice, but instead found the row empty. He relaxed some as he looked toward the other two, signaling to them that it was clear, but when he turned back around he was startled to find that Nikki had emerged from between the containers and was standing directly in front of him, pistol raised.

The 7.62 round from Nikki's Makarov entered the man's skull just above his left eye. Maxwell's man dropped to the floor with a thud. The remaining men scrambled backward, taking up a more defensive posture, only to find that Nikki had ducked away, disappearing into the inventory of containers.

Maxwell called out to Ramsey, "I didn't want this to go down like this. Call your people off or you will all die. You have one chance to leave here breathing. This is it."

Paul Jackson stood crouched, his back to Ramsey. "He says you should give up."

Ramsey spoke over his shoulder to Paul. "So I heard," he replied, just as the first of the four men who had flanked right came into view. Ramsey's pistol was raised head height, waiting. He yelled over his protection to Maxwell. "And then what? You kill us all anyway. I don't think so."

The men stopped moving, poised at the ready, trying to discern the direction of Ramsey's voice in the echoing chamber as Ramsey crouched against the shipping container.

"Call them back," Ramsey said again, yelling toward the rear of the cave. This time the echo didn't help. The first of the team on the right spun toward Ramsey, motioning to the others to follow.

In the shadows of the metal boxes Ramsey tapped Paul to spin him around. Jackson repositioned himself to stand with his right shoulder pressed hard against the steel of the container, his pistol held steady above the head of his partner, just as the third man of the four man team stepped into the row.

The lead man peered into the shadows of the boxes. He'd heard the voice and was sure it had come from this row. He moved forward allowing the men behind him to pull in tight around the containers and pulled his AK up, just as his men rounded the corner. He heard the sound of shuffling feet and thought he saw movement. Without hesitating he fired into the shadows, the muzzle blast illuminating the faces of Ramsey and Jackson.

"Shit!" Jackson blurted out as the round from the AK zipped past him, so close he swore he could feel the change in air pressure.

Ramsey didn't wait to respond to the threat. He had the first man in his sites and squeezed the trigger, firing off two rounds from his nine mil and shooting the startled man in the face and neck. The lead team member fell to the floor, weapon clattering and then becoming silent as the man stopped moving.

The second of the team was too startled to shoot and fumbled with his AK trying to get into a good position. Jackson squeezed off several rounds, growling as his shots struck home, driving through center mass of the target in front of him, two of the four rounds embedding into the shoulder of the third man as he and the last of the team struggled to take cover.

As the smoke cleared from the doorway and the echoes of the first few gunshots diminished, Bob Matthews spun around the edge of the opening with Rick White immediately behind him and Anatoly taking up the rear. Matthews moved his ragtag group to the far right and began making his way toward the rear of the cave. He stopped at the T80 tank to regroup when the firefight between Ramsey and Maxwell's men erupted, stopping nearly as quickly as it began.

He peered around the gooseneck of a flatbed trailer to see two of Maxwell's team running for cover, one of the two obviously injured. Still the man was engaged with the mission, regrouping with Maxwell and the remainder of his group, five in all, four of whom had AK-47s.

Bob Matthews looked around at the amount of weapons and equipment in the cave. So much to choose from, he thought as he tried to spot something he could use to even the odds against the AK-47s. He looked up at the T80's turret and the 7.62 PKT machine gun perched on the mount.

He turned to Rick White. "You two wait here. I'm going up to take a look around. He holstered his pistol and quietly climbed up onto the trailer and then to the deck of the tank, standing so that the turret was between him and Maxwell's men. He paused to take a look at what was happening, peering stealthily around the machine gun and over the turret. The taller of Maxwell's group was tending to the wounded man, fabricating a pressure bandage.

Matthews examined the machine gun. He had some tactical weapon training, but little on foreign weapons. Other than a few UZI submachine guns and the AK-47 and its variants all of his training was relegated to American weaponry. Still, this weapon was made by Kalashnikov and shared similarities with the AK, such as the safety and firing selector. As he studied it briefly he noted that it was a belt fed machine, top loaded like an M60 Machine gun, or a SAW, both of which he knew.

He spotted a 200 round box of ammo in the cradle of the mount and carefully unlatched the ammo box's bale. To his amazement the box was full. After a few more minutes of fumbling with the weapon's receiver lid and feed mechanism, Matthews had the belt of ammo in place.

He pulled the charging handle on the weapon backward slowly, then released the charging handle to move the bolt forward. There was a problem. The handle slid forward, but the bolt mechanism was locked to the rear. After a couple of seconds Matthews realized that the bolt had a mechanical lock for loading. He reached down and pressed the lock to release the bolt, realizing as soon as he pressed the release that it was the wrong thing to do. He winced as the first round from the belt loaded into the chamber and the bolt assembly slammed home with a resounding clank.

Maxwell was the first to respond to the noise. Without hesitation he began firing at Matthews and yelling to his people to concentrate fire on the tank turret.

Matthews spun the weapon to the left and without aiming, yanked the trigger sending a burst of about eight rounds flying in Maxwell's direction. The rounds slammed into the metal containers and ricocheted off the concrete, missing by a long shot any of Maxwell's men as Matthews tried to get a feel for the weapon. Maxwell nor his men wanted anything to do with the business end of the machine gun and scrambled for cover.

Ramsey, startled by the loud and sudden report from the machine gun, stood and carefully looked over the top of his cover. He glanced along the huge door and then to his left, catching movement from the top of the tank to see Matthews clutching the control handles of the PKT.

Jackson slid over next to Ramsey and raised himself to his boss' level. He spotted Bob Matthews and the smoking barrel of the PKT in the distance, turned to Ramsey and calmly stated, "Well, what do you know. Bob's here."

On the opposite side of the cave Nikki and Vostav took the opportunity to reposition. Nikki scanned the rows to her left and right as she ran forward, catching a glimpse of Anatoly as he ducked behind the trailer with the American. She turned left down the second to last row and was moving quickly toward Maxwell's last position when suddenly she was grabbed and nearly yanked her off her feet as she was drawn into the opening between two crates.

Nikki spun her weapon around at head height only to find that it was Alan Ramsey who had hold of her. Still pointing her pistol at him, alternating it between Jackson and Ramsey, she glared at Ramsey as she yanked away from him.

Ramsey wasn't intimidated by the pistol, in fact, he was getting used to it. "You're going to get yourself killed. Those guys are all armed with AK's and there's five of them,…"

Nikki wouldn't let him finish, "…And there's now seven of us. Anatoly and your man White are at the tank along with the tall one. We have the opportunity to finish him. You can stay here and hide, but I am going after him."

Gordon Maxwell was breathing heavily as he ducked behind one of the metal engine containers. His people were spread out, taking cover behind anything substantial. He looked around for his lead man, Charlie, but couldn't see him. He was sure he was right behind him. Maxwell peered back the way he'd come, but saw nothing but empty concrete leading to the tank perched on the flatbed. He turned to look back the other direction and was startled by Charlie's sudden reappearance.

"I found a little something to even the odds," Charlie growled, and without hesitating. stepped out into the open, raised an RPG and fired. The round jumped from the launcher and rocketed away, screaming across the distance to the tank and impacting near the back lower section of the turret.

Matthews saw the round coming and instinctively ducked, taking cover next to the thick steel of the turret as the tank shuddered from the explosion. A huge fireball rose to the cave's ceiling, a glowing incandescent pall of smoke and debris that encompassed the turret. He could feel the hot expanding gasses on his shoulders, his neck, and the back of his head. The smell of his singed hair added to the aroma of hot steel and burning gasses, as he pressed himself as low as possible against the tank's turret.

Ramsey cringed. The noise was deafening. He spun in time to see the glowing cloud of smoke rising from the tank turret and then turned to look down the length of the row of crates and containers to the open blast doors of the nuke storage area and then turned back to face Nikki and Jackson.

"We've got to get that thing closed up. If Maxwell sends another one of those the wrong direction and takes out those warheads this place and everything above it will disappear."

Vostav stepped forward, "I will go. I know how to work the controls." He looked toward Nikki, as if trying to get her approval.

She waved a hand and sighed, "Go. Close it. We will cover you."

Vostav took off toward the control panel amid the sound of gunfire that was directed toward the T80 tank. The Russian dodged and weaved from crate to crate, sprinting and stopping, looking left and right, then moving ahead once more until he reached the end of the row where he stopped to catch his breath.

He carefully scanned the area for Maxwell's men, looking back in the direction of the source of gunfire. He glanced to his right and saw Matthews pinned down next to the turret of the T80. Every time the agent tried to get back up another volley of rounds was fired in his direction. He saw Anatoly and the other agent, White, pulled up tight against the trailer.

Vostav looked at the controller, now about thirty meters away and to his left, then back at Matthews, White and Anatoly just as a second RPG screeched across the cave, missing the tank completely and exploding against the cave's wall.

Anatoly and White crouched behind the trailer. White turned to Anatoly, "We need to draw their fire away from Matthews so he can get back on that machine gun." He looked around trying to come up with a plan. He saw the rows of containers and the open doors of the bunker. "There. That way!" White pointed with his pistol. "We can take cover behind those crates or in that room."

Anatoly's eye's widened, but before he could protest White rushed to the front of the truck and fired in Maxwell's direction. Maxwell and his men immediately shifted their aim to the front of the truck.

White ran several feet to the amazement of Anatoly then realized that there was no way he could make it to the open storage room with fire concentrated on his movement. He spun and ran back, amid the ricocheting bullets, and threw himself at the truck. He crouched low against the right front wheel of the truck and breathing hard, said, "Ok, that's not going to work."

White's distraction, however short lived, was all that Vostav needed. He sprinted the thirty meters to the console, sliding to a stop on his knees, grabbing the console's podium as not to slide past. He reached up, tapping repeatedly on the touch screen to wake it from its electronic sleep and selected the command to close the doors. The hum of the electric motors could barely be heard over the exchange of gunfire reverberating throughout the cave.

From his position he could see that Maxwell and his people were advancing on Nikki's position and the tank. Maxwell led two of his men along the crates while his lead man and the wounded man moved toward the tank. He could tell that the taller of the two had military training, staying low, firing and then moving between bursts. Vostav glanced toward the T80. Both White and Anatoly were taking cover and Mathews was pinned down. If Maxwell's thugs got to them they wouldn't have a chance. Without hesitation he checked his ammo and rushed to their position.

White watched as Vostav jumped to his feet and began running in the direction of the tank. The Russian held his pistol high and pointed in Maxwell's direction as he ran. Bullets hit the floor and pinged against metal and wooden containers all around Maxwell as Vostav moved swiftly across the smooth concrete floor.

White jumped up from his crouched position against the truck, threw his arms over the bumper of the vehicle and began firing at the three men moving toward Ramsey's position when he saw the two others moving around to the back of the trailer. He turned to Anatoly and shouted as he pointed to the back of the truck, "We've got company!"

CHAPTER 61

CULMINATION

MAXWELL'S men crouched at the left rear of the flatbed, hidden from those crouched on the opposite side. Charlie contemplated the next move. His main concern was getting the agent away from the machine gun. The other two could wait. Kill the machine gunner and move in. Textbook, he thought. His wounded partner was moving far too slowly for the action that was happening all around them. He could hold a pistol, but the AK-47 was out. Charlie grabbed the AK from the man and shoved his pistol into the wounded man's right hand.

"Here, you'll do better with this," he said as he racked the charging handle on the AK to ensure a round was loaded in the chamber.

The wounded man was shaking. Blood soaked his shirt from his left shoulder, the makeshift bandage having already come undone. Charlie barked orders that the man heard, but didn't fully understand. He was thinking of his survival and the fact that he was losing so much blood. Charlie snapped his fingers in front of the man's face, "Did you hear what I said? You go for the two down low, I've got the one on the top. Got it?"

The wounded man acknowledged that he understood, and with a grimace, raised his weapon and stepped toward the opposite corner of the trailer with Charlie crouched low behind him. He tapped the man's shoulder, signaling him to move, as he sprung up from his position and took aim at Bob Matthews.

Vostav had just come to a stop when the wounded man appeared around the corner of the trailer firing successively in their direction. Anatoly felt the impact of two of the rounds as they slammed into his right arm, causing him to drop his pistol as he fell backward out in the open, in front of the truck, writhing in pain as he scrambled to get back on his feet.

Rick White was frozen for a moment, then he pulled the trigger, sending several rounds toward the wounded man, striking him in the torso and chest. Vostav ran past White, weapon firing, rounds slamming into the face of the wounded man as he pitched backward and fell to the floor. He spun to his right, found his next target and fired.

Charlie didn't anticipate the fourth man. His eyes were wide with surprise as the first round fired at him from Vostav's nine mil found its mark, ripping through the operative's neck. Blood spurted from the gaping tear in his flesh and artery as he dropped the AK to grab at his neck.

Vostav didn't hesitate, firing again and again, through Charlie's hands and face and neck, neutralizing any threat the tall mercenary may have posed.

Maxwell watched from his vantage point near the crates as he moved closer to Ramsey's position. He cursed as he saw first one, then the other man go down. He ordered his men to move in, but he was more interested in the man on the floor in front of the truck. He was wounded, but still in the fight as he tried desperately to get to his feet. Maxwell raised his AK-47 in Anatoly's direction, but before he could squeeze the trigger Nikki jumped from one of the crates, slamming into Maxwell, disarming him.

Maxwell recovered, grabbing at Nikki's pistol hand, pulling it down to his awaiting knee, forcing her hand open and the pistol to the floor. The Makarov clattered to the concrete. Maxwell kicked at it, causing it to slide out of reach.

Nikki spun around, kicking Maxwell in the groin several times. She punched him hard in the side of the head only to receive a well placed punch to her right ribcage and a high elbow to her left cheek by Maxwell, causing Nikki to fall back.

The last of Maxwell's men raised their weapons as they moved around the last obstacle, ready to meet Ramsey and Jackson head on, only to see the two Americans move deeper into the stacks of crated weapons. Jackson sprinted past an open box of grenades, sliding to a stop to grab two of the lemon shaped fragmentation grenades. He ran to where Ramsey had taken up a defensive posture. "Cover me," he yelled, but didn't stop running, instead moving to a gap in the row of steel containers and disappearing between them only to come out nearly back where he started, closer to the end of the row near the tank.

Jackson pulled the pin of the first grenade and threw it underhanded along the floor toward the two men. The clatter of the grenade caused one of the two to turn. Seeing the grenade roll to a stop he reacted, reaching down, grabbing the grenade and tossing it as hard as he could deeper into the cave away from them.

The second grenade landed in nearly the same spot as the first, but there was no way to get to it in time. One of the men dove between the metal crates as the first grenade rolled to a stop against several tank shells. The grenade's explosion created a secondary detonation of the 120 millimeter shells. The concussive force of the blast and the pressure from the exploding shells caused the cave to tremble. Huge chunks of rock fell from the cave's ceiling. The containers of engine parts and other weapon systems blew away from the center of the explosion as the resounding thud from the second grenade rocked the cave and peppered the closest of Maxwell's men with shrapnel.

Jackson looked at the results of his attack and cringed. The far end of the cave illuminated brightly with each successive explosion. Large pieces of rock and infrastructure, as well as steel parts and weapon system components rained down, landing on other crates, clanging loudly all around them. Several light fixtures crashed to the ground while others flickered and went dark or shattered from the shockwaves, sending cascades of sparks down from above.

"Oh, shit," he cursed as he saw the second of the two men jump up and run from his position toward the open service door of the cave, something that he also thought might be a good idea as another large explosion rocked the cave, sending several large containers flying. One of the containers, empty, but still easily weighing three-hundred pounds flew overhead and crashed against the steel entry door, smashing the fleeing operative and blocking the only way out on foot.

It seemed as if the whole cave were coming down around them. The noise of the explosion and the sound of the steel container slamming against the cave's entrance door startled Vostav, who was standing between the only exit and the tractor trailer. Tank rounds, artillery shells, parts, containers and all manner of debris rained down as the explosions grew more intense and worked from the back of the structure toward the front. Vostav looked around for any place that would offer protection from the raining debris. There was no place to go to escape, except the T80 tank.

Vostav ran over to White who was helping Anatoly get to his feet and yelled for them to get in the tank. He was in extreme pain, but knew that to stay where he was would prove deadly as another round of deafening explosions blasted more hardware across the confines of the cave.

Ramsey looked for Paul Jackson as he ran to escape the toppling crates and shelving, dodging left and right. He was getting disoriented running through the maze of crates and boxes. He was running at full speed between two twenty-foot shipping containers when he ran head-on into Jackson, slamming hard into him, knocking Jackson off his feet.

"What the hell did you do?" He yelled at Jackson as he helped him back up off the concrete.

"I had a bad grenade toss." Jackson yelled back, "I'll tell you about it later. Let's get the hell out of here before this whole place comes down."

The repeated concussions brought Maxwell and Nikki's fight to a sudden end. For a brief moment they stared at each other and then looked around at the events going on around them. Nikki spotted Ramsey and Jackson moving quickly toward the exit, stopping at a frantic, arm waving Vostav at the front of the semi, motioning to the end of the cave.

Nikki looked to where Vostav was motioning and saw that the exit was blocked. She glanced up to see a wounded Anatoly being lowered through the gunner's hatch by the American, Rick White. They were getting in the tank. Vostav was going to drive out. That had to be the plan, she thought, as another huge explosion rocked the cave. She had to get to the tank.

Nikki ran past Maxwell, heading toward Vostav, but Maxwell wasn't finished yet. He grabbed at her as she ran by, pulling her off her feet, causing her to crash to the concrete as he retrieved one of the AK-47s, aimed it at her and pulled the trigger. Nothing happened. He yanked the charging handle rearward to clear the weapon and load another round in the chamber.

Nikki got to her feet and lunged for the Makarov, kicked away by Maxwell earlier. In one swift move she raked the pistol from the floor and, while running back toward Maxwell, fired, hitting him in the stomach and sending him reeling backward to fall through the yellow tape that encompassed the WWII ammunition. Maxwell tried to recover, pushing himself up from the crates where he'd landed. He pulled at the yellow cordoning tape, remembering suddenly why it was there.

Ramsey was the last to get into the tank through the gunner's hatch. Vostav had just fired up the engine and was putting the tank in a left neutral steer, the tracks spinning in opposite directions, turning the forty-five ton tank to a ninety degree angle on the heavy transporter's flatbed trailer. Alan Ramsey called to Vostav below, pointing to Nikki who was running full speed toward the T80.

Vostav gunned the eleven-hundred horsepower engine. The T80 tank pitched forward and down as it drove off the edge of the trailer and onto the concrete with a thud, then picked up speed quickly. Vostav pulled hard on the left lateral control turning the vehicle hard to the left, then braked hard causing the huge vehicle to slide sideways to a stop directly in front of Nikki.

As she reached for a handhold several rounds from Maxwell's AK-47 ricocheted off the curved thick steel of the turret startling her and causing her to lose her footing as she climbed onto the road wheels and up the side of the tank.

Ramsey spun the PKT on its mount and released the gunner's ring, spinning the machine gun to settle in Maxwell's direction. Ramsey knew that hitting him at two hundred yards with a weapon he was unfamiliar with was probably an impossibility, but if he could buy Nikki some time, then what the hell.

He slammed down on the trigger, releasing a burst toward Maxwell. The rounds careened off the concrete as Ramsey adjusted his fire, walking the rounds to Maxwell's position. He missed Maxwell, but hit the decaying wooden crate of WWII hand grenades, detonating the TNT and causing the first of a succession of chain reaction explosions with the volatile World War II stock.

In a blinding flash Maxwell was gone, incinerated in an expanding, rolling explosion that rocked the ninety-thousand pound tank as if it were a ship on a stormy ocean.

Ramsey leaned down extending a hand to Nikki and pulled her up, then dropped down into the hatch as Vostav accelerated away from the onrushing explosions now taking place everywhere. Nikki threw herself into the opening, grabbing the cupola cover and locking it down as debris from the collapsing complex rained down on the T80 tank.

Vostav held the accelerator to the floor hoping that the huge corrugated door would be no match for the forty-five ton, eleven-hundred horsepower tank. He reached down and released the latch to drop the drivers seat into the cupola fully and braced himself for the impact with the door. The T80 blasted through the corrugated steel door without slowing, creating a huge gaping hole in the steel structure.

Brandon felt the ground tremble and saw the flash of multiple explosions. He could tell that all hell had broken loose inside the cave, but had no idea of just how volatile the situation was. He was getting worried for the others and fearful that he may have to face Nikki, or worse, Maxwell, on his own. He gathered his courage and decided he would go in.

Just as he opened the door and stepped into the darkness, he heard the huge crash of the collapsing corrugated steel door and watched as the Soviet tank crashed through, a huge fireball following the tank's exit, expanding out of the opening and encompassing the fast moving vehicle, looking as if the devil's fiery hand was reaching out to pull the tank back into the hell from which it had come.

Explosion after explosion rocked the cave, sending large debris outward, careening off the tank and smashing against Maxwell's vehicles that were parked near the opening as the tank clattered to a stop about a hundred meters outside the cave's entrance.

Inside the cave multiple small fires burned, illuminating the carnage from the powerful explosions as smaller detonations from crates of small arms ammunition continued to cook off. For the most part the explosions were immediate and powerful, each one creating huge pressure waves, removing any oxygen that fed the fires. Brandon cringed as another large explosion sent another wave of pressure, blowing out several of the smaller fires and sending more debris out of the cave's opening.

Vostav stepped up on the driver's seat, clambered out onto the pitched top surface and down to the dirt to stand next to the tank. He looked back into the cave, raising both of his hands to wipe the sweat and grime from his face, sliding them back and locking them behind his head. He sighed a deep sigh and fell to his knees on the ground, exhausted, and thankful for the successful escape.

Paul Jackson was the first to emerge from inside the tank, popping the commander's cupola cover and throwing it back to lock it in place. He looked back to the cave as the gunner's position hatch cover sprung upward.

Alan Ramsey pushed himself up and out to sit on the edge of the cupola's opening. He eyed Paul first, then turned to look at the smoke billowing from the cave's destroyed door. A fairly loud detonation echoed through the interior of the cave as one more grenade detonated somewhere inside. "Looks like the worst is over."

Paul Jackson smiled. "I'm just glad those blast doors held," he said, with an obvious look of relief. Jackson turned to find Vostav getting back on his feet. "Hey, You OK over there?"

Vostav leaned on the tank as he held up a thumb. "Never better, considering…"

Ramsey got to his feet as Anatoly climbed up and out. Ramsey offered a hand that Anatoly took.

"Lover boy," Jackson quipped, "I'm afraid Vostav over there just stole your MVP status from you."

Anatoly cracked a slight smile, "He deserves it, and if this is what you have to do to get it, then he can have it," his remark causing Jackson to laugh out loud. As soon as Anatoly cleared the hatch, Nikki's hand with her painted fingernails appeared.

Nikki lifted herself out of the cupola to sit on the rim as Ramsey had earlier, her face and arms showing bruises. She looked up at the three men standing over her. She had a split lip and dried, caked blood under her nose. Her hair was covered in dirt and tossed in all directions and signs of a darkening bruise surrounding one of her eyes revealed itself, the effect of a well place punch by Maxwell.

Nikki leaned back against the hatch cover and looked at her hand, grimacing and moaning. She held up her hand, middle finger raised at Jackson and said in an exasperated tone, "Shit. Wouldn't you know it. I broke a nail."

—

CHAPTER 62

OUT OF HELL

THE first of three Ukrainian Mi24 Helicopters landed in the clearing in front of the cave's entrance. The others hovered above the area, slowly circling, their flood lamps lighting the ground below, concentrating on the tank and illuminating the cave's opening. Alan Ramsey met with the commander of the helicopter and the two walked around as Ramsey described the chaos of the last two hours.

It took several attempts before Alan Ramsey could convince the Ukrainian commander that he was who he claimed to be and was allowed to use the satellite phone on board the helicopter to call Gabe Anderson.

In Washington, D.C. Gabe answered the phone, glad to hear Ramsey on the other end. Ramsey quickly briefed him on the events. Gabe reciprocated, explaining the incident with the Secretary of State and his suicide.

"Alan, I spoke with the President. He wants you to know that he was unaware of the measures taken by his Secretary of State in regards to you and your team's safety. He never intended for you to be placed in harm's way. That was all Erickson. He asked that you accept his apology." Gabe added, "For whatever that's worth."

Alan was quiet for a moment. He knew that President Carlton was only doing what he thought was best for the country. Sometimes, he thought, secrets of state are best kept secret. Unfortunately, his position in the T2T made him privy to the secrets now.

"That actually does mean a lot to me, but, I'm afraid that won't help him in the long run. He'll be lucky if he doesn't end up in prison after all is said and done."

Gabe Anderson agreed, "Oh, by the way, Gene Patterson got the State department to contact the Ukrainian defense ministry. He cleared the way for you and your team to be returned to Moscow. You'll probably be there a few more days while they debrief you on Maxwell and your Russian R.S.S. liaison. They're going to want to know details. Don't be afraid to tell them what they need to know, but leave the events here at home out of your brief. What's happened here is none of their business. No need to air our dirty laundry."

Alan agreed, taking the guidance without questions. Ramsey handed the satellite receiver back to the Ukrainian commander and looked out the open cargo door. Kiev police, as well as Ukrainian government agency personnel were now swarming around the cave's entrance. The Commander of the Mi24 tapped Ramsey letting him know that the first helicopter to Kiev was about to lift off.

Vostav sat quietly next to Rick White, eying the T80 tank, not wanting to leave it behind, when suddenly White jumped out of the helicopter.

Jackson saw the move and tapped Vostav on the shoulder to get his attention, yelling over the sound of the spinning five blade rotor, "Where's he going?"

Vostav shrugged and answered sarcastically, "I don't know. It is not my day to babysit."

Jackson stared at the grinning Russian. "You try way too hard, dude. It needs to come naturally. Don't be forcing it."

Jackson sat back to see what White was doing. He walked to Maxwell's vehicle, reached inside and pulled something off the dashboard, and then ran back to the helicopter, strapping himself in just as the aircraft began to lift off. Jackson was looking at him questioningly.

White pulled up the phone that Maxwell had taken from him and held it out for Jackson to see. "It's my phone," he said in a matter of fact way, then turned and started poking at the screen. Jackson smiled to himself.

Ramsey was sitting next to Nikki who was wearing the hearing protection offered to her by the aircraft's commander. He leaned over and motioned for her to take off her hearing protection. She lifted one side to listen to what he had to say.

"Where are you going to go?"

Nikki looked skyward as if contemplating her options. After a few seconds she answered with a sigh, "Anywhere but Russia." She leaned closer to Ramsey, "The question is, where are you going, Mr. Ramsey?" She pointed to the cave. "It seems to me your investigation is over. What are you going to do now?"

Ramsey looked at her and grinned, "I don't suppose you are going to let me arrest you. You know, bring you back to the States."

Nikki smiled a broad smile, her green eyes sparkling in the dim light of the helicopter's interior. She looked at Ramsey somewhat playfully, as the rotors picked up speed, lifting the craft straight up. Suddenly the towers of the monastery could be seen. Nikki had to yell over the beating of the rotor blades, "You cannot arrest me in the Ukraine or Bosnia. I'm afraid you will be going home empty handed."

Ramsey yelled back as the Mi24 pitched forward, "No, Nikki. You're wrong," he said, shaking his head. He looked down at the huge pall of smoke billowing from the ground. "I may not be able to arrest you, but we are not leaving empty handed. Maxwell is dead, the weapons are destroyed and the nukes are safe." He leaned a bit closer to Nikki's unprotected ear, smiled, and said, "....and we still have your laptop."

That caused a frown to appear on Nikki's face, but only briefly. Then, she gave him a slight smile and shrugged, as if the news didn't really matter.

He continued, "We'll use that, along with some other information we gathered, to set things right at home." He sat back as Nikki let the ear muff fall back into place. He stared outward, thinking about Erickson's death and wondering what would happen to the President. Another black eye for the U.S., he thought. He looked back at Nikki who pulled the hearing protection up again, "You never answered my question. What about you? What's next?"

Nikki looked at Anatoly who was conscious and sitting up next to her. "Me? I think I am going to retire." She smiled at Anatoly then turned back to face Ramsey.

"I have Gregorov's money. I will use it to go to Bosnia and look for my father and my brother." She stopped to correct herself, "...for their bodies, I mean."

She cocked her head to the side, the bruises from her fight with Maxwell starting to show even in the dim light. "Perhaps you will share some information with me. I have a strong suspicion that your President may have some answers."

She paused and then added, yelling loud enough for even Paul Jackson to hear, "...or I can always go to America and ask him myself." She smiled wickedly.

Paul Jackson spoke up quickly, "Uh, no thanks, that's ok. I like that whole retirement idea you had, better." Paul shot a glance at Ramsey. "What do you think, Mr. Ramsey? Think we can help a sister out?"

Ramsey stared out into the darkness before answering his partner. "I'll see what I can do...As long as you promise me you won't go hunting anymore live persons. Seems to me, you still haven't found a particular general."

Nikki smiled. "Ah, yes. Well, I do not think I want to make that promise, Mr. Ramsey. I'm afraid I might not be able to keep it, and I like to think of myself as a woman of my word."

Ramsey was too tired to keep yelling over the noise of the helicopter. He smiled again and leaned back against the seat and closed his eyes before replying to her. "Fair enough, I suppose. Fair enough."

Kenneth Wash

EPILOGUE

STAKE OUT

THE intermittent beeping of the back-up warning stopped and the operator stepped down out of the backhoe. Anatoly was tired of the noise of the excavation at the burial sites. They had been at it for months, each promising lead turning up more of the same. In all, more than 200 dead.

They had reopened the site at Cerska Valley, west of Konjevic Polje, last excavated in 2001. That site alone revealed forty newly identified bodies, all found in a mass gravesite where over one hundred and fifty others had been found in the first excavations after the July 1995 massacre. The newly revealed bodies were also between the ages of fourteen and fifty, all wearing civilian clothing and with their hands tied behind their backs.

There were more victims of the atrocity known as the Srebrenica Massacre, found with information gleaned from the millions of bytes of data on Secretary Erickson's external hard drive.

All of the information condemned the already dead ex-President Milosevic. Damning documents from the secret negotiations that proved the existence, and more importantly, the exact meaning of Directive Seven, a presidential directive from Milosevic, successfully proven to the tribunal by his defense council early in his prosecution to have been misinterpreted by his commanders, thereby releasing him from the full responsibility of the massacres.

Yet, Erickson's external drive held the copies of the proof, signed documents to his commanders in the field that spelled out the actions that were to take place starting on the morning of July 13, 1995, and a promise by then Secretary of State, President James Lincoln Carlton, to suppress the evidence in return for the war's end. Among the agreed-to-terms was the disposal of Serbia's thousands of enemy combatants, to be dealt with however the military and political mechanisms felt necessary.

Anatoly pondered the anonymous help that Nikki had received. Paper documents and digital information on a single DVD, pieces to the puzzle that led to the three month search for Nikkolai and Zlatco Sidorova, and delivered, by courier, to Nikki Sidorova's well hidden location, a small home in the forests of the Drina Valley, a quaint homestead abandoned by its previous owner during the escape from Srebrenica.

But this site was different than the rest. Originally excavated after reports of a thirty vehicle convoy of trucks and busses arriving on the morning of the July 14, 1995, delivering additional prisoners to the nearly one-thousand men and boys already held there, the Grbavci School in Orahovac was host to the mass killings and executions of more than 600 people.

The forensic evidence that was not available for the war crimes tribunal and subsequent jury, the information that resided in the RAID array of Erickson's external drive, showed evidence on restricted-from-view aerial and satellite photos that the ground at the school in Orahovac was disturbed on more than one occasion.

Known as Lazete one and Lazete two, the photographs showed that the first gravesite was dug sometime between the 5th and the 27th of July, 1995 and was exhumed between July and August 2000. The second site was originally exhumed between 1996 and 2000 by the Office of the Prosecutor and Physicians for Human Rights, revealing some 240 or so victims. What the prosecution's information didn't show was the proof that a third gravesite, Lazete Three, and now the location of Nikki's current efforts, existed on the grounds.

It was at that site that eyewitness accounts placed the Serbian General, Ratko Mladic. According to one survivor, a political prisoner who survived the shooting by pretending to be dead, he and thirty others were taken by bus to the grounds of the school. Upon arrival, the men and several boys were lined up along a ditch. There they stood, in the direct sun, for over an hour. Fatigued and barely able to stand, they waited, for what they didn't know. At one point a red car drove up and General Mladic exited the vehicle.

The witness said that the general walked the line of men, stopping to face a tall blonde man. "Well, your government doesn't want you, and now I have to take care of you."

The stocky figure returned to his car and drove out of sight, after which the men were forced to turn around and all were shot in the back.

It was the personal writings of the witness who, after being wounded and lying in the shallow end of the ditch, wrote,

"When the shooting started I immediately fell into the ditch. Two men fell on top of me. I thought for sure I was going to be shot a second time or be buried alive. I waited, staring into the unmoving green eyes of the tall blonde to whom the general spoke. As night fell we still were uncovered. I managed to pull myself up and out of the ditch where I hid in the tall hedges. At one point I heard the voices of Americans and thought I would be saved, but

they dropped off bags and instructed the Serbian soldiers to dig the ditch deeper. By the time morning came I had made it to the road and was able to crawl away to a nearby farmhouse."

The words of the witness came to life as Anatoly stared across the meadow at the farmhouse, easily a mile away, and then back to the excavation at the edge of Grbavci soccer field. The ground held the secrets of the dead he was sure, at one point revealing a bundle of material that was thought to be blindfolds, thirty-one in all. For each bit of dirt they moved more clues were uncovered. A shoe, a belt, and then, finally, the dark colored plastic bags.

Unlike the last sites, where the bodies were a tangled mess of clothing, bones and rotted flesh, these bodies were encased in body bags. The ones that the witness spoke of, Anatoly thought. And the depth of the site was different as well, also corroborating the witness' tale of survival.

As the dirt was carefully removed and brushed away, one of the men moved from bag to bag, unzipping them to view the human remains inside. After opening several of the bags the man stopped and stood, the blonde hair of the corpse within revealing itself in the sunlight that had not touched it in over fifteen years. After a brief discussion he and Anatoly walked to a construction trailer where both men stepped in out of sight.

Bob Matthews handed the radio back to Villacruze after watching for any change and reporting in with his boss. He could see that Vee was chomping at the bit to break in on whatever meeting was taking place in the small structure. Matthews had already placed several teams in locations around the site and was just waiting on word to move them in. He broke the news to Vee. "Ramsey said we wait. You need to learn to be patient, my friend."

Villacruze liked working with Matthews, but the guy was so methodical. "All I'm saying is we know who's in there. We could go right now and get it over with. I really don't see why we have to wait for them all to be outside the building."

Matthews glared at his partner. "We wait, because the boss said we wait." He sat back in his seat trying to get more comfortable and then turned his head in Vee's direction. "I'm not sure how you prior Special Forces guys work, but the C.I.A. has procedures."

Anatoly closed the door behind him and stepped up to the desk where Nikki Sidorova was looking at documents and maps splayed out in front of her, each new location marked with the results of each excavation. She looked up to see Anatoly and the site foreman and lead forensics investigator standing in front of her.

"I think the next dig should be here," she stated as she tapped the pencil she had been gnawing on against the paper.

Anatoly stepped closer. He reached out and grabbed her hand and stared into her green eyes. For a moment there was silence as Nikki tried to understand what emotion Anatoly hid behind his tight lipped smile. He seemed happy, yet his eyes showed a sadness that Nikki hadn't yet experienced with the man. A feeling of butterflies churned in her stomach.

"What? What is it? Have you found something?"

Anatoly put his arms around her and whispered quietly, "I think we found them."

Nikki pulled away from his embrace. She turned to the other man who seemed to be affected. His eyes were red and his expression was one of relief. "He has blonde hair. The first since we started looking."

She threw the door open and looked across the open expanse to the worksite. She paused for a few moments then stepped down to walk toward the opened grave.

Villacruze saw movement at the door. He sat up straight and hit Matthews lightly to get his attention, pointing toward the group that was now exiting the building. "We might not have to wait long. Look, Manno, something's going on down there. You better call the boss back."

Matthews saw the faces, recognizing one as the person they had been looking for. The others were important to the investigation, but if they resisted there would be no hesitation from his men. As long as they didn't kill the main subject everything would be fine. He picked up the radio and spoke the words the teams had all been waiting for, "All teams move in."

A group of six armed men moved in, surrounding the small building as two agents approached those who had just stepped outside.

Villacruze and Matthews approached the teams as they took the two men down to the ground, securing their hands behind them. Villacruze yanked up his badge, flashing it to them, then turned to the older of the men. There was no mistaking his blue eyes. "It's him. We got him."

Bob Matthew's looked into the eyes of the most wanted man in Eastern Europe and asked simply, "Do you speak English?"

The boxy figure of the infamous general nodded his head. He asked Matthews in perfect English, "Who are you?" Then, motioning with a nod toward the cameraman recording the event asked, "What is... all of this?"

Matthews looked around at his team and, having heard the account of Mladic's meeting with the Dutch commander at the gates of Potocari, twisted Mladic's own words around.

"This is history in the making, General. We are recording for the people of Srebrenica and for the world, their triumph to rid itself of a wretched person like you."

The words garnered a scowl from Mladic as Bob Matthews read him the charges. "General Ratko Mladic, you are under arrest for crimes against humanity. You are being extradited by the United States government and are being placed in our custody..."

At the dig site over four hundred miles away Nikki was unaware of the successful operation to find and secure General Mladic. She looked past the crew as she approached the dig site, an uncovered ditch at least fifty feet long, dusty black body bags visible just below the surface of the excavated layers. On the ground was a partially open bag, and inside, a mummified corpse of a once tall, blonde-haired man.

Nikki recognized the plaid shirt, and below it, under the collar, the chain of the necklace he was wearing. She suddenly dropped to her knees next to the bag, unzipping it to reveal a crucifix protruding through the rotted fabric of his shirt.

Nikki's eyes welled with tears as she drew her hand to her own chest for the millionth time, feeling for the crucifix. She looked up at Anatoly, tears streaming down her face, and sobbed, "He wasn't even Muslim." She rested her hand back on the crucifix, thinking back to the day she gave it to him, in the warehouse, the last day she would ever see him, until today.

Anatoly couldn't imagine what Nikki must be feeling. After not knowing for so long what had become of her father, and then, to find him here among the murdered. He stood at the edge of the mass grave, scanning the row of barely visible bags, searching for any that could hold the smaller body of Nikki's brother, Zlatco.

Sadly Anatoly's gaze returned to Nikki and the body of her father, and that was when he saw it, the shape of a second body,… in the same bag as Nikki's father.

"Nikki!" Anatoly suddenly blurted out, "It's Zlatco. He's there."

Nikki looked up, scanning the area surrounding the uncovered bodies. She looked back at Anatoly, "Where? Where is he? What are you saying?"

Anatoly plowed through the workers, "Move, get out of the way," he said as he maneuvered himself next to Nikki and knelt down next to her. She looked frustrated, angry and confused until Anatoly took her hand and placed it on the zipper. Then suddenly she understood and she too saw the odd shape of the bag.

Nikki hesitantly pulled the zipper further down, opening the bag to expose first the dark brown hair and then, a second body, the body of her brother, Zlatco, wearing the striped shirt he had on the day he disappeared. "Oh, Zlatco," she sobbed.

Anatoly pulled her up to embrace her as she sobbed uncontrollably. He could feel her letting go. Finally, he thought to himself. Finally, she can put her past behind her.

Parked on a road overlooking the Grbavci excavation site, Alan Ramsey lowered his binoculars. He turned to face Paul Jackson in the driver's seat. "Looks like they found them."

Jackson was smiling. "That's really why you wanted to come here, to see that she was digging in the right place?"

"Yes, I told you of all the places this site's information matched up the best. I had a feeling."

Jackson smiled again, "Uh huh, and those feelings are scary sometimes. I'm betting Vee wishes he had your feelings. He bet Matthews that it would be the last site." Jackson thought for a minute, "That guy never wins a bet." He laughed thinking about Marks and Vee and the constant betting that always seemed to turn out bad for Vee. There was a momentary silence. "Well, then I guess that's that... unless you are going to go down there to arrest her and start this shit all over again."

Ramsey looked at Jackson quizzically, "Arrest who?"

"What do you mean, who? Nikki."

Alan Ramsey feigned a look of confusion, "Wait, do you mean, Nikki Sidorova? That can't be her down there. She died in an explosion while fighting Maxwell."

"So, is that the official story?"

Alan gave Jackson a hard stare, to which Jackson replied to his own question, "Oh yeah, in that cave. I seem to remember that now. You're right, that can't be her. My bad."

Jackson placed the car into gear and again looked toward Ramsey and said, "Seriously though, she could be a big help to the T2T. We might want to keep tabs on her." He smiled a crooked grin.

Suddenly a voice from the rear seat chimed in. "You should always keep your friends close and your enemies close, also."

Paul Jackson looked in his mirror, sighing at Vostav's version of the famous line from the Godfather.

"It's, keep your friends close, but your enemies closer."

He turned and rolled his eyes at Ramsey and pointed a thumb in Vostav's direction. "Are we really taking this guy with us? You sure do have some strange criteria for selecting your agents."

Alan Ramsey laughed at Paul's statement. "Hey, I picked you, didn't I?" He placed the binoculars in the glove box and then gestured toward the road ahead. "Drive on, Mr. Jackson, we've got a plane to catch."

ABOUT THE AUTHOR

Ken Wash lives in St. Louis, Missouri. He is an Army Reserve soldier who has served over 35 years in Active Army and Army Reserve, enjoying a career in the ordnance branch as a 915E Senior Logistician, having attained the rank of Chief Warrant Officer Five.

Mr. Wash has worked in the civilian automotive repair industry for over 30 years as an ASE Certified Master Technician, publishing numerous technical investigative reports as a professional technical writer, subject matter expert and mechanical claims witness for major insurance companies in the areas of automotive forensic investigations of fraud and theft.

Mr. Wash has been writing as a hobby for about fifteen years. He has written several short stories, edited and produced documents for military publications and directed, produced and edited military videos and keynote presentations for high visibility military staff functions.

Flags of Vengeance is Mr. Wash's second novel in the Alan Ramsey series.

OTHER BOOKS BY KENNETH WASH

THE FINAL DEFENSE

The first book in the Alan Ramsey series.

A skirmish in the desert on the Texas/Mexico border set events in motion that put Alan Ramsey, a prior Special Operations captain turned terrorism subject matter expert, and his newly recruited partner, Paul Jackson, on high alert as they follow a criminal pattern that indicates the immediate war on terror isn't exactly over.

When it is suspected that a nuclear warhead has made it onto American soil and is in the hands of a group of terrorists led by a ruthless Iraqi insurgent, Leaja bin-Masri, the stage is set for a race against time to stop the terrorists before the weapon can be deployed.

With Alan Ramsey's team on the heels of the terrorists at every turn, bin-Masri must decide to keep moving or use the weapon before reaching its destination, taking the C.I.A., F.B.I., and the local police on a wild ride down several different and sometimes simultaneous paths in a final act of defense that culminates with a heart pounding, white knuckle ride to beat the clock.

Fast Paced Thriller – *"Enjoyable thriller with terrorists and a nuke in the USA. Relentless action and some cool characters make this an imaginative and satisfying read."*

Outstanding action, memorable characters, realistic terrorist threat – *"An excellent series beginning with complex yet realistic surprise twists as the action moves with lethal terrorist sleepers and ruthless extremist zeal. Good grasp of weapons and tactics, great flow and page-turning suspense and action. International scope. Looking forward to the sequel. Well worth the time."*

Made in the USA
San Bernardino, CA
06 March 2016